MURMURS OF EVIL

The Possession Chronicles #2

By
Carrie Dalby

For Sean Connell, my first editor and the one who said I had "serious horror chops."
This possession is all your fault—thank you!

And Tom Scholz and the music of Boston.
The songs "Magdalene," "Surrender to Me," "Higher Power,"
and "If You Were in Love," directly influenced this manuscript,
and many other tunes and inspirations through the years.

One

"Miss Jones, we're at your service." The captain gave a jovial bow and took Magdalene by the elbow across the wide gangplank of *Miss Mary Louella* amid the line of steam ships on the Mobile River.

Magdalene clutched her worn carpet bag. "This is nicer than the ferry, I'm sure. You keep a lovely ship, Captain Walker."

"Many thanks, Miss Jones. She's smaller than the public boats, but just the right size for tying up at private docks. Make yourself at home. We'll be off shortly."

Magdalene climbed the stairs to the upper deck, passing a draped cargo pile on the main floor. Its strange shape seemed more fitted to an import ship than a bay runner. The craft puffed eastward into a blanket of clouds while she settled on a bench and questioned the haste of her employment. She had no experience and not much in the way of references. Why did Mr. George Melling hire an unknown woman to be in the closest confidence of his wife?

Halfway across Mobile Bay, one of the deckhands came by. "Are you in need of anything, Miss Jones?"

"Is all the freight on the lower deck for Mr. Melling's house?" Magdalene asked.

A shadow crossed his tanned face. "Every last bit of it, though it's larger than usual today with the headstone and all the samples."

Her hand went to her throat. "Headstone?"

"For Miss Melling. Are you not acquainted with the family?"

"Only Mr. Melling. He said his daughter recently departed, but he failed to mention a timeline or cause. Was she very young?"

"Nineteen and right nice to look at." The deckhand lifted his cap to Magdalene. "I must continue my checks now."

Last month, after she entered Melling and Associates law office for an interview, Mr. Melling told Magdalene a melancholy tale of his daughter gone without warning and the need for his wife to have constant fellowship. Magdalene attributed the lack of details in the story to Mr. Melling's grief. Now trapped between the gray sky and bay, she wasn't sure. Keeping house with a society lady was one thing, but to have the employer in mourning brought a whole other dynamic—one Magdalene didn't know if she felt equipped to deal with because the prick of her own loss still stung. As the steamer drew closer to the looming red cliffs of Montrose, she second guessed her choice of leaving behind her role as the spurned daughter of the widower blacksmith of Seven Hills.

After seeing the boat secured to the pier, Captain Walker found Magdalene. "I'd like to bring you to the house before we unload the delivery. Mr. Melling should be there by now, so everything will be set." He took her bag and offered his assistance down the stairs.

"Captain, if I may ask, why was I brought with the cargo?"

"He must have wanted to avoid the talk of him bringing a young woman across the bay. The ferry is ripe for gossip and his family has been attached to scandals in the past. It's likely people would be unpleasant to you if you were to travel alone with Mr. Melling."

While she appreciated his honesty, it caused a flutter in her stomach. "I don't recall reading anything about Mr. Melling in the newspaper."

The captain's expression betrayed his youthful amusement. *He can't be more than half a dozen years my senior.*

"He's the type of man people know better than to write about. He's got friends in all the right places, but I can see your concern, Miss Jones. As long as you stick with Mrs. Melling, you should be in no danger of scandal. I've been doing weekly deliveries to the household for months and I'd be happy to look after your welfare when I stop in, if you'd like."

They started up the pier. "Yes, thank you. Then you know about the death of Miss Melling?"

"My first trip was weeks before her passing so I only met her once. Her hair was darker than yours and her eyes a striking blue."

Magdalene fumbled through awkward foot placements as she climbed the path beyond the red clay cliff of Ecor Rouge. Captain Walker kept a hand at Magdalene's elbow to help her. She tried her best to keep her mind on the placement of her feet rather than morbid ideas of being a replacement for a deceased daughter as they neared the house.

What Mr. Melling referred to as his cottage was nothing short of a manor to Magdalene. It might be smaller than his mansion in Mobile, but the looming spires atop the gables of the columned white house were beyond anything she thought possible in the wilds of the Eastern Shore. The only things higher than the peaks of the roof were a few towering southern pines amid the deciduous trees. The clearing around the house made for a tidy yard, offset with a scalloped sweep of white pickets as ornamental as the building's gothic windows. But the little fence around the yard seemed incapable of holding back the weight of the forest. The house itself appeared powerful enough to stop any intrusion, natural or not. It possessed the grace of a cathedral, the charm of a country church, and the oppressive mystery of mortality all in one glance.

Magdalene's apprehension sat heavy in her chest, but she put on a brave face when Captain Walker opened the gate. He led her around to the huge back porch and knocked on the screen door of the kitchen.

A tiny form approached them, her heart-shaped face cherubic and her gingham dress crisp as a picnic blanket. Behind the girl, a woman with an oval face the same dark hue as the child's came to the door.

"Captain Walker, this will never do." The woman wiped her hands on her apron and opened the door. "Give me her bag, but present her at the front."

The open door showed the kitchen housed a modern stove, icebox, and sink with plumbing—all extravagant compared to Magdalene's country home. She was pleased to see her trunk in the far corner, which had been collected from her aunt's house two days before. At least she'd have her familiar things that night.

"You know I always wish to call on the most important lady of the house first." The captain reached into his coat pocket and retrieved a candy stick. He held it out to the young girl. "My compliments to Miss Priscilla."

Her face beamed as her hand clutched the treat. "Thank you, Captain Walker!"

He tipped his hat to her.

"You're a scoundrel to give that to her before supper, but I'm not one to take it away from her now." The cook's words were harsh, but her dark eyes revealed tenderness for her daughter.

"Now, Miss Rosemary," he said in response, "let me introduce you to Miss Magdalene Jones before I bring her 'round. Miss Jones, this here is Rosemary Watts, the best cook this side of the bay."

"Hush with your compliments, Captain. Just get her to the front door before Mr. Melling accuses you of dilly dallying with your important load."

Magdalene smiled. "It's very nice to meet you, Miss Rosemary."

Then a maid with curly brunette hair bustled toward the door, swinging her coin purse as she pushed passed the cook. Magdalene stepped behind Captain Walker to get out of her way.

"Excuse me, Captain. I'm running late today." Upon seeing Magdalene behind him, she paused and scrutinized every inch of her. "You must be Magdalene. You're much prettier than Mr. Melling hinted at. I'm Lydia."

"It's good to meet you." Magdalene smiled.

"That remains to be seen." Lydia hurried down the lane.

"She's not the most amiable one in the lot," Rosemary said, "but she does work well."

Captain Walker took Magdalene's arm. "I'll see you shortly, Miss Rosemary."

At the front step, Magdalene placed each booted foot carefully before the other as she prepared for entry into the next chapter of her life. The captain raised the knocker on the front door and let it rap upon the metal strike plate three ominous times before removing his hand from the lion's mouth that held the ring.

Moments later, the door opened inward with a slight squeal as if the house fought to allow more into its fold. A butler, dark and mustached, stepped to the side and motioned them in. Behind them, the door shut with a sigh. The newcomers were shown into an ornate crimson parlor. Mr. Melling rose from one of the wingback chairs by the unlit fireplace, over which hung a giant, veiled mirror. His drooping mustache and long face framed by the receding line of his bronze hair tainted his expression from ever looking cheerful.

"Miss Jones and Captain Walker, at last. I trust everything went smoothly for you."

Magdalene, relieved to see a familiar face after her journey by wagon, streetcar, and boat, focused on Mr. Melling rather than the dreary room. "Yes, sir. Thank you."

"And you've brought the monument and samples, Captain Walker?"

"Everything's at the dock. I wanted to bring Miss Jones to the house before overseeing the delivery."

"Then I shall accompany you myself." Mr. Melling turned to the far corner of the room with what appeared to be a smile. "Alexander, I'm sure you would be happy to entertain Miss Jones until I return."

"Yes, Father." From a small settee, a solemn young man with wheaten hair and a square jaw stood.

While Mr. Melling commanded distance and respect, the fresh, clean-shaven face of Alexander Melling drew her in, despite his seriousness. Mr. Melling and Captain Walker took their leave and Alexander came to Magdalene's side.

"Welcome to Seacliff Cottage. Where would you be more comfortable?" Alexander motioned to both a chair and the matching settee in the corner he'd vacated.

"Here's fine, thank you."

Alexander followed Magdalene to the settee, and then took a seat in the armchair across from her. She tried not to study him, but with his coloring at odds with the luxurious reds and mahogany furniture that filled the space, it proved difficult to not turn toward the brightest spot in the room. His blue eyes were the color of the sky on a cloudy day, but they weren't cold—though Magdalene was certain they could be. Alexander's pleasing looks caused an ache to open within. Her social time the last few years consisted of her father and his apprentices at mealtimes, church functions, and occasional dinners with extended family. Being this close to a man stirred memories of William and the future she could have had if he hadn't left her the week before their wedding.

As though seeing the melancholy on her face, Alexander offered his assistance. "I'm sure it's been a long day for you, Miss Jones. Since Father is gone and no one needs to be the wiser, would you care for a tonic to help you through the remainder of your day?" He motioned to the side table, where a silver trimmed decanter trio stood at the ready. "We aren't a household to shy away from the occasional drink."

Magdalene clasped her hands in her lap. "No, thank you. I'm quite comfortable for the time. I understand sympathies are in order."

"I need no one's sympathy, but thank you nonetheless."

"I'm sorry to speak out of turn. I know it's difficult to lose someone."

Alexander walked to the mantel and retrieved a framed photograph that was tucked under the drape of the veiled mirror. "You have no idea of the oppression, but you will soon enough."

Hesitant to touch the gilded frame, Magdalene took the cold thing in her hands, but the face staring back chilled her more. Large, haunting eyes, like her brother's—but accompanied by the piercing glare of Mr. Melling—was an image she would not soon forget.

"That was taken on her fifteenth birthday. A painting in her cotillion gown hangs in the upstairs hallway, but Mother has it veiled. And, of course, she has Eliza's final photograph by her bedside. There are some things Mother doesn't like to share."

"She's lovely. Do you both take after your mother?" she asked as he took his seat.

His laugh sounded bitter, but the smile that broke the grief on his face was worth the awkwardness between them. "You'll be hard-pressed to find out anytime soon."

"I was under the impression Mrs. Melling is here, as I am to be her companion."

Alexander scoffed. "But of course she's here. I assess Father did a poor job interviewing you. He was probably afraid to scare off a naïve country girl and conveniently forgot to supply you with all the details about the lady of the house, you poor soul."

Magdalene sprung off her seat, fists clenched at her side and her pert head high. "You can be sure I'm neither naïve nor to be pitied."

Alexander rose, meeting her fierce gaze with an expression near admiration. He turned to the side table and opened a decanter. "It's good to see you have pluck. You'll need it in the days ahead." He offered her a crystal chalice of amber liquid.

Magdalene saw it as a challenge. Trying to prove she wasn't a girl to be pushed around, she took the glass. Their hands touched in the exchange of the goblet. She never knew a man's hand to be so soft, un-callused. A thrill went up her arm and she kept her eyes on his as she slung back the drink and returned the empty glass into his still outstretched hand.

Then the burn inside her empty stomach struck, followed by coughing. Alexander took her elbow and eased her to the settee.

After the racking coughs subsided, he touched a strand of her brunette hair that had shaken loose, tucked it behind her ear, and then rested his hand on her shoulder. "We were supposed to toast and then sip, you impulsive thing."

If her chest wasn't already seized with burning, it would have engulfed in flames. Not since William had someone touched her so tenderly. Breathless from coughing, Alexander's nearness flooded her with yearning to absorb all the sensations around her. She wanted to stroke the velvet of the cushion and inhale the different scents of the various decanters. Then dizziness struck, causing her to close her eyes and lean her cheek on the top of Alexander's hand.

He gently removed his hand from her shoulder, and though in that moment she wished he wouldn't let go, relief enveloped her when he did. A tear welled in her eye and she turned away from him.

"Guess you aren't up to brandy." Alexander patted her knee. "Here, take this. It will help clear your head and hide the odor. We don't want Father or Mother thinking you have trouble with the bottle."

Magdalene discretely wiped her eye and turned to accept the mint. After it melted on her tongue, she could breathe easier and ventured to speak. "I hope you don't think less of me."

"On the contrary. I have more respect for you than when you arrived." Alexander poured himself a drink. "And respect is no cheap thing. It's something you have to earn, and many people find the price to win the respect of a Melling too high."

He raised the leaded crystal glass and leaned toward her. "This is how it's done properly."

It was easy for Magdalene to watch him drink. Soon one of her fingers followed the scrolling pattern on the settee and ventured closer to Alexander on the other end. He set the empty glass on the table and smiled.

"You need to pace yourself, Miss Jones."

She hiccupped, covered her mouth with her wandering hand, and smiled. "Please call me Magdalene."

"The Lord will strike me down for getting you drunk on your first day." He crossed himself.

The feeling of lightness Magdalene first experienced turned heavy. She gripped the armrest with her left hand and used her right to brace herself from falling onto Alexander.

"Oh, for the sake of all things holy, please don't pass out." Alexander rang a silver bell from the side table. When the butler came, he gave swift instructions to fetch food and tea from the kitchen.

"Come on, Miss Jones." He stood in front of her and held out his hands. "You need to get up and moving."

"I'd rather take a nap." Her arms went limp and she started to lean to the right.

"Oh, no, you don't." Alexander caught the weight of her upper body as he dropped to the settee beside her. His left arm went around her waist and his right nudged her head so it nestled on his chest rather than slipping toward his lap.

She looked up at him, brown eyes dewy and wide. "I feel fuzzy, like a peach."

"Miss Jones." He leaned forward with her. "If we don't stand up now, I may regret whatever I do next even more than I do giving you that drink."

She wobbled so much he had no choice but to tuck her against him, pulling her to his chest as he stood. "Mother Mary, make me strong," he muttered as he fought to distance himself from her without letting her fall.

"Are we dancing, Mr. Melling?"

He slowly shuffled her toward the fireplace. "Mr. Melling is my father. Call me Alexander, Miss Jones."

"And I told you to call me Magdalene." She straightened her back so she wasn't completely dependent on him.

"That's possible only when we're alone."

She looked up at him. "And how often is that going to happen?"

"Not often enough."

Two

The butler returned with a tea service tray. If he thought anything of the embrace between the younger Mr. Melling and the new help, he kept it to himself.

"Watts," Alexander said, "you're just in time."

Alexander led Magdalene to one of the leather chairs by the fireplace and saw to her comfort before retrieving a teacup.

"Eliza held her drink so well, I forget not all ladies are up to it," Alexander muttered as he stirred a teaspoon of sugar into the hot tea. He put both Magdalene's hands around the china cup before letting go. "It was only a shot because you looked so weary."

Mr. Watts cleared his throat, but said nothing.

After she took her first sip and he saw her hands were steady, Alexander collected a shortbread cookie from the tray Mr. Watts still held and handed it to Magdalene. "You do forgive me, don't you?"

"Since I'm the ninny who accepted it, there's nothing to fret over."

Alexander smiled in relief. "A spirited team player is just what I need."

Magdalene sipped the tea, but kept an eye on Alexander as he poured himself a cup. She still had the urge to reach out to him, but felt weighed down and didn't trust herself to speak. He settled across from her in the matching chair and took a bite of a teacake.

"If it were ten degrees cooler, I'd light the fire." Alexander stared into the hearth. "There's still a chance for a cozy fire or two before summer sets in. After that, it will be bonfires on the beach. Do you enjoy a good fire?"

The memory of her father's screams, followed by the terrified shouts of his apprentice seared through Magdalene. By the time she'd run to the forge, the stench of her father's burning flesh filled the air of the lean-to next to the barn. She shuddered.

"If you've caught a chill, I'd be happy to light it now."

"No, thank you." Magdalene paused to lift the black-and-gold cup to her lips. "It's nothing that can be warmed."

Alexander turned to Mr. Watts. "Thank you for your assistance. I trust none of this will reach Father."

Mr. Watts nodded and turned to Magdalene. "See my wife in the kitchen if you need something later."

Magdalene managed a smile of gratitude. "Thank you. I've already been acquainted with Rosemary and Priscilla."

"Did that scoundrel of a captain present you at the back door?" Alexander asked as the butler left the room.

Trying to displace the animosity in his voice, she wasted no time. "Captain Walker meant no disrespect. He was merely bringing the little girl some candy."

Alexander scoffed. "That shows he's adopted too much of his wife's personality. I wonder if Father knows how familiar the captain is with the help. If he keeps this up, it won't be good for him. His wife ruined her own father's business because of her interactions with the coloreds during the Spanish-American War. She's liable to do the same to him."

Talk of wars and ruinations were too much for Magdalene to wrap her head around while fighting to stay upright. "As long as he does his job well, what harm can be done in showing kindness to a little girl?"

Alexander stared at Magdalene's face, but when she betrayed no emotions of guilt, his gaze traveled down until it settled on the lone piece of her mother's chatelaine that hung from the waist of her skirt—a pair of folding scissors. "What is the story behind your partial chatelaine?"

Her teacup rattled and she quickly placed the saucer onto the side table. "It was my mother's. She often wore it to church, to snip wayward threads from Sunday clothes. My father was to buy me the rest of a set when word that Will—"

Her hand covered her mouth, closing off the sentence before she could betray the rejection she'd received.

"Will what? Or who?" Alexander detected the blush on her cheeks. "So you aren't a young spinster, are you? You've had a lover or two, I dare say."

Magdalene stood to admonish him, but the room spun. Up in an instant, Alexander placed one hand on her elbow and eased her into the chair before returning to his own. After taking another sip, Magdalene leaned her head against the back of the chair, thinking of her bandaged father laid up in her aunt's house with no room for her. "Lost loves don't count. At least you have your parents."

"So you're an orphan?"

"No, my father still lives and breathes, though he doesn't do much else." She paused. "I'd rather not say more."

Alexander let out a long breath. "Tragic events, they haunt us all."

Magdalene finished her tea and cookie but continued to hold the cup as if staring into the dredges would reveal the best way to keep her secrets. "Life seems ever so lonely these days."

"We have each other now." Alexander leaned across the space, reaching for her knee.

The front door swung open and the scent of evening air blew in from the hall. Alexander looked at Magdalene, his blue eyes shining, before he stood at attention. Two of the deckhands from the boat shuffled in, red-faced, with a crude wooden crate suspended from poles lifted by each of their hands.

"In front of the fireplace, boys," Mr. Melling ordered.

Alexander came around the back of Magdalene's chair and slid it to the side to prevent her from becoming trapped when the crate lowered between the two chairs. With a fluid motion, he ran his fingers across her shoulders. Magdalene's body surged with energy and she fought the instinct to reach for his hand. Never had she been so in need of touch from another person—it unsettled her to think of attaching herself to a man she just met.

"Alex, go fetch your mother." Mr. Melling stood in the entrance overseeing the room. "Make sure she has appropriate footwear because we are all going to see the headstone laid properly. That means you as well, Miss Jones."

Alexander paused under a crucifix hanging over the doorway, its dark wood nearly invisible against the deep red wallpaper. "Father, Miss Jones never knew Eliza. Does she have to come?"

"Of course she's going," he barked. "We're all going, now get your mother!"

Mr. Melling's hostile attitude when he turned back to the room further chilled Magdalene. It would have been nice to have seen this side of him as a warning before she took the position.

Magdalene put either hand on the armrests and willed herself to stand.

When she knew the room wasn't going to spin, she raised her voice. "Mr. Melling, might I fetch a wrap from my luggage before we go?"

In response, he waved a hand as if to dismiss her. "Tell the Wattses to put dinner in the warming oven and ready themselves as well."

Magdalene held her breath, trusting he wouldn't smell the alcohol or witness a tremor in her limbs. "Of course, sir."

Captain Walker and the deckhands were on the front porch. She hoped they would accompany the household to the graveside so she wouldn't be the only outsider present. Going for the back of the house, she walked the dark hall and tried the last door on the right.

As soon as she pushed through the swinging door, the smells and sounds of the kitchen engulfed her. Priscilla sat at the small corner table, happily playing with a rag doll. Rosemary stirred a pot on the stove but looked over at Magdalene.

"Leroy told me what happened. Are you feeling well?"

"Well enough, though embarrassed, to say the least. Does he do that to all the newcomers?"

"Not hardly, but there've been few guests in recent months."

"I was sent to fetch your family. We're all to accompany the Mellings to the graveside for the headstone placement."

Rosemary shook her head. "It'd be too practical for the Mellings to wait for the Sabbath. I suppose I'm to keep supper from spoiling?" She prattled on, not waiting for a response. "But at least we're dressed presentably today, seeing as how Prissy and I made a call to the ladies' group from our church this afternoon. Hurry on back now, sugar. Mr. Melling isn't one to be kept waiting."

"I came to fetch a wrap. Is it all right to get into my trunk here?"

"Leroy's been too busy to haul it up the stairs yet so help yourself. I'll be sure he gets it situated during supper."

Magdalene was careful not to rummage through her clothing in a rush. The urgency of the situation sobered her as she secured her green shawl over her arm. Rosemary shuffled the pots and pans into the warming oven and Magdalene left the kitchen without speaking, passing under yet another carving of the Lord upon the cross. The hall was cleared save one individual near the stairs.

"Let me help you." Alexander pulled the shawl from her arm and spread the triangular ends out like a welcoming embrace. Magdalene couldn't help the sigh that escaped her lips when his arms brought the shawl around her shoulders. "And Lord send help to me."

"You have guardian angels to watch over you," a deep, feminine voice spoke from the top of the stairwell.

The formidable outline of the lady of the house descended the carved stairs in a shroud of black. The drape of the fabrics created a bell shape from the billowing skirt to the intricate Victorian mourning veil over her head in a crown of cascaded webbing.

"Come, Alex." Mrs. Melling held out her black lace-covered hand when she reached the last step. "You must not allow your sister's memory to be spoiled by the arrival of the hired girl."

Alexander, his face as stony as it had been when Magdalene arrived, took his mother's arm. The coldness in his demeanor dispirited her more than Mrs. Melling's biting remarks. Pulling her shawl tighter, she followed the Mellings out the front door.

Three

Though the nippy air felt pleasant, the motion of the wagon on the dirt roads further irritated Magdalene's wobbly head. She rode in the back of the Watts's family wagon, the end position of the mourning train from house to graveside. Those from the ship carried the stone in another wagon and a fine carriage driven by the stable hand transported the Melling family from Seacliff Cottage to the cemetery through two miles of trees tangled with palmettos and vines until they reached Montrose proper.

Magdalene found it odd a family with so many reminders of faith in their home did not bury their loved one in a church graveyard rather than the far corner of the community cemetery. The deckhands and Captain Walker assisted in lowering the granite headstone into place on the barren site. As the weather warmed, the grass would spread over the resting place, but for now the early spring blossoms would have to cheer from afar.

Beloved daughter and sister
Eliza Rose Melling
November 11, 1886 - January 10, 1906

A wave of nausea swept over Magdalene during Mr. Melling's graveside remarks. She steadied her swaying frame with a trembling hand on the trunk of an unsuspecting pine. Mr. Watts noticed her struggles and shifted his position to shield her from the Mellings' view. Whether he did it to help her or to fulfil his duty to hide Alexander's transgression, Magdalene didn't know, but she appreciated the respite. Eyes closed, she bowed her aching head and distanced herself from the praises Mr. Melling spewed about his daughter.

What felt like seconds later, a gentle hand tugged on her shawl. "Mama says you need to come," Priscilla whispered.

Startled, Magdalene stepped away from the tree. Dusk had grown deeper and the rest of the group moved closer to the grave to pay respects to Eliza Melling. Rosemary urged Magdalene in front of her family. After Captain Walker and his men, hats in hands, bowed their heads beside the grave, Magdalene stepped forward to do the same. She'd seen several of the others cross themselves when they finished, but since she wasn't Catholic, she merely clutched at her shawl and nodded her head. A gust of wind rustled through the woods behind her and brought a blanketing of the winter's fallen oak leaves across the mourners. Dread, pure and heavy, settled in Magdalene's chest and she wanted nothing more than to run home to Seven Hills.

When she stepped back, she glanced at Alexander. He stood at his mother's elbow, a smirk on his pale face. A flustered blush swept across her cheeks but she stood tall.

After the Watts family paid their respects, the group returned to the waiting horses in the navy twilight. Lanterns were lit and hung on the front sides of the wagons and carriage before the wagon rattled its way back to Seacliff Cottage. When Magdalene lowered herself to the ground outside the Mellings' stable, the blackness of the forested property tucked around the gleaming white house did little to comfort her in the starless night.

The Mellings were already inside, the Watts family quickly headed for the kitchen, and the men from the boat gathered near the out building for a smoke while the gray-haired stable hand saw to the horses. Magdalene wondered why the man had stayed with the carriage when the rest of the household went to the gravesite and why he didn't talk to anyone as he went about his work with a solemn expression. As though he felt her watching, he looked up and tipped his hat to her.

Captain Walker came to Magdalene. "Let me see you to the house."

"Thank you. I wasn't sure if I should enter the front or the back."

"If you're on errand from Mr. or Mrs. Melling, the front should be fine."

He saw Magdalene to the porch. "I'll be back next Friday and will ask Rosemary how you're doing."

Overwhelmed by someone caring about her well-being threatened to spill out as tears. "Thank you, Captain Walker. I'm much obliged."

Before Magdalene could shut the carved door, Alexander came up behind her and sealed the entrance himself. With his hand still on the knob, he whispered in her ear. "From now until bed, don't leave Mother's sight. She's suspicious, and that's never a good thing."

"Suspicious of what?"

Alexander ignored her question and she reluctantly followed him to the parlor. Mr. and Mrs. Melling sat in the chairs on either side of the hearth, which now housed a crackling fire. The young flames shone upon the fragments of stones that Mrs. Melling sorted through from the crate while Mr. Melling watched from the opposite chair. Alexander took her shawl and motioned Magdalene to the large settee in the center of the room while he claimed an armchair between her and his parents.

Magdalene watched the veiled lady of the house hold each pallid stone to the light with rigid movements under the drapes of black fabric. It wasn't until Mrs. Melling removed a gleaming piece of marble that she relaxed back into her seat, set the stone in her lap, and stroked the polished side as though it were a kitten. When Mr. Watts came in to announce supper, Mrs. Melling kept the marble in one hand as she took the arm of her husband. Not knowing what else to do, Magdalene accepted Alexander's offered arm and followed the couple.

With each new room of the house she entered, Magdalene further understood the immense wealth of the family and failed to see how she could ever be comfortable among them. The wallpaper in the dining room offset the arched molding that extended above the height of the doorways. It was opulent in a way that almost mocked God because it seemed a more sacred space than the whitewashed walls of the Methodist church Magdalene attended in Seven Hills.

Mr. and Mrs. Melling settled at either end of the massive table, and Alexander helped Magdalene into a carved chair in the center of one of the long sides, taking the seat opposite. She wished the flowers of the centerpiece were taller so she could block his incisive gaze. The wood chandelier taunted gravity over the table and its gas lights burned bright, though far from cheery in the ominous room that was watched over by another crucifix.

As Mrs. Melling folded the black lace mourning veil over her head, Magdalene muffled her shock at seeing a nearly smooth complexion and sad blue eyes. Mrs. Melling lifted the marble sample and peered at the details of the rock.

"This is the whitest of the lot. The veins are almost translucent and I want Eliza's house as pure as she was." She flipped over the sample and looked at the engraved plate. "And the quarry is close so it should not delay the building. Georgia Marble Company in Pickens."

"Then it's settled." Mr. Melling lifted his fork. "I'll speak to Parker myself when I get to town Monday."

"I want to bring it to the location to see how the sunlight affects it to be sure." Mrs. Melling looked at Magdalene. "The new girl shall come with me tomorrow."

Throughout supper Magdalene remained quiet, easy to do because the Mellings didn't speak much, even among themselves. She ate her flounder and rice, but picked at her asparagus. Some things didn't keep well in a warming oven.

After supper, the group returned to the parlor, Mrs. Melling once again covered by her mourning veil. The meal had taken the edge off Magdalene's headache, but when Alexander poured drinks for himself and his father, her stomach churned. As if sensing her discomfort, Alexander gave a brief smile that further set her on edge. His bright eyes were once again kind, but she didn't trust them to stay that way for long.

"Come, let the girl sit with me a moment." Mrs. Melling motioned for Magdalene to sit opposite her.

Grateful for the crate of stone between her and the ethereal lady of the house, Magdalene eased herself into the wingback chair and leaned away from the fireplace, picking an invisible piece of lint off the skirt of her plain dress.

"Seeing as how my husband does little more than speak a few sentences to me each day, I worry that the choice he's made to select you as my companion is a poor one. How can a man who barely knows my temperament select someone with whom I can have amiable conversations? Do you see my dilemma?"

Magdalene could feel the stares of the men from across the room even though she couldn't see the face of the one she must answer. She swallowed with difficulty.

"I understand completely. The last nine years I've suffered through what other people thought best for me. It's not something I'd wish on friend or foe. I wouldn't be angry if you decided to release me. I can be on the ferry tomorrow if you wish." As much as the option appealed to her on one level, Magdalene prayed she wouldn't be turned away without a chance.

Mrs. Melling's delicate hands fingered the cross that hung from the gold chain around her neck. From the tilt of her covered head, it looked as though she gazed down at it through the lace. "Come now, leave the dramatics across the bay. There is no need to rush off. You must stay the weekend on trial."

"That's very kind of you." Magdalene, simultaneously overcome with worry and relief, yearned to lean her aching head on the back of the chair.

"Sundays after I am ready for Mass would be your personal time until supper, but I insist on keeping you around this time, to see how you get on." Mrs. Melling's head tilted. "You look travel weary. I dismiss you for the remainder of the night. Go on and see if Rosemary is still here and have her show you to your room by way of the back stairs."

Mr. Melling and Alexander stood as Magdalene rose to her feet.

"Thank you, Miss Jones." Mr. Melling inclined his head when she passed.

"Good night, Miss Jones." Alexander, though his voice sounded kind, refused to make eye contact.

Magdalene found Rosemary putting food away while Priscilla and Leroy finished cleaning the dishes. The cook showed the way through another door off the kitchen. It led to a narrow flight of stairs lit by a single gaslight on the wainscot wall.

"You're not on a separate floor, and there's no door between this hallway and the rest of the second-floor rooms, so be sure to guard your modesty when traveling to and from the washroom."

Rosemary opened the door at the top of the stairs and stepped into a red hall darker than the parlor. Wood paneling stretched halfway up the walls and across the ceiling in decorative molding lit by gas chandeliers. Magdalene tried to focus on the craftsmanship of the interior, but instead felt she'd been swallowed by the house and traveled down its throat.

Rosemary pointed to the first door on the left as they passed. "That's your private bath. It's nice, but hasn't been updated this decade. Your bedroom is the brightest room of the house, having been transformed to meet the standards of a proper guest room."

"How long have you been working here?"

"Since I was sixteen, but back then I was just the assistant to the cook. In the past decade, the Mellings have let most of the staff go. They keep a full staff at their Government Street mansion, but things have slid on this side of the bay." She fingered the woodwork around the mirror on the door. "No more governess, of course, but there used to be a live-in maid and a butler who kept the house even when the family was in town, as well as a fulltime cook. Now it's just Leroy and me, and the part-time maid, Lydia, who you saw this afternoon. Plus, there's Mr. Campbell, who lives in the little house beside the stable. He's been here since Mr. Melling's father ran the place and looks after everything when the family isn't here. The roads around here are improving and Mr. Melling is supposed to get an automobile for this side of the bay like he has in the city. Since Miss Eliza's accident, no one's ridden for fun except Master Melling."

Magdalene, facing the mirrored bedroom door, could see the disquiet on her own face. "What type of accident?"

"Don't worry yourself none. The horse had to be put down."

She felt the urge to cling to Rosemary rather than be left alone with the Mellings. "And where does your family live?"

"Up towards Daphne, in a little bungalow. Now the family is late risers and not much for breakfast so help yourself in the mornings. I keep the basics on the sideboard, so it should be easy to find what you need. Leroy and I arrive by nine, and stay until supper is cleaned, but we come and go in the afternoons if we aren't needed for something. Before the noon dinner, I usually have to see to making beds and changing out towels on the days the maid isn't here. On Sundays, we don't come until it's time to fix supper, but I prepare a cold luncheon the day before. Not a bad lot. You should be more than comfortable. I aired the room earlier today when the sun was out."

When Rosemary swung open the door, brightness flooded Magdalene's eyes. The room was decorated in the aesthetic style with touches of the orient. The robin's egg blue wallpaper was covered with leaves and flowers, and the furniture was light enough to enjoy the carvings without being suppressed by the richness.

"Oh, it's heavenly, the perfect respite from the gloom out there! I've never been in such a pleasant room."

Rosemary nodded. "You should have everything you need, let's hope you are given enough downtime to enjoy it. I'm off now, but I'll see you in the morning."

"Please, just one more thing."

Rosemary paused at the door, her hand on the knob.

"Those stone samples delivered today, what are they for?"

"For Miss Eliza."

"But they just laid her marker. What more does she need?"

"These Mellings have more money than sense. They're building a mausoleum on the property. That poor girl had no break in life and can't even rest in peace. That's why she's temporarily laid to rest in the community cemetery rather than at the cathedral they attend in Mobile or the one up in Daphne she was so fond of. Those priests would never allow her body to be removed once it's placed."

A frigid sensation slithered down her spine and Magdalene shivered.

Taking notice, Rosemary pointed to the empty fireplace. "There are no makings for a fire, but if you're cold tonight, I'll have Leroy prep one tomorrow. For now, there's an extra blanket in the bureau. I'll see you in the morning."

"Thank you." Magdalene wanted to say something else to keep Rosemary longer but couldn't find the words, even when staring at the door long after it closed.

Four

After allowing herself a few minutes of woeful thinking, Magdalene unpacked. She removed enough clothing from her trunk to get her through the weekend—uncertain she would survive the scrutiny of Mrs. Melling. She placed her sketchbook on the little desk and her brush and comb on the dressing table. The damp chill in the air made her reach for her shawl, but she withdrew empty handed. Playing back the events of the evening, she recalled Alexander taking it from her in the parlor upon their return from the cemetery. Her reluctance to go downstairs after being dismissed for the evening was real, but the thought of facing the night and morning without proper warmth gave her no choice.

The kitchen had only a dim gaslight burning on the far wall, creating monstrous shapes out of the stoves and ice box. The light gleamed off the shiny tiles, making her path easier to navigate through the looming shadows along the edges of the room. Magdalene paused at the door and deliberately nudged it open enough to peek out.

The downstairs hall stood empty but was lit by the glowing lamp at the base of the front stairs. No sounds of conversation or the movement of bodies reached her ears, so Magdalene pushed the door the rest of the way open and stepped onto the oriental runner. The pocket doors to the parlor were open. A dying fire in the hearth turned the red room a mass of burnt orange flickering shadows. Both chairs flanking the hideous crate were unoccupied. Curiosity overruling her better judgement, Magdalene started toward the box.

She stared at the stones, allowing the warmth of the nearby fire to remove the chill that had its hold on her since Rosemary told her of the mausoleum. The top piece of marble, deeply veined with black lines slashing across the pale surface like claw marks from a wild beast, was violent in appearance. The contrast to the creamy white of the other stones begged Magdalene to know what the lines felt like.

Her hand trembled slightly as she reached for the marble. At the first touch she wanted to jerk her fingers off the icy stone. Instead, she ran them down the length of the slash marks, and then across to the light parts of the stone. Polished so expertly, there was no difference between the colors, only a continuous, smooth surface. Surprised that they absorbed no heat from the nearby fire, Magdalene ran her hands over more of the samples, her fingers continuously cold though her arms warmed with each passing second.

"It's a peculiar thing to spend one's time feeling rocks."

Magdalene froze but her heart raced on. The first face she saw when raising her head was the likeness of Eliza Melling. Her large, sharp eyes stared from the mantel.

"If geology is a hobby of yours, I'll bring you to explore the cliffs. Its color isn't the only thing spectacular about it. Ecor Rouge is the tallest spot of coastline between Texas and Maine."

On this second remark, Magdalene recognized Alexander's voice and turned to the far corner by the decanter set where she'd first met him hours before. He placed a pink hardcover book on the side table and stood.

"I came for my shawl. I'm sorry to disturb you."

They both moved toward the center of the room and their hands laid claim to what draped across the back of the settee at the same time.

"On the contrary, I hoped you'd return, Magdalene." His voice, low and soothing, was at odds with the Melling gleam Magdalene grew wary of already. "I've kept watch on this old thing since we came in after supper. I didn't remind you when you left because I wanted to see if you'd return for it. It must be special for you to roam around in the dark to find it."

Magdalene looked down at the shawl and then back at Alexander. A lump formed in her throat. "It was my mother's."

"May she rest in peace," he whispered back. "Allow me."

For the second time that day, Alexander draped the shawl over her shoulders. Silently, they stood facing the fireplace—Alexander behind Magdalene, his hands on her shoulders.

"She stares at us." Alexander tightened his grip before removing his hands from the shawl. At the mantel, he tucked the picture of Eliza under the veil that hung from the mirror. "Mother had it out earlier."

Though the portrait was covered, the young woman's gaze burned in Magdalene's vision. She pulled the shawl tight, keeping her hands clasped on the ends and her arms crossed protectively across her chest. "Good night, Alexander."

A look akin to fear flittered over his face and he crossed back to her in three quick strides. "You can stay awhile, if you wish."

"I suppose you want to offer me another drink." Her tone, light and teasing, was something she hadn't used for months.

Alexander ran a hand through his blond hair. "Not until I know if you're staying. I won't do anything to put your job in jeopardy."

Magdalene shifted, releasing her arms and placing one hand on her hip. Even with his face shadowed, backlit by the fireplace, their closeness allowed her to see his bloodshot eyes. "As much as I'd like to believe that, I'm not sure I can."

His head bowed in a show of humility. "I'd never hurt you, Magdalene. I need you here."

She couldn't stop the tug of mercy that pulled at her. To keep from reaching out, she clasped her hands behind her. The movement shifted the corner of the shawl off her right shoulder. Alexander closed what little space separated them. He reached the dangling edge of the shawl and placed it around her. Then he took the opposite end and brought the two together before her heart.

"I'm beginning to think Father knew exactly what he was doing when he hired you. Your purpose is clear," he whispered.

Magdalene took a step back but he didn't release the shawl. She mustered all the boldness she could, which didn't amount to much in her current state. "And just what is that?"

He tied the shawl with a loose knot. "A peace offering to help save me from her memory."

The shock of his words and the pleading tone sobered Magdalene. She needed to escape. Whether from Alexander or the house, she didn't know.

"I'm here for your mother, not you or the memory of your sister." She stepped back, grateful he released the knotted shawl that time.

"I don't speak of my sister but of the woman whose heart I broke, and she in turn broke mine."

His piercing gaze returned to show his resolve, but to Magdalene it only made it look as if he wished to own her. After her experience with William, determination not to be played by another man loomed foremost in her mind. But the struggle was real. Her heart said that broken Alexander needed her caring touch to help him through his sorrows. She could be the means of bringing peace and happiness to him, but her head shouted of his drunkenness and haunted eyes. He was untrustworthy and playing her.

That night, she listened to her head.

"Think what you will. Good night, *Mr.* Melling."

Magdalene didn't wait for a response. She hurried down the hall and through the kitchen, her boots clacking against the tiles. Not until she reached the back stairwell did she allow herself to breathe. She gathered her toiletries and clothes and locked herself in the bathroom. After adjusting the gas chandelier and sconces on either side of the sink to their brightest settings, Magdalene turned her attention to the taps. Though tired, the thought of a hot bath she didn't have to fill by bucket was alluring to no end. After trial and error with the controls, she had a bath running that wouldn't scald her upon entering.

She approached the full-length mirror in the far corner and saw she didn't look as frumpy as she felt, which brought a smile to her face. The wrinkles on her blue dress were hardly noticeable from a few feet away, but when she stepped closer, the truth revealed itself. She was travel-weary and dusty. Her dowdy bun was nothing like the high pompadour style she saw in the city and her plain dress was inches shorter than fashionable. Alexander must have mocked her to be so flattering.

Disheartened, Magdalene undressed. She had never seen her full body reflected and she stared at her alabaster curves in wonder. Never thinking much of her own looks, pleasure at being reminded of Renaissance paintings of figures like Venus and Aphrodite by her own figure warmed her cheeks before embarrassment over her immodesty moved her toward the tub. The feeling of warm water enveloping her from toes to chest as she stretched across the porcelain created a stir of excitement. She doubted she'd ever be able to hunch over in a tin tub in a kitchen again.

Intoxicated with the luxury, she pulled the pins from her hair and submerged herself fully. Washing her hair when it wasn't in preparation for the Sabbath was something she'd never done. She fought the feeling of indulgence in prideful behavior with the defensive thought that cleanliness was next to Godliness.

A noise from the hallway caught her attention.

She stared at the closed door and held her breath. The crystal cut knob turned. Magdalene sunk lower into the water and prayed she'd locked the door correctly when she entered. The thought that whoever was out there could have a key struck panic through her previously relaxed body. Suds ran down her forehead and stung her eyes but she didn't wipe them away.

When the knob rotated back without opening the door, Magdalene exhaled in relief. A rustle of movement sounded in the hallway, followed by stillness.

Hastily, she rinsed and drained the water. She shivered as she dried with one of the thick gold towels and squeezed the moisture out of her hair. Once dressed in her linen nightgown, she thought of her situation of being trapped in the bath with no proper covering. She couldn't make herself redress in her dusty clothing. If she stayed on, she would have to purchase a robe, for she couldn't roam the hall in her nightgown each time she bathed.

She left her laundry and pulled a dry towel around her white nightgown like a cape. Opening the door, she checked the hallway and dashed into her room. A new wave of dismay overpowered her upon discovering no lock upon her chamber door.

Not knowing who—or what—tried to enter the bathroom, Magdalene picked up the dressing table bench and placed it in front of the door. If someone opened it, the noise of the door striking the bench should rouse her, if she managed to sleep. It would be a long, cold night with damp hair and unknown hands trying to reach her.

Five

Up at daybreak, Magdalene opened the drapes on her window. The forest surrounding the house blocked most of the indirect light as though wishing to keep the inhabitants in gloom, but the sun infused the room with more cheerfulness than the gaslights the evening before. Though she'd spent the night chilly and frightened, her room by morning was glorious—the polished furniture gleamed and the flowered wallpaper shone with a metallic quality. She dressed in a plain skirt, ruffled shirt waist, and boots. Sitting at the dressing table, she undid the braid she'd created before crawling into bed.

The alcove behind her reflected in the mirror, the crucifix above the headboard prominent. Seeing the dark wood of the cross against the wallpaper by daylight troubled her. She'd seen matching crucifixes in all the rooms she'd visited thus far and wondered if their numbers served as a constant reminder of the Lord's way for the inhabitants, or if they became blind to them, seeing as how most of the crosses blended in with the dark wall coverings.

At seven o'clock, Magdalene paced the room a few times, thinking about all her gaffs the day before. Most of them revolved around Alexander. She dreaded the thought of being caught alone with him because she wasn't sure how she would hold up with the waves of emotions that besieged her since her arrival. Remembering what a fool she had made of herself after one drink caused a noticeable blush.

She was certain she'd grow to dislike all the mirrors in the room because she couldn't hide from herself. Besides the vanity mirror, there was a beveled mirror above the fireplace. It wasn't quite as tall as the dressing table mirror, but it made her conscious of her outfit, more specifically, how trim her waist looked. Though against her personal preference, she thought it best to wear a corset because Mrs. Melling seemed the type that would expect the ladies in her presence to be suitably attired from foundation to trimmings. The corset had been her mother's and was ridged with traditional whale bone—meant for formal occasions—but Magdalene didn't have many options when it came to finery and proper attire. The laces were long enough so she could cinch herself closed in the front. Even though it wasn't the fashionable serpent curve, the slight enhancement was welcomed in her current efforts to impress the Mellings.

Magdalene sat back at the dressing table and took her brush. Determined to replicate the pompadour hairstyles she'd seen in town yesterday, she set to work to create the soft pouf of hair to frame her face with height. It took several tries, and once she completed the front, she realized she didn't know how to twist the back up. She ended up doing a loose bun and pinned it to be sure it held through the day.

Pleased with her updated look, she took the back stairs to the kitchen and helped herself to a slice of bread and butter while she waited for water to boil for tea. Magdalene set a place at the square table in the corner of the room. Her bread was half nibbled away when the kettle whistled. As she turned off the burner, the door to the front hallway swung open.

"Miss Jones, it's good to see you up and looking fresh. I'll take a coffee."

She turned to her employer. "Good morning, Mr. Melling. I'd be happy to help, but I'm afraid I've never mastered the skill of brewing coffee. My first try nearly a decade ago caused my father to grimace and he never allowed me to touch his coffee beans again. I'd be happy to make you a strong cup of tea."

Mr. Melling harrumphed. "It will have to do for now, but be sure Lydia teaches you the art of coffee making next week. I cannot be expected to continue with no coffee when I'm here. Ever since…" He looked about and ran a hand down his white shirt sleeve as though brushing off a memory. "Ever since the accident, my wife refuses to leave her rooms before noon except for church and I've done without coffee in the mornings in this house. That is all very well for Lent, but Easter is coming and I want back what I've done without."

Seeing an opportunity to better understand her responsibilities, Magdalene set to work with another teacup. "Sir, Rosemary informed me the house maid, Lydia, comes but three times a week. Will I be expected to help around the house in her absence?"

"You're to do whatever my wife tells you to and nothing more." He sliced a piece of bread from the loaf. "That is, if you happen to meet me or Alex in the kitchen some morning, like right now, it would be agreeable if you assisted with coffee or tea as we aren't much acquainted with these preparations. Typically, we wait for the Wattses to arrive, but some days that's hours after I'm about."

Surprised that Rosemary had her information wrong, Magdalene continued her questions as she carried the tea to the sideboard. "So you're an early riser?"

"Yes, but I'll be in the city more often than not." He nodded his thanks for the cup and took his items in hand. "I'll be back to Mobile first thing Monday morning and won't return until Friday afternoon."

"And when should I expect to assist Mrs. Melling in the mornings? How will I know she's ready for me?"

"After you're prepared for the day, you may wait in her sitting room and anticipate her calling for you." Mr. Melling stepped toward the door.

"And where is her sitting room?"

He paused and seemed to search for the answer. "Two doors down from yours. There are several comfortable chairs. Make yourself at home." He pushed through the hall door with his food and drink.

Magdalene sat at the table with her tea and a fresh slice of bread, in no rush to attend the lady of the house, though she knew that if she lingered too long, it wouldn't be good for her prospects of staying employed. Nor did she wish for Alexander to happen into the kitchen while she ate. Mr. Melling was surprise enough.

After rinsing her dishes, she stopped in her room to make sure she'd left everything tidy. Not knowing how long she'd wait to be called for, Magdalene thought about bringing her sketchbook, but decided against it because many people looked down on ladies who spent time on frivolous pursuits.

In the hall, gloomier by day than by night, she looked down the red expanse of closed doors. All were the same—twin mirrored panels on the fronts and scrolling carvings above. She stopped before the second door beyond hers, across from the front stairs. The soft glow of the gaslight in the stairwell haloed her reflection in the mirrored door.

The knob turned easily and she stepped across a small section of bare hardwood onto a luxurious carpet, shutting the door behind her. She started to feel her way along the paneled wall searching for a light control while trying to make sense of the looming shapes in the dark room. Her fingers struck the edge of a switch plate the same moment her eyes adjusted enough to realize that the bulk of shadowed angles with touches of lighter areas to her right was a canopied bed.

In her shock, she gasped and her hand flew to cover her mouth. She could see Alexander's blond hair and bare chest tousled amid white sheets. With haste, Magdalene clawed for the doorknob and threw it open. She stumbled on the transition to the hall runner and found herself grabbing for the stair banister to stop her momentum.

Behind her, Alexander jumped out of bed. She silently cursed herself for reacting impulsively. If she'd kept her composure, she could have exited without him ever knowing.

"Magda—Miss Jones. Are you all right?"

"Yes." She kept her eyes down, looking at his bare feet below his sleep pants. "I suffered a fright is all. I'm sorry to disturb you. I came into the wrong room."

"Did you now?"

The mocking tone of his voice was too much to ignore. Magdalene raised her gaze past his lean torso to his smirking face topped with ruffled locks.

"Yes, it seems Mr. Melling lost track of the doors. He mistakenly directed me here rather than your mother's sitting room."

Alexander leaned against the doorframe and kept his voice low. "I find that hard to believe."

I'm beginning to think Father knew exactly what he was doing when he hired you. The words blazed through her mind, but still she found it impossible to believe Mr. Melling would send her into his son's bedroom when he seemed to wish her to stay on.

"Nevertheless, it's what happened." Magdalene stepped forward, ignoring the blush she felt creeping up her cheeks and the sense of unease in her middle. "Now, if you would be so kind as to point me to your mother's sitting room, I'd appreciate it."

"No need to hurry." Alexander crossed his arms. "She won't be up for another hour, but I'd be happy to keep you company until then."

"I'm sorry for disturbing you, but I don't think you're properly attired to respectfully entertain at the moment."

"Is it a shock for you to see a man like this?"

Magdalene scoffed. "If you're implying your thin pallor is beyond my field of experience, then yes."

A hearty laugh escaped before he could muffle it. He took her by the shoulders and pulled her just far enough into his room so she wouldn't be seen by someone looking down the hallway. He took a robe off the coat rack and slipped his arms into the sleeves.

"You're good for me, Magdalene, even if you pretend otherwise. Though I've been with dozens of women, I compare you to only one lady from my past. How many men am I to be compared with?"

Ignoring the reference to his experience, she played indifferent. "Do you so soon forget that I'm but a naïve country girl? Being raised amid the fields has afforded me ample time to study the strength and workings of numerous men as they tend their farms and livestock."

"I fear I'm no match for muscled farmhands and will have to win you over with my charm and wit."

His smile was impish and stirred feelings Magdalene did not wish to feel. She stepped backwards into the hall, her heart pounding more from her own flirtations than Alexander's intentions. "You'll need all the luck you can get with that. If you could point the way to your mother's sitting room, I'd be forever grateful."

"One more door." He pointed to the next room. "It's the last door on the left, something Father couldn't get wrong, but I'm okay with you thinking it was an honest mistake. I'll take whatever means brought you here, especially with you looking lovelier than you did yesterday."

Forcing herself not to run, Magdalene walked as composed as possible, forever feeling the weight of Alexander's gaze on her with each step. Between the two rooms, a veil hung over a picture. Tiers of blue fabric painted on the lower half within the carved mahogany frame peeked out from the edge of the black shroud. She could only assume it was the portrait of Eliza he'd mentioned yesterday.

Her own reflection in the mirror on the next door revealed what she feared—blotchy red cheeks advertising her embarrassment.

Still, Magdalene couldn't help but look back at Alexander, the winning smile yet upon his face. Once certain she was in the correct room, she shut the door and leaned against it in defeat. There seemed no way to safeguard against the magnetism that pulled her toward Alexander. Her heart beat faster with the anxiety of the situation. Surely, she couldn't have turned into a swooning girl from the attentions of one man. She couldn't be that desperate, that needy for love. But something must be going on within these walls, for she wasn't herself since arriving.

Six

Not wanting to dwell on her meeting with Alexander, Magdalene acquainted herself with Mrs. Melling's sitting room. The curtains were open with only sheers holding back the morning sun. Besides the large window and hall door, a second door stood closed on the other side of the sitting area. The furniture throughout was an eclectic mix, as were the frames on the wall that held everything from Madonna and child paintings to old family daguerreotypes.

Magdalene paced the mauve room and looked at all the pictures and china figurines—mostly birds and religious artifacts—by far the most cluttered room she'd ever been in. She pitied the housemaid who had to dust it all. In one corner, under a dark cover hiding something tall, came a flutter and two cheeps. She hadn't pictured Mrs. Melling as one to keep animals, but birds weren't ones to roam the house or leave fur behind.

Avoiding the veiled frame over the fireplace, Magdalene settled in a chair at the round table in front of the window. She pulled back the sheer curtain so she could observe the backyard. A clear view of the small cottage where Mr. Campbell lived and a path into the forest were easily seen. The deciduous trees budded new leaves but the gaps in the foliage afforded a handful of views of the bay, the blue water sparkling in the morning sun.

Magdalene sat until half-past nine, memorizing the lines of the forest so she could later sketch them. Then she heard the tinkling of a bell. She looked around the room, her gaze settling on the mantel clock, but the sound had not come from that direction. The second time it rang she knew it came from behind the closed door at the opposite end of the room. Assuming it to be the lady of the house, Magdalene crossed the room and turned the knob to open the door a crack.

"Mrs. Melling?" she called.

"Magdalene Jones, come in." Her voice was thick with sleep.

Bracing herself to enter a tomb-like room, Magdalene was relieved to find another rose-colored space. Mrs. Melling lay in an oak half-tester bed adorned with crosses along the three peaks of the headboard. Her white nightgown brightened her face and she didn't look half as old as she did in black.

"I'm glad to see you're ready for the day." Mrs. Melling shifted herself higher against her pillows. "You must be dressed before me every day."

"Yes, ma'am."

"I bathe in the mornings. Since I've been weak these months, I ask that you stay nearby while I am in the bathroom, in the event I have to call for help. Now please fetch my robe."

Magdalene retrieved the silk robe from the bench at the foot of the bed and held it open for the woman.

"Come." Mrs. Melling waved to her so she followed into the next room.

"Run the taps, please." Mrs. Melling motioned to the claw-foot tub. "I like it hot with two dashes of fragrance."

Magdalene plugged the drain, started the water, and then searched the wicker shelves for the right bath perfume. A mourning dress already hung on a hook on the far wall and the lady of the house added her robe to the collection. With the tub more than half full, she motioned to Magdalene to shut the water off.

"Stay sharp," Mrs. Melling told her on her way out.

In the next room, Magdalene made the bed to keep busy. A pile of ruffled pillows in various shades of pink crowded the corner next to the side table. When she bent over to retrieve one, she found herself staring at a skull. A square, marble footing held an ebony cross that supported a gleaming white Christ. At the base of the crucifix was a skull and cross bones. With a shiver, she took hold of the cross and lifted the heavy object to the table top. There she found a postcard sized frame face down. Magdalene placed the crucifix statue in the center of the square table and lifted the picture. The skull should have warned her not to meddle with those things. She found herself holding a postmortem photograph of Eliza Melling. Alexander had mentioned his mother kept the final portrait of his sister by her bed, but Magdalene had no idea it was a picture of an empty vessel of a girl.

The silver plated frame vibrated in Magdalene's hand but she couldn't let it go. Nor could she look away. Much like what she could make out of the cotillion gown in her veiled painting in the hall, in this portrait, Eliza wore an evening gown with more embroidery and details than she had ever seen on a person. Her hands were crossed on her chest and her dark hair was pulled up, her face veiled by a pale lace covering.

"Sugar," Rosemary rushed in from the sitting room, "don't let her catch you looking on that."

The cook pried the frame from Magdalene's hands, placing it facedown at the base of the crucifix. Rosemary kept her voice low. "You've had a fright, to be sure, but that picture is only for Mrs. Melling. Not that anyone else would like to gaze upon that unholy sight."

"I thought I'd make the bed while she bathed, but I noticed everything from the side table knocked over."

"You might as well know Mrs. Melling's been having night fits. She's likely to have thrashed about in her sleep. At least the glass didn't break this time. And thank you for helping with the housework. That lightens my load when Lydia isn't here." Rosemary put the finishing touches on the placement of the pillows, fluffing them accordingly.

"I fear I'm in over my head."

"Oh, she's not all bad," Rosemary said. "Being peculiar never hurt no one."

"But fits in the night?" Magdalene's whisper betrayed her unease.

"Oh, she's no danger. Just troubled sleep is all. Mr. Melling was able to get some medicine from their doctor in Mobile last week and that's helped settle her down from what I hear."

Thinking back to the rustling noise in the hall and the attempt to enter the bathroom while she bathed, Magdalene leaned closer to Rosemary. "Do her fits ever start her roaming the halls?"

"Mind you, I've never been here for one, but from the state of her room in the morning, it involves thrashing about in her sleep, not walkabouts. But you could ask Mr. Melling to be sure."

Asking Mr. Melling if his wife tried to interrupt her bathing? Not at all. Magdalene knew the options other than it being Mrs. Melling were truly more disturbing. And after she'd entered

Alexander's chamber this morning... No! She was certain she'd rather go on thinking it was Mrs. Melling. After all, the noise she'd heard afterward was assuredly that of a skirt rustling.

Rosemary touched her sleeve. "Don't worry none. Her tea and biscuits are on a covered tray in the sitting room. She likes two spoons of sugar and a slice of lemon in her cup. Just leave it where it is and I'll clear it after a while."

With that, Rosemary left and the *whooshing* sound of the water draining from the tub gurgled on the other side of the wall.

Magdalene paced the floor between the dressing table and the bed, trying her best not to look at the skull-decorated crucifix on the far table. This room, with all its ominous trinkets, was enough to steer her to melancholy and despair. Magdalene saw how it would not be healthy for Mrs. Melling and silently vowed to keep her out of it as often as she could.

On her next pass by the vanity, Magdalene focused on a delicate black wire shaped into a flower with a lone pearl as the center amid the looping petals. It rested upon an oval mirrored tray, all the decorative perfume bottles pushed to the edge, creating a circle around it. Unsure of the medium, she reached her hand out to touch it.

The bathroom door opened next to her.

"I was planning on wearing that today. Please pass it over, Miss Jones." Mrs. Melling's gray-streaked chestnut hair tumbled over the shoulders of her smartly tailored black walking suit.

"Yes, ma'am." As soon as her fingers touched the flower stem, she knew exactly what it was made of and wished to drop it. Fearing unemployment more than a dead girl's hair, she kept a light grip and handed it to Mrs. Melling. "It's...lovely."

Mrs. Melling sat on the stool and carefully slid the stem into a buttonhole at her chest. Then she reached for the cross she wore yesterday. It hung on its long chain from one of the carved scrolls on the mirror and her mourning veil hung from the other. She stroked the polished wood, but shook her head. Opening one of the tiny drawers of the dressing table, she retrieved a gold cross decorated with blood-red garnets. It filled her hands, the black satin ribbon spilling over her fingers.

"Please tie this on." She passed it to Magdalene. She marveled over its lightness despite its formidable size. Mrs. Melling held up her hair while Magdalene worked the ribbon into a decent bow at the base of Mrs. Melling's neck.

Once on, Mrs. Melling lifted it to her lips and kissed it.

"It was my mother's, and her mother's before that. It was to be Eliza's one day, but I suppose I'll have to be buried in it if Alex does not produce heirs before my demise."

Magdalene held Mrs. Melling's gaze in the looking glass, checking her reflex at wanting to flinch at his name.

"That son of mine has had several opportunities to marry since he finished his law degree, but my Alex needs perfection. One would think he could find an acceptable debutante in his years in Tuscaloosa, but apparently there were not as many Catholics there as I had hoped. Last year's carnival season was a debacle with that writer I tried to warn him away from. The drama of that insufferable woman—it nearly broke my boy. And, of course, this year's season was out because he was in mourning. But he's not one to settle for lesser things." With the last remark, Mrs. Melling narrowed her eyes at Magdalene. "Now, please see to the tray I am sure Rosemary has brought up by now and ready my tea."

"Yes, ma'am." With bowed head, she took refuge in the sitting room.

While Mrs. Melling arranged her hair, Magdalene added the sugar and lemon to a teacup as pink and flowery as the set of rooms themselves. But her mind wasn't on tea—it was on Alexander's extra years of bachelorhood. Of course his mother claimed his pickiness, but maybe the women turned him aside because they feared him too much like his father.

Mrs. Melling, still unveiled, sat in a velvet armchair opposite the window. "Just my tea for the moment. I want to be sure it's prepared to my taste."

With quiet resolve, Magdalene delivered the saucer and cup, and then stepped back to await the pronouncement.

After a timid sip, Mrs. Melling took another. "You do surprise me."

Magdalene breathed a sigh of relief, grateful for Rosemary sharing her insight. Her shoulders squared, confident that the tea was a key step toward secured employment.

"But no one can make tea like Eliza did. You may bring me a biscuit now."

And Magdalene was back to being less than human—compared to the ghost of a girl within the murky shadow of Seacliff Cottage.

Seven

Satisfied with food and drink, Mrs. Melling saw to her canaries and told Magdalene to fetch the marble sample and meet her by the front door. After she disappeared into her bedroom, Magdalene gathered the dishes onto the tray and carried it toward the back stairs. As she neared Alexander's open door, he positioned himself in the center of the hall so she'd have to squeeze around him to pass. Magdalene stopped short and met his gaze.

"Did you pass the tea test?"

"Yes, thank you for your concern." She stepped to the right and motioned with the tray that she'd like to pass.

Expecting to have to fight her way through, Magdalene was pleased when he stepped aside. "Are you off to the cliffs now?"

"Yes." She continued to the end of the hall without looking back.

"Let me get the door for you." Alexander hurried ahead to reach the stair door first, holding it open her.

The door at the base of the stairs was slightly ajar, so she nudged her foot into the kitchen. Rosemary looked up from the chopping block where she cut carrots. "Sugar, you should have left those for me. I'll be spoiled within the week."

"It's no trouble," Magdalene said. "I was coming downstairs anyway. We're off to the mausoleum site."

Rosemary gave her a look that spoke of sympathy. "Take care, then. I'll see you for dinner."

Entering the front hall, Magdalene was grateful Mrs. Melling wasn't already waiting. In the parlor, she went to the crate, expecting to find the piece on top of the pile, but it wasn't there. The deeply veined sample which she'd touched the night before still held the highest position. She looked around Mrs. Melling's chair, but came up emptyhanded. Refocusing her search on the room at large, Magdalene easily spotted the white stone on the mantel by Eliza's veiled picture.

Not wanting to touch the cold marble, she removed her embroidered handkerchief from her skirt pocket and wrapped it around the polished square like a present.

"How good of you to treat it with such respect." The veil did not mask the appreciation in her voice. "You may carry it for me."

"Yes, ma'am." Magdalene opened the front door, eager to escape into the sun from the gloom of the house.

From the umbrella stand next to the door Mrs. Melling took a thin, straight walking stick. With the veil and cane, she aged several decades. Magdalene shut the heavy door behind them and stepped into the morning, the house's imminent strength behind them only as powerful as a phantom in the sunlight. Under Mrs. Melling's direction, they exited the gated lawn and took a trail into the forest on the northwest side of the house as the windows of her suite looked down on them with gaping eyes.

As they stepped through the winter softened carpet of leaves, the chorus of birds quieted. The eerie stillness surrounded Magdalene in a shroud of anxiety. She clutched the marble, its coldness seeping through her handkerchief. She ran her thumb over the embroidered vines and morning glories that she'd stitched, and willed her heart to stop racing.

After walking a few minutes in the forest, they came across several freshly cut stumps scarring the land. Mrs. Melling stood in the center of the space and held out her gloved hand. Magdalene unwrapped the marble and placed it on the black satin. The contrast between the fabric of Mrs. Melling's glove and the gleam of the white stone in the sun was spectacular.

"This shall do perfectly, don't you think?"

"Yes, ma'am. It's beautiful."

Mrs. Melling nodded, then tucked the marble under her veil next to her heart and took a seat on a wrought iron bench beneath an oak. "You may wander for a few minutes, but stay close."

"Thank you, Mrs. Melling."

Beyond a thicket and the final towering trees was Ecor Rouge's edge. Magdalene could see the smokestacks of Mobile a dozen miles to the northwest, and between her and the city the water sparkled like a million stars. Her mind was clear, her body free. On top of the world, Magdalene spread her arms and filled her lungs with the coastal air.

Feeling brave, she stepped closer to the edge of the cliff and looked down. Below the sheer red clay lay a strip of beach, not twenty feet wide in the high tide. The gentle lapping of Mobile Bay reached for the cypress trees that grew to the edge of the water. Their roots appeared more claw than anchor as their trunks stood nearly as far above the sand as Alexander's shoulders, who waved up at her. Seeking comfort, she reached for her shawl that wasn't there. Not knowing what else to do, she waved in return before stepping back so she wouldn't be visible from the shore.

A little way to the south was a spot along the cliff with a boulder sheltered by a massive hemlock and welcoming ferns that survived the mild winter—the perfect spot to sit and ponder the world. Magdalene sat and tucked her knees up under her skirt, resting her chin on them. Below, she could see the end of the Mellings' private pier and across the inlet, Fairhope's public wharf.

Magdalene sat in the sun for several minutes, one ear listening for Mrs. Melling's call. What came instead was the snapping of a stick to her left. She turned, expecting to see a breathless Alexander after a run up the trail. Instead, a young priest in a dark cassock stared at her, eyes wide on his olive face.

"I thought you were a ghost." His whispered voice held an exotic accent. "She liked to sit here. I came to feel closer to her one more time."

Magdalene's body froze over despite the spring sunshine. "I'm sorry to disappoint."

"You must not think me foolish." He stepped closer. "She often came here to draw. Through the trees I saw you and my dreams became a reality for a moment."

She tilted her head, studying him. His hair was cut much shorter than current fashion dictated, but his Italian accent and coloring was a handsome match for his earnest, yet troubled countenance. There in his gaze, she saw the unguarded yearning of someone who held profound loss, different than what she saw in the Melling family. It was deeper, guilt-ridden.

He must have sensed her deduction, for in an apparent grab for control he closed the gap between them and took her wrist. In that instant, she feared for her life—so close to the cliff and captured by a stranger—and wished Alexander would come.

"No, *signorina*," he pleaded. "Do not think bad of me for my admiration of Eliza."

Magdalene tugged her hand loose and stepped from the rock to the other side, using it as a barrier. She brushed her skirt off and stared at his brown eyes once more. "I said no such thing."

"One need not speak. The eyes have all the language we need, and your eyes pierce the soul. Where Eliza could seduce with a glance, you can read the secrets within. You have seen the depths of my despair and know me as guilty."

"You're mistaken." Magdalene stepped toward the trees, hoping the quiver in her voice wasn't noticeable. "I know nothing more than what you yourself just declared."

His knees struck the dirt as he clutched at the cross hanging from his neck. He slumped over the boulder and muttered prayers that were unintelligible to Magdalene as he spilled them in his native tongue. But the tears were that of anguish and pleading, a universal language of the heart. While she had feared his intentions moments before, she now felt nothing but pity for him.

She gingerly placed a hand on his shoulder. "I don't judge you. Only the Lord knows your heart."

His breath steadied and he removed a handkerchief from a pocket. "The natural man is too strong in me to continue my training, but if I am sent home without receiving the full priesthood, I will be shamed."

"Do you not practice confession? Is there nothing you can do to lighten your load?"

"*Sí*, but I have been too ashamed of my actions to speak. It is because of me she is no longer here."

Magdalene wanted to run from the grief-stricken man and the ghost of Eliza Melling that kept appearing in conversations, but she held her ground—at least for the moment. She patted his shoulder, and then distanced herself a half a step. "She died by your hands? I was under the impression that she had an accident on her horse."

The priest quieted further, wiping his eyes with his handkerchief. "Not my physical hands, but she—"

"Magdalene!" Mrs. Melling's voice rang through the trees.

He blanched and looked at her with pleading eyes. "*Signora* is here with you?"

Magdalene nodded. "She's sitting in the clearing. Are you a source of comfort for her?"

"*Sí*, she clung to me in the early weeks because she thought Eliza saw me as a spiritual leader." He shook his head. "But no, Eliza was my teacher."

Hearing more than she bargained for, she wished to learn no more of the scandalous tale. Magdalene shook her skirt to remove any debris and the memories of the letter she'd received from William years ago, which brushed her off with much the same wording—he'd found a special woman who'd taught him how fun life could be and that was the end of their engagement. *Why must females be the vessel of such disgrace to decent men? Or were there such things as chaste and decent men these days?*

"I must go, but I think you should come with me. It would do your spirit good to lift that of another," Magdalene said.

With a solemn expression on his face, he nodded. "You are right. Just as Eliza, you are knowledgeable in the ways of the heart."

Her laugh was soft, bitter. "Not at all. I've been troubled since I arrived. I'm not in control of my faculties as I should be when with the Mellings. Maybe you can help me as well."

He offered his arm. "I will try, *signorina*. But first I need to see to *Signora* Melling."

Eight

"My dear Claudio!" Mrs. Melling held her hands out to him as Magdalene and the man came into the clearing. "I knew you would come to me today."

He kissed each gloved hand and his countenance shone with the urge to help. Magdalene gathered a small sense of pride for having been correct about his need to comfort others, especially the grieving family.

"I see you have met our hired girl." Mrs. Melling motioned toward Magdalene.

"Not properly. I took the scenic route and stumbled upon her on my way here."

"Mr. Melling took her on as a companion for me, and though she might not possess the dignified ways we are used to, I think she will do well." From the close range in the natural light Magdalene could tell which way Mrs. Melling's eyes peered through the veil— she looked straight at her. "But you must not go walking in the woods with strangers, do you hear?"

"Yes, ma'am." Magdalene's cheeks burned but she kept from uttering anything in retort.

"Magdalene Jones, this is Deacon Claudio De Fiore from Church of the Assumption in Daphne. Eliza was fond of going there and he has been a great comfort to me since my own Father is across the bay, though Bishop Allen himself came to pay his respects last month."

"He is most magnanimous," Deacon De Fiore said.

Mrs. Melling nodded. "Claudio, this is where it is to be. And this," she said as she held out the sample, "is what it shall be built with. Now, if you can secure permission to anoint this ground hallowed, everything will be ready."

Deacon De Fiore shifted his weight between feet and bowed his head. While waiting for a reply, Mrs. Melling patted the bench next to herself. "Come, Magdalene, you make me nervous as you pace about."

With steepled fingers under his chin, the deacon looked up. "God knows the yearnings of the heart. We need not seek approval to consecrate this land, especially since she will not go into it, but rest upon it."

Though she was admittedly naïve about their church, the situation did not sit right with Magdalene. To the contrary, Mrs. Melling clasped her hands over her heart.

"Then you must do it now!" She spoke with such enthusiasm Magdalene did not know how Deacon De Fiore could refuse.

"I must...I must prepare myself spiritually. Allow me some time to fast and pray."

"Nonsense, it must be done today, on the two-month anniversary! Why, it is even a full moon. Do you remember the night? The moon shone bright enough Eliza wanted to take a winter night's ride."

"Yes," his voice caught in his throat. "I remember that night well."

Mrs. Melling was too lost in her own sorrows to notice the anguish of the other. "I should have never let her leave. Who in their right mind allows their daughter to gallop about after supper?"

"You must not blame yourself, *signora*. You could not have known the danger lurking."

And was that danger you? Magdalene wanted to ask.

"It was a blessing you were nearby and heard the scream, dearest Claudio. There is no telling how long she would have been lost. It could have taken hours after she did not return home for someone to locate her."

The deacon's sigh was long and deep. With a breaking voice, he managed to reply, "I do what I can, but I am just a man."

"The dearest of them, to be sure." Mrs. Melling smiled under her veil.

Magdalene folded her hands together and willed herself to keep out of the conversation, though there were many questions she wanted to ask relating to the deacon and Eliza.

"I must go and prepare," Deacon De Fiore told Mrs. Melling.

"You must dine with us today. Come for supper and we shall break your fast and then come here."

He opened his mouth to protest.

"No, I insist, and the carriage will pick you up and bring you home. I shall send word to Father Angelo that we require your assistance on this mournful day. He will not tell me no. We have been too generous to the parish."

"*Sí, signora.* Then allow me take my leave." He bowed his head.

"You will be picked up at five thirty, Claudio. I need you to comfort me this night."

He nodded to Mrs. Melling, and then turned to Magdalene, a pleading look in his dark eyes. "It was a pleasure to meet you, *signorina.*"

She managed a smile though her mind continued to scream questions about the situation. With his earlier revelation, Magdalene half expected him to disappear and never return.

Mrs. Melling sat quietly for all of a minute after the deacon left. Then she sprung up like a young girl and called to Magdalene over her shoulder. "We must return so I can write the letter to Father Angelo."

Magdalene hurried at her heels, surprised at the speed with which Mrs. Melling moved along the path without the use of the walking stick she carried in her hand. When they entered the front door, Magdalene felt the weight of the interior crushing her body. Mrs. Melling instructed her to tell Rosemary to send fresh tea upstairs. She waded through the shadows in the hall to the kitchen and afterward ascended the back stairs.

When Magdalene passed her open bedroom door, her eyes fell upon the middle of the floor. Her sketchbook lay in the rectangle of sunlight. She placed it back on her desk, longing for the peace she'd felt on the cliffs. Hurrying down the dreary space, she made it to the sitting room physically intact.

At the corner desk, Mrs. Melling penned a letter on embossed floral stationery. "Do sit, Miss Jones. I do not abide pacing."

As she settled in a chair near the window, a shudder went down her spine as she recalled the person roaming the hall last night while she bathed. The rustling sound, like that of a woman's skirt, was clear. Rosemary had already left, and if Mrs. Melling was so opposed to pacing, why would she trouble herself with going to the far end of the long hall? The absurd thought that it was Eliza flittered into her mind. Once there, it anchored itself and chased all rational opinions into the last century.

Mrs. Melling wrote for several minutes, the scratching of her pen on the paper setting Magdalene's nerves further on edge. Just as she sealed the envelope, Alexander walked into the room, his hair rumpled from the wind.

He winked at Magdalene before addressing his mother. "Good morning, Mother."

She stood and turned, letter in hand. "Alex, dear. Have you anything to occupy yourself with the next hour?"

"Not at all. I'm completely at your disposal."

"Good, then you can bring this letter to Father Angelo." She held out the envelope. "I am requesting Claudio at supper. He is going to bless the mausoleum site for Eliza."

Alexander's bright smile faded and he slowly took the envelope from her. "I'd be happy to, Mother. Is there anything you need from town while I'm there?"

"Not unless they have decent flowers at any of the markets. A fresh arrangement to adorn the clearing would be nice."

"Any certain type?"

"No, you have a good eye for beauty. I trust your judgement."

He turned to Magdalene, a wolfish look in his eye. "And for you?"

Magdalene wished for a robe, but would never put Alexander in charge of something so personal. "No, thank you. I'm perfectly fine."

To Magdalene's relief, Rosemary came in with the tea tray. She looked over Alexander then addressed Mrs. Melling. "I only brought settings for two. Do I need to fetch another cup?"

Mrs. Melling crossed the room. "Alex is leaving on an errand. We are hosting Claudio for supper. Do you need anything from town to support the menu?"

"I shouldn't like to put Master Melling through any trouble. If I need something, I can fetch it myself this afternoon, but thank you kindly." Rosemary placed the tray on the table in front of the window. She picked up the teapot to pour, but Mrs. Melling interrupted her.

"Magdalene can see to that."

Rosemary nodded. "I'll ready the other rooms while I'm up here."

Magdalene waited until both Rosemary and Alexander left before approaching the tray. With a steady hand—though her mind raced with scandalous thoughts about the deacon and Eliza—she fixed Mrs. Melling's cup of tea and delivered it to her in the armchair next to the fireplace. While preparing her own drink, Magdalene mulled over the possibilities of Alexander's obvious distaste at the mention of the deacon. Was it possible he knew about his sister's inappropriate relationship? Did he blame the deacon for her death? If that was the case, Magdalene was certain Alexander would have told her about the deacon during one of their conversations yesterday. Maybe he had hoped to pass the morning with her and his mother, and it was only annoyance at being sent away that caused his smile to leave.

Magdalene sat with her tea across from Mrs. Melling. She did not wish to seem impertinent by asking personal questions, so she sipped her drink and gazed about the room, avoiding the unveiled face of the lady of the house.

"What did you do to keep yourself busy before coming here?" Mrs. Melling set down her cup.

"My mother was taken by the angel of death during the yellow fever epidemic of 1897. At fourteen I became the lady of the house for my father. That lasted until his accident."

"When was that?"

"The day after Christmas."

"And what sort of accident was it?"

"He was a blacksmith, the most respected in Seven Hills. His apprentice was giddy from his Christmas Day off and didn't follow directions. I wasn't there, so I'm not sure exactly how it happened, but the fire didn't stay in the kiln and my father tried to help right the boy's mistake and ended up engulfed in flames." Magdalene caught her breath before continuing. "I heard the shrieks. He was rolling on the ground by the time I came from the kitchen. When the apprentice saw me, he ran away. No one has been able to find him to question what exactly happened."

"You poor dear. So your father passed away?"

"No, he survived but is severely burned and his hands are useless. He all but lost the right side of his face, and suffered throat injuries such that he still couldn't speak when I left. He's bandaged and bedbound at his sister's home. She took him away after it happened, convinced I was unable to care for him properly."

Mrs. Melling's eyes were soft, kindness displayed on her face. "She left you alone in the house?"

"No, she made me come along with him, but never could there be room for a second woman of the house where Agnes Newell is concerned. I wasn't allowed to cook, help with my father, or leave the house without a member of the family, which only happened on Sundays. I was reduced to doing needlework in her front room."

"Such a setback for you after running a household." Mrs. Melling shook her head.

Magdalene, unhappy about being laid bare, did her best not to look pathetic when telling her mournful tale. "Yes, I was most anxious to be out from her thumb. I felt it a sign from God when I saw the advertisement for this position. The paper was three days old before I happened upon it, and I feared my letter would be too late when I sent an inquiry, but it all worked out in the end. Or so I hope."

Even before she lowered her veil, Mrs. Melling's face darkened with despair. "It is said when one door closes, a window opens. The door of Eliza's life shut so your window of freedom could open. Who am I to stand in the way of fate? Whatever reason you are now here with us, you must prove worthy. Eliza's death must not be in vain."

Nine

Mrs. Melling stayed silent the rest of the morning. Even during the noon dinner with Mr. Melling and Alexander—just back from his errands and late to the table—she only whispered an "Amen" after the prayer her husband offered over the meal. Mrs. Melling picked at her food and finally motioned for Magdalene to follow her back to the upstairs sitting room before lowering her veil.

Alexander had delivered the flowers after the ladies went to the dining room. The round table in front of the window held several buckets with numerous bundles of white lily of the valley flowers against the broad, shiny green blades of the plant. The fragrance from the blossoms filled the room with spring passion.

"Our Lady's Tears," Mrs. Melling said. "Alexander has outdone himself. Tell me, Magdalene, where do your talents lie?"

Caught off guard, Magdalene stumbled over her words. "I sing fairly well and—"

"Come now, no modesty needed."

"I'm good with a needle, too, but what I enjoy best is drawing." She held her breath, hoping she wouldn't be laughed at.

"So you have an artist's eye like my Eliza. She was often with her sketchbook on the cliffs or in the parks around Mobile." It sounded like she stopped a trembling lip with a sharp intake of breath. "I should like to see your work and show you Eliza's at some point, but for now, I need you to arrange these flowers."

Overwhelmed at the mass of tiny bell-shaped flowers, Magdalene took a step back. "I've done nothing more than arrange a few wildflowers in a bottle from time to time, Mrs. Melling. Surely someone—"

"If there is anything I have learned in my life, it is that an artist, no matter their preferred medium, can work wonders with a fresh palette." She spread her arms open. "Here is your project for the afternoon. Create!"

Before Magdalene could respond, Alexander entered.

"Alex!" Mrs. Melling embraced her son. "Your choice to honor your sister is perfect. I need you to help Magdalene with whatever she desires while arranging them. Fetch her supplies, help keep the flowers hydrated, and whatever else is deemed necessary. I leave this up to the two of you while I rest." Mrs. Melling turned toward her bedroom with a *shush* of her skirt.

As soon as her door shut, Alexander turned to Magdalene with the familiar gleam in his eye.

"And what do you desire, Magdalene?" He touched her shoulder and ran his finger down her sleeve, stopping briefly on her bare hand before she could jerk it away.

Overwhelmed with the enticing fragrance and Alexander's daring, Magdalene sighed in frustration. "I wish to work. To do a job well done and please your mother."

His icy stare warmed as he brushed his finger on the tip of her nose and smiled. "Then a glorious work you'll do, Magdalene, I'm most certain."

Seeing there was no room to work at the table, and unsure of what exactly she needed to do, Magdalene thought a change of scene would be best. "Should we work somewhere else, so we don't disturb your mother?"

With raised eyebrows and parting lips, Alexander closed the space between them. "Your room has plenty of space, as does mine, as you well know."

She clenched her fists and huffed. "That's in no way what I was referring to and you know it."

Alexander smiled as he leaned in. "You're simply breathtaking when you're ruffled. I'll try to contain myself."

With the slightest of touches, like a murmur of feeling, he fingered the spot below her right ear and traced the line across her jaw. When he got to her chin, he tilted it up. Magdalene, gasping at the tender sensation, arched her back in response—all the while screaming at herself to stomp his foot. She held his clear blue gaze while he glanced between her brown eyes and rosy lips, caught between willing him to kiss her and praying he wouldn't.

Alexander brought his face down at an angle, pausing inches away. "Woman, must you torment me?"

Then he dropped his hand from her chin and turned away.

The expectant tension in Magdalene's body deflated in an instant, leaving her craving his touch all the more. She was certain she wanted him to kiss her—and she wanted to kiss him in return. The thought itself infuriated her and she wished him never to know her feelings. But was it possible to hide her wants from the penetrating eyes of a Melling?

They brought the bundles of lilies to the back porch so they could easily fetch other greenery for the arrangements if needed. Magdalene, wearing a striped apron borrowed from the kitchen, eyed the quaint sitting area under the attached gazebo at the back corner of the porch, wishing she had the luxury of sitting on the swing. Rosemary wiped off the yellow oak pollen that coated the rectangular table and chairs in front of the outdoor fireplace with a damp rag before setting off on errands with her family.

Out in the sun and fresh air, Alexander didn't radiate with the same sense of urgency he did in the house, but still a lingering attraction niggled at the corner of Magdalene's mind. His blond hair shone in the natural light, his eager smile pleasant. She untied the twine holding the flower bunches together and reminded herself to stay on task.

"I need to see why the wagon is out. I'll be back in a jiffy." Alexander hopped off the back step with a boyish gait and disappeared into the stable yard.

Magdalene watched him go, wondering why she no longer felt the yearnings that tugged her toward him minutes ago. Having been so isolated before coming here, she must be going mad with the nearness of a handsome man—the first one she'd been around for more than a few minutes since William jilted her.

By the time she had freed all the blooms, Mr. Melling, dressed for a gentleman's day off in his brown walking suit, paused in front of Magdalene.

"I'm off to Fairhope for the afternoon. If Ruth begins to fret, please reassure her I'll be back before supper. Expect me by five."

"Yes, sir. She's resting now."

"Just as well." With that, he departed toward the stable.

When the open wagon drove past a minute later, Mr. Melling was at the reins. He didn't seem the type to ride about in crude transportation when he had a fine carriage and driver at his disposal, especially when he was used to an automobile in the city. Wherever he was headed, he must not want the stable hand privy to his destination.

Alexander returned with his jacket gone and cuffs rolled to his sleeves. Perched on the edge of the large work table, he smiled mischievously. "Now it's just us."

A shuffle in the yard caught his eye and he frowned. Mr. Campbell stopped before the porch steps, his hands behind his back.

"Master Melling, sir." His weathered face was tight, serious.

"Yes, Campbell." Alexander huffed with annoyance.

"I came to inquire about your trip to town earlier." His speech was slow, a hint of the Scottish brogue from his childhood tugging at the edge of his words, though it blended into the Southern accent of those around him from his years in Alabama.

"I don't believe I'm beholden to you for my whereabouts." Alexander looked toward the porch swing, feigning indifference though his body remained stiff.

The old man brought his hand out from behind his back, clutching a sprig of the lily of the valley with a soiled handkerchief. "As long as I'm responsible for the horses, it's my business if someone brings poison around them." He motioned to the table filled with flowers with his free hand. "That there's enough to kill the whole house, but this here piece I found in the dirt by the stable is enough to do in a horse."

Magdalene dropped the lily she'd held.

Alexander jumped from his seat. "What do you mean?"

"I mean to say these lilies are poisonous to eat. I've heard of humans and animals dying from these plants and I don't aim to lose another horse on my watch, however long it lasts."

Alexander looked over the white blooms covering the table then turned back to Mr. Campbell. "Do you think that's what caused Flora to—"

"A horse would've been crippled with pain and convulsions, not able to rear and bolt like one possessed. And there's no way she could have run that far after—"

"I see." Alexander brought his hand over his hair. "You can be assured I'll never bring the flowers around the horses again."

"Thank you, sir. And you, miss," he motioned to Magdalene, "you best be careful handling so much of it. Can't be good for you. Mark my words."

"Well, that was something," Alexander said after Mr. Campbell returned to the stable.

Magdalene, too shocked to move, continued staring into the backyard. He took her hand and rubbed it as though cold. Chilled to the soul would be accurate.

"Come now, we're all safe. There's no harm in the plant unless we turn animal and start eating. Of course, if I had known, I would have chosen roses or something safer. But even roses have thorns." He retrieved a stalk from the table, holding it up so the dainty bell-shaped blossoms hung down. "But they're still a perfect fit for Eliza. Their beauty holds a toxic secret."

Ten

In a hurry to be done handling the noxious plants, Magdalene rushed through three arrangements. Alexander provided two low profile bowls and a tall blown-glass vase. Once they were filled, Magdalene carried the centerpiece and Alexander took the two smaller arrangements into the dining room. She did not have to point out where to place them. Alexander knew what to do, especially when he cornered her against the sideboard when she stepped back to observe the setting. A hand on her neck, his thumb stroked as her blood raced beneath her skin. She was sure it was all in her mind, but his touch seemed to burn.

"Please," she said, breathless, "your hands. You've been handling the flowers."

Alexander's frost blue eyes crinkled at the edges as he smiled. "It's a shame. I should have thought about that before. Now I won't be able to taste your neck."

He closed the space between them and moved his hand to her waist, which she could scarcely feel though her layers of clothes. His exhale, hot on her already warm face, brought the immediacy of the moment to the forefront. Magdalene leaned against the table, bracing her hands on the slick wood on either side of her hips to keep them from reaching for Alexander. But her own eyes betrayed her yearnings, famished from years of neglect. She could only think of William, how she'd remove his hat whenever they pressed together, and held it behind his neck. It kept her hands from roaming, it kept her safe. Or so she thought.

"May I?"

His question, merely a whisper, startled her more than any shout ever could. She expected him to take—a spoiled, rich boy that took more than he gave. Someone who needed to control those around him. He was supposed to be easy to despise, but his tender ways and the voice within kept eroding her resolve to walk away.

The heat from his hand on her waist began to make its way through her clothing. He rested the other lightly on her shoulder. "Just a kiss."

It was more question than statement, but in response, Magdalene unwillingly leaned toward him, eyes closing.

His kiss—barely there in its softness—she left as his alone, fighting the intense desires that churned within. He pulled away and rested his forehead against hers, the sensation more affectionate than the kiss.

"You don't need to be afraid." Each whispered word prickled across her cheeks.

Aren't people who tell us not to be afraid the ones we need to fear?

She straightened her posture, thereby breaking Alexander's connection and freeing her hands from the table. They stood, staring at each other for seconds, minutes, seemingly hours. With a slight acknowledgement—the tilt of her head, unnoticeable to an outsider—Alexander returned, both arms around her.

"But your mother is upstairs," she said after another brief kiss.

He spun her around as though they danced to an unheard song. They ended, breathless, before the fireplace. Magdalene distanced herself, and turned to the mirror over the mantel. Her cheeks were flushed, and a few strands had come undone from her up-do. She tucked them behind her ear and smoothed them back toward the bun.

"No, wait." Alexander took both her arms and lowered them to her side with a smile. His hands were all over her hair, undoing her hard work from the morning. He toiled as though he were racing against himself, trying to finish before it registered that what he did was against all rules of decorum. Alexander stood to the side of her when finished.

Magdalene, too shocked to move, stared at her reflection. Brunette waves trailed over her shoulders and around her waist. The vision of a forest nymph in a Renaissance painting filled her mind. She yearned to pull free her corset and run barefoot through the woods, her hair streaming behind her.

"A glimpse of freedom passed through your head, didn't it?" Alexander stepped before her, blocking the view of the mirror. "We can be free, together."

As if possessed by that woodland spirit, she spun around. Her locks trailed out like ribbons in a May pole dance. Magdalene reached for Alexander as she slowed. He took her in his arms and stroked her hair. Watching his reflection in the mirror, she battled with herself over what to do next. Just as she succumbed to initiate a kiss of her own, Alexander stiffened, his gaze on something across the room. Using the mirror, she followed his stare and settled on the crucifix over the hall door.

"Forgive me." He released her from his grasp and turned toward the door to the kitchen.

"You asked. There is nothing to forgive." *This time.*

Alexander turned back to her. "You enchant me to such a level I can't trust myself. Nor can I trust your beguiling ways. We're a treacherous pair, but I don't want to be apart even though I know one of us will be dreadfully damaged by the time this is over."

He must have seen the light go from her eyes as he spoke the words. As though he didn't want her passion displaced, he took her into his arms and spun her around. Nuzzling his head into her loose hair, he spoke softly against her shoulder. "Since you walked into this house, my mind is not my own. Don't think me rash or forward, I simply have no control when it comes to you. You remind me too much of my first and last love affair."

Fear took power over Magdalene's body and mind long enough for her to free herself from the embrace she'd just found pleasure in.

"I need to see to the remainder of the flowers."

Alexander lifted a finger to trace her jaw line. "Such a shame."

"You're supposed to help me, remember?"

"Yes, of course." He stepped back, both hands behind his back. "Do you need more vases?"

"No, I have an idea. I'll need twine or wire to help me make wreaths."

His gaze, though full of adoration, held a shadow of regret. "Beautiful *and* clever. I'll see what I can find."

Magdalene paused at the mirror long enough to twist her hair into a simple bun. Alexander gathered her hairpins and she tucked the excess into her pocket. He held the doors open for her when she went back to the porch but he didn't join her until he'd found what she required. By then Magdalene had two long garlands of the lilies delicately woven together with the twine from the bunches. With Alexander's help in holding the greenery, she secured the weak points and tied them into wreaths.

"Is it a headpiece for you? Let your hair down once more and I'll crown you with it."

"No, it's for your mother and father to lay at the sepulcher location, unless they'd like one for her temporary grave."

"Father won't want to carry around a wreath. Why don't we take the second one to the cemetery right now?" His hand held out for hers, a fervent look on his face.

"No, I wouldn't feel right leaving Mrs. Melling. After all, that's my job. I'm supposed to be her companion, not yours."

"We'll see about that."

Magdalene easily brushed him aside as she stepped around him. "These wreaths need to stay cool. Do you think we could set them in the kitchen sink for now?"

He huffed in defeat. "Yes, you bring them in and I'll gather up the clippings."

"What will you do to dispose of the remaining plants?"

Alexander paused, tilting his head in thought. "I'll box them to save for my next bonfire."

"But where will you store—"

"I'm the one who brought poison to the house so I'll be the one to dispose of it." He held open the kitchen screen and motioned to the wreaths. "Bring those in and ready yourself for dinner. Mother will want us all to dress for the occasion."

Magdalene picked up a wreath in each hand and stepped toward the door, turning back once she'd stepped inside. With the gathering gray clouds behind him, Alexander stood like a burning candle against the gloom. If her hands weren't full, she would have thrown her arms around him. She hurried to the sink to free herself from the flowers, expecting him to rush to her because he was moved by similar feelings.

When she came back to the door, he was gone. Magdalene thought she heard laughter behind her, but when she turned, the room was empty. Questioning her sanity, her memories flitted over the longings Alexander stirred and the strange happenings that surrounded her since arriving at Seacliff Cottage. She committed to talk things over with the deacon when he arrived. The thought of his return helped her remain level-headed for the time being, though chilled. She climbed the back stairs, the sudden urge to make herself irresistible for the evening driving her to prepare herself.

Yes, we'll win them all, but most especially Alexander.

***

Magdalene washed her hands thoroughly before going to her room to gather a change of clothes. Out of the corner of her eye, she spied her sketchbook at the foot of the pale bedspread, like someone had lounged there to browse it. Had Alexander come in at some point? He had been with her most of the afternoon. Priscilla? But the Wattses were gone as well.

She tossed it back onto her desk and settled for her light blue cotton dress, even though more suited for a spring Sunday. The embroidered details on the sleeves, wrists, and neck were lovely, though too pale for an evening affair.

After she restyled her hair to resemble how it had looked that morning, she took her sketchbook to Mrs. Melling's sitting room and sat by the window, drawing the forest while she tried to figure out how to approach the subject of her uninhibited desires when she met the deacon.

Just after four, the door to the bedroom opened. Mrs. Melling emerged wearing a black silk dress decorated with velvet ribbons and organza ruffles. One glance at Magdalene and she shook her veiled head.

"That will never do. Do you not have an evening gown?"

"No, ma'am. I've never had need of one." Magdalene laid aside her drawing and stood.

"A mourning dress?"

"I outgrew mine years ago. I'm sorry I have nothing suitable. I can stay in my room if needed."

Mrs. Melling examined her. "Turn around."

"You may wear that to church tomorrow, but not to my table tonight." She rubbed her hands together as though they were cold. "I think there might be something. Come, you must accompany me upstairs."

Magdalene, having been told all the bedrooms were on this floor, assumed it was all the house had to offer. Upon further reflection, she remembered the dormer windows in the gabled roof.

But surely Mrs. Melling wasn't going to tromp around an attic in her evening gown.

She followed her employer down the grotesque hall. Mrs. Melling opened the door across from Magdalene's room, revealing a narrow staircase. She fiddled with the switch, waiting for the gaslight to brighten in the stairwell.

"Come along."

Magdalene followed two steps behind, her right hand using the railing and her left holding up her skirt. When Mrs. Melling opened the door at the top of the stairs, an unearthly cold draft wafted down.

Goosebumps prickled her arms. "Did you feel—"

"Come," Mrs. Melling commanded.

Except for the chill in the air, it felt as if Magdalene was inside an Arabian tent. She turned around to see all the sights in the massive room. The angled ceiling, swathed with yards of bold, Turkish prints hung down the walls in puddles of lush colors. The windows were draped with sheer fuchsia panels and also acted as privacy curtains around the untraditional pallet bed of purple silk. In the center of the room, a low table encircled by large, jewel-toned pillows held court, and near one of the windows, an artist's easel.

"It's most extraordinary."

"Eliza decorated it herself for her eighteenth birthday. She begged to be up here, in her own space, blanketed against the sounds of the house so she could paint and draw without distraction. The last several months of her life, she stayed up most of the night working. At least I believe she did, as she slept most of the day." Mrs. Melling opened a teak wardrobe on the far side of the room. "I can't stand the thought of someone wearing one of her dresses, but this one she received for Christmas and never had the opportunity to wear. I think it will do well for you."

Luxurious cream and black, with lace and puffed elbow-length sleeves filled Magdalene's vision. The embroidered detailing on the skirt and the ruffled train were more glorious than she'd ever dreamed of wearing.

"Hurry down and change." Mrs. Melling handed her the padded hanger, the dress draped over one arm to keep it off the floor. "Mind it on the stairs. And don't spill anything on it."

"Yes, ma'am. Thank you."

The gown was heavier than Magdalene expected, but once on her body, she felt she'd rise to the moon. Staring into the full-length bathroom mirror, she remembered the earlier thought of winning over everyone in the house, and she knew it to be possible. Even with her old-fashioned slippers, she knew Alexander would only have eyes for her.

Eleven

As soon as Magdalene dressed, Mrs. Melling wanted to go to the parlor. Once they were settled in the dim room, she rang for Mr. Watts. "Find my husband and let him know we are here."

Magdalene, pleased at winning the first family member's approval, ran her hands over the silky taffeta cascading over her lap. She'd never sat in such ladylike repose with ankles crossed, elbows directly below her shoulders, and chin up. Since Alexander found her pretty in her regular clothes, he would be sure to find her beautiful in the new dress. At the thought of all the good things to come, she smiled softly amid the oppressive air of the room.

Mr. Watts returned. "He's not here, Mrs. Melling."

"What? He knows we have Claudio coming for supper." Anger surged in her voice though her face could not be read through the veil.

Magdalene frowned, upset over having forgotten the message. "He went to Fairhope. He left while I was arranging the flowers and told me to let you know he would be back by five."

"Well, he has fifteen minutes to return." Mrs. Melling dismissed Mr. Watts and stared toward the fireplace.

The crate of rock samples still occupied the center area before the hearth. From afar, Magdalene studied the marble sample on top of the pile—the veined one she'd touched last night—and thought of Alexander's caressing words and touch. Tonight, she pledged to be the beguiling one, to stay immune to his sway.

"Magdalene." Mrs. Melling's voice broke through her fanciful daydream like a lantern in darkness. She pointed to the mirror over the mantel. "Remove that veil and tuck aside the sheers over the window, please."

Magdalene addressed the windows first. It didn't change the appearance of the room much with the sun already low in the sky, but it did give the feeling of openness.

"It has been two long months." Mrs. Melling sighed. "I do not want things to be dreary this evening, especially for Claudio. I want this to be more a celebration for her life than continued sadness over her death. After all, this is her coming home party. The work will begin on her new house soon."

A tingle in Magdalene's spine caused her to pause as she reached for the corner of the veil. She tugged at the lace but it caught one of the finials atop the mirror's frame. Then a hand touched the small of her back.

"Allow me." Alexander reached beyond her extended arm, his body lightly pressing against hers as he took hold of the black lace and lifted it off. He handed it to her with a smile.

She clutched the lace to her chest, hoping to hide her throbbing heart from his determined gaze. "Thank you," she managed to say.

"My pleasure."

"Alexander, please turn on the clock's chimes," Mrs. Melling spoke behind them. "I'd like to hear them once again. We've been silent too long."

Magdalene stepped aside, folding the veil. She kept track of Alexander's movements as he rotated the mantel clock and slid open the back. The drop of an interior lever was followed by the tinny sound of a bell being partially rung. His hand rested briefly on the photograph of his sister.

"Bring it to me, Alex." His mother reached her hand out for the framed likeness. She brought it under her veil to study the portrait in solitude.

"Is it time for your covering to be removed as well, Mother?"

"Almost, dear. Almost."

Aside from the ticking of the clock and the beating of Magdalene's heart, a reverent quiet settled in the room. She used it to study the smart cut of Alexander's dinner suit. The crisp black lines against the white of his shirt splendidly offset the royal blue tie at his neck. He caught her staring and nodded his mutual approval and she mentally berated herself for falling under his spell.

"Excuse me, but where shall I place the veil, ma'am?"

Mrs. Melling waved a hand, as if she wanted to be left alone. "Bring it to my sitting room."

In hopes of regaining her faculties, she sought to put distance between herself and Alexander. Magdalene hurried up the front stairs. By the time she'd laid the folded veil on a table near the bedroom door, she realized she wasn't alone.

"I thought she was suspicious." Magdalene spoke when she turned to face Alexander. "How could you risk following me?"

"She's lost in memories for the moment and I couldn't stay away." He placed his hands at her waist and pulled her to him.

Magdalene put a hand on his chest in order to put some distance between them. They gazed at each other, their eyes seeming to dare the other to make the next move. Emboldened by his following her, Magdalene moved the hand she'd meant to stop him with to his neck. His blue eyes widened as she reached around and gently guided his head to hers.

"Then kiss me if you can't stay away. That's what you want, isn't it?" The sound of her own voice, breathy and brash, scared Magdalene.

Alexander's lips were hot against hers. He started to pull away as soon as they made contact, like he'd done earlier that afternoon, but Magdalene kept him there. He surrendered and his hands roamed from her waist up her back, pressing her closer while their kiss lengthened.

Magdalene pulled away. "I must go back before she misses me."

He grasped her hand when she turned toward the door. "After supper, when they've all gone to bed, meet me in the parlor."

A smile curved up the corner of her mouth—pleased with the success of winning the second Melling—and she couldn't stop the flow of power swelling within from being wanted.

***

Magdalene returned to the settee in the parlor as the mantel clock chimed loudly for such a small clock. When the first gong struck, Mrs. Melling removed the photograph from beneath her veil.

"Take it back." She held it out to no one in particular.

Magdalene jumped from her seat and took the portrait. When she replaced the picture on the mantel, she couldn't help but see the sharp gaze of Eliza Melling. The iciness in her eyes seemed directed at her, as well as her shrewd smile.

"Alex, dear."

Magdalene startled at Mrs. Melling's voice and turned to see Alexander in the doorway.

"Please set a fire. Our Magdalene has a chill and I will not have her cover that gown with a homely shawl." Magdalene's cheeks colored as she slipped back to the settee. When Alexander knelt over the fireplace, his mother stopped him. "No, have Watts look after it so you do not get ashes on your clothes."

"I'm perfectly capable of lighting a fire without spoiling my sleeves, Mother."

"Yes, I forget you enjoy it. I shall not deprive you of your playthings."

It could have been Magdalene's imagination, but Mrs. Melling turned toward her and she felt her stare through the black lace. Had she been reduced to a plaything? Did the Mellings know how Alexander frolicked when he thought no one looked? She'd felt helpless to her whims, but she must admit she didn't mind the flirtations and contact—at least not while they happened. But the thought of her pulling Alexander toward her for the kiss soured her stomach. The aftermath spoiled the memory.

Magdalene switched the cross of her ankles and clasped her hands in her lap, doing her best not to watch Alexander building up the fire. Seeing him so close to the young flames with his hair cast in an orangey glow caused fear to leap in her chest. The vision of her father's accident was grueling to displace and she did not fancy seeing flames so near Alexander. Once the fire crackled contently, he stood.

"Do not hide yourself in the corner tonight," Mrs. Melling spoke to him. "Go on and sit by Magdalene for now."

The three sat in awkward silence. Magdalene thought about the previous afternoon. It seemed like a lifetime ago she'd been tipsy with drink and practically threw herself on Alexander. But if the alcohol was to blame, why did she feel the same way now? She could feel the tug—no, the heaving pull—of his body calling to hers. The inches separating them felt like miles, and the desire to rush to him primal.

Alexander sat rigidly, but allowed his head to turn toward her. At first his gaze was soft, inviting. A moment later, a panicked look of terror froze his features. His hand reached for her, but he stopped it with his other as if he were battling to control his own reflexes, all the while staring at Magdalene, who sat wide-eyed, watching his battle for control.

He looked away, but his right hand trembled. "Mother, would you care for a drink?"

"No, thank you, dear. But help yourself. Magdalene, too, if she wishes."

Coming to the conclusion that it wasn't the drink, but some stronger force at work, Magdalene caught Alexander's gaze. She held up her fingers a smidgen apart and nodded.

A look of relief washed over him, and he hurried to the decanters in the corner. The clock chimed the quarter hour. Mrs. Melling sighed in exasperation just as the sound of the front door opening reached the parlor.

"We've been waiting for you, George. How could you!" Mrs. Melling called out.

"At least let me change before you berate me, Ruth," he answered from the front hall.

Magdalene found it odd that Mr. Melling didn't come speak to them, and Mrs. Melling seemed to take it hard. She brought her hands under the veil, possibly wiping tears.

"The scoundrel," Alexander whispered so low Magdalene wouldn't swear to what she thought she heard him say.

She accepted the wine glass he offered before sitting next to her. Chancing a brief look over, Alexander raised his glass to her and winked. With his playfulness returned, she lost her nerve to drink. She held the glass and stared out the window into the gray evening.

As the clock chimed half-past five, footsteps descended the stairs. Mrs. Melling straightened to give the appearance of control, though she'd spent the last fifteen minutes mercilessly twisting a handkerchief, the wrinkled square of cloth now wedged under the cushion of her chair. Mr. Melling entered without a word and poured himself a drink before sitting in his regular place by the fire. He took his first sip and stared at his veiled wife.

"Everyone mourns differently, Ruth. I have no need of your judgement today." He finished the contents of his glass with one swallow and held it toward the settee. "Alex, if you would."

Alexander took his father's glass and refilled it in the corner. Mr. Melling's eyes met Magdalene's and he twisted the curl on the tip of his mustache. "You look exceptionally lovely this evening, Miss Jones. I hope all went well today."

"Yes, thank you." Magdalene had to fight not to squirm under his heavy-lidded gaze. Many drinks were undoubtedly part of his afternoon out.

"Tonight is a celebration," he said. "Be sure you enjoy all we have to offer at Seacliff Cottage."

Alexander deliberately walked in front of Magdalene when bringing his father the drink, taking the long way around the room to his destination. No one commented on his act, but Magdalene was relieved that the physical barrier, though brief, appeared to refocus Mr. Melling's attention away from her.

"Please, no more, unless Claudio wishes for a pre-supper drink." Mrs. Melling's voice was quiet but firm. She turned to Alexander, who had refilled his own glass when helping his father. "That goes for you as well."

"Yes, Mother." Merriment sparkled in his eyes as he looked to Magdalene. "You haven't touched yours. Don't be shy."

"I'm taking my time, thank you." She took a tentative sip of the red wine. Though she didn't exactly care for the taste, she found it better than the liquid fire that had burned her the previous day. Resolved not to get drunk—or throw herself at Alexander that evening—she held tight to her glass and contemplated the clouds outside the darkening window.

Twelve

The master and mistress of the house sat in stony silence for the better part of half an hour. Magdalene looked forward to Deacon De Fiore's companionship, eager to no longer be alone with the Mellings, for even she and Alexander could not talk without drawing unwanted attention from his moody parents.

A knock at the door coincided with the tolling of the mantel clock. Mr. Watts passed the parlor and Magdalene waited for the deacon to enter, but what she heard instead were the words "*Padre Santissimo.*"

As she was closest to the hall, Magdalene left the parlor and found Deacon De Fiore leaning against the wall muttering, "*Madre Maria*, save me," as well as a slew of Italian she could not understand.

Mr. Watts had stepped to the side, unsure what to do. "He came in and looked scared."

Magdalene placed a hand on his back. "Deacon De Fiore, I'm here to help. Why don't we get some fresh air?"

He continued his pleading in Italian as if he didn't recognize her as she walked him to the porch.

"Better?" she asked once they were in the cool evening air.

Deacon De Fiore nodded and stepped down into the yard, Magdalene following him.

Not wanting to waste what little private time they might have, Magdalene spoke. "I'm beginning to think something is going on inside the house. I'm not myself when I'm in there for long periods of time and it's beginning to scare me."

"I feel it, too." He looked her in the eye for the first time. "I feel Eliza here. It is a warning. You must not follow her path."

Alexander came onto the porch. "For the love of all things holy, both of you get inside!"

Keeping one hand on the deacon, she waved Alexander away with the other. "Go to your family and leave us a moment." She looked at the butler, standing just beyond Alexander. "Mr. Watts, could you prepare tea in case the deacon should need it?"

"Of course, Miss Jones." Mr. Watts left for the kitchen.

"Tea? He needs a stiff drink to pull himself together." Alexander looked pointedly at Deacon De Fiore. "Claudio, you don't want to upset Mother by coming in late, she might suspect something."

Magdalene glared after Alexander as he sauntered inside. He knew about the deacon and his sister, but as much as she wanted to stop Alexander from possibly uttering something to his parents, she stayed with the deacon, an arm around his shoulders.

"Deacon De Fiore, I'm here and we can help each other, but you must come in to see the Mellings."

His body heaved with a sigh that rattled the soul, and he whispered a prayer in Italian. She straightened herself and closed her eyes in reverence for his pleading.

After a moment, his words slowed.

Magdalene took his arm and they stepped into the house. Concerned by the fear she saw on his countenance, she wanted nothing more than to appease him and calm from the distress pulling at her as the temperature in the hallway noticeably dropped.

"This house has been turned into a—"

"Claudio," Alexander said as he joined them, "they're about to come looking for you. Pull yourself together."

The deacon released Magdalene's arm to do the sign of the cross over himself and then her. Once she was free, Alexander placed his hand on Magdalene in a show of ownership. The look on the deacon's face wasn't jealousy—he looked repulsed by the action. The blush of remembrance from her weakness with Alexander warmed her cheeks.

"Enter with me." She sought to redeem herself, holding a hand to Deacon De Fiore. "All will settle down."

The deacon took her arm to escort her into the parlor, and Alexander rushed ahead to claim his favorite spot in the back corner, unheeding his mother's previous instructions. While the deacon greeted Mr. and Mrs. Melling, Magdalene returned to the settee. The deacon declined a drink and sat beside Magdalene, wiggling his right leg in nervousness. The relief when Mr. Watts announced dinner was visible to everyone in the room.

Alexander, the fifth member of the dinner party, followed the two other couples into the dining room. Magdalene could feel his eyes cutting into her back as she walked with her hand lightly resting on Deacon De Fiore's arm. The two sat together on one side of the table, Alexander across from them, eyeing their every move.

Gesturing to the centerpieces, the deacon whispered to Magdalene. "*Giglio nella valle.* They are very beautiful, but dangerous. Where did they come from?"

She nodded toward Alexander, who appeared to be trying to follow their conversation. "He bought them today."

After the food was blessed, Mrs. Melling started in with their guest. "Claudio, I have the most splendid plans for Eliza's mausoleum. She shall have glorious white marble and a stain glass window. I have been trying to narrow down choices for the window art, but it is difficult."

"She loved nature," the deacon said.

"Yes, flowers would be an obvious choice, but I want something more. Something beautiful and pure, like my daughter."

Alexander's scowl spoke louder than anything he could possibly say.

"Then go with a bird, dear." Mr. Melling took another bite of steak. "You love birds and they are found in nature, among other places."

Mrs. Melling dabbed at her mouth. "Eliza was not fond of my birds, she liked the exotic ones, but those would not be appropriate on her resting spot."

"A dove," Deacon De Fiore offered.

"That is a possibility. A dove holding a rose maybe. I shall think on it. Thank you, Claudio."

At the close of the meal, Mrs. Melling decided they should postpone dessert to walk to the mausoleum site. She sent Magdalene to the kitchen to spread the word.

"We need to be on our way," Rosemary said. "We'll tidy up the supper things and prepare the dinner for tomorrow. The cake is on the sideboard there. Mrs. Melling will probably want it served with coffee and tea in the parlor when y'all return."

"I can't do coffee."

Rosemary laughed. "I'll prep for both so all's you've got to do is pour."

"Thank you."

"Now you get your lovely self out there, sugar. But be careful. The mischief of the full moon is out tonight."

Mrs. Melling and Deacon De Fiore took the lead. They each held one of the wreaths Magdalene had fashioned, their opposite arms linked together. Mr. Melling traveled behind them, carrying a lantern against the cloudy night. Last in the group were Magdalene and a moody Alexander, who didn't seem to enjoy having Magdalene's hand on his arm.

"Why should that insufferable fop escort my mother?" Alexander muttered.

Sensing his anger, Magdalene tried to reason with him. "He's a spiritual leader and she finds comfort in having him nearby."

His laugh was dry, bitter to the ear, but was nothing compared to his venomous whisper. "He's nothing more than a wolf in a deacon's cassock. It might as well be me with a robe and rosary."

The image caused a giggle to escape. Magdalene quickly covered her mouth with her free hand, but Alexander brushed her off his arm and stomped a few steps ahead. The darkness of the forest enveloped her senses. Though she was separated from the lantern by only twenty feet, the distance between her and the party seemed vast in the dark night. Her foot caught the root of an oak and she stumbled forward.

Alexander hurried to her side. "Can you forgive me for leaving you?"

Magdalene took his offered arm, a stiff gesture made from someone raised to be a gentleman. She was just as formal in return. "Of course."

In the solemn clearing, Mr. Melling's lantern illuminated only the center spot where he stood. Alexander stepped forward to fill the void left by the deacon when he distanced himself to lead the others in prayer. Magdalene stood in the shadowy edge near the bench, trying to ignore the scuttling sounds beyond the dark trees.

"In the name of the Father"—Deacon De Fiore did the sign of the cross as he spoke—"and the Son, and the Holy Ghost, we call upon thee to bless this ground."

Magdalene, hands clasped before her, watched the Melling family follow his lead, some more sensitive to the outpouring of the deacon's emotions than others. Though the words of the prayer filled the clearing, they seemed to flow around her without touching her ears. Her eyes closed and her mind whirled with the oddness of

Alexander's behavior and their combined flirtations. The press of his body, his hands in her hair, the feel of his lips... She shivered as she relived the sensations, so out of her perceived normal character. Or were they? Magdalene had felt the temptations with William, but she was able to overcome them at that point in her life.

"*Signorina*, are you unwell?" The deacon touched her arm. "You are freezing."

She opened her eyes, casting off the memories of shame that bound her. "I'm fine."

He straightened as Alexander approached.

"It appears my parents are ready to return to the house. I trust the two of you wish to accompany us rather than consort in the forest."

A look between anger and shock turned Deacon De Fiore's face to stone.

"You are correct." Magdalene reached out a hand. "Deacon?"

"Allow me," Alexander stepped between the two and tucked Magdalene's hand around his arm.

Mr. and Mrs. Melling led the way with the lantern, followed by Alexander and Magdalene. The deacon trailed behind, muttering in Italian. Magdalene wasn't sure if a prayer or a curse flowed from his tongue. As they approached the out buildings, Mr. Campbell peered from the front window of his little house as though he'd been watching for them. Magdalene waved a hand in greeting but he didn't return the gesture.

At Seacliff Cottage, Mrs. Melling sent Magdalene to fetch the food and drinks while the others gathered in the parlor. Magdalene removed the lemon iced cake from the glass cover and placed it in the center of the silver tray. As she set the teacups around the cake, the hall door swung open and Deacon De Fiore entered.

"Have you come to help? You could carry the coffee pot."

"Yes, I may help." His English was jumbled, showing his concern.

"What is it?" Magdalene set down the tray. "You did well at the mausoleum site, if that's what you're worried about."

He shook his head, sorrow in his eyes.

"Are you worried about Alexander? About how he taunts you? I don't think he'd tell his parents." Magdalene continued preparing the trays.

Deacon De Fiore slumped into a chair at the corner table. "I did not know he knew, but it makes sense. We were good friends,

Alex and I, when I first arrived. I met him on the ferry when I came to Daphne for training after visiting the archdiocese. Alex had fresh wounds from a broken engagement and was on his way to Seacliff Cottage for the weekend to ride Janus. I spent my free time with him. Then Eliza started coming with us on our excursions, and before long she made excuses for why Alexander could not be there, though I now believe she lied about him ever being invited."

"I don't think he'd betray a friend, but you need to clear your conscience."

"That's what I'm trying to do." He placed his hands on hers. "Preventing the mistakes of another would clear my heart better than anything else. Eliza is here. She wants—"

The door swung open. "What I want is for you to keep your hands off what isn't yours, Claudio." Alexander stalked into the room.

Magdalene turned to him. "It's not like that. He wasn't trying—"

"I know full well what he's trying. I've seen it before." Alexander stepped between Magdalene and the deacon, shielding her from his view.

"Alexander, you do not understand." Deacon De Fiore clutched the cross around his neck. "I am here to warn her."

"What? Warn her that not everyone in holy garments is saintly?"

Magdalene tried to push around Alexander to get to the deacon but he held his place, blocking her.

Deacon De Fiore's countenance sunk into despair. "I am a man and have made mistakes."

Alexander smirked. "I guess it's the holy ones who fall the furthest."

"Eliza loved me, I loved her. Our love was beautiful, though sinful."

Alexander laughed. "She played you for a fool, as she'd strung men along before. Eliza loved the thrill of the chase, the drive of forbidden love, the beauty of the human form, not you."

A sickness rose in Magdalene's stomach. She gripped Alexander's arm. "He's pained enough!"

The deacon, ashen, placed a hand on the back of the chair next to him. "Eliza loved me."

Alexander's laugh was bawdy. Disgusted with his harassment, Magdalene shoved him and crossed the room to the deacon, laying a hand on his shoulder.

Seemingly strengthened by her touch, Deacon De Fiore returned Alexander's bitter glare. "Our love was real."

"I guess we'll never know because she took that secret to the grave." Alexander's face tightened.

"No, Alex, I know, and you will, too."

One of the black-and-gold teacups began clinking. It soon turned into a rattle and then flew off the tray, shattering on the tile at Alexander's feet. Blue eyes wide, he looked at the shards on the floor and then at Claudio.

The deacon pointed to the destruction at his feet. "She is here. That is your proof she loved me."

"Does Father Angelo know you dabble in magic?" Alexander stepped over the broken china, his chin defiantly raised. "Magdalene, fetch another cup. I'll carry the tray for you."

The teacup replaced, Magdalene took the coffee pot in one hand, the teapot in the other.

"Come, both of you." Alexander led the way through the swinging door. In the hall, he turned to Magdalene. "And not a word of this to my parents."

Thirteen

Huddled under the cream-colored blankets in bed, Magdalene's body tried to unwind from the stress of the day. She'd been dismissed for the night not long after serving the cake. Thinking it better to prepare for bed while the others were still entertaining, she completed a hasty bath and changed into her white night dress. Though she felt sorry for leaving the deacon at the mercy of Alexander, she thought he'd be safe with Mrs. Melling around.

From the shelter of her bedroom—the bench once again against her door—she listened intently for sounds from the hall. In her mind, she heard the rattle of the teacup against the silver tray. How an unseen hand shattered it upon the floor she did not know, but the ghostly scene would not leave her mind. The teacup made her remember her displaced sketchbook, moved twice that day without her permission. Eliza was an artist. Was she peeking at her drawings? She pulled the brocade bedcover over her head. If Eliza were to make an appearance, Magdalene did not wish to see her because the eyes of a dead Melling must surely be worse than those of the living.

An hour after she last heard doors closing down the hall, Magdalene still cowered under the blankets. She fancied the sound of footsteps in the attic room and prayed for sleep. Though no longer chilled, she had the feeling something was wrong, similar to the impression she experienced before her mother took a turn for the worse all those years ago. After the fact, she knew she should've sent for the doctor the hour before. By then, it was too late.

Unable to lie still, she clambered out of bed and opened her curtains to let in the full moonlight in the now clear sky. While she paced, she re-braided her hair and avoided looking at herself in any of the mirrors. She didn't want to mistakenly see Eliza's reflection instead of her own. When she passed the desk, the inert sketchbook caught her eye. She fingered the spine, and then spied the bottle of black ink, pulling her memory to another black container.

The broken teacup needed her attention. With tomorrow being Sunday, Rosemary wouldn't be there until time to fix supper, and Magdalene didn't think it right for the shattered china to be on display for the family to step over. Nor did she wish to answer any questions Mr. Melling might have, as he could possibly see it before she woke in the morning. She must clean it to avoid the explanation of how it broke in the first place. Though she wanted to stay safe in bed, the urge to attend to the cup pulled stronger than her comfort.

She forewent her house shoes and placed her mother's shawl around her nightgown as a makeshift robe. Moving the bench aside so she could exit the room, she entered the dim hallway that hummed with the glow of the low-burning chandeliers. She tiptoed down the back stairs and nudged open the door at the bottom.

In the middle of the tile floor the fragmented teacup lay. Though she thought it beyond repair, she swept the pieces into a dustpan and set it under the work bench for Rosemary to see on the morrow. The squeal of the hinges on the hall door sounded menacing as she replaced the broom on the hook in the corner. From down the hallway, the clock struck midnight and its ominous bongs echoed through the open door. Magdalene hugged the shawl across her chest and turned.

Alexander, still dressed, though his tie and dinner jacket were missing and the top two buttons on his shirt were undone, stepped toward the middle of the room. He placed an empty tumbler on the cutting block.

"I hoped you were on your way to the parlor." He motioned to the empty floor. "But keeping things tidy is a good habit to have when you don't wish to leave a trail."

There in the moonlight, his eyes shone like the hottest part of a fire—pale blue and bright. Compelled to see them closer, Magdalene approached the square of light. The cold tile beneath her feet heightened the sensations her body felt with each step under his gaze. She stopped more than an arm's reach away, fixed upon his intense stare.

"Come," he whispered.

Magdalene had to move, but didn't want to obey. She took a tentative step forward. Her skin felt as though kissed by the sun. A warm glow spread from her feet to her scalp and she heard the sounds of rushing wind like a summer storm.

Alexander stepped in to meet her, his hand skimming her fingers and then traveling up the thin sleeve of her night dress until it cradled her neck beneath her braid. His breath, woodsy with the smell of roasted fruits, aroused the image Magdalene had that afternoon of running free through the forest. She reached for him.

He brought both his hands to his side and smiled in invitation. "What will you do to me, Magdalene?"

Not meaning to be coy, she shrugged and her shawl slipped to a heap behind her. Alexander's hands gripped into fists, but relaxed when she stepped behind him. She draped her arms over his shoulders.

"What is it you want from me?" she whispered in his ear, though she already knew the answer.

He turned slowly, keeping her arms about his shoulders, and gripped her waist, surely feeling her hot skin through the nightgown. "There is no want, only need."

His mouth covered hers and she tasted his brandy-lips. The sweetness caused her to cling to him longer, but the thought of his possible drunkenness gave her pause enough to notice the redness around his eyes.

She traced a finger along his brow. "Did you behave yourself the rest of the deacon's visit?"

He forcibly exhaled. The air he expelled bewitched her further. "I was a gentleman, same as always. Claudio is the animal twisting you around his will by seeming helpless in sorrow."

Alexander lifted her braid and slowly kissed her neck above her lace collar as his other hand pulled her against him. Tingling all over, Magdalene gripped his shoulders. He nuzzled into her as she shuffled backward toward the counter. The side of her foot pricked something on the way.

"Ouch!" Magdalene lifted the affected foot and wobbled slightly.

Alexander leaned back to look at her. "What's wrong?"

"I stepped on something." The formerly hot air turned chill and Magdalene felt exposed.

He accompanied her to a chair at the corner table. "Sit and let's take a look."

"Please"—she pointed to her shawl on the ground—"will you get it for me?"

She pulled her left foot onto her right knee and lifted her nightgown enough to look while his back was turned. A sliver of china stuck into the arch of her foot. She plucked it out easily, a small dot of blood marked where it had been.

"You're bleeding."

Magdalene dropped her foot and gown as he placed the shawl around her shoulders. "It's nothing, just a prick from a piece of the teacup."

Alexander found a clean dishtowel and knelt before her. Without speaking, he reached for her left ankle and raised her foot. He pressed the folded towel against the tiny wound with both hands.

"Thank you, but I'm sure it's fine." She tried to lower her foot, but Alexander kept it straight.

"It needs pressure for a few minutes to make sure."

"Truly, it's a small cut, more like a nick. You're overdoing it."

"Better to err on the side of safety than to leave things undone." He took one hand and followed the curve of her ankle around her leg. With an impish smile, he studied her face for a reaction.

Afraid to speak, Magdalene shook her head.

"Shame." He kissed the top of her foot before lowering it to the floor. Standing, he tossed the towel into the sink and held his hands out to Magdalene. "You're freezing."

Magdalene couldn't fib her way out of the truth. She stood, looking him in the eye. "I'll be fine once I get to my room."

"Is there a fire going?"

"No, but I'm comfortable in there." She looked toward the stair door, suddenly wanting nothing more than to escape.

"Let me come with you." He came to her side, one arm around her. "I'll build a fire."

Magdalene stepped out of his grasp. "There's no need," she said over her shoulder.

Alexander followed and took her braid into his hands. He undid the bottom ribbon and methodically raked his fingers through the twists.

"Is there no need," he whispered, "because of the fire between us?"

In response, Magdalene turned and placed her lips against his before she could talk herself out of it. With her hair spilling around her shoulders, she felt it would protect her from immodesty, like a cloak. Her logic was as muddled as her feelings, but she gave in to the enticement because with William she had always held back, kept their kisses chaste. Now as she played in Alexander's hair and ran her hands across his shoulders, she wondered if she hadn't been so pious, if she'd be long married to William now. But her moments with Alexander were otherworldly in their intensity, something different than what she ever had with her former fiancé. And in the moment, she was fine with it.

"What spell have you cast on me?" Alexander's words scorched her neck from where he nestled into her hair.

They were in a breathless tangle against the wall between the doors to the stairs and front hall. Magdalene endeavored to straighten herself, but feeling more wildcat than young woman, arched in a stretch and pressed against Alexander. He stroked the length of her hair to smooth what he had previously tousled.

"We need to keep our wits, Magdalene. How about a drink? The fire's still going in the parlor."

"All right."

Alexander once again retrieved her shawl from the floor and they walked hand in hand to the other room. He left her in front of the fire and got his dinner jacket from the corner of the room. The way he looked at her from head to toe while she was backlit by the fire caused Magdalene to blush.

"You make it difficult to keep away." Alexander took her shawl and helped her into his black suit jacket, taking the time to button it closed. Before going to fix the drinks, he sat her in the chair to the left of the fireplace and tucked the green shawl over her lap.

Feeling like Eve with nothing but a triangle of fig leaves to cover her nakedness, Magdalene couldn't help but be ashamed of her lustful actions. At the age of twenty-two, she finally understood the real pull of the natural man and found herself behaving like one of the women she despised for ruining men like William. While thankful to have reached that point in her life unscathed, she feared for what the future held, especially when Alexander placed the glass of brandy in her hand.

He sat on the rug at her feet, rested an arm on her knee, and sipped from his glass as he stared at the fire.

Magdalene brought her own cup to her lips—the woodsy aroma once again made her head spin. When she'd first drunk it yesterday, she hadn't taken the time to smell or taste it. She only remembered the burn and coughing. Now that she'd tasted it on Alexander's lips, curiosity got the better of her. Warily, she tilted the glass and drank a mouthful. The heavy smoothness went down easily and burned like fire in her belly.

Alexander squeezed her knee. "Much better this time."

She laughed softly and tried another. That time, she coughed.

"Pace yourself, Magdalene. We have all night."

After her third swig, she'd grown accustomed to the burn and found it vaguely comforting. It drowned the nagging voice that told her to run away before she was completely ruined. Soon enough, buzzing hummed in her head and she no longer cared. She leaned back against the chair with a sigh.

"Warm and relaxed, are we?" Alexander took her almost empty tumbler and set both of their glasses on the nearby coffee table. He rested a hand on each of her knees, his thumbs caressing them with circular motions through her gown. "You've filled such a void in my life, it's difficult to believe you only arrived yesterday."

"You need not lack anything." She grasped the open collar of his shirt.

Before she realized her actions, she found herself on the edge of the chair wrapped in another kiss. Alexander's hands went up from her knees to her hips, and then under his jacket to her waist all while their lips roamed each other's mouths, jaws, and necks. Needing to breathe, Magdalene collapsed against the back of the chair, her loose hair fanned around her shoulders. The room practically spun around Alexander, whom she tried to stay focused on, but in her dizzy vision he appeared to have two heads.

No man can serve two masters. She found the verse ingrained from her earliest Bible studies comical when it came to her, but if she could only choose one, she knew in that moment which side her loyalties lay.

Magdalene straightened herself and looked him in the eye. "Your passion is my master."

A grin played across his lips as the gleam in his eye took on a wicked hue. The shift sobered Magdalene, and as the clock struck the half hour, she took the interruption as a way out.

"It's later than I thought. I'm sure we both need rest."

"There's only one thing I need…"

Alexander pulled her to her feet and smothered her with caresses meant to be her undoing. But from where she stood, she stared at the photograph of Eliza on the mantel. A cold shiver ran down her spine. Alexander took it as electricity from his efforts and unbuttoned the jacket.

To get his attention, she kissed him on the mouth and then spoke. "Not here, not now."

He smirked. "But my passion is your—"

"Not here—"

"But now?"

She needed to stop the play of lust before things went too far. Without a word, she rushed for the door and down the hall. Her bare feet slapped across the kitchen tile and pattered up the stairs. Lightheaded from her flight when she reached her room, she took a moment to steady herself by placing a hand on the doorframe.

Alexander, having taken the closer front staircase, stood calmly inside her moonlit bedroom. "I'm here for my jacket."

Fourteen

Magdalene first thought Alexander looked sinister standing defiantly in her room. With a softening heart, she found it romantic that he'd rushed ahead to surprise her. She hesitated only a second before closing the door. The faint click seemed louder than it was, signaling the next step on her path to ruination.

Untroubled—or beyond caring because she only listened to her new master—Magdalene unhooked the final button on Alexander's dinner jacket and willed him to take it from her. She watched in the dressing table mirror as he deftly removed the dark covering, exposing the full pureness of her nightgown. It wasn't herself she saw reflected, but a temptress with flowing tresses and yearning in her eyes.

Alexander tossed the jacket onto the bench, which stood by itself near the door, an awkward reminder that earlier Magdalene had feared her safety. Again, the windless breeze blew, but this time it caught her physically, rippling her gown and lifting her hair off her shoulders. It cooled her fiery skin so that when Alexander took her hand, his touch warmed her. The air ruffled his hair, but he didn't seem to notice during his efforts to unfasten the buttons on the upper back of her gown. The top two buttons open, he nudged down the eyelet at the front to expose her collarbone.

His lips on that tender spot previously untouched by a man caused a moaning gasp to escape Magdalene. She stiffened in his arms, fearing the appetite that coursed through each layer of her body and urged her to behave in such a manner. Somewhere, deep inside, she heard a faint scream of *Stop!* But all the other voices implored her to proceed. She wanted more of the strength she felt from being wanted, so she didn't resist when he led her toward the alcove and sat her on the edge of the bed.

Magdalene smiled up at Alexander as she reached for the bottom button of his untucked shirt. Her hands quivered with trepidation, but the whirling air stirred sensation across her skin and whispered to her body desires she never knew she had. Outwardly, it was a small draft, but inside, a gale of craving raged. With the front of his shirt free, Magdalene reached her arms around his back and hugged him, resting the side of her face against his bare stomach. She fought herself to stay that way, unmoving, to absorb all the sensations of the moment. Alexander leaned against her, seeming to enjoy the respite as well.

But it was short-lived.

Magdalene's curiosity to how he would react to her lips on his body heightened with the wailing of the cyclone inside her. Her fingers traced his torso and led the way for her to take a nibbling kiss on one of his ribs. With a sharp intake of breath, Alexander pushed his body against her and threw his head back. She looked up to see his face as he lowered his gaze. She expected his hungry eyes to fall upon her and then he would take control. Instead, his body went slack in her arms. Eyes closed, he bowed his head and stepped away from Magdalene.

"Lord, forgive me." His voice, obscured by the whirlwind that filled the space, dripped with regret.

The squall flapped the curtains and caught Alexander's shirttails. No longer able to ignore the ghostly wind, Alexander opened his eyes and looked around the room. The pages of Magdalene's sketchbook fluttered on her desk and the borrowed dress she had worn that evening nearly ripped off the hanger where it hung on the front of the wardrobe.

Horror paled his astonished face as he looked to Magdalene. "What have we done?"

The blowing calmed, but a mischievous laugh from unknown origins replaced the void.

"No more games!" he shouted before snatching his dinner jacket off the bench and flinging the door open. He half-ran, half-stumbled down the hall and slammed his bedroom door shut.

With tears in her eyes, Magdalene quietly closed her own door, replacing the bench in its nighttime location. Then she threw herself on the bed and sobbed. Afraid to scrutinize her crying because on the surface she wasn't sure if they were tears of shame or frustration. Even admitting that much caused a fresh sob to rack her body. Physically, she'd traveled a scarce thirty miles from Seven Hills, but emotionally she'd plunged into outer darkness.

Exhausted and her pillow soaked, she finally fell asleep.

***

It was light outside but overcast when Magdalene opened her bloodshot eyes, face crusty with dried tears and her hair a matted brown mass. The image she saw when she passed the dressing table wasn't hopeful, but she gathered her blue Sunday dress and locked herself in the bathroom until she made herself presentable. When she was satisfied that she did not look as if she'd spent most of the night in passion and tears, she descended the stairs to the kitchen.

Halfway through a leftover dinner roll and cup of tea, Magdalene turned when the hall door swung open. Veiled in all black, the soft green of Magdalene's shawl was a stark contrast to the gloves that held them.

"I found this on the parlor floor when I came down this morning. You were not wearing it at the dinner party. How did it come to be there?" Mrs. Melling didn't accuse her, but there was an edge of knowing something was amiss in her voice.

Magdalene tentatively reached for the shawl while her brain spun possible excuses. "I'm sorry I was careless. I had a chill after everyone went to bed and I'm not good with lighting a fire. I came down to see if one still burned and warmed myself for a few minutes."

With the partial lie spoken, she clutched her mother's shawl to her chest and held her breath until she knew if it would pass judgement.

"Be sure to have Mr. Watts kindle one for you after supper this evening. It is so damp today, I expect there to be rain before long."

With a relieved exhale, Magdalene smiled. "Yes, thank you, Mrs. Melling."

"Be in the yard in half an hour. You are riding with the family this time. After today, you will have to find your own means to whichever congregation you wish to attend."

"Do you need any help before we leave?"

"No, Sundays give me new hope and energy. I take care of myself quite well this one day each week. A small miracle if there ever was one." Mrs. Melling disappeared into the front hall.

Magdalene, having lost what little appetite she previously had, poured her tea into the sink and left her half-eaten roll in the rubbish container. When she turned to leave, something white on the floor near the work table caught her attention. The hair ribbon Alexander removed when he'd unraveled her braid—another reminder of her recklessness. What would the deacon say about the experiences she had in the night with Alexander?

Not wishing to run into another Melling, she retreated to her room. She fastened her chatelaine to the sash on her dress and added a tiny coin purse adjacent to the lone scissors dangling against her side. A knock on her door startled her while she debated how much would be appropriate to leave in a collection plate. Crossing the room, her heart quickened at the thought of it being Alexander. She tried not to let her disappointment—or concern—show when she saw Mrs. Melling.

"Would you like to come in?" she asked.

"No, I merely assumed you might need a head covering for church. I did not know if you were acquainted with our traditions, and I want to make sure you are appropriately attired to avoid any discomfort."

"Thank you. I hadn't thought of that." Magdalene accepted the white lace mantilla.

"It was Eliza's, but you must use it while you are here. Go ahead and situate it. Adding a pin or comb will help keep it steady."

"Thank you. I'll be down shortly."

Unsure what to do with the head veil, Magdalene placed it on the dressing table and gazed out the window while she tried to recall how Catholics adorned their heads when attending church. Outside, Mr. Campbell readied the black carriage, dusting and shining the trim. Magdalene had never ridden in anything so fine, and she imagined she'd feel like a princess, with Alexander as her prince. She wondered if he'd sit next to her or across, so he could admire her more readily. She fingered her neckline and sighed in remembrance of his lips and hands caressing her.

But I mustn't!

She had to sweep the thoughts away—her job depended on it. Disappointed with herself for behaving like a mad woman her first time away from home, she held back tears as she arranged the covering over her head. The reflection of herself in white lace caused the memories of her planned wedding with William to scamper through her mind. Would Alexander think of wedding bells when he saw her? Would he think it improper for her to wear white after the fervent moments they'd shared?

Magdalene didn't need to ask herself those questions because leaving her shawl and ribbon behind revealed that she wasn't thinking things through properly. Concern for the future hadn't been part of her experiences—only quenching her desires ruled those moments. She slipped a few pins through the lace, and felt an overwhelming sense of gratitude for Alexander's forethought in taking his jacket on his way out of her room last night. His clothing in her room would be much harder to explain than her outerwear in the parlor.

But that could be solved with more discretion. No need to stop what feels good when we all want it.

Shuddering, Magdalene jumped, the voice in her head more distinct that time. The now familiar wind whirled, stirring her passionate memories to the surface. Magdalene rushed down the back stairs, the edges of the mantilla fluttering behind her like wings.

Fifteen

The heavy air barely held its moisture in the gray clouds. Magdalene paced the length of the back porch when the man and woman of the house came around from the front arm in arm. Mr. Melling, his drooping mustache souring his expression, walked by without looking her way, but Mrs. Melling waved her along.

"None of that pacing, Magdalene. You are not a circus animal."

Though she'd behaved no better than a wild one, Magdalene managed to look calm as she fell into step behind her employers. As they reached the carriage, Mr. Campbell led a fine, saddled chestnut horse out of the stable.

"What's this about?" Mr. Melling asked. "We're all going in the carriage today."

"It's for me."

Magdalene caught her breath when she heard Alexander behind her. She had longed to see him just minutes before, but now she dreaded their first exchange after last night.

"Alexander Randolph," Mrs. Melling said when she turned to him, "you cannot ride to church like a traveling man. Why, you are almost dressed as one!"

He wore a simple brown suit and derby hat, which he removed to address his mother. Magdalene, relieved not to have grown weak in the knees at his respectful gesture, linked her arms behind her back. "That Italian congregation is not my own. It was Eliza's fancy and it only brings me pain to keep revisiting it. I'd rather take Mass in Fairhope."

Mrs. Melling's hand went to her heart. "With the progressives? I have never heard such nonsense! You have not been yourself this weekend. It is all too much with the anniversary for me to lose you now to the utopians. You must accompany us one more time."

"Do it for your mother and let's be on with it." Mr. Melling turned to the stable hand. "Put Janus back. Alexander is coming with us. Now, Miss Jones, if you will." Mr. Melling opened the carriage door and held out his hand to help her up.

She followed the direction of his pointing finger and sat herself on the cushioned seat at the front of the enclosure, so she'd ride backward. Mrs. Melling sat across from Magdalene, close enough to see fleeting glances from behind the veil.

Alexander settled on the seat next to Magdalene, making special effort not to brush against her in any way. Upon seeing that he kept his eyes averted, Magdalene vowed to do the same, which proved easier than she expected, in part from the coldness his eyes betrayed the few times he glanced her way. He was insufferably full of himself.

Once Mr. Melling entered there was a minute of silence, then the carriage swayed as Mr. Campbell climbed into the driver's seat. While the Mellings' lane was smooth, the dirt road to Daphne jostled the riders. Magdalene, unused to the springs in fine transportation, nearly turned green from the movement. Receiving a nudge from her elbow each time she bounced and swayed most unbecomingly, Alexander moved against the side wall and focused his attention out the window.

"Alex, dear." Magdalene would swear Mrs. Melling looked at her as she spoke. "I saw your blue tie from dinner last night by the decanter set in the parlor. And that horrid novel. Be sure they are put away properly when we get home."

"Yes, Mother."

"And do be more mindful of your drinks. There were more glasses than necessary. I do not want the staff to think us disheveled or immoral as to leave clothing lying around and drinking too much on a Saturday night, dinner party or no."

Magdalene tried to sit straight as she continued to totter on the cushion next to him.

"And, Alex," Mrs. Melling continued, "I had word from Cousin Edwin on Friday. With all the happenings the past few days, I forgot to mention it. He and Edith are stopped over in Atlanta, on their way from Sarasota to their cottage in Newport. They've invited you to join them for the summer season. They'll be in Atlanta for another week, then to New York for business before going on to Rhode Island. I think it'd be wise for you to accept."

"Come now, Ruth," Mr. Melling joined in. "I planned on Alex taking up more responsibility at the firm again. He needs to gather new clients and regroup the old ones since he's been absent these two months. Being established is more important than running off to play."

"Nonsense. It is the perfect time for him to go." Mrs. Melling spoke as if Alexander wasn't there. "A few months' delay will not hurt a thing. In fact, it could surely help his business prospects if he were to collect a sophisticated fiancée in Newport and return ready to settle into marriage *and* business."

"It did work well last time he was engaged, but really, Ruth, a Yankee?" Mr. Melling's sharp eyes stared at his wife as though she'd suggested becoming a cannibal.

"How dare you mention that unfortunate event, George?" Mrs. Melling shifted away from her husband.

"That Easton girl was his best asset for the time it lasted until he had to mess things up."

"Father, that's enough." Alexander's lips were thin and his knuckles white.

An uneasy silence filled the tottering carriage a moment.

"I suppose if Alva Smith of Mobile can marry into the Vanderbilt family," Mrs. Melling continued, "and still end up with Marble House as her Newport cottage after a divorce, then the reverse should apply. Not that a Melling would ever be so crass as to divorce."

"It's a fine plan and I need to get away." Alexander crossed his arms. "I think it would do us all good. But I'd feel better if you would settle back in Mobile, Mother. You could take Mass with your established friends, and Father wouldn't have to hire someone to keep you company."

Losing Alexander and trying to be forced out of her job was too much for Magdalene to wrap her head around while bouncing down the oak canopied road. She leaned against the back of the upholstered seat and tried to follow every word since they insisted on keeping her out of their conversation.

Mrs. Melling shook her head. "I am not leaving until Eliza is housed in the mausoleum. Furthermore, I am used to spending summers here. We all are. I shall stay put until you return, then we will all go back to Mobile together in the fall."

"Sounds sensible enough." Mr. Melling adjusted his gold cufflinks.

"And if you are ready this week, Alex," Mrs. Melling said, clasping her gloved hands, "you could attend to the mausoleum business in person. Stop in at the marble quarry office on your way to Atlanta and make sure they prepare and send the proper stone."

"Yes, come to town with me tomorrow and talk with the architect so you know exactly how much to buy." Mr. Melling good-naturedly slapped his son on the knee. "The perfect chance for more responsibility."

"I'll do as you wish," he replied.

***

The Church of the Assumption was populated by a throng of Italian immigrants and there were more hushed conversations in that tongue than in English. Magdalene straightened the mantilla on her head as they walked down the main aisle to a row near the front of the wooden chapel. She raised a hand in greeting when she spotted Deacon De Fiore seated in a special section to the side. He gave a curt nod to her in return and stared down Alexander—who refused to turn his way.

From the Mass he led, Magdalene sensed Father Angelo's kind heart, though his face appeared wrinkled and stern. She hoped Deacon De Fiore would speak with him soon and relieve some of his suffering. When she met Father Angelo officially after Mass, his warm handshake—complete with a kiss to both of her cheeks—was genuine. In hopes of urging the deacon to confess, she searched for him on their way to the carriage. He stood near the front corner outside the church and she waved him over.

"Deacon De Fiore," she whispered as she took his arm, "you must confess to Father Angelo. Surely he is kind and filled with the love of God. Nothing could be worse than what you are going through right now."

After a dark-eyed glare toward Alexander, the deacon nodded. "I will try, *signorina*. Was all well for you last night?"

"It was worse than ever."

"Miss Jones," Mr. Melling called, "it's time to leave."

Deacon De Fiore frowned. "I come Wednesday. Pray fervently until then for your safety."

On the ride home, Mrs. Melling sprung another bit of news at her captive audience.

"Mr. Campbell heard from his nephew on Friday. Yes, it was a good day for the post." The cheerfulness in her voice seemed proof to Magdalene that the lady of the house needed to get out from its oppression more often. "The boy has arrived in New York and should be here within the week. He's supposedly an excellent driver, so you may purchase our Eastern Shore automobile now, George. Having a chauffeur and an automobile will be wonderful for Magdalene and me this summer, won't it, dear?"

"Yes, Ruth. It will give me great comfort to know you and Miss Jones will be able to see the sights of Baldwin County with greater ease. I'll check with the salesman we bought the Lyman from first thing tomorrow."

"No, George, the second thing. Our first concern is Eliza's homecoming. You and Alex need to see that it happens. If that stone isn't in transit soon, I shall suffer."

Not sure if she should respond to Mrs. Melling's warning, Magdalene waited in hopes that one of the men would say something to reassure her. Seconds went by and Magdalene finally had to speak.

"Suffering isn't allowed on my watch, Mrs. Melling. We'll take that new automobile and go to the quarry ourselves if need be."

A smile cracked Alexander's face as he turned to her. "Do you drive, then?"

"No, but that won't stop us, will it, Mrs. Melling?"

A real laugh escaped her veiled body. "Apparently not. But just in case, I think we should arrange for you to have some driving instruction, once we see if the chauffeur is sufficient. That way we ladies can have even more independence."

"Are you to become a suffragette, Mother? Shall the day come when you don purple and demand voting rights as well as drive yourself?"

"No, but I do not see why the younger set should not have more independence than women my age. But, Alex, do keep your father on task before you leave. Please see to the marble and the automobile with him."

Alexander reached across to take her hand. "Yes, Mother." He said it with such sweetness, not an ounce of annoyance to his voice, that Magdalene thought the hour at church good for him as well.

By the time Magdalene carried the first tray into the dining room, the Mellings had settled into a stony silence. Did the house affect them as it did her or were they always that indifferent to each other?

Frustration bloomed when the thought to brush Alexander's arm with hers burst upon Magdalene as she approached the table with a plate of bread. Fighting the sudden urge, she held her breath as she stopped beside him.

Just as she leaned over, he stopped her. Taking her wrist with one hand and the tray in the other, he looked up at her with adoration. "Allow me."

Magdalene released her hold on the platter and Alexander deftly ran his thumb across her wrist as he freed her. When she stepped back, Magdalene chanced a look at Mrs. Melling at the end of the table, unveiled to eat. Her head was cocked to the side in rapt contemplation as she studied her son. Magdalene caught a glimpse of herself in the mirror and noticed she still wore the mantilla. Before collecting the final tray of food in the kitchen, she paused by the hall table and left the head covering folded with her pins neatly on top.

When Magdalene returned with the fruit, Mrs. Melling rushed through her final words. "…and you must not underestimate your potency, Alex."

Alexander looked pink in the face and Mr. Melling smirked.

Mrs. Melling gave Magdalene a knowing gaze and sighed as she placed the tray of cheese and fruits in front of her. "Lord forgive the natural man." She crossed herself, and then closed her eyes in preparation for the mealtime prayer.

An awkward silence ensued as the platters were passed around the table and the food eaten.

As the group finished their meal, Mrs. Melling addressed her son. "You must begin packing at once. It will be more efficient if you take the train directly from Mobile once the plans are in order. There will be no need to spend the time re-crossing the bay to say goodbye. We can have our farewell after supper."

While Alexander had looked more than happy to leave when they discussed the plan in the carriage, here in the dining room he appeared sullen. "Of course. I'll see to it straight away."

Not long after Alexander excused himself from the table, Mr. Melling retreated into his den. Mrs. Melling stayed, watching

Magdalene clear the table one armload at a time. When she'd gathered up the final plate, Mrs. Melling spoke.

"We'll go to the sitting room when you're done. Be sure to wash up while you're in the kitchen."

"Yes, ma'am."

Mrs. Melling's intense gaze in her previously soft eyes warned Magdalene of a potential problem. Not wanting to face her—and possible unemployment—Magdalene took her time lathering her hands at the kitchen sink, the plates piled around her. She'd much rather tackle the dishes than commune with Mrs. Melling in her over-decorated room.

Resigned to whatever fate the conversation must hold, Magdalene collected Mrs. Melling from the dining room. To her surprise, her veil was still upturned. On the way to the stairs, Magdalene noticed her borrowed mantilla wasn't where she left it. She checked the floor as they passed the table, but neither the lace nor the pins were in sight. Would Mr. Melling have taken it? Alexander? The latter was more likely, but Magdalene couldn't rule out a third, more sinister, option.

In his room at the top of the stairs, Alexander leaned over a suitcase that sat open at the foot of his bed. He carefully placed the pink book Magdalene had seen him with the first day into his luggage.

Mrs. Melling paused. "Alex, be sure to come see me if you finish before supper. I am going to rest, but tap on my door. I might not sleep."

"Of course, Mother."

With the door closed behind them, Mrs. Melling fussed over her canaries for a minute as Magdalene stood near the window, hands clasped behind her back. Her mind raced between the missing lace and the coming news from Mrs. Melling.

"Well, Magdalene," she said as she turned to the young woman, "I'm sure you understand why I am sending Alexander away."

Magdalene blanched and a hand went to her heart.

"Whether it's the timing or having a fresh face about the house, Alex is ready to move on from mourning. I see the inkling of interest as he passes you, but it could never be. For one thing, your coloring is off. He always fancied blonde hair, not your mousey brown. And I need not bring up the difference in social class. Magdalene, dear, don't mistake his chivalry for flirtation."

Magdalene opened her mouth to defend herself but no sound escaped. On second thought, she found that to be to her benefit. If she started to spout the numerous times Alexander had come to her, dismissal for being a liar or worse would be upon her.

"That shawl of yours," Mrs. Melling continued. "Did you go down in hopes of catching a glimpse of him after hours? Did you see him?"

"No." Magdalene answered the first question truthfully, for it was the shattered teacup she descended the stairs, but made it appear as if she were answering both.

"Well, you must have missed him. He does like a drink before bed, and for that reason, I ask you to not go to the parlor after you're dismissed for the day. I can tell you are not deceitful, so I shall trust your word if you promise."

"Yes, ma'am, I promise not to go in the parlor at night unless I'm with you." Her steady voice hid the shaking inside her caused by indignation for being placed solely with the blame. Even if Mrs. Melling didn't guess the half of it, Magdalene did not like being accused of chasing Alexander.

"Very well, Magdalene. At any rate, we can thank your pleasant complexion and supple form for awakening Alex from his depression. You are agreeable to have around, there is no doubting that, and I expect you would like to stay on with me, even though it will be quite different starting tomorrow, with Alex leaving and George in the city all week."

Her head whirling with all she'd heard, Magdalene nodded before she could speak. Seacliff Cottage without the Melling men would be an improvement. "I'd very much like to stay. Thank you."

"Good. You can take your leave until four o'clock. No loitering downstairs, but you may stay in here or your room, as well as walk about the yard, so long as you stay near the house. I do not want you getting lost in the forest or down on the beach alone."

"Yes, ma'am. I'll check with you at four. I hope you get some rest."

Sixteen

For half an hour, Magdalene worked on settling her belongings into her room. She felt confident in filling the wardrobe with her clothing and arranging her books and stationery in the desk. Even her folding scissors and coin purse found a home in a little dresser drawer. Mrs. Melling was keeping her on and Alexander would leave the next day—two blessings Magdalene felt would make the new week wonderful.

With her empty trunk tucked between the fireplace and the armchair, she settled at the desk. Lifting the lid with one hand, she retrieved her pen and stationery with the other. As she was about to begin a letter to her father, a soft knock sounded on the door, so faint she paused to see if it would come again before moving. When it did, Magdalene crossed the room with a racing heart. When she opened the door, Alexander slipped in and closed it behind him before she could blink.

"I brought you this." He held out her mantilla and pins with a suave smile.

"Thank you." She placed them in one of the empty drawers in the dressing table. "Would you like to sit down?" she asked out of politeness, though she knew it wasn't proper to have him there. At least she hadn't told Mrs. Melling she wouldn't have company in her room. She broke no promise in that regard.

He stepped toward the armchair by the window—its curtains pulled back to allow in the most possible light on the cloudy afternoon—but shook his head. "Here's as good a place as any."

Taking her hand, he twirled her in the middle of the room. Magdalene resisted the urge to return his smile when she stopped spinning, his arms folding around her.

"This morning in the carriage, I was more than happy to agree to leave. I could barely keep myself seated in that monstrous little chapel during Mass. I wanted nothing more than to pack my bags and be gone. And then"—he leaned against her and dropped his voice—"there you were, bringing me plates of food, like Ceres reaping a bounteous harvest."

He ran a finger along her jaw and touched the high lace collar of her dress. The tingling in her body scared her because it represented a threat to her new job, but the longing tugged harder than the fear. Magdalene wrapped her arms around him and breathed in his sandalwood scent—just as intoxicating as his rich brandy.

With a clap of thunder, the sky opened. Large drops of rain pelted the window and ran down the panes like the tears Magdalene had cried in the early morning hours. Tucking herself deeper into his arms, she spoke. "Even after...whatever it was that happened last night?"

He walked her backward toward the bed. "You mean me leaving you so suddenly? Shall we—"

"No!" Magdalene planted her feet and refused to be moved. "I mean the wind and the laughter."

Alexander ran a hand through his hair and paced. "I was drunk, I admit it."

"But I saw and heard it, too." Magdalene sank onto the vanity bench.

Alexander laughed. "You were also drunk. We were two impassioned bodies, overcome with needs." He dropped to his knees before her and rested his elbows on her lap.

"And how do you explain us both feeling, seeing, and hearing the same thing?"

"I haven't agreed that we have." He raised his eyebrows, framing his mischievous blue eyes with mirth. "This is the first we've spoken of it, and you've only admitted to there being a draft and the possible sound of laughter."

Magdalene struggled to control her exasperation. "It was a tempest! It pulled at the curtains and moved your hair and shirt. You had to have felt that."

Alexander's hands went to her shoulders, gently pulling her closer. "I felt your hands unbuttoning my shirt and your fingers running through my hair. That much I remember."

Their faces inches apart, Magdalene searched for the truth. "But after the laughter, you shouted, 'No more games!' like you were speaking to the wind."

"More like you and your games. Why else would I repeatedly throw myself at you if you weren't playing a winning hand?" His lips hovered over hers, his breath warm on her face. "I surrender to you."

Amid the sounds of the thunderstorm outside, Magdalene's personal storm swelled within. When his kisses began to roam, Magdalene leaned against the dressing table to escape. Alexander still knelt before her, now positioned between her knees. She pushed him back so she could situate herself into a more ladylike way.

Alexander laughed. "Yes, Miss Jones. I'm sorry to rumple your dress. Allow me."

As soon as his hands were on her lap, Magdalene jumped. "That won't be necessary, Mr. Melling." Her voice crinkled with flirtation as a misty breeze fluttered through the room, across their intent faces.

"I'm happy to assist you with any of your wardrobe concerns," he assured her.

Magdalene played with the embroidery on her left sleeve while deciding what to do about the man in her bedroom. She stopped near the empty fireplace. She looked over her shoulder at him. "And what of your parents, also within this house?"

"Mother sleeps like a baby during a storm and Father smokes an after dinner cigar and naps on the couch in his study every Sunday afternoon. They're very accommodating in that regard." He stayed behind her and kissed her earlobe. His gaze in the mirror witnessed her reflection quiver under his touch.

As much as she wanted to give in to his caressing, she willed herself to think of reality. She turned to him, placing her arms around his neck as the room darkened further from the storm. With daring, she corralled the frenzied passion and called upon that stubborn streak Aunt Agnes accused her of having. Either she would call his bluff or sacrifice her innocence to understand what powers played between them.

"So, here we are again. What will we do about our needs this time?"

Alexander leaned away, a dazed look upon his face. He searched her countenance for insight to her aspiration. Then smiling in approval, his impetuous hands grasped her waist. "You're braver than me. You speak of what I can only fantasize. No more words, no more games."

Magdalene, her guard worn by his tender whisperings and the vortex of aching, found herself pressed between Alexander and the silky wallpaper. Lips already sore from the strength of his lust-driven kisses, she gasped for air while he burrowed into her neck, tugging at her dress. Momentarily, she closed her eyes and welcomed the tantalizing sensation of his whole body against hers. She felt the wind blowing her skirt around her ankles, then her calves above her laced boots.

But it wasn't the wind.

Alexander had finally performed the winning hand because she played the wrong card. Dread over the situation she'd gotten herself into made her go limp. Her eyes still shut against reality, she blindly grasped at what might bring him pause.

"Do you feel the wind now?" she asked as he rubbed his leg against hers.

"Magdalene." His hands trailed over her sheer dress. "I want to feel everything."

Frantic because she'd lost control, Magdalene's eyes flew open. Her gaze immediately seized upon the crucifix across the room. She knew what she must do, even if it placed her more in his control in the interim.

Pressing her body further against his, Magdalene pushed off the wall. Her new freedom allowed Alexander to caress her back with his wandering hands, but it also gave her the space to maneuver. Under the guise of being enticed with his attention, Magdalene grazed around his body until behind him. Taking the bait, he also turned, but his eyes were only on her. As he advanced, she retreated toward the alcove.

Halfway there, she paused, allowing him to catch her. Her apprehension soon turned to rapture as he stroked up her arms, neck, and cheeks in unison. Caught in his grasp, he drew her into a kiss so unfathomable she felt it in her soul. The ghostly wind swelled to a crescendo as lightning lit the room. Internally, Magdalene raged with terrible hunger, her mouth all over Alexander's, while outwardly her hair and dress danced as if caught in the bay's breeze. Perhaps the soul-stirring kiss was a warning—one meant to provoke her fear rather than her passions—but she succumbed to the thirst as the rain beat upon the window. Before Magdalene knew what happened, Alexander lowered her to the bed.

In a final, desperate effort to gain the upper hand, she arched into him to keep him upright, propping herself with her arms. "Do you remember what's caused you to stop each time we're too far gone?"

"No"—he towered above her with the icy Melling gaze—"don't talk. Accept that we've won you."

Despite the breathless abandon she'd just experienced as they embraced, dread enveloped her whole body. She heard the laughter from last night, cold and cruel, over her predicament. Then the gale returned, lifting Alexander's shirttail.

"Can you not see the effects of the wind now?" She raised herself to sitting.

"The only thing I see is you."

Intercepting his moving to envelop her, Magdalene landed in his arms. "There is something you see, every time."

In order to get him to relax his hold, Magdalene tugged at his shirt, undoing the top button as she fumbled with an anguished kiss. Then she hiked her skirt and kneeled on the soft bedding. From there she held one of his hands and stood triumphantly over him. Speculation flitted across Alexander's expression, but in a flash of lightning it turned to a burning need. He scrambled onto the bed, his eyes roaming up Magdalene's body as if he didn't know where to begin. She smiled, pulled him to her, and shuffled toward the headboard while he clung to her.

"There's one," she said, "who stops you every time, and it isn't me."

Hoping she calculated her position correctly, she took a final step back against the headboard. His eyes on hers, she slowly turned to her right so he would follow her gaze.

"The one with power to forgive all sin," she whispered, eyeing the crucifix.

Instinctively, she wrapped her arms around him before he sank onto the bed. For the first time, it felt as though they were truly alone. No appetites yelling for attention, just two remorseful bodies wrapped together.

"You left me no choice." Sorrow filled her voice as she briefly nestled into his chest. Then she stood and held her hand out to him.

Alexander knocked it aside. Resentment burned in his eyes as he looked at her with disgust. "I need no pity from the one who placed me in this position."

He started for the door, and then turned back. "Did Claudio teach you this? Is this what you whispered about last night?"

"It's not like that, and you know it!" Magdalene matched his anger. "You're so full of yourself you can't believe it when a lowly blacksmith's daughter rejects your advances."

He looked down his nose at her. "As if I'd ever want you."

Magdalene marched forward defiantly. "Well, your mother seems to think you do. That's why she wants you to go with your cousins this summer—to get away from me."

His fury hastened to fervor in one last attempt to prove conqueror. Magdalene wrestled to keep her arms free as he searched with wandering hands for the fasteners on the back of her dress, their heavy breathing eclipsed only by the thunder.

With her left hand gripping his shoulder to keep from falling to the floor, she fumbled to use her right hand to do the sign of the cross while he pursued an entrance to her gown. Alexander froze, his eyes momentarily rolling back. With a deliberate motion, he untangled first one arm, then the other, from his ardent hold on her.

"You turned my own beliefs against me." Agony filled his voice. "I'll never forgive that."

Magdalene watched him leave. Exhausted from her struggles, she fell onto her bed and sobbed as the dismal rain beat against the house.

Seventeen

Just before four o'clock, Magdalene arose and made herself presentable, washing her face and arranging her hair. She settled by the window in Mrs. Melling's sitting room with her sketchbook. To keep the memory of her shameful actions from overwhelming her senses, she set to work drawing the contents of the mantel shelf. Concentrating on the items kept her from mulling over Alexander, even though the thoughts were as constant as the drizzling rain. She behaved wickedly. No longer could she trust her judgement or claim he wasn't her type—not after all she'd done and wanted to do with him.

Magdalene continued to draw after Mrs. Melling joined her. The lady of the house kept her mourning veil off and entertained herself by flipping through books of poetry. At five thirty, the ladies descended the front stairs and convened in the parlor. Mr. Melling was already there, a drink in hand.

"I hope you two had a restful afternoon." He stood from his seat by the fire and offered a hand to his wife to help her around the crate still occupying a predominant place in the room. "I'll be sure to have Captain Walker collect this as soon as possible."

"Not until Alex has the order secured in Georgia." Mrs. Melling adjusted her skirt after sitting. "If for some reason I need to choose another stone, I want the samples here."

"Of course, though I have faith in Alexander securing everything we need. Don't you agree, Miss Jones?"

Startled, Magdalene stared at Mr. Melling from her place on the settee. "Yes, he appears quite capable."

Mr. Melling winked at her before tilting his glass back to take the last swallow of the amber liquid. He set it down with a laugh.

Magdalene's stomach soured as she remembered how Alexander alluded to his father steering her to his bedroom yesterday morning. She blushed when she understood how her remarks could be taken by someone expecting her to have intimate knowledge of Alexander. *Quite capable, indeed!* Tomorrow would bring freedom from these liquored men and Magdalene couldn't wait to be rid of them.

Alexander had still not arrived when Leroy came to announce supper.

"Please go see if he needs assistance with packing so he can join us for supper," Mrs. Melling addressed the butler. "While you are up there, Magdalene requires a fire in her room."

"Yes, ma'am."

Magdalene lingered in the parlor as long as possible after the Mellings exited. She didn't look forward to sitting across from Alexander's wrath for the duration of the meal. Perhaps he'd calmed down in the last few hours, but she didn't hold out hope.

When Rosemary entered the dining room with the first serving platter, Mr. Melling held his hand up to stop her. "Give us three minutes, to see if Alexander joins us."

"Yes, sir."

Magdalene shifted in her seat and stared at the lilies. They were beginning to brown around the edges of the delicate white flowers and would need to be disposed of soon. The maid would probably see to them tomorrow, but if she did not know of their poison, she might haphazardly toss them away. Magdalene needed to warn her.

Alexander entered the room behind Magdalene, his scent falling over her like cooling rain as he rounded the table. "Sorry I'm late. There was more to see to than expected." He kissed Mrs. Melling's cheek as he passed her chair.

"Were you able to finish so you may spend the evening with us?" Mrs. Melling asked.

"Yes, I'm set for the morning."

With prayers spoken and the food served, the four settled into their meal. Alexander kept his eyes from Magdalene as he ate, addressing only his mother. It didn't bother her at first because she knew it would be difficult to hide any loathing from Mrs. Melling's keen eyes, but as the minutes ticked by and the food slowly disappeared, Magdalene recognized her longing.

"Is there anything you wish me to tell Edith or Edwin when I see them?" Alexander asked his mother.

"Just that I hope they can stop in this winter when they return south. They've yet to see our new home in the city."

"I'll be sure to invite them, Mother. Thanksgiving might be a good option. The weather is usually fine then."

Being ignored did not sit well with Magdalene. She'd gazed across the floral arrangements, hoping to catch his eye. Uncrossing her legs under the table, she tried stretching her foot toward Alexander's but she bumped into the table's central pedestal with a knock from her booted toe. Mr. and Mrs. Melling didn't notice, but Alexander looked up. Their gazes finally connected and Magdalene was pleased to see the absence of malice.

Exploring the table with her foot, she learned the squared column was much too large to get around. As a slight frown of disappointment touched her mouth, a smile curved the corner of Alexander's. He tilted his head to his right and looked down. Understanding his meaning, Magdalene stretched her left foot as far as it would go along that side of the pedestal. Just as she was sure she could stretch no more without sliding down in her seat, the tip of her boot touched something less hard than the wood base. The obstacle tapped her foot three times as Alexander did his best not to pay her attention.

They completed the meal with numerous exchanges of foot nudges. A simple liaison, but it solidified their mutual enticement. Magdalene wished for nothing more than to curl up with Alexander on the settee in the parlor, his arms around her for warmth. She sighed as she stood at the end of the meal, the yearning escaping with her breath.

"You sound tired, Miss Jones," Mr. Melling remarked.

"Yes." Mrs. Melling fingered the cross around her neck. "You are dismissed for the day. Get the rest you need. I will see you in the morning."

"I need to write a letter home to let my family know I made it safely and how they can reach me. Is it possible to get it to a post office tomorrow?" she asked as they entered the hall.

"We could bring it on the ferry and post it from downtown tomorrow," Mr. Melling offered. "It would be quicker than sending it through the Montrose post office as you'd have to wait an extra day for it to cross the bay. Pass it on to Alexander when it's ready. He'll see to it."

"You may place it here." Mrs. Melling's pointed to the credenza in the hall.

"Yes, thank you. I'll leave it there shortly," Magdalene replied. "Safe travels, Mr. Melling, Alexander. I'll see you in the morning, Mrs. Melling."

Once in her room, Magdalene turned her back to the fire in the hearth and sat at the small desk to work on the letter she'd planned to write that afternoon. She closed her eyes, remembering Alexander's fragrance and touch. Distracted by her thoughts, she set down her pen and undid her hair, which ruffled in the mysterious breeze. The tendrils brushed her neck and brought her craving for Alexander's touch to a throbbing need. She wanted to rush to his room and fling herself upon his bed, absorbing his scent and wrapping herself in the blankets that cradled him at night.

Covering her face with her hands, she cried aloud. "He's not even here! Please leave me!"

Miraculously, the wind settled, but her emotions did not. Magdalene paced the room until she calmed enough to focus on writing. Upon sealing the note, she descended the back stairs. She boldly placed the letter upon the appointed table, across from the parlor's open doors. When she turned, she glanced into the room. Alexander had his back to her, but Mrs. Melling narrowed her eyes. Magdalene hurried back the way she'd come to avoid a reprimand.

She closed the curtains in her room against the cloudy night and brushed her hair until it shone. Once in her nightgown, she tried sleeping, but gave up after half an hour. Magdalene pulled the armchair toward the fire and settled there, waiting for the knock she knew would come.

***

No knock came to Magdalene's door, but at midnight, the knob turned and Alexander entered. He carried a small crate and went straight to the dozing figure in white. After looking upon her a moment, he settled cross-legged on the rug before the fire. He took a handful of lily clippings from the box and tossed them onto the dying hearth. With a hiss and a pop, the greenery expelled extra smoke. Poker in hand, he nudged the ashes and logs about the space to rekindle the fire.

Magdalene shifted in the chair, not quite aroused from the happenings next to her. The hem of her nightgown caught between the arm of the chair and her knee, so her bare leg stretched out beneath her gown. Alexander tossed another handful of clippings onto the hearth then placed a finger on the underside of Magdalene's knee. With the lightest of touches, he gradually traced the curve of her calf. She opened her eyes with a smile and flexed her bare foot to bring tautness to her leg muscle. When his finger reached her heel, he lifted her foot and kissed the top of her toes before releasing his hold and turning back to the fire.

"You're supposed to stay asleep." His voice sounded strained, which caused Magdalene to stir. Still drowsy, she leaned forward as she freed the hem of nightgown and pulled it back into place around her legs. "What's that you're burning? It smells different."

He added another fistful. "The clippings. I was going to do a bonfire this week on the beach, but I needed to take care of them before I leave."

"No, Alexander!" She dropped to his side and grabbed his arm. "You'll poison us!"

He looked into her brown eyes, wide with alarm, and smiled in such a way that made him not look himself. "If I'm not here with you, what difference does it make if you're alive?"

The look on his face—more sinister than the Melling gaze—was something straight from Hell. Magdalene shivered before the blaze.

"Let me warm you." His voice was deep with a rumbly quality that set her nerves on edge. He put both hands on her shoulders and eased her to the floor beneath him.

A chill wind originated behind him, tugging at the fire and leading the toxic smoke into the room with a tornadic circulation. Magdalene watched it shape and shift behind Alexander as he straddled her.

Her fists beat against his chest as she struggled to wiggle out from under him. "No, don't do this! You're hurting yourself, not just me!"

Dropping upon her, he pinned her arms between their chests, squashing her rebellion. "I feel no pain," he whispered into her ear as he ran a hand over her throat before clutching the ruffled neckline of her gown.

The sound of the ripping fabric soured Magdalene's stomach with the reality of her circumstance. No romance, no seduction to sway the mind to the will of the flesh. Alexander had control, taking what he wanted, no matter the cost.

Rising a few inches to pull the damaged neckline open, Alexander paused to lick her cheek. An ungodly smirk tainted his lips. "You taste like fear."

Magdalene mentally grappled for anything she could use as leverage to break free. "The Lord is my shepherd…" Her voice trembled.

Startled, Alexander shifted off her, shaking his head. The swirling smoke lifted toward the ceiling in disorganized plumes. Magdalene rolled away from the fire and crawled toward the window. Behind her, the smothering hiss of the remainder of the clippings piling upon the fire brought urgency to her plight. Crouching, she lunged to the space between the chair and the window.

A cold hand grasped her ankle and yanked her back with inhuman strength. Pulling her toward the fireplace, the friction of her nightgown against the rug caused it to bunch around her thighs by the time she came to a stop. When he flipped her over, she saw the thick smoke encircling his body and reaching out to her with snake-like feelers.

Seized with tremors, she shut her eyes against the vision of the flames reflected in his callous stare. "Alexander, please! We'll both die in this air. What would it do to your mother to find us here in the morning, killed by the flowers meant to honor your sister?"

"Then she'll know we're damned because we died in sin." His voice was raspy from the smoke.

He ran a hand up her leg, and then he fell upon her. Tonight, it wasn't the warm-bodied Alexander with physical longings who could be persuaded to follow her lead—this was a tenacious leviathan with cold hands, shrewd eyes, and incalculable needs. Magdalene squirmed under his touch enough to free a hand so she could do the sign of the cross. As soon as her hand left her forehead, he forced it to the floor above her head. With venomous breath, he took to her neck with fierce kisses that were a source of torment to an entrapped soul.

She recited, though with each word it grew harder to speak. "The Lord is my shepherd; I shall not want. He maketh me to lie down in green pastures: he leadeth me beside the still waters."

With a jerk, Alexander reared back, stumbling over her legs. When free, she kept delivering the scripture verses as she heaved herself toward the window. Magdalene threw open the curtains. She wrestled with the latch before she was able to push up the glass.

Alexander's cold hand brushed against her foot. She stuck her head outside to gasp for fresh air while she had the chance, then uttered, "Surely goodness and mercy shall follow me all the days of my life: and I will dwell in the house of the Lord forever."

When he didn't grab for her, Magdalene chanced to open the window all the way. The damp night air pushed into the room and blew her nightgown against her searing body. Hesitantly, she turned, a fist at the ready, but Alexander struggled to breathe. Above him, the smoke dispersed, rising up the flue or diluting against the ceiling as it mixed with the outside air. Magdalene took a careful step forward. Seeing him in genuine pain, she dropped to her knees beside him.

Ashen and clammy to the touch, his body covered in a cold sweat that made his white shirt transparent with the moisture. His breath barely lifted his chest and his body shook enough to rattle his teeth.

"Alexander," she nudged his arm to see if he'd respond. "What can I do to help?"

A moan escaped his parted lips. "Lord"—his teeth chattered between each word—"deliver us from evil."

And then he went deathly still.

"Alexander!" Terror gripped her anew. She felt his damp cheeks and hands before placing a hand on his heart. A faint beat thumped within his chest. "Wake up, please wake up!"

Magdalene stood and moved behind his head. She maneuvered her arms under his shoulders, hooking them through his armpits for the arduous task of dragging him to the window. Once there, she was able to prop him against the wall so his face could be near the rain-freshened air.

An alarming cough set his frame quaking. Magdalene— forgiving his earlier ill intentions—encircled Alexander to keep him from crashing to the floor or banging his head against the windowsill. After the cough subsided, his teeth went back to chattering. She knew the dampness of his clothing wasn't good for the chill and unbuttoned his shirt. When her warm hands skimmed around his ribs to unstick the back of his shirt, another moan escaped him. She winced, thinking that even in his weakened state he could still be a threat to her. But once she removed his shirt, she hugged him to her chest.

"Please, Alexander, don't die."

"Blanket," he rasped.

Alexander slumped to the side when she left. Magdalene wadded the heavy bedspread into her arms and brought it to him, dropping it at his feet.

"You're going to need to roll onto it or lift off the floor enough for me to slip it under you."

"Down," he gasped.

Magdalene spread the cover on the floor in front of him, pushing the armchair out of the way.

"Get as close as you can to the center."

After watching a few of his labored movements, Magdalene placed a hand on his back and the other on his arm. She steadied him so he didn't spend as much energy righting himself when he lost balance as he inched onto the bedspread. When he was close to centered, he collapsed and she wrapped the side of the blanket closest to the window around his left side, and then tucked the other edge over his right, overlapping the other from foot to chin. Finally, she helped him slide back under the window.

Exhausted from her own efforts, Magdalene leaned against the wall in the corner. Relief to see the lingering smoke was sparse allowed her to relax somewhat. She pulled her knees under her nightgown, tucking the edges underneath before hugging her knees to her chest.

Alexander turned his head to her. "Thank you." His voice was still raspy and labored.

Pleased with his improved coloring, Magdalene smiled. "You would have done the same."

A look of discontent shadowed his face. "We tried to kill you."

Dread filled Magdalene's bones. "Alexander—"

His blue eyes were wide and bright with fear. "We came in with the flowers and were going to smoke you in your sleep because you chased us out this afternoon. When you woke, we decided to finish what you started when you came to this house, radiant with innocence and desires."

"*We?*" her voice squeaked. "You were alone."

Alexander thrashed within his blanket cocoon. "It's in me—in these walls! In you!"

Magdalene cowered in the corner. "What is?"

He scrambled to stand, the blanket falling around his feet like a rent chrysalis. "Eliza, the devil, it doesn't matter!" He clawed at his bare chest. "It's in here, corrupting me."

The angry scratches bled and spread into rips as he tore at his chest.

"Alexander, stop!"

His look of pure desolation filled Magdalene with compassion. She snatched his discarded shirt off the floor and with a desperate plunge fell against him, covering his wounds with his shirt in an attempt to stop the bleeding and prevent further injury. Alexander enclosed her with his arms so she was pinned against him.

"Why must you try to help?" His voice rumbled. "I told you what we meant to do, yet you run to me with respite for my sins."

His arms slackened, but immediately his hands were in her hair. He stroked the length of it, and then grabbed a fistful with one hand as the other pulled the small of her back toward him. His damp lips were over hers, his pressing needs evident in his actions.

Each exhale of Alexander's contaminated breath defiled Magdalene. Rather than pushing him away, she kissed in return. Once again, he was warm and willing. She needed his touch to prove her worth in this life as more than a servant or statuesque niece.

Their groping movements brought them against the wall of the alcove, Alexander's shirt long since fallen to the floor. The metallic tang of his wounds further drove Magdalene in her frenzy. She wasn't a girl to be spurned by William a week before their marriage or by haughty Alexander in his family's carriage. He was there—in *her* room—because he desired her. Swollen with lust and pride, she fell onto the bed in the bloodstained gown.

Alexander touched his chest and brought his hand to his face, the seeping blood tacky on his fingers.

"No..." He shook his head and backed away. "It's in you now."

Magdalene gripped the sheet with a fist as she leaned toward him. "There's nothing but you and me. All these feelings and emotions." Magdalene leapt up and pressed against Alexander. "They're nothing without consummation."

The beguiling way she spoke the final word seemed to wrap Alexander back into the fog. His blood dampened hand went to her neck, further ripping aside the torn hem. What first was ecstasy for Magdalene suddenly turned to distress as Alexander's previously warm hands turned reptilian against her skin. His body became like stone, his kisses painfully hard and detached. Like when he burned the lilies, he pressed on with a conquering will to dominate, not reciprocate.

Grateful to have her clarity back, Magdalene struggled against Alexander, but that only made whatever drove him more enticed. How dizzying the reversal of roles played out, but because of this Magdalene knew the devil labored against both of them. She opened her mouth to recite, but he fell upon her lips to stop the words as he backed her toward the bed. Before she could be pinned beneath him, Magdalene pulled back an arm and punched his shoulder, hoping to jar him awake from his trance. He raised his face from hers, a vile sneer upon his face.

"If we had followed through one of the other times," a guttural voice came through his words, "there wouldn't be the need for us to force things along. We need this."

Before Alexander exposed either of them to something that could not be unseen or undone, Magdalene gathered her strength for her final effort. With a knee to his groin and an elbow in his gut, she shoved him away and kicked his soiled shirt to him.

"Go, Alexander, before it's too late! You're leaving this house in a few hours, but leave me now to be sure we survive the night!"

With quivering lips, he looked over her blood smeared gown, focusing on the handprint at her neck. "What have I done?" His voice quaked.

Fearing to touch him, lest the urges pulse through them again, Magdalene pointed to the door. "Nothing that can't be cleaned, but leave me before it's too late."

He snatched his shirt off the floor, fumbled out the door and down the hall. Magdalene waited until she heard his door close and then locked herself in the bathroom.

Eighteen

Magdalene woke with a start when her chin fell to her chest. Feeling disoriented, she looked around the bathroom and tried to piece together what happened. She sat in the wicker chair, wrapped in two fluffy towels. Nothing more. She found her sleepwear soaking in the sink.

Then she remembered.

When she'd looked in the mirror after locking herself in the bathroom, the sight of her bloodstained gown had caused her to sob. While she cried, she'd stood naked at the sink, rinsing and scrubbing her once spotless clothing. Twice, someone—or something—tried to enter the room. Through muttered prayers and good bolts, the door held.

Recalling the rapture and fear, Magdalene didn't know how she'd managed any rest. Fortunately, her clothes had come clean and she hung them in the shower. Unsure of the time and with nothing to wear, she tightened the towels around her and peeked out the door. All was quiet.

She dashed for her room, shocked to see its chaotic state. The bedspread near the opened window, rumpled sheets, windblown items on the desk, and the box Alexander had brought near the fireplace all needed to be set to rights. It was comforting to see the promise of a sunny day in the morning glow, but she shivered upon recalling Alexander's agony when he ripped his flesh. Something sinister was in Seacliff Cottage and it revolved around Alexander Melling.

After dressing, she set to cleaning the room. Magdalene saw to everything except the crate. Unsure what to do with the box, she decided to leave it beside Alexander's closed bedroom door before going to the kitchen. It was only seven but the smell of coffee filled the air and there were two dirty cups at the table. Surely the coffee meant the maid, and two cups meant Mr. Melling and Alexander were awake, possibly already gone to catch the ferry in Montrose.

She pushed open the hall door and looked to see if anyone was about. From the closed door across the hall came the faint sound of furniture scraping against the wood floor. Mr. Melling's den. She'd yet to have cause to go in there and she didn't feel the need to do so now.

When she settled at the kitchen table with her tea, the kitchen door swung open behind her. The swirl of electricity in the air announced Alexander before she could turn.

"Stay where you are," he warned. "I don't want to hurt you. I just wanted to say that I'm sorry."

When she looked upon him, Magdalene's hand went to her mouth. His skin had a grayish cast to it and the dark circles around his eyes advertised he'd not slept. He held his suitcase at an odd angle, denoting pain. Her hand dropped from her face to her chest, with a questioning tilt to her head.

"I wrapped it as best I could, but I plan to stop at the doctor's office to have it tended properly, and then seek an appointment with Father Quinn. He's familiar with my confessions and shouldn't be too shocked at my actions."

Magdalene sank to the chair with trembling hands. Alexander stepped forward but stopped abruptly. "Something devilish drove me last night. Drink, flirt, and seduce—that I'll admit I do. Not those…unspeakable events that transpired last night."

She hugged herself and looked away from the agony on his pallid face.

"Please, Magdalene, I beg you to keep my mother safe. If whatever is at odds with me I'm leaving behind, it's up to you to be attentive. If things aren't right, involve Claudio if you must. No matter what I think about him, I know he cares for her like a second mother. I'll never forgive myself if she's harmed."

Nodding, Magdalene looked to him. "I promise, Alexander. God keep you on your journey."

Just as one of his boyish smiles was about to break through his downcast countenance, the hall door swung in behind him. Lydia in a black uniform strolled in while tying her white apron around her ample curves.

"Now there's a surprise." Finished with her apron, Lydia straightened her stiff white collar and smoothed the white head covering over her curly hair knotted at the back of her head. "Your father wants you at the carriage in five minutes, Alex."

Alexander glared at the maid. "I told you never to call me that."

"Oh my! Someone needs his coffee this morning." With an exaggerated curtsey, she batted her eyelashes. "May I pour you a cup, *Master* Melling?"

The grip he had on his suitcase turned his knuckles white. Through gritted teeth he growled his response. "Leave the room."

To Magdalene's surprise, the woman darted out.

Alexander stomped through the kitchen. Before he reached the back door, he turned to Magdalene with his icy glare. "Whatever you do, don't trust her."

He slammed the door, leaving Magdalene alone with her now tepid tea.

As though she'd listened in the hall, Lydia came in with a smile on her pleasant face. "Don't take it personally. He's been like that as long as I've been around."

"It's been an interesting weekend." Magdalene added a splash of hot water to her cup and stirred.

Mr. Melling rushed in from the hall, his eyes focused on Lydia. When he noticed Magdalene at the counter, his smile faltered. "Well, goodbye, ladies. It's good to know I have such an industrious team, bright and eager to work. Be sure to show her how to make coffee this week, Lydia. I'll want a fresh cup come Saturday morning." He winked before leaving.

All signs of joy drained from Lydia. She turned to Magdalene, her hazel eyes narrowed. "I hear Mr. Melling can be a bit of a scoundrel. I hope he didn't require too much from you in the way of…references."

"No, never!" The heat of embarrassment colored Magdalene's cheeks. "It was a trying weekend, but not in that regard. Most of my time is spent in the company of Mrs. Melling. The few times I was around Mr. Melling he was a gentleman."

She wished she could say the same for Alexander, but fortunately he wasn't the topic of their conversation. Outside, the carriage rolled by the open window and a load lightened from Magdalene.

The spark returned to Lydia's eyes as well. "Good. Be sure to keep it that way, Mags. I'd hate for there to be an incident with such a nice girl like you."

Lydia set about gathering used glasses from the parlor, and Magdalene, not wanting to see the reminders of Alexander's late nights, tried to retreat upstairs.

"I hear they entertained this weekend." Lydia remarked before Magdalene could disappear.

"The deacon blessed the site for Eliza's mausoleum Saturday night."

"How awful for you to have to go through that on your first full day here." She twirled a loose piece of hair around her finger. "But I suppose it could have been worse—you could've known the chit."

Magdalene gasped at hearing her speak ill of the dead. It wasn't as shocking when Alexander said something negative—that sort of thing tended to be normal between siblings—but to hear such a slur from the maid was blasphemous.

"Oh, don't mind me." Lydia waved a dusting cloth at her. "I'm nothing but a clucking chicken. Rosemary's used to my biting remarks, but I'm not fool enough to speak such things before the family. I suppose you're the innocent, sheltered type. I'll try to hold my tongue, but I don't make any promises. Did you go to finishing school?"

Magdalene laughed. "Not at all. I went to the one-room schoolhouse in Seven Hills until I was twelve, and then learned from my mother at home until she passed away two years later."

"Older, distinguished brothers or sisters? Young'uns to raise?" Lydia twisted the cloth around her hand and snapped it at the rung on the back of the nearest chair.

Never having been around a woman as spirited as Lydia, Magdalene eyed her with trepidation. "No, just my father and me. It wasn't so bad."

"What, he go remarry and the wicked stepmother kicked you out?" She snapped the towel again.

Magdalene took a wary step away. "No, he had an accident and his sister took him in. I came of my own will."

"Well, let's hope you don't regret it. It's good to have a new face around this dreary house. We'll be good friend, Mags, I'm sure."

***

By the time Rosemary served dinner, Magdalene had been accosted with questions from the maid at least half a dozen times. Whenever she passed Lydia in a hallway she heard, "Why isn't she wearing her veil?" or "When did the chimes get turned back on?" and "Aren't you the ray of sunshine in Mrs. Melling's *mourning*." Magdalene looked forward to a calm midday meal in the dining room with Mrs. Melling who, though unveiled, still dressed in black.

Halfway through their soup, Lydia rushed in squealing like a little girl. She flung Alexander's blood-stained shirt onto the floor in a fit of disgust.

"I can't be handling things like this, Mrs. Melling. If I didn't know better, I'd say he murdered someone up there. It's on his bed and clothing. I can't make heads or tails of the mess, but I sure can't be expected to clean all that by myself."

Lydia glanced at Magdalene, but she looked away.

"My poor boy! Did either of you see him this morning? Was he okay?"

Magdalene lifted her chin. "He seemed al—"

"He looked putrid!" Lydia screeched. "He looked like death, with all those bloodshot eyes and dark circles."

"Enough with the hysterics, Lydia. You did not come until the autumn, but Alexander gets nose bleeds every spring and autumn. That is how we know the weather is about to change. They are so regular farmers could plant their crops by his bleeds. He must have had one after he went to bed. I am sorry for the mess, but there is nothing I can do about it. Rosemary has cleaned them up a time or two. She will know what to soak the linens in until the laundry is picked up. Now," she said as she waved her hand at the maid, "get that out of here so we can finish our meal. I hope from now on you will be able to hold your peace until I am finished eating."

Mrs. Melling turned back to her bowl as if nothing had happened, but Magdalene saw the rage on Lydia's face. She stared down her sharp nose at Magdalene before leaving with the shirt. When Mrs. Melling and Magdalene finished eating, they retreated to the upstairs sitting room. Mrs. Melling twittered with her canaries before settling down with a book on the saints. Lydia could be heard several times, coming and going from the other upstairs rooms, but she didn't approach the sitting room until three o'clock. With her hands meekly behind her back, she stood in the open doorway and cleared her throat.

"Yes, Lydia, you may enter." Mrs. Melling's voice sounded sharp, though she'd not previously displayed annoyance.

"I finished Master Melling's room. I understand he's to be gone for some time. Would you like me to shut it properly before leaving?"

"I suppose you think it easier to accomplish with a helper." Lydia nodded.

"Magdalene, you may go with her."

As soon as they were in the hall, Lydia clutched Magdalene's arm. "You're just what I wanted. Now, what do you think *really* happened with Alex last night?"

"I…I couldn't say. I was sent to my room directly after supper. When I brought my letter down for the mail, the family was still in the parlor."

"Oh, just as well." Lydia dropped Magdalene's arm. "Let me fetch the covers. I'll be right back."

Alexander's room by the full light of day wasn't as brooding as Magdalene expected. The paneling was tasteful and most of the furnishings plain. Only the massive bed, its wood almost black and carved with unnecessary ornamentation, loomed ominously. She touched one of the posts rising from the footboard and followed the undulating thickness up to the solid wood canopy. A touch of fabric would have softened the frame, but it was decidedly masculine and overpowered the space—a perfect representation of Alexander Melling. Leaning over the bare mattress, she gazed up at the carved ceiling of the bed. The notion crept seductively to lie on the bed and imagine Alexander with her. She clung to the post and shut her eyes in prayer.

"If you love that monstrosity, it's the end of our friendship." Lydia dropped a heavy pile of canvas in the middle of the floor. "It's horrific to dust."

Magdalene's laughter helped drive out the sinful thoughts. She set to work helping Lydia drape the furniture with the large sheets to keep them free from the dust of disuse.

"I'd never in my life met a more pompous man than this one. Did he make you feel like an old shoe?"

"He called me a naïve country girl my first day and did seem arrogant a good deal of the time." Magdalene tossed a sheet over the roof of the bed to Lydia, hanging on to one end so they could drape it equally.

"Figured as much. He gets that from his mother."

Magdalene wanted to help Lydia, but coming into Alexander's room and speaking of him made her insides prickle. She pursed her lips and tried to change the subject. "Where did you work before you came here?"

"The Point Clear Hotel, still do actually. I meet all types there, including the Mellings and folks from New Orleans and Atlanta and beyond. The Mellings came for Saturday supper one day I was filling in at the dining room last September. I'm typically a chamber maid, but I'm always willing to work wherever I'm needed for extra money."

They finished draping the bed and moved on to the dresser.

"It was just the two of them—Alex and Eliza were at some society dance—and there I was, trying to balance a tray with two drinks a piece. I lost my footing at the end and spilled the wine all over Ruth's satin dress."

"Oh my!" Magdalene, as shocked at hearing Lydia call Mrs. Melling by her Christian name as well as by the accident, understood how such a first impression could account for Mrs. Melling's sharpness with the maid.

"She put up such a fuss, the hotel docked my pay and threatened to dismiss me. I was in tears by the back door when George found me. He laughed, gave me his handkerchief, and offered me a position at his house in Mobile. When I told him I lived with elderly relatives and couldn't go that far, he put me in here as a maid, only asking that I provide my own clothes because he liked to see a woman in uniform about the house. I'm still at the hotel most weekends, but no longer allowed in the dining room."

Magdalene covered an armchair by herself. Seeking to nudge her back to the task at hand, she questioned the maid. "Where about is your family?"

"East of Fairhope. They've got one hundred acres of corn and cotton fields, but it doesn't do much to feed and clothe me. I have to help supplement the income. All our generation does. I get a ride into town from one of my cousins on his way to the pottery kiln and can usually find a passing wagon to the get the rest of the way to my destination. Otherwise, it's these old boots doing the walking."

"Is there nothing closer to you, employment wise?"

"Nothing with prospects like these. I aim to catch myself a gentleman and be a kept woman one day." Lydia wrapped a sheet around herself as though it was a mink stole and sashayed across the Oriental rug.

Magdalene's good-natured laugh rang out.

"It's no joke! I'm closer than ever to getting what I want. I'll be well to do and you'll still be sitting by old ladies with their needlework."

"I was only laughing at you prancing around. I didn't mean anything by it. I'm sorry."

"Finish covering things and close up the windows, then I might forgive you." She turned on the heel of her worn boot and exited the room like she owned the place.

Though shaken by Lydia's moodiness, Magdalene knew it would be better to comply than walk away with it undone. Making an enemy of one of the only young women she'd likely have regular contact with wasn't an option, no matter that Alexander warned her to not trust Lydia. She draped the coat rack behind the door, knocking it shut in the process. A menacing click sounded when the door slid into place, followed by a gentle breeze filled with sandalwood and brandy. Rousing Magdalene's impassioned memories of the weekend with Alexander, she opened the wardrobe. She ran her hands over the clothing Alexander left behind and inhaled his fiery scent. With a moan of pleasure, she buried her face in the lone gray suit.

Coming to her senses, Magdalene tossed a canvas over the wardrobe. Then, rushing to the window, she pulled both the sheers and the heavy velvet curtains closed at the middle. The room turned dark as midnight. Pale shapes of the covered furniture stood like eerie sentinels along the path to the door. She had to conquer the infernal room to gain her freedom, treading through the thickening atmosphere as she lifted one foot, then the other. A trick of her mind made the room lengthen and tripled the distance, as well as her anxiety. Each step caused the once-white covers to darken until she no longer had the luxury of the furniture as guideposts. The room a uniform black space surrounding her, smothering her inch by inch.

When she felt she must be halfway, she paused. The evidence that stopping was the worst thing she could have done assaulted her senses. A howling wind encircled her, creating chill bumps on her skin. From within the gust, she heard the words that created the most fear from the horrors of last night.

We tried to kill you.

Over and over, Alexander's haunting words whispered threateningly as she stood in the darkened room without hope of escape. What could the wind—and the voice—do without a body for a vessel? Or was she the form it would now take? Would she need to scratch her skin to relieve the sensation as Alexander had done? She didn't think herself capable. But hurting herself, she realized, is what she'd done all along through the sins of the flesh she was willing to commit. Alexander sought the help of a priest in Mobile, maybe she needed outside help as well. Deacon De Fiore? Desperate, Magdalene fought for a way out of her dire situation.

"You cannot have me!" Her voice rose with each word. "I give myself to the Lord!"

The darkness dissipated enough for Magdalene to see the path to the door. Distress still pounding in her chest, she crossed to it in three strides, but no amount of tugging would allow her exit. Petrified with apprehension, she banged on the door for help.

Nineteen

After pulling at the door without success, Magdalene again beat on it with her fists as a last resort.

The door yanked open as Lydia's laughter filtered in from the hallway. "You're easy to rile up. Scared of a dark room, are you? There are lots of them in Seacliff Cottage."

Magdalene stumbled out of Alexander's bedroom and tried to control her rage.

"Girls!" Mrs. Melling called from her room. "Is everything all right?"

"Yes, ma'am. Just a little trouble with the door is all." Lydia turned to Magdalene, and in a softer voice spoke. "Don't waste time being poked up. It was only in jest. How was I to know you'd start pounding the door like that?"

Magdalene ignored her and went straight to her bathroom to splash water on her sweaty face.

Lydia leaned against the attic door when she emerged. "You aren't sore, are you?"

"No," Magdalene forced a smile, "it's okay. A little scare never hurt anyone."

"That's right, Mags." She patted her arm. "You're a good sport. Now, I'm off. You can tell the missus for me."

After Lydia's departure, the house seemed to calm. Supper with Mrs. Melling—an hour earlier because the men were gone—was uneventful, as was their time in the parlor afterward. With the airing the room received that day, the lingering scents of the men's drinks had vanished. If only Magdalene could rid herself of the image of Alexander, all would be well.

The mantel clock struck eight and Mrs. Melling shifted in her chair by the fire, resting her book on her lap. Magdalene put her sketchbook aside and addressed the lady of the house.

"Does Deacon De Fiore come often?"

"He does not come as often as he did when Eliza was about, but he visits me Wednesdays. My middle of the week check-in. He wants to be sure I am comfortable and cared for while George is in town. Alex stayed with me until now, but he was prone to brood. Of course, since the accident, I have been out of sorts myself. I do not know why I wanted to stay here, it seemed fitting somehow. Eliza often asked to stay here during the week, so I indulged that a time or two. Either Alex or I stayed with her, but she was often alone in her room or out on the cliffs."

But maybe not as alone as her mother thinks.

"The coast is inspiring. I understand why she wished to stay."

"Yes. She kept a sketchbook with her at all times in the final days and filled many, but I have not found her last one. I am worried about its fate, but George and Alex think me eccentric to fret over it. A mother wants to know what captivated her daughter in her final days as a way to hold her closer."

They were captivated by sin.

Magdalene didn't think Mrs. Melling would want to know what held Eliza's interests her final weeks—at least for the sake of her friendship with the deacon—but she nodded, wondering if Alexander had found the book and kept it from his mother.

"Come closer to the fire, Magdalene. I won't be up much longer. Oh, it is quiet without the men," Mrs. Melling mused, "but better in many ways. I do think I will be able to rest this week. Especially once Alex secures the marble."

"Do you ever feel scared to be out here alone?" Magdalene asked as she sat in Mr. Melling's wingback chair.

"I am never alone." She fingered the cross around her neck. "Besides, this house somehow does not feel barren. We are watched over."

A knock sounded. Magdalene's pulse quickened and her eyes widened.

"Get the door, please, Magdalene."

"Ma'am?"

"The front door. Someone is there."

Her hand went to her heart. "But is it safe at this hour?"

Mrs. Melling laughed. "I see now how Lydia was able to spook you this afternoon. Yes, I heard the commotion. Now go."

Embarrassed, Magdalene did her best to hold her head high when she left the room. With a hand on the oval knob, she held her breath before opening the house to the unknown.

Mr. Campbell, cap in hand, stood on the front porch. Relieved it wasn't a stranger, Magdalene smiled and waved him in. "Hello, Mr. Campbell. Mrs. Melling is in the parlor."

He nodded, solemn faced. Magdalene hoped he didn't have bad news from his nephew because she looked forward to getting out of the house as often as possible with Mrs. Melling and the new driver. She closed the door and followed him, waiting by the settee while he approached Mrs. Melling.

"Good evening, Mr. Campbell. I hope all is well in the stables."

"Yes, ma'am. I just wanted to make sure you ladies were fine before I turned in for the night. It's been a while since Seacliff Cottage was without a man."

"We are quite comfortable. We need not fear with you around."

Mr. Campbell took a handkerchief from his back pocket and wiped his wrinkled forehead with a trembling hand. No wonder he was bringing in a nephew to help him. He didn't seem strong enough to hitch or saddle a horse.

"You send the girl around if you need anything, Mrs. Melling."

Magdalene dug her nails into the palms of her hands. Why must people think her a child because she was female and unmarried?

"I will, Mr. Campbell. Thank you for checking with us." She nodded to Magdalene, who released the tension in her hands and smiled politely as she walked him to the door.

As she reached for the knob, Mr. Campbell's weathered hand touched her sleeve. "Are you safe?" he whispered.

"Yes, thank you." She politely pulled her arm away.

The wrinkled skin around his gray eyes softened. "I felt there was something wrong, and coming inside, I know it to be true. Evil spirits are at play."

Magdalene took a moment to answer. "How can you tell?"

"You feel it, too? Your bedroom window was open for hours early this morning. I thought you might have been trying to rid the space of some foulness."

Her stomach lurched with worry that Mr. Campbell knew what was going on with her and Alexander. He knew of the lilies, did he guess Alexander had burned them? Considering the lilies, Magdalene gasped.

"The lilies! Lydia cleaned out the vases but I don't know what she did with them. I'd forgotten to speak to her about their removal. And the wreaths in the woods, what if an animal has eaten them?"

He patted her shoulder with grandfatherly affection. "I'll see to it, miss. Keep your wits about."

Shaken, and only partially comforted, Magdalene returned to the parlor. Before she could sit, Mrs. Melling stood.

"Let us retire. It has been a strenuous day with the changes and that maid grates my nerves. I am always most tired on the days I have to put up with her." She sighed. "At least George was right with one of his hires. He did well with you."

"Thank you, it's kind of you to say."

"Please see to the fire."

"Yes, ma'am. Good night, Mrs. Melling."

Magdalene used the poker to spread the remaining logs amid the ashes and then replaced the screen before the hearth. She dimmed the gaslights along the path to her room. Not fearing for her modesty, she went about comfortably in her second best nightgown. After mending the ripped neckline of her other gown, she pulled the window curtain aside and peered into the darkness. Mr. Campbell emerged from the forest, a lantern in one gloved hand and the wilted wreathes in the other. A new sense of respect for the humble man warmed her heart.

***

Just as Mrs. Melling hoped, Tuesday was a restful day. In the morning, they read in the sitting room. Not long after the midday dinner, the lady of the house received a telegram from Alexander. He had secured the order from the architect and his ticket to Georgia. He would be leaving the next morning on the first leg of his journey.

Encouraged by the news, Mrs. Melling and Magdalene walked to the mausoleum site and enjoyed the spring air. Magdalene took her sketchbook to the cliffs and drew different views of the bay. When her mind wandered, it fell to Deacon De Fiore and how haunted he'd seemed by his memories when she first met him there. Now that Alexander was gone, she felt she should tell the deacon about what happened Sunday night, as well as discuss what he felt when he'd arrived at the house for supper Saturday and the incident with the tea cup.

That evening, Magdalene found herself alone in her bedroom for the duration of the long night. She decided to ready a bath. While the tub filled she gathered fresh laundry from her bedroom, and then shut herself in the bathroom. Though it was just her and Mrs. Melling in the house, she kept the habit of locking herself in.

Once in the water, just as the first night she came, she heard a rustling noise from the hall and the doorknob turned. To escape the sound and sight, she submerged completely. Lying on the bottom of the tub, she opened her eyes and looked through the wavy surface at the paneled ceiling. After several seconds, the ceiling appeared to be dropping on her. Then she realized she was rising—her body's instinct to return to the surface—but she kept herself heavy, a desire to see how long she would last underneath compelling her precarious decision. When her lungs burned, she could not fight nature any longer. She burst from the water gasping, took hold of a towel hanging beside the tub, and dried her face.

We tried to kill you.

Hastily, she pulled the plug to drain the bath. Her chest heaved for air. Was she supposed to die in the tub, not at the hands of Alexander, but alone? Would she prove to be her own undoing? She slid under again and water poured into her mouth. Spattering, she bolted up, slipping in the half-drained bath so that she had to grab the towel rack to keep from falling.

In her dripping state she froze as an invisible tentacle wrapped her ankles. It slithered around her calves, knees, and thighs. Shivering, her heart seized as the sensation continued up her hips and waist. Like a slug, it slowed as it wrapped her chest not once, but three times, catching her loose hair as it snaked to a stop around her pale neck. When the wind started, her locks were invisibly tied to her body. Her chill escalated to quaking, but she couldn't move. Her teeth rattled and her eyes rolled back—causing her vision to go black.

You taste like fear.

"Alexander!" she cried with gasping breath.

Her eyes blinked against the light of the bathroom to search for him because it was his voice she heard. His tongue she felt on her cheek. But Alexander wasn't there. It was never him, his words or actions. The cravings, temptations, and needs did not belong to him or her. They were driven by something within the house, of that Magdalene now knew.

Still unable to move, Magdalene spoke. "In the name of the Father, and of the Son, and of the Holy Spirit, I command you to leave!"

The unseen tentacle loosened its hold on her throat and slid down her body. Once free, she collapsed on her knees in the empty bath. She vomited as she shook. Afraid she would bang her head on the tub, she crawled out, pulling a towel with her. Lying on the rug, she wrapped the golden towel around her shaking body as best she could and closed her eyes.

When the taste of bile overruled the chills and fear, she stood. After rinsing the tub with hot water, she climbed into the shower. Magdalene washed her mouth, hair, and scrubbed her body wherever the invisible thing touched her, staying until the water turned cold.

Once dressed in her fresh night clothes, she prayed for protection and dashed to her bedroom. Magdalene set the bench by the door like she had the first few nights. Upon turning to her bed, she found her sketchbook there once again. It was open to a page near the back—one she knew she hadn't used. When she stepped closer, she caught her breath. A sketch of her in Alexander's arms covered the page.

Looking upon his handsome profile caused the tug of longing to return. Magdalene ripped the page out of the book and studied it. The style was not her own—it was more practiced. Someone with more time to devote to art rather than running a household had drawn it, but the only one in the house with her was Mrs. Melling, and she admitted to not being skilled with drawing. Not knowing what to do with the possibly cursed picture, she dropped it into her fireplace and watched as the page curled and the image of her unrighteous time with Alexander vanished.

During the night, when the stirring winds of Alexander's scent didn't arouse her from sleep, the whisperings began. She thrashed about in nightmares, waking at two in the morning covered in a cold sweat and tangled in the blankets.

We tried to kill you.

Accept that we've won you.

Her muttered prayers created an invisible barrier around her bed, but the rest of the room tossed with chaos. Magdalene, damp with fear, huddled beneath the covers to block the sight of the curtains billowing in the foul wind. The voice quieted but still whispered at the corner of her mind like a mosquito vying for blood. After an hour of cowering, exhaustion took hold. Magdalene fell into a dream-ridden slumber.

***

Magdalene gazed out the attic window. A silk evening gown of midnight blue adorned her serpentine curves with tasteful lace overlays that broke the sheen just enough to keep it from overpowering the dress. Hair in a sophisticated pompadour style, décolletage lower than ever, and lacey cap sleeves exposed her as never before.

From the window, she watched carriages and automobiles arrive. The handsomely dressed guests disappeared onto the porch as they approached the front door below, silky trains trailing behind the women. When the lull between guests lengthened, she turned from the dormer and paced Eliza's old room. Magdalene's sultry hue was artistic glory amid the fuchsia, gold, and emerald fabric that draped from the sloped ceiling and flowed down the walls in silky waterfalls.

It was here that Alexander found her, in the exotic nest of colors. He slipped into the room with the click of the door lock. She kept pacing, but stole glances at him as she turned about, first eyeing his top hat, then his black coat tails and slim-fitting slacks. His bowtie was snowy white, shoes gleaming black.

After watching each other in silence, Alexander finally spoke. "Why haven't you come to my party, Magdalene?"

She paused, fingering the sheer fuchsia hanging around the pallet bed in the far corner. "I'm not keen on attending a party celebrating your coming nuptials."

He made his way deftly across the room, past the jewel-toned cushions scattered about the low table in the middle of the tented space, and turned her to him.

"You've bought that gown and readied yourself for the party. Come, join us."

"I've done this for you, not a houseful of people I've never met. And certainly not your fiancée everyone will be toasting."

"She pales in comparison to you." As she turned from his touch, he trailed his lowering hand across the tender skin above her low neckline. "And that, Magdalene, is what I wanted to see and do when you came here all those months ago. You and your proper high

---

collars! Who knew I only had to get engaged to see your perfection? Join us, and you shall be celebrated. Let the world see you as I do."

Magdalene dodged around him and circled—their old flirtations back with enthusiasm. "And what if I fancy myself a spurned lover?"

Alexander laughed. His eyes were sparkling blue in the glow of the fanciful room. He tossed his top hat onto the table and quickened his gait. "It was only one weekend, after all, but we could build upon what we started." He caught her hand and traced his touch up her bare arm, once again focusing on the expansion of skin below her chin. His other hand slid around her cinched waist and pulled her into his embrace.

"Stay with me," she whispered as he nuzzled against her pounding heart.

He loosened his hold so he could lean away. "If only it were that easy."

With the grace of a swan, her slim arms encircled his neck as she pressed upon him with a satisfying kiss that left his hands caressing the bare skin of her upper back. She sighed, wondering who would first change into the lust-driven beast that drove out all semblance of romance. Or maybe they were beyond that while they were within the attic. Here, they were equals in dress and manner. Passion could linger easily amid these shades, without the need of dominating strength.

Enjoying the chase, Magdalene pulled away and circled toward the wardrobe. Leaning against the teak wood, she fingered the lace ruffles at her chest and held Alexander's stare. "It's easier than you think. We're halfway there because you locked the door on your way in. You planned it all along."

Incredulous, he doubled back to the entrance to check the door. He turned around, smiling like a boy caught in a lie. "My mind knows my ambitions before I do. Or possibly my heart knew what vision I'd find here."

He strode toward her, a new purpose in his merry eyes. His hands rested against the wardrobe on either side of her shoulders and he leaned in for a kiss. Her lust coerced her into danger, but this time she didn't think she would mind because she knew how to conquer should things get too heated.

Seductive and gentle it was until Magdalene's hands went to Alexander's chest and pursued the deep U-cut of his white vest to the bottom of the three closed buttons. With ravenous force, his kisses probed before working their way down her neck. Magdalene was devoted to his touch—to the needs it fulfilled inside her essence.

One hand on the curve of her lower back, and the other holding aside a lace sleeve so he could kiss her shoulder, he lured her toward the sheers surrounding the bed. Once there, he lifted a panel of the fuchsia drapery and tossed it around her like a mantel. Where the deep pink overlapped the gown, it manifested a violent purple.

"My queen." He kissed her hand and bowed. "What do you ask of your humble subject?"

"Make me yours." With a provocative embrace, she breathed into him all her desires as his sinuous hands swept across her supple skin.

Magdalene drove herself against him, pushing toward the bed with unrelenting need. She was now the monster and the fall was far. Alexander's heel caught the mattress and he went straight back, effortlessly landing on the sumptuous Turkish blanket covering the bed. Magdalene hiked her satin gown to kneel over his legs and slink up his torso.

Alexander's eyes feasted upon her cleavage as a hand ran across her unadorned neck. "Who taught you the art of seduction?"

"My tutor is everywhere." Resting her weight on him, she kissed under his ear.

He reflexively thrust against her and seized the beguiling curve of her waist. "It has you, but not for long." Alexander grasped her hips and leaned into her as he overturned their positions and fell upon her with unyielding power.

"Air." She gasped and settled in his lap, running her hands through his hair while looking over his shoulder for her salvation.

He loosened her bound hair, pulling her closer to breathe in its scent. "Get my jacket. Loosen my tie."

Alexander shimmied out of his tuxedo jacket and she tossed it away. Running her hands along the white expanse of shirt and vest, she settled at his collar. Pausing, her eyes darted around the room once more.

Alexander laughed and nibbled her jaw. "What you seek isn't here."

Her fingers stumbled over the knot and tried to look innocent—a difficult task for one who'd given into pleasure. "What?"

His hands over hers, he pulled the wide bowtie so it unraveled through her fingers before dropping to the bed.

"There is no cross within this room. Eliza knew better than to invite carnal pleasure where a sacred symbol resides." Magdalene sighed as he eased her back down. "I wonder if my dear sister realized she cleared obstacles for me as well."

Magdalene knew Alexander could sense her throbbing heart as he tasted first an earlobe, then her neck, shoulder. A moan of pleasure escaped. Then the craving to arch into him pulsated through her, beginning with a shiver of desire. Perceiving her yearnings, his hands explored downward.

With a gasp, she clung to his shirt and then pushed his body away. Frantically trying to get out from beneath him, she panted between words. "Our Father, who—"

"Easy, Magdalene. You're no prisoner." He rose off and she slid to the side of the bed.

Stroking her hair, he shushed her. "There's no need to fear your emotions. Those appetites are natural—the way we were created since the time of Adam and Eve. Man needs woman, woman desires man 'and they twain shall be one flesh.'"

"That's marriage, this is..."

"Consummation, I believe you called it that spring night." He kissed her shoulder, caressed her arm—his hand growing colder by the second. "Let me protect us so we can finally have all we desire."

From behind her, he brought his undone bowtie around her neck and playfully ran it across her chest, relaxing her guard. With the swift movement of a striking snake, he had the length of the tie in her mouth as a gag and knotted it at the back of her head.

With groping hands, he laid her down. "There, Magdalene. No symbols, no script. We have you now."

Twenty

Magdalene rose from bed screaming and ripped the blanket off her body. No one heard her pleas for help. She was alone in the vast house—too many unoccupied doors between her and Mrs. Melling. But she wouldn't have let the lady in even if she did come knocking because she'd promised Alexander she would protect his mother. Admitting to her employer the strange happenings and nightmarish fantasies wasn't an option. She collapsed at the foot of the bed, curled into herself, and cried.

A heavy sense of oppression weighed on her chest like an anvil. Fear or guilt? Fear because something similar to the seduction and then conquering of her by Alexander in her dream could happen. Guilt because they already had explored too much of each other. Both it would seem by the strength of her misery. At times she wanted Alexander. His flirtations in the parlor, the feel of his hands in her hair for the first time in the dining room, his passionate kisses in the kitchen, bedroom… But she loathed him! How he often spoke down to her, how he spurned her in the forest, and his coldness in the carriage. And the poisonous lilies.

No! Alexander wasn't the one for her, no matter if her body told her otherwise when they were together. She would continue to fight to control her yearnings, tainted by swirling winds and aching desires that seemed to swell within the house. She needed to keep herself pure and stay on the straight path—if it wasn't too late already.

Still trembling from the dream and the encounter in the bathroom the night before, Magdalene forced herself to rise and prepare for the day. Because Deacon De Fiore was coming, she dressed in her best black skirt and a crisp white shirtwaist. Everyday her skill improved at styling her hair into the pompadour she admired in the city last Friday. She thought of her hair in the dream and knew that sophisticated arrangement was beyond her current knowhow. Thinking of her appearance and all her exposed skin in the midnight blue gown caused her to shiver. Would she ever be comfortable in evening wear such as that? It would probably take several months' pay to even purchase a dress so fine, so it was senseless to envision such magnificence.

The mantel clock in the parlor struck a quarter after eight when Magdalene went downstairs. The Wattses weren't expected until the next hour, but there was no sign of Lydia. Curious, she checked the other rooms downstairs. The parlor and dining room were empty, as was the tiny wash room. Though Lydia appeared to have cleaned Mr. Melling's study Monday morning, she thought to check for her there.

Apprehension crossed her mind, the weight she still carried from the nightmare increased as she turned the knob. A foul presence seeped out as the door swung in. Magdalene could sense the sinister feelers creeping around her from head to toe, drawing her into the dark space, pulling the memories of being wrapped in Alexander's arms to the front of her mind. She waded through the musky atmosphere to the window and pulled the heavy curtains aside. The flood of sunshine caused a collective hiss within the room. Magdalene nearly fell over from the tension seized within her body.

Reaching out to steady herself, her hand fell upon the oak frame of a free-standing shadow box. The display had two pairs of clawed feet, like a full-length mirror. When the dizziness passed, she angled her head to look within. She caught her breath, stepping away from the dozens of taxidermy birds. Cardinals, finches, and every bright thing with lovely songs were stuffed, glassy eyes forever staring from their faux perches into the menacing case.

A green chaise lounge and full-size sofa sat across from each other like they were plotting someone's demise. Possibly, they already had. The velvet upholstery of the chaise held several dark stains. Magdalene turned to flee the vulgar space and nearly ran into Lydia in the doorway.

"What are you doing in here?" Lydia's voice was full of bitterness.

"I was looking for you." She put a hand on Lydia's arm, in part to feel something human to contrast the unbodied evil she felt in

the room. "I thought you'd be working already but didn't see you anywhere."

"Mr. Melling doesn't like anyone here unless they're invited."

"I don't see why anyone would want to come in." Magdalene shuddered. "Do you not feel it?"

Lydia stared at her. "Are you turned in the head? It's just a room, like any other in this house."

Magdalene stumbled into the hall. "I need some tea."

Behind her, Lydia closed the curtains and then the door. "Don't ever go back in there. Mr. Melling won't stand for it."

"You needn't worry on that account."

Her initial irritation calmed, Lydia accompanied Magdalene to the kitchen and showed her how to prepare Mr. Melling's coffee while they waited for the water to boil.

"Who will drink it?" Magdalene asked as she turned the handle of the coffee bean grinder.

Lydia shrugged. "Guess I can."

"Should we make enough for Leroy and Rosemary?"

"I don't serve them."

Still grasping for a friendly conversation to dispel the unearthly terrors of the past few hours, Magdalene tried again. "Did you use to work more days here?"

Lydia shook her curly head. "I've always been part time. One of these days I hope to make it to the big house in the city, or an even better situation."

They poured the hot water into the respective cups and stirred. The dainty silver spoons made tinkling sounds against the china as the aromas of English tea and Brazilian coffee merged in the air.

"Taste it before drinking your tea, just so you know what it's supposed to be like." Lydia gave the cup to Magdalene.

"Strong *and* bitter. Does he not like it with sugar?"

Lydia smiled demurely. "Not usually. He'll let you know if he's in the mood for sweet."

To get the taste out of her mouth, Magdalene took a sip of tea. After setting it on the table, she buttered herself a leftover hunk of cornbread and sliced an imported banana before sitting down.

"Since you're only here during the week when Mr. Melling is gone, how did you come to learn how he likes his coffee?"

Lydia threw her stirring spoon into the sink. "You ask the most infernal questions. A regular busybody you are, first sneaking around and then asking things like you're a blooming detective. Does the missus have you on errand to find things out?"

Taken aback, Magdalene paled. "No, Lydia. I'm trying to understand how everything works around here and you're the only person I have to talk to. Once Rosemary's here, I'm with Mrs. Melling the whole time. These mornings and you are all I have."

Lydia sauntered to the table, resting a condescending hand on Magdalene's arm before taking her seat. "You poor dear. Don't mind me, I'm temperamental today."

"Did you oversleep?"

"No, why do you ask?" Lydia held the coffee to her nose before drinking.

"You were here so early Monday, I thought you reported that time every day."

Lydia snorted. "Not hardly."

"Your ride must head to town early Mondays."

"If you must know, my cousin comes in early every day for his job. I just take that ride Mondays because Mr. Melling pays me then, unless I happen to still be working when he comes in on the ferry Friday afternoons."

"It'll be nice to have my first salary. I never thought to ask when I'll be given it, though."

"Friday evenings, most likely. That's when everyone else gets paid." Lydia set her cup down. "But don't you go into his room to collect it, Mags. You stay with Mrs. Melling or wait in the hall."

"I don't wish to go in there anyway."

"Good."

Settling into quiet, Magdalene tried to make sense of it all. Waiting a little longer on a Friday to have money over the weekend would be in a person's best interest, wouldn't it? Unless she had to rush to her job at the hotel for the evening. But Lydia left after Mr. Melling was home Friday, so she had to have been paid last week. And her being upset over Magdalene looking in the study seemed territorial. Thinking back to the hideous stains made Magdalene's skin prickle. No, she wouldn't even think it—not of Lydia or her employer. Just because dark thoughts and fancies overpowered her, didn't mean the same for others.

Wishing to be out of the way, Magdalene quickly finished her breakfast and stood to leave.

"I suppose the deacon is coming today," Lydia remarked.

"Yes, that's what Mrs. Melling told me."

"I'll see to the parlor first, and hope to be gone before he arrives."

"You don't like him?" Magdalene paused by the stair door.

"He's right nice to look at, but I can't abide listening to him speak. His accent squashes all thoughts immediately. I couldn't even dust around him if my life depended on it."

Magdalene checked her laughter, not wanting to give Lydia reason for a temper flare. "What time do you expect him?"

"Two o'clock is his usual." Lydia gathered a few cleaning supplies from the far corner of the kitchen.

"You must have a lighter load today."

"Yes, Wednesdays I focus on the entertaining areas downstairs. Mondays are mostly beds and baths. Fridays are that horribly cluttered pink sitting room and touch-ups as needed. Why, are you looking to change professions?"

"Not at all, but I can help keep Mrs. Melling out of your way easier now that I know where to expect you."

"Oh, you're a dear. I can't stand the old thing."

Magdalene smiled, knowing it would be just as much a service to Mrs. Melling to keep her out of Lydia's sight as the other way around.

***

Magdalene took another cup of tea with Mrs. Melling in the upstairs sitting room, brought to them by Rosemary at half-past nine. Mrs. Melling fussed over her canaries and worked a flowery needlepoint scene while Magdalene read poems by Emily Dickinson aloud.

"Do you think Alexander is doing well?" Mrs. Melling asked in the long pause between poems.

Startled back to the image of Alexander in his top hat and tails from her dream, Magdalene tried to refocus her thoughts. "Y-yes. With the weather being nice, I don't think there would be any issues while traveling, especially by train."

"He always loved to be out and about. I worried about him staying with me these past months. George stayed the first few weeks as well, but Alexander refused to leave me alone after that and I did not wish to go back to Mobile. I see now it was wrong to keep Alexander here, though it was his choice to do so." She sighed. "This is my home now. It will be strange to go back to the bustle of the city and having people pay visits every day. I have decided I like being a hermit."

"You might feel different when the time comes," Magdalene said.

"Perhaps. Continue reading, please."

They took their dinner at noon, and then headed for the parlor. Seeing Lydia out of the corner of her eye, Magdalene took Mrs. Melling by the arm. "It's a lovely day. Why don't we wait for the deacon on the back porch? There's a swing in the gazebo I'd like to try, if that's all right."

Patting her arm as though she were a child, Mrs. Melling indulged her. "Yes, that is a splendid idea."

The sun and fresh air were welcoming as they emerged from the shadow of the house. When they approached the back porch from the yard, the Wattses came out the kitchen door, rags in hand to clean the yellow pollen off the furniture—coated, yet again, since Saturday. Rosemary and Leroy washed and little Priscilla dried. While they waited, Mrs. Melling inspected the rose bushes at the corner of the house that were beginning to bud.

"All set, Mrs. Melling. You send Magdalene in if you need anything," Rosemary said.

"Thank you." She turned to the butler. "And when Claudio comes, please bring him to us."

"Yes, ma'am." Leroy held his hand toward Priscilla to usher her inside.

"Leave her be, Mr. Watts." Mrs. Melling smiled down at the girl. "I bet you would like to swing with Magdalene."

Priscilla nodded, the little bows at the tips of her braids dancing with her enthusiasm.

"Go on, then. You show Miss Magdalene how to do it."

"Thank you, ma'am." She started to skip toward the gazebo, but stopped. "You look much nicer with your face showing."

"Priscilla!" her father boomed.

Rosemary covered her mouth to hide a smile and Magdalene bit the inside of her own cheek to keep from laughing.

"Now, now." Mrs. Melling waved her hand. "I never fault a child her honesty. Truth be told, it feels wonderful, though I do hope it is not a shock to Claudio."

"I'm sure he'll be pleased to know your heart is healing," Magdalene told Mrs. Melling as she took Priscilla by the hand and followed the girl to the swing.

The wisteria vine climbing the white columns and lattice of the gazebo had fresh green sprouts and she looked forward to smelling their flowers when they bloomed. After allowing Priscilla to climb on, Magdalene sat beside her. While her feet touched the floorboards, Priscilla's shiny black shoes stuck straight out from under her calico dress. Not allowing her size to prohibit her goal, Priscilla leaned forward and back from her position on the double swing.

"You gotta do like this," she told Magdalene.

Magdalene followed her lead, with the addition of one of her booted feet pushing them back from the ground. The other foot she kept stretched in front, like Priscilla's, and the girl squealed with delight.

"Higher!"

Magdalene indulged Priscilla until it appeared they would crash into the lattice behind them. Then she lifted her other foot and allowed their momentum to keep swinging them, carefree in the moment.

Twenty-One

Deacon De Fiore arrived at precisely two. Magdalene, looking for bugs in the side yard with Priscilla, saw him walking up the path from the main road in his dark cassock that nearly touched his feet. Lydia had left the same way not fifteen minutes before, happy to have finished her job before he arrived.

Magdalene placed a hand lightly on the top of Priscilla's braids. "Company's here. Run in and tell your mama." The girl took off and Magdalene went out the picket fence and met the deacon in the lane. "Deacon De Fiore, I'm happy to see you again."

"Call me Claudio, like everyone else here." He took both her hands in his, squeezing them lightly, then leaned in to kiss both cheeks. "The sun agrees with you, you look well."

Seeing her dazed look, he apologized. "Where I'm from, we kiss everyone. The spring air has me feeling nostalgic for home. I left there two springs past, though I didn't arrive in Daphne until last year."

Magdalene smiled, pausing at the gate. "It's good to see you happy. What changed?"

"I took your advice and confessed to Father Angelo about everything. I am, how do you say...*un uomo nuovoa*. A new man. But there is one item of concern." He handed Magdalene a letter. "This came just before I left and I read it on my way here. Take a moment and read it, please."

Claudio held the gate open for her and offered his arm as they followed the path around to the back porch.

"Mrs. Melling is much improved as well, but there's something I need to speak with you about, when we're able."

"I will work to find the time and place, especially after you read the note." Upon seeing the lady of the house sitting in the rocking chair unveiled, he crossed himself and uttered a prayer in Italian. "Some of *signora*'s features are just like Eliza's."

Magdalene patted his arm and let him approach the porch alone, while she hung back by the corner of the house.

"A portrait of glory to the Lord, you are." He took Mrs. Melling's hands and kissed her cheeks as he did to Magdalene. "Father wants to see his children happy and enjoying the sun."

"Dear Claudio." She kept hold of his hands and pulled them to her heart. "You are God's gift to this family. Thank you for coming to me."

"How may I be of service today?" Claudio asked.

"Magdalene and I have been out here the last hour, but I would like to walk now. Would you accompany us to the shore? I would feel safe if you were there with us. I have not been to the beach since before the accident."

"Shall we take a picnic tea?" Magdalene asked.

"No, we shall go with empty arms, but ask Rosemary, if they are not leaving on errand, if they would bring one to us."

Magdalene found Rosemary kneading dough in the kitchen and told her the plan.

"We'll be there. Ask if she would like lemonade or tea."

Magdalene stuck her head out the screen door. Claudio and Mrs. Melling were not in conversation so she spoke. "Lemonade or tea?"

"Tea because there is still a nip in the air," Mrs. Melling replied. "And tell her to bring Priscilla. There's no need for the girl to hide in the house when she's here."

Upon hearing the message, Rosemary raised a doughy hand, pointing a finger at Magdalene. "You're good for her, there's no doubt. I've kept Priscilla tiptoeing around here the past two months, but she's got spring itching in her shoes now. It's been hard to keep here quiet the past week. Tell her Leroy will be down with the camp chairs and I'll bring the tea within the hour."

Magdalene passed along the information.

"Allow me to fetch my hat before we leave," Mrs. Melling said as she stood.

Claudio walked her to the front of the house and Magdalene settled on the gazebo swing with the letter.

March 12, 1906
   Claudio,
   I write to you today on urgent matters. Having met Magdalene, I know you will want to protect her, just as she has showed compassion for you. It has come to my attention that forces beyond our control are at work within the walls of Seacliff Cottage. I need not spell out the details, but let it suffice to say that I had improper intentions toward Magdalene. I behaved in most ungentlemanly ways and it culminated in an act of violence my final night within those walls. It is most fortunate I was not successful in any of my carnal attempts, for I am sure I would be more wretched a creature than I am at this very moment had I stayed in that house an hour longer.

   Upon reaching Mobile, I sought medical attention for self-inflicted wounds and then went to Father Quinn for confession. It brought back all the pain and agony of what I went through over my beloved Lucy. Part of what draws me to Magdalene is that she reminds me of her. Forgive my language, Claudio, but given time, I would have taken Magdalene—of that I have no doubt—and then she would have been as wounded as dear Lucy. Truly, I'm a monster, but fortunately, Magdalene is strong. Though she appeared affected by desires of her own at times, she was always able to gain control and drive away the evil within me.

   Please use whatever is in your powers to pray over and protect Magdalene—and do apologize to her for me as I dare not send her a letter directly—and more especially Mother. Perhaps it is better there are no men in the house with them all the time, but nonetheless, they could still be in danger. I know you typically visit on Wednesdays, but please stop in on the weekends when you can because I do not completely trust Father. His intentions are not always chaste when it comes to his admiration of young women, and Magdalene, though a simple country girl, is pleasant to look at. I would never forgive myself if something happened to her that I could have prevented. And dear Mother, she did show improvements in the first two days under Magdalene's watchful care, but she needs to be out from that oppressive house. Mother looks to you for comfort. See that you encourage her to be of good cheer and see the beauty of the earth firsthand, not through books in her sitting room.

You may write to me courtesy of my cousin, Edwin Warrington, in New York City, and then, come May, in Newport, Rhode Island. Also, I trust you to burn this letter upon reading it, for I will deny any of these details if they are to become known to others. I aim to return with a wife once and for all, and she need not hear tales such as these from any source.

Regards,
Alexander

Magdalene, hands trembling, dropped the letter on her lap. Whether she quaked from fear or anger, she knew not at that moment. Claudio, having returned from escorting Mrs. Melling, quieted her hands with a few gentle strokes and looked into her brown eyes.

Forgetting her fears and the shocking truths the letter held, Magdalene focused on her indignation. "I have half a mind to march this letter upstairs to his mother!"

"But you would not, *signorina*, because you wish to protect her, too."

A dry sob heaved in her chest and escaped as a hiccup. "He's the most insufferable—"

"Yes, he is vain and wealthy. Two things easy to despise, but he is my friend. And like it or not, you are connected to him as well."

"This uncultured country girl is bound in shame!" She slapped the letter.

"Be calm, Magdalene." She shivered at the way he spoke her name. Noticing her reaction, he stepped back, bringing the letter with him. "You are, as he said, both strong and pleasant to look at. And his apology is nothing to take lightly. He respects you, no matter how flippant he comes across. I am here to help you, *signora*, and this house."

Recalling the evil that found its way into the bathroom last night, Magdalene grabbed his hand. "I must have protection! The evil came for me again last night. It…it touched me, though I could not see it." A cold shiver ran the length of her spine. "How am I to bathe or dress if it is always there, always waiting? Can you not stay with us?"

Freeing his right hand from her grip, the brush of Claudio's fingers both calmed and excited as he blessed her.

"I am not yet strong enough to withstand prolonged contact with the devil's power. Especially not with someone like you involved. My experience with Eliza provided me with a roadmap to my weakness. You and I must never be alone."

A tear rolled down her cheek like a spark escaping a fire. "I'm a ruined woman now. I should never have come here."

"No, *signora* needs you. You coming is a blessing for her. And you still have that which is most precious in the sight of the Lord. You are strong enough to withstand temptation, and I am here to help."

From a pocket he withdrew a small string of brown beads. He laid it across his hand and held it to her. Hanging in the middle of the delicate wooden beads was an exquisitely carved crucifix, the body of Jesus Christ no longer than her thumbnail.

"My grandfather carved this for my sister, Gabriella, as a gift for her first Communion. She died from fever just weeks before my journey to priesthood. Her passing helped me decide it was the right thing for me to do. I had been unsure for many months, but losing her showed me the suffering in the world needs ministering and I wanted to help." He motioned for Magdalene to hold out her arm and secured it to her right wrist. "I held it when blessed by the pope in Vatican City and it pilgrimaged with me through all the holy sites I saw before crossing the ocean. It should serve you well."

"But I can't take something of such sentimental value."

"No, no, I insist. You need it more than I."

"How odd does it look for a Methodist to wear a symbol so steeped in Catholicism?"

The deacon smiled. "God does not differentiate his children. All who seek to overcome evil, all who try their best, are on the path to Him."

"And what of this purgatory your church so often mentions that we might end up in?"

"As they say, the road to Hell is filled with good intentions. We must try our best and have faith in the grace and mercy offered by Christ."

Mrs. Melling returned in a huge sunbonnet and Claudio took the lead with her on his arm. Magdalene followed them down the sloping path toward Rock Creek. It was the same path she'd climbed with Captain Walker just five days ago but it seemed like a lifetime. With the sun out and the sparrows chirping, the atmosphere was completely different than the cloudy afternoon she arrived.

The foot of the path intersected with the hard-packed shore of the mouth of the creek, the end of the Mellings' private pier, and the sandy beach. Claudio kept Mrs. Melling near the base of the sheer front of Ecor Rouge and walked her toward a wooden Adirondack chair near a clump of cypress trees that provided shade. Removing a handkerchief from his pocket, he dusted the chair before she settled into it.

Magdalene, taking her first step into the sand, was surprised by its depth. She tottered across, following the concave spots left by the others.

Mrs. Melling laughed when Magdalene reached the tree line.

"Claudio, you should have helped her instead of me. One would think you have never walked in sand before, Magdalene."

"I haven't. It's my first time on a beach."

"You dear! Why didn't you say something? I would have sent you down here Saturday with Alexander. The bay isn't as glorious as the gulf, but you must get your feet wet. When we have our driver this summer, we'll go to the shore. The white sand is truly splendid. But for now, take off your shoes and stockings."

At the mention of stockings, Claudio turned toward the water to give her privacy and Mrs. Melling stood so Magdalene could sit while she unlaced her boots. She was grateful to be there with Mrs. Melling and the deacon as opposed to unsupervised with Alexander. Her face grew hot at the thought of unrolling her stockings in the same vicinity as him, but recalling how he'd ignored her on nearly all accounts when they were away from the house, maybe she would have been safe. Her stockings tucked into the boots and set beside the trunk of the nearest cypress, Magdalene stood.

"Oh, it's much different than dirt, I'll give it that." Her toes wiggled through the warm top layer and dug into the cool underside of the sand. "I never knew such wonders."

Reclaiming her seat, Mrs. Melling waved her off. "Go on. Claudio will join you, won't you?"

The deacon turned, a radiant smile on his olive face. "Anything for *signorina*."

Claudio began the arduous task of unfastening two dozen buttons that ran the length of his cassock. Once his priestly coat hung on a branch of the tree, he stood a changed man. Gone was the formality of the cloth. In its stead was a handsome man with a charming smile. His complexion contrasted with his white shirt most becomingly. He untied a shoe while leaning against the tree and

Magdalene could not remove her gaze. For the first time she understood how Eliza could consider a physical attachment to a man in the process of dedicating his life to God.

As though he felt her stare, the deacon glanced up while he switched to undoing the other shoe. His jaw tightened and his smile faded. He took his time rolling his black pants up to the knees. Then he tucked his crucifix into the space between two of the buttons on the chest of his shirt and took Magdalene's arm.

"Come, the water is yours."

Magdalene held his strong arm tighter than necessary. When they reached the compacted sand by the shoreline, Claudio gingerly removed her hand and took a step away.

"You must never look upon me like that again," he said. "I am cleansed, but not yet healed."

Gladness filled her at finding a friend who knew the pulls of temptation and could help her better understand what was going on inside of her—and within the house. The sense of urgency intensified.

"That's what I need to speak to you about."

"Not now. First you must experience the water. Take hold of your skirt."

Without worrying over advances, Magdalene folded her skirt to her calves and held it to one side. Claudio took her other hand and walked with her toward the gentle lapping of the water brushing the shore.

She squealed when the first wave tickled her toes.

"Do not stop now, just a little more." Claudio led her on until she had to raise the height of her skirt further.

Up to her knees in the gentle bay, Magdalene felt she would burst from happiness. All those busybodies in Seven Hills would be chattering up a storm if they knew she was standing in the bay with bare legs, holding hands with a Catholic deacon. The absurdity of the situation, paired with the delicious sensation of the water and sun, caused a giggle to escape.

"I haven't had fun like this in a long time." She looked at Claudio and her joy further increased to see him smiling.

"It is most pleasant." He swung their joined hands like they were children, then, dropping his grip, he kicked his leg sideways to send a spray of water at her.

Shouting with surprise, Magdalene lunged for him, but he ran north, sending splashes of water in all directions. With water dripping into her eyes, she stumbled a few steps toward the shore. Not caring who saw, she lifted her skirt to wipe her face. Mrs. Melling's laughter rolled to the shoreline, which further escalated the bubbles within Magdalene. She took off after Claudio, her skirt held above her knees to allow her freedom to run—something she hadn't done since before her mother died.

Magdalene ran until she caught up with Claudio, who had stopped in the water beyond the cypress trees. Part of her wanted to keep running—past Claudio, the Montrose pier, and beyond Daphne until she stumbled into the wilds of the delta. But the deacon, as if sensing her need to flee, reached out.

"*Signorina*, you must stop." His strong hands on both of her upper arms reminded her of Alexander. He led them out of the surf, and then he took her skirt into his own hands and gave it a few strong shakes to clear it of lingering sand and water. They turned back south, his arm around Magdalene's shoulder in a display of camaraderie.

They only had a hundred yards to walk and Magdalene knew she needed to open the conversation before they returned to Mrs. Melling. "I need to tell you that beside what Alexander said in his letter about the weekend, I've been besieged at other times when alone. But when we were together in the house, we had several passionate moments," her voice trembled. "I was not myself."

Dropping his arm from around her, Claudio pulled his crucifix from where he had tucked it into his shirt and clasped it with both hands. "Then it is worse than I feared. Father Angelo warned me that the devil was at play with me thinking Eliza was in the house and the episode of the flying tea cup."

"Was it not her ghost?"

"No, only the mischief of the devil."

"There's been ghostly winds, cold spots, and…" Magdalene hugged her arms across her chest. "And Alexander tried to kill me Sunday night."

"*Dio ci aiuti!* God help us!" He hastily crossed himself, and then Magdalene. "You must leave this cursed place before you are dead like Eliza."

Slowly, as if trying to convince herself, she spoke. "But he's gone now, so I'll be safe."

"You have seen and felt nothing since Alex left?"

"There's been the ghostly wind, which happened before he left, and voices. I'd had overpowering feelings of oppression and doom in two of the rooms. And a terrible, vivid dream." She felt the hair rising on her arms just thinking about it. "And then what touched me in the bath last night. I heard Alexander's voice and was wrapped like a bound prisoner."

"Yet you think you are safe? This cannot be! You must leave." He stopped her with a hand, and stood in front of her.

"But I can't! I promised Alexander I'd keep his mother safe. She's made up her mind to stay here through the summer. What will happen to her if I leave?"

His brown eyes filled with compassion. "Does *signora* know of what is going on? Is she affected?"

"She doesn't know what's happened between Alexander and me. I'd probably be let go if she did. But she suffers from melancholy, at the very least. Rosemary did mention she had night fits and Mr. Melling got medicine for her, which she started last week, but I've yet to see signs of the fits."

"It is no good. I must protect all of you."

"Tell me, Claudio, do you have one of Eliza's sketchbooks? Mrs. Melling says the last one she had is missing."

"No, but I know of which one you speak. It had a red leather cover, and for the sake of Mrs. Melling, I hope she never finds it." With a pained looked on his face, he muttered a few things in his native tongue.

"Someone has been messing with my sketchbook. It keeps getting moved around my room, and last night...last night there was a sketch in it I didn't do. Someone drew a picture of Alexander and me embracing, but no one was there to see our moments together."

"Nothing is safe in the house, most assuredly not you."

Laughter came for them in the form of little Priscilla. She flung her arms around Magdalene's skirt. "The tea is here and I can play!"

"Thank you, Priscilla." Magdalene, to keep from toppling over, removed her grip and took her by the hand.

The deacon followed them to where Mrs. Melling waited under the trees. There were now four additional chairs, a blanket, a basket of food, and tea supplies. Priscilla ran to the shore with her father while Rosemary served the others.

"You seemed to enjoy the water," Mrs. Melling remarked.

"Yes, it was most refreshing. I hope I wasn't too childish." Magdalene looked at her shyly.

"Nonsense. You think I have never seen the ruffled edges of underdrawers? If a woman cannot enjoy her first time at the shore, then what type of world do we live in?"

Magdalene felt her face go hot and Rosemary looked at her sideways.

Claudio took an awkward sip of his tea. "I am to blame, no? For getting her wet and causing her to chase me?"

Mrs. Melling waved her hand. "There was nothing wrong. You enjoyed yourselves and the beach is ours. Though if we make this a regular occurrence, I suggest investing in a wading suit."

"My shopping list grows longer each day."

Mrs. Melling smiled. "Fear not, Magdalene. There are worse concerns for a young woman than not having appropriate beachwear."

To clear her head of the conversation with Claudio, Magdalene looked up, but that only solidified the vision of evil. Ecor Rouge loomed behind their tea party. Her eyes followed the red elevation as she recalled how she first stood on those cliffs and looked across the sweeping expanse of the bay only to find Alexander on the beach looking up at her. She shivered in the warm sunlight for what was to come.

Twenty-Two

All Thursday morning Magdalene sat by as Mrs. Melling puttered around her sitting room. Though the day started sunny, clouds moved in and a blanket of dampness hung over the cliffs. She didn't attempt to take the lady of the house outdoors, and the sitting room was more cheerful than the parlor. Magdalene sat complacently with the forbearing that something headed her way while trying to hold to the pleasant memory of the time she spent with Claudio the day before.

Rosemary entered the dining room to clear the midday dinner dishes and stopped by Mrs. Melling's side. "Mr. Campbell wanted me to inform you his nephew arrived last hour. He wants to know if you would like to meet him straight away."

"Our driver!" She clapped her hands like a young girl pleased with her bounty on Christmas morning. "As much as I would like to, I think it would be best to let him rest and clean up from his journey. Tell them to come after supper. We shall wait for them in the parlor this evening."

"Very good, Mrs. Melling." The cook left with a smile.

As the ladies ascended the front stairs, Mrs. Melling spoke. "I slept surprisingly well last night. I think the afternoon at the beach agreed with me. We should do that more often, if we are not too busy traveling about in our motor coach. I do hope George followed through with his promise to secure an automobile for this side of the bay."

Not long after they settled upstairs, Rosemary brought in an envelope. "A telegram and the laundry is back, so I'll be putting it away."

Mrs. Melling set aside her book and took the message with anxious hands.

"It is news from Alex!" She skimmed the note, and then a second time, before holding it to her chest. "He secured the order. The marble will be here within two weeks!"

"That's wonderful," Magdalene said.

Rosemary, who had waited by the door to hear the news, slipped into the hall.

Mrs. Melling stood, her black dress sharp against the pink room. "Now I think I will rest for a while. Magdalene, feel free to roam. I do not need you until supper."

"Thank you. Let me know if you change your mind."

Magdalene retreated to her bedroom. What she thought upon entering it her first day—that it would be a place of refuge against the darkness of the house—had proven false. Everywhere she looked held a sordid memory. Burning flowers in the fireplace, Alexander on the floor by the window, their liaisons in the alcove—all of it soiled from the plague of evil. To stop the lurking emotions, she pulled the bracelet from under her sleeve and fingered the beads as she whispered the twenty-third Psalm. It helped calm her, but she needed air that hadn't festered inside Seacliff Cottage. She tossed her green shawl around her shoulders and exited the front door.

Wanting to take the winding lane to the main road but thinking it too far to go alone, she settled her mind to lounge at the cliff. While approaching the stable, she heard the nervous whinny of a horse, and a Scottish accent trying to soothe the animal.

"Mr. Campbell," she called from the doorway. "Do you need assistance?"

From the shadows of a stall, a man in khaki work pants, white shirt, and dark boots emerged. His russet hair was tousled and a hint of a red beard on his unshaven jaw caused Magdalene to take a step closer for a better look.

"My uncle's resting, but I think I have it under control." The chestnut horse behind him nudged him the rest of the way out of the stall with its muzzle. He stumbled forward and looked at Magdalene with a sheepish grin as he rubbed the back of his head. "This one doesn't like me, but Uncle Simon warned me Janus doesn't take well to strangers."

It was Alexander's horse, the one he tried to ride away on Sunday morning. Magdalene took another step into the stable. "What needs to be done with him?"

"Exercise and grooming." He joined Magdalene in the center of the main space, and held out his hand. "I'm Douglas, by the way. You must be Magdalene."

Surprised that Mr. Campbell would have mentioned her by name, Magdalene blushed at Douglas's touch. His handshake was work-hardened and firm, like she was used to. She made a point to look him in the eyes while they greeted and was met with the intensity of a clear summer sky. Before he let go of her hand, she knew Douglas was someone she could trust.

"It's good to meet you. I was around horses before coming here. Could I try to get him out for you?"

"Aye, by all means." Douglas raised his hands in frustration. "I've been trying for a quarter of an hour."

Magdalene slowly approached the open stall. "Hey, old boy. Let's get you outside for some pampering." In the entry she paused and held out a hand, palm side up. "Janus, old boy, let's get you some brushing and fun."

The stallion shook its head and nickered, but came to a rest near Magdalene. She raised her hand and Janus let her stroke its neck. She whispered encouragement and allowed the horse to nuzzle her arm. "We're here to help, Janus. Come now. The bridle, please, Douglas." Magdalene stretched her free hand behind her to take it from him. "Try not to rattle it or move too quickly."

The feel of his fingers against hers as he passed the tack cheered her gloomy mood. Once she had the bridle secure, she guided Janus out of the stall. "We're ready for the reins now. See if he'll let you do it."

They exchanged places in the main stable doorway and Douglas successfully clipped the reins to the bridle.

"Thank you." Douglas looked at her with admiration.

Magdalene, glad to have met him while free from the oppression of the house, adjusted her shawl over her shirtwaist. "Happy to help."

"We make a good team. You sure they need you inside?" The arch of his left eyebrow and good-natured grin created a genuine smile from Magdalene in return.

"Unfortunately, they do."

"Aye, I'm sure you're most indispensable to the lady of the house. Thank you again, Magdalene. I hope to see you soon." He nodded to her before turning his attention to the horse.

Magdalene, feeling warm despite the dampness, smiled to herself and turned toward the forest path. The bay looked as if it had been painted silver from the reflection from the sky. After watching a steamer make its way toward Mobile, she settled herself on Eliza's old rock, pulled her knees under her chin, and continued to gaze across the gray water. A few minutes later she rested her cheek on her knee and closed her eyes.

***

Magdalene awoke with a jolt, almost falling off her perch. Her legs were stiff unfolding and her tailbone sore from the hardness of the rock. Seeing the sky noticeably darker, but having no way to tell time, she took off at a run through the darkening woods. The stable yard was empty and the glow of the gaslights in the parlor flooded the shadows in the front yard.

She slowed approaching the front steps, then gingerly let herself in the door. All was quiet in the main hall. Peeking around the corner to the parlor, Magdalene released her breath because it was unoccupied and the mantel clock only showed a quarter to five. With the few remaining minutes before the weekday supper, she went in the guest bathroom. After washing her face and hands and then wrapping her hair into a fresh bun, she stashed her shawl on the little towel shelf, so the lady of the house wouldn't be annoyed with its shabbiness. She returned to the hallway just as Mrs. Melling descended the stairs.

Over her bowl of gumbo, Magdalene remarked that she had met the chauffeur that afternoon.

Mrs. Melling set down her spoon. "And is he amiable? Someone we shall not tire of on long trips?"

"Yes, Douglas is very pleasant and isn't afraid to show gratitude or admit defeat." She wanted to add *unlike Alexander*, but she kept quiet in that regard. "I helped him get Janus in the yard for exercise and grooming."

"Most excellent, but where was Mr. Campbell?"

"Resting." Magdalene pulled a loose string from the napkin in her lap and hoped she would not get in trouble for helping out.

"The dear old man has been here since before I came as a new bride. Back then, Seacliff Cottage did not have its own pier. He used to wait for us with the carriage in Montrose. He still does if we do not use a hired boat. Of course, George is happy to take the ferry.

I think he enjoys the admiration of the fellow passengers. That reminds me. A telegram came while you were out this afternoon. Captain Walker is to stop in tomorrow to collect the crate of samples and do his weekly delivery and we are to expect a surprise as well. No time was given, but it will most likely be after dinner."

"The automobile?"

Mrs. Melling checked her smile. "One never knows with George."

After supper, the women settled in the parlor to wait for their callers. By seven o'clock the Wattses were gone for the day, so Magdalene had to answer the door when the knock came.

"Welcome, Mr. Campbell, and Mr...Douglas?" Magdalene stood to the side to let them in.

"Just call 'im Douglas, Miss Magdalene. But it's Campbell, too. He's my youngest brother's lad, from his second, more youthful wife. She's proven good stock—lived past forty, unlike her predecessor."

Douglas shrugged, an amused smile on his newly shaved face.

"Well, he's most welcome, as are you, Mr. Campbell. Mrs. Melling's in the parlor."

Mr. Campbell led the way while Douglas waited for Magdalene to secure the door before venturing forward with her. Mr. Campbell approached the lady of the house.

"Where is the charming nephew of yours who will open the doors of Baldwin County to Magdalene and I this season? We want to see it all before the end of summer."

When Mr. Campbell stepped to the side, Mrs. Melling's eyes widened with pleasure as she drank in the form of Douglas Campbell. Though not in a suit jacket, he wore a navy, emerald, and yellow tartan vest with a gold pocket watch chain looped over one of the buttons, paired with a white shirt and dark trousers.

"I do not suppose," Mrs. Melling said, "you brought bagpipes or a kilt by any chance."

Magdalene had to turn toward the wall to hide laughter that threatened to erupt.

"There wasn't room for bagpipes, Mrs. Melling, but I did pack a kilt for special occasions."

"How delightful! I am afraid Mr. Campbell's Scottish roots had withered away by the time I met him, so it will be nice to have a bit of new flavor around here."

Mr. Campbell cleared his throat. "My days of leading the village to victory in a game of shinty are long gone."

"But there's still talk of the great win of '75." Douglas clapped his uncle on the shoulder.

"Please, gentlemen." Mrs. Melling motioned to the settee. "Make yourself comfortable. Magdalene, you may sit across from me."

After she settled in Mr. Melling's chair, the men took the settee.

"Excuse our mess, but the crate will be gone tomorrow. Now, would you like anything to drink? Eat?" Mr. Campbell and Douglas respectfully declined, so Mrs. Melling continued. "Douglas, your first item of business will be to learn the area so we do not fall into the wilds on our adventures. I suppose a trip to Daphne would acquaint you with those who could point out the landmarks and possibly supply you with a map."

"I'll bring him as soon as possible," Mr. Campbell said. "This lad's a quick study."

Mrs. Melling nodded. "I would expect nothing less. Once you are comfortable with the automobile and familiar with the roads, I want to begin lessons for Magdalene. I dare say she is a quick study, too."

All eyes looked at Magdalene.

"I can say she has a way with horses." Douglas smiled encouragingly. "She came to my aid this afternoon with the stallion."

"So I heard." Mrs. Melling smiled wider than anything Magdalene had seen.

"If you would, ma'am, does Douglas need to secure a special uniform?" Mr. Campbell inquired.

"We are not so full of pretense on this side of the bay. I have not required uniforms here since we dropped from a full staff. Rosemary and Watts wear what they want, but keep it respectable. Lydia gives herself airs with her maid's uniform, but I think that is only because she has it from working at the hotel."

Remembering what Lydia had told her about her uniform made Magdalene's stomach churn. With the feelings she experienced in Mr. Melling's study, she knew he was up to something most unbecoming. She could feel it reaching out to her and shifted uneasily in the chair.

Mrs. Melling drew the meeting to a close. "I am sure a busy day was had by all. We can speak more at length at a later time. Do let me know if my husband tells you anything contrary to my specifications. I aim to be in control of the transportation situation as I am the primary family member in residence. Stop in another evening during the week. It does get quiet here."

As soon as Magdalene returned from letting the Campbells out, Mrs. Melling burst. "You and Douglas would make a lovely couple!"

Magdalene felt the color rise to her cheeks. "I'm sorry, Mrs. Melling. Did I hear you correctly?"

"He is handsome, isn't he?"

She thought of the shy way he looked at her in the stable, with the rough stubble of a beard burning red. "Well…yes, but—"

"It is a perfect match. Just like Leroy and Rosemary, it shall be Douglas and Magdalene. I find it tidier to have the help paired off. There is less likelihood of dramatics when the workers are happily married and actively employed."

Thinking of the possible den of iniquity down the hall, Magdalene shivered. Did Mrs. Melling suspect her husband of wrongdoing with Lydia?

"At any rate, I think it is time to retire upstairs." Mrs. Melling stood. "It is lonely down here without anyone else. You may stay in my sitting room for a while, if you wish."

"Thank you, Mrs. Melling."

Magdalene saw to the fireplace and dimmed the gaslights. Mrs. Melling was already upstairs, so she retrieved her shawl from the hall bath before going upstairs. At the top of the landing, Magdalene turned left for her room but something the color of blue hydrangeas caught her eye. To the right, just beyond Alexander's closed door, the life-sized portrait of Eliza Melling hung unveiled. The rich tiers of blue fabric on the full skirt of her dress pulled one's gaze higher within the mahogany frame. Above the slim waist was a flounce of ruffles around an opened neckline adorned with pearls. Over the whole fashionable ensemble shined the enticing smile and piercing Melling stare that she shared with her bother. In place of Alexander's golden hair, Eliza's head was topped with a delicate swirl of glossy black.

Stepping out of her room, Mrs. Melling stood beside Magdalene. "She was striking, was she not?"

Unable to turn away from the painted eyes that matched the color of the dress, Magdalene nodded. "Yes, most definitely."

Mrs. Melling fingered the intricate carvings of flowers on the frame and sighed. "I feel a headache coming on. I need to take my medication and lay down. I'll see you tomorrow."

Abandoned in the throat of the house, Magdalene felt powerless to do anything but stare at the chilling reminder of the one who caused so much misery. Just as when she saw Claudio without his cassock—seeing him as a man apart from his calling—she now saw how that man could have lost his way with a beckoning face such as Eliza's toying with his emotions. There was much to be said about the prowess of a young Melling's charisma.

Twenty-Three

Upon waking Friday, Magdalene found herself knotted in her blankets and wrapped in the memory of the same nightmare she'd had the previous night—her and Alexander in the attic room tangled in passion on the night of his engagement party. With a pounding in her chest, she prepared for the day, grateful she didn't have to pass Eliza's portrait for over an hour. While finishing up her breakfast, both the Wattses and Lydia arrived.

"Rosemary tells me the driver's here." Lydia ground a scoop of coffee beans. "Is he handsome?"

Magdalene, unsure whether or not to let her opinion be known, nodded.

Lydia whooped. "About time we got ourselves something fine to look at."

Magdalene colored, and stepped toward the stair door.

"Don't you worry none. I ain't gonna step between you and him." Lydia snapped a towel toward her. "I've got my eye on a bigger fish, but that don't mean I can't enjoy the scenery. How do you suppose he takes his coffee, bitter or sweet?"

"I could hardly say," Magdalene stuttered. "I just met the man."

Lydia brandished the dish towel. "Come now, Mags. Don't be a ninny. How do you imagine he takes his coffee?"

"Honestly!" Rosemary stepped between the two women. "You'd think there were better things to discuss than a man's coffee preference."

"But coffee is the key to everything." Lydia winked at Magdalene. "What do you say?"

Wanting to get away from Lydia's innuendos, Magdalene sputtered, "Cream and sugar," and rushed up the back stairs.

The sound of Lydia's laughter clawed at her heels all the way past Eliza's portrait and into the sitting room. It was Lydia's day to clean the room so Magdalene encouraged a morning walk after Mrs. Melling saw to her birds and breakfast.

"We must stay near the house in case Captain Walker comes," Mrs. Melling reminded her.

They settled on a stroll to the main road and back, with promises of being fetched should the captain arrive. It wasn't until after their midday dinner that Captain Walker presented himself at the front door just as Priscilla ran by the parlor window with a peppermint stick. Magdalene smiled over his kindness.

"I'm almost sorry to see it go," Mrs. Melling remarked as the deck hands nailed the crate shut.

Captain Walker checked his watch. "Now, ladies, I must insist on you stepping out to the porch to make sure you don't get hurt when they bring the crate out."

He led Mrs. Melling out the front door and to the side. Just as Magdalene joined them, the peculiar sound of a horn rang through the air, followed by the rumble of an engine coming up the lane.

"It's here!" Mrs. Melling clapped her hands. "George didn't disappoint me!"

"We had to drop it at the Montrose pier. The oxen pulled it up the incline and Mr. Melling started it up on Sibley Street to drive over." Captain Walker held his arm out to Mrs. Melling. "Would you like to come to the lane?"

Magdalene stayed on the porch until the automobile was in sight, a luxurious black touring car with a canopy and small windshield trimmed in brass to match the headlamps. The sound of the vehicle brought both the Campbell men around from the stables, as well as the household staff. She joined Lydia and the Wattses near the back fence while Mr. Melling showed his wife the automobile.

"I can just picture myself riding in the backseat, a giant straw hat tied to my head with a pink scarf." Lydia sighed. "Some people get all the breaks."

When Mr. Melling helped his wife into the front passenger seat, Lydia huffed and went back inside. Mr. Melling took the wheel, turned around in the stable yard, and went down the lane in a swirl of dust. Rosemary and Leroy wandered back to the kitchen porch with

Priscilla to unpack the groceries and supplies Captain Walker delivered.

The captain made his way to Magdalene.

"I trust your first week at Seacliff Cottage went well."

Relieved that the stresses she'd encountered in her time there didn't show on her face, Magdalene smiled. "Well enough, thank you."

"Mrs. Melling looks right cheerful." He held Magdalene's eye with a straight, friendly gaze.

"She's been looking forward to the automobile all week. I'm glad it's here for her. She's been in the house far too much."

"It's good to see her out from the veil." Captain Walker tipped his hat. "You take care of yourself, and the missus. And let me know if you ever need anything from the city."

"Thank you, Captain."

Captain Walker followed his deckhands down the cliff path and out of sight. Magdalene met with Mr. Campbell and Douglas in the stable yard, conscious of Lydia watching from the kitchen porch and the freedom she enjoyed compared to the maid.

"It's a fine automobile." Douglas's smile held pure excitement. "A Pierce Great Arrow like that won the Glidden Tour endurance run last year with a near perfect score with Pierce himself as driver. I never thought I'd be in charge of one when Uncle Simon offered me the position."

"Don't get your hopes up with handling it anytime soon." Mr. Campbell shook his head. "Mr. Melling looks a mite too pleased about that toy to want to share it this weekend."

"She'll be worth the wait, I'm sure," Douglas replied, still smiling as he turned to Magdalene. "And you'll be spoiled the rest of your life with that being your first experience behind the wheel."

Magdalene clasped her hands behind her back, her countenance shining.

Lydia stepped onto the back porch and hollered, "Anyone want coffee? I aim to make a pot for Mr. Melling."

Douglas opened his mouth, but Mr. Campbell spoke first. "No, thank you. We don't make a habit of intruding on the house's kitchen."

The automobile rumbled into the yard, halting all discussion. Mr. Melling sprung out of his seat and helped his wife down.

"It runs like a dream!" she exclaimed. "Much smoother on the roads than the carriage and it is breathtakingly quick! We rode all the way to Montrose Post Office and back."

The couple came in the gate, their eyes roaming those still assembled.

"Lydia," Mrs. Melling said, "tell Rosemary to put on tea for everyone, including the Campbells. We'll have it on the porch to admire the glorious addition to our cottage transportation collection."

"I'd be happy to brew some coffee, too, if anyone is interested."

A glint of mischievousness passed Mr. Melling's eyes. "By all means. You do make the best coffee."

"Perhaps you would like to meet Douglas, and show him around the new car." Mrs. Melling's voice sounded strained and her earlier jubilation all but gone, causing Magdalene to feel her suspicions about Lydia and Mr. Melling were true.

While Mr. Melling met with Douglas in the yard, Magdalene took Mrs. Melling to the porch and allowed her first choice of the seating. She chose a rocker and patted the one next to her for Magdalene.

"At least he kept his word about the automobile." The look of defeat on her face was better suited for a stormy night than a sunny afternoon.

"And where do you think we should we go first for a grand adventure?" Magdalene questioned, hoping to get Mrs. Melling's mind thinking of joyful things to come.

"The gulf and whatever we find on the way. We can secure hotel rooms and make a proper trip of it. Maybe we could even take Claudio along. Surely he gets vacation."

"I don't know how it all works, but we could try." Magdalene doubted it would be proper for a deacon to travel about with women without a chaperone and didn't think Douglas would be a proper fit for that role. "Maybe we should stick to short trips for the time being."

Mrs. Melling rocked, eyes closed, mouth shut in an almost frown. Not knowing what to say, Magdalene watched Douglas on the other side of the fence as his hands roamed the vehicle's trim and he tinkered with things under the hood. He was the type of man comfortable with machines or horses, a brilliant blend of the old ways and industrialization, sure to make something of himself no matter his station.

Rosemary and Lydia brought tea, coffee, bread, and cookies and set the spread on the table. Mr. Campbell had to drag Douglas away from the automobile. While Rosemary served Mrs. Melling, Magdalene helped herself.

"Are you sure you don't need me to pour for you?" Lydia scowled.

"I'm capable, thank you." She ignored the cold stare until Douglas arrived. Then she wanted to run away, but Mr. Melling was with him, so she stood to block Mrs. Melling's view of the food table.

Lydia was all smiles and twinkling eyes as she readied coffee and a small plate for Mr. Melling, then she set her sights on the chauffeur. "I don't think we've been introduced. I'm Lydia, and you must be Douglas Campbell, fresh off the boat. Mags and I have a wager on how you take your coffee. Not that we gamble." She inclined her head toward the Mellings.

"American women have strange pastimes." He accepted a plate and placed a few cookies on it.

"I simply must know, to ready it for you." Lydia held the empty cup, an alligator smile on her lips.

"It depends on the time of day. For right now, I'll take it with a splash of milk. Thank you."

Lydia giggled, but set to preparing his coffee. "She was half right."

Mr. Melling took the rocker beside his wife, so Magdalene ambled to the gazebo and leaned against the railing. Leroy stood, offering his spot on the swing, but she declined. He fetched a straight back chair from the other end of the porch for her.

"Lydia will ruin you if you let her," Rosemary whispered. "She's up to no good."

Magdalene huffed as she set her teacup on the railing. "I want no part in her schemes, thank you."

Mr. Campbell and Douglas came into the gazebo, standing near Magdalene while Lydia loitered near the table—and Mr. Melling.

"What do you get for guessing half my coffee preference?" Douglas asked.

Magdalene set her plate on her lap and waved her hand. "It's nothing. Just a game Lydia started. I have no stake in it nor wish to play."

"Oh." Douglas took a sip and settled back a step. "Well, I like it with sugar in the mornings, just in case she asks."

Her cheeks burned, but she couldn't hide a grin.

After tea, Magdalene saw Mrs. Melling to her room for a rest. She sat in the armchair in her own bedroom and sketched. After her thoughts swirled to drawing Alexander, she hurried down the back stairs in search of cleansing air on the porch. She sat on the swing and was soon joined by Priscilla, who wandered in from the side yard. Mr. Campbell and Douglas had the carriage horses out of the stable for grooming, and the younger man raised his hand in greeting. Magdalene returned the gesture as she pushed the swing higher.

Quarter of an hour later, Lydia emerged from the kitchen. Her head piece and apron were folded neatly in her hand but her curls were coming undone.

"It's a good week when he comes home early." She rattled her coin purse. "I can enjoy myself a bit this weekend."

"Wait!" Mr. Melling came around from the front side of the house. "I want to see how this new fellow drives. Why don't we take you over to Fairhope, Lydia, and save you some walking." He hollered to Douglas in the yard, and then, seeing Magdalene on the porch, he extended the invitation for a ride.

"No, thank you. I best stay in case Mrs. Melling needs me."

"But let me get your week's wages while I'm thinking about it. Come with me."

Reluctantly, Magdalene followed him to his study. A wave of nausea, like what struck her in the room the other morning, threatened to dislodge her tea and cookies. She waited outside the threshold, conscious of the kitchen door opening behind her, just enough for someone to peer out.

"Ruth seemed in better spirits today." He handed Magdalene an envelope. "You've been a big help to her. I trust it's not too quiet around here with Alex and me gone."

"Not at all. Thank you." She turned about and marched into the kitchen, the door bonking Lydia square on the shoulder because she couldn't get out of the way quick enough.

"There's no reason to spy. I told you I'd not step foot in that room."

"You're just jealous I get to ride in the automobile before you."

Over her shoulder she said, "Don't be petty, Lydia. It doesn't look good on you."

Despite not caring, Magdalene watched from her bedroom window as the group readied to leave. Mr. Melling helped Lydia into the backseat with what appeared to involve more touching than necessary. Douglas settled behind the wheel and Mr. Melling took the front passenger seat. They went in a swooping circle around the yard and then out of sight.

Twenty-Four

"I sat in the front with Douglas in case I needed to grab the wheel, but he's a splendid driver," Mr. Melling told his wife over the supper table. "And he's willing to work with the horses, which is a good thing with Campbell up in years. Whatever knowledge he can pass to the boy will be a blessing."

"Magdalene helped with Janus yesterday while Mr. Campbell rested."

"We can't have our house girls in the stable."

Mrs. Melling's smile faded. "I like for Magdalene to be about. She is my eyes and ears when I am not able to be everywhere."

"So you feel the need to have her snoop? Is that what Alex did for you?"

"Alexander looked out for himself and me. I expect Magdalene to do the same. She knows her way around horses and there is no reason for her not to stop in the stable when she has the time."

Mr. Melling crossed his arms and glared at his wife. "And I say it's not proper for the house girls to hang around the stable. There's no telling what might happen in there."

Mrs. Melling laughed. "Magdalene is completely respectable, even if some of your other hires are not."

Magdalene shrunk in her seat with the burn of shame over her improperness with Alexander, as well as fear for what might happen between the Mellings. Mr. Melling's red face looked ready to explode. Instead, he stood and excused himself.

After picking at her food for several minutes, Mrs. Melling placed her napkin on the side of her plate. "I feel a headache coming on and am going to bed for the night. Please tell Rosemary we are finished in here."

Magdalene gathered a few plates to bring along with her when she spoke to Rosemary. The Watts family was seated around the small kitchen table eating their own supper.

"Don't get up now. There was a bit of a fuss and they've both gone their separate ways for the evening. Mrs. Melling went to bed for the night with a headache." Magdalene set the dishes by the sink and sighed.

"Oh!" Rosemary cried. "Her medicine was in the delivery this afternoon but with serving the tea for everyone, I forgot to bring it upstairs."

"I can bring it to her." Magdalene retrieved the bottle off the counter and said her goodbyes.

As Magdalene passed the portrait of Eliza in the hallway, a gust of wind struck her with the force of heat from an opened furnace, but this wind chilled. Her hand that reached for the knob of the sitting room door had a bluish tint and she had difficultly maneuvering it.

While struggling, one of the doors behind her opened. She turned and gasped. "Sorry, Mr. Melling. You gave me a fright."

"There, there." He patted her forearm. "I don't mean any harm. I'm on my way out. I need to test the car at night, to make sure all is working properly."

"Yes, I suppose you must." Magdalene turned back to the sitting room door, bringing her arm out from under his overbearing reach.

"Ruth needn't know, if she doesn't ask." His voice was eerily calm as it crept up her back. He started walking away but paused. "And don't you mind what she said at the table. Whether she likes it or not, I control what goes on under this roof, not her."

Two large strides brought him back to her and he placed a domineering hand on her arm. Magdalene's insides shriveled under his touch. She did her best not to outwardly flinch, but she couldn't look at his icy stare as the frigid wind stirred around her.

"Tell me, you aren't as respectable now as you were when you arrived, are you? Ruth pretends that you're above any games that others might play, but I saw the glances between you and Alex. She did as well, and to protect you, sent him away for the summer season while it's yet spring. She didn't want to tarnish your purity, like those snow-white lilies that wilted and died on our supper table."

Magdalene already knew as much, but hearing the words from Mr. Melling's haughty mouth made it more shameful. He ran his hand up her arm. Then he took her chin to force her to look up at him.

"I chose you with Alex in mind. Did he appreciate my offer before he left?"

Surging with the rage of once again being reduced to a plaything, Magdalene knocked Mr. Melling's hand aside. "Obviously he would have bragged, proud of his conquests, if he had."

"A true gentleman never brags, my dear, just as a real lady never mentions indiscretions." He leaned toward her with a deadly stare. "Ruth broke the mold with that this evening. Have you been filling her head with stories?"

"There's nothing I need to say because she's not blind. Now if you will excuse me…" This time, the knob turned. She slipped into the sitting room and was about to shut the door when Mr. Melling stuck his foot in to stop it.

"Your time will come, Magdalene, and it won't be by the hands of a stable boy."

Magdalene leaned against the door after he walked away, willing her lips to stop trembling. She dry-heaved a few sobs and hugged herself, the medicine bottle clutched against her chest.

"Magdalene," Mrs. Melling's voice came from her bedroom, "is that you?"

She took a few deep breaths to get her breathing under control. "Yes, Mrs. Melling. I brought your medicine."

Mrs. Melling peered into the dim sitting area from her bedroom. In the low light she rushed out, her sheer robe fluttering behind her.

"My dear…" She put her arms around Magdalene like only a mother could, which set Magdalene to tears. "He crossed a line, didn't he? No, do not answer. You need not be ashamed." She took the bottle with one hand and steered Magdalene toward the sofa with the other, sitting down with her.

Magdalene hadn't been cared for by a mother figure in almost a decade and relished the moment. But as much as she felt safe in Mrs. Melling's motherly arms, if it were not for her promise to Alexander—or the possibility of running into Mr. Melling in the dark—Magdalene would have escaped the house at that moment.

"Is he gone?"

Magdalene nodded, still unable to speak through the tears.

"That means you shall be safe tonight." Mrs. Melling took her hand. "Something in him changed last summer. After having been here at the cottage with us all June, he went to work in the office one Monday in the middle of July and stayed at home, not wanting to commute across the bay each day. When he came back that Friday afternoon, he was a different man. I could not place the change right away because it was subtle, but by fall he no longer visited my room. Then I knew for sure he had found satisfaction elsewhere. At least it appears he was thoughtful enough to wait until the children were grown. Some husbands roam while there are yet babes under the roof." Mrs. Melling sniffed.

It was Magdalene's turn to squeeze her hand reassuringly. "I vow to you not to be part of the problem. I won't be another name on someone's roster of iniquity."

But the thought that the evil in the house could seduce her toward Mr. Melling as it did Alexander sent a chill to her bones and nausea to her stomach. She reached under her sleeve to finger Claudio's rosary and felt a small sense of relief to know he'd promised to come the next day.

***

Never before had Magdalene been so glad to see the sunrise. Every time she fell asleep the nightmare of her with Alexander in formal attire and dripping with want woke her. Between the reoccurring dream and Mr. Melling's words last night, her brain worried continuously, though it lessened a tad when she settled on the back porch with her morning tea. Upon seeing the automobile parked haphazardly in the side yard, her feelings resurfaced knowing Mr. Melling was in the house. She prayed he wouldn't wake up before the Wattses were there and demand coffee.

Or something else.

After a few minutes, the solitary figure of Claudio in his familiar cassock trudged up the lane. Magdalene ran out to meet him. His usual empty hands carried a black leather bag, much like a doctor's kit.

"Claudio!" His name rolled off her tongue as she ran to him. She slowed seeing the grim set to his jaw, similar to when he rebuked her for staring at him while he defrocked on the beach.

He took her forearm with one hand and kissed her cheeks with distracted force. There were smudges of a sleepless night around his eyes and immediacy in his grip—which continued after the greeting. "I came as early as I dared, *signorina*. We must speak. You do not look rested. Are things worse?"

"Yes, but I believe I found the source of evil." She walked with him toward the yard.

He set his bag on the porch table. "This is what I need to heal the house and drive out the demons."

"Demons?"

"They are the source of the evil here."

"Is there a demon in me now, trying to capture you?"

With a slight tilt to his head, he studied her face, pulled his crucifix the length of its chain and touched it to her forehead. It felt like a cooling relief.

"It is as I expected. You are not possessed. Every so often, there is a fleeting glance in your eyes that reminds me that you and I are both natural man and woman, fallen creatures subject to the whims of our flesh."

"But what Alexander said is true. I urged him along several times. Are you repulsed?"

"No, *signorina*, you are good. Now where is the source of evil?"

"Mr. Melling, but I don't think he'll be cooperative."

"The demons are with him?" Claudio's eyes widened. Magdalene nodded. "*Santissimo padre!*"

"He's been having affairs since last summer. And it appears"—Magdalene shivered—"his current infidelity is taking place here, in his den."

"*Peccati del padre*. The sins of the father." Claudio shook his head. "Most unfortunate. He invited evil within these walls when he first committed adultery here. We must cleanse that room, bless the house, and expel the demonic infestation."

Magdalene wanted to be joyful over the plan the deacon laid out, but it seemed too simple a task for such deep-rooted evil. "That's all there is to it?"

"Depends on the level of infestation and how cooperative those within the house are at confessing sin and their willingness to deny sin in the future."

"If it doesn't work, will it make the situation worse by stirring up the spirits?" Her brown eyes were wide, her voice strained.

Claudio took her hands in his. "We can only pray it helps. Let me begin with one."

Still holding hands, Claudio bowed his head and uttered the most beautiful words Magdalene had ever heard. The spirit flowed over her like warm water as he prayed in Italian. He moved his hands to the top of her head and blessed Magdalene and closed with the sign of the cross on them both.

The reverent pause afterwards was broken by the most authentic smile Magdalene had ever seen. Her heart leapt from righteous joy over seeing Claudio so full of the spirit of God rather than squalid yearnings. She wanted nothing more than to dwell with the source of the light within him at that moment. Her own countenance became a mirror for Claudio's benevolence and she experienced the lightest sensation she'd ever felt.

"We must prepare what we need." Claudio squeezed her hand and then opened his bag.

He removed a linen surplice, purple stole, the holy Bible in Latin, two crucifixes, three glass jars individually wrapped in purple velvet, and something that looked like a baby rattle. Claudio placed the white surplice over his cassock. Then he draped the purple stole with an embroidered gold cross on either end around his shoulders and handed her one of the crucifixes.

"Saint Benedict's crucifix is the best for expelling demons," he said.

"You are official now, but what's that?" She pointed to the rattle-shaped object on the table.

"An aspergillum, for the sprinkling of exorcised water." Claudio motioned with his hand to show how it worked, then took the first bottle out and filled the silver reservoir with the holy water. Slipping the filled bottle into a pocket, along with one that looked to be filled with oil, he smiled at her. "We might not need it, but better to have it on hand."

The third bottle was filled with salt. He tucked the holy Bible under his arm and opened the salt. "Now we start on the exterior doors, so the devil may send no more to distract us. Then we will concentrate on the den."

They moved to the front door, Magdalene watching while Claudio prayed in Latin and sprinkled water and held the cross to the door. He motioned for her to open the door, and then he sprinkled a dash of salt across the threshold.

"Exorcised salt," he told her as they walked back around the house.

Uneasiness waivered over her when they approached the back door. With the final exit blessed and the salt sprinkled, Magdalene thought she felt the porch tremble beneath her. Claudio looked over his shoulder at her, a determined look on his face.

"Do you want to wait out here?"

"No, I must go with you."

"Then keep a prayer in your heart and do not give in to the darkness."

As they went through the kitchen, Claudio chanted and sprinkled the water. Afterward, he dropped a few dashes of salt in each of the corners. Then they went through to the hallway. When the first drops of water touched the den's door, there was an audible hiss. Using the purple stole as a mediator, Claudio turned the knob. Almost visible to the naked eye, the foul air billowed through the opening door.

"*Santissimo padre!*" Claudio whispered before starting back to the Rites and stepping into the room.

Magdalene, seeing Mr. Melling face down on his sofa still wearing his shoes and disheveled clothing, put a hand on Claudio's arm and pointed across the room. Continuing to speak, he backed out and Magdalene pulled the door shut, turning the knob so it wouldn't click into place.

"What do we do now?" Magdalene asked. "Can you expel the evil while he's asleep?"

"Depending on the grievousness of his sins, it can be as gentle as a confession or as violent as a brawl, but he needs to be an active participant for it to work. I am not the proper one to seek that from him, but the house I believe I can help. Let us continue to cleanse the other rooms, and then the evil will be sealed within the den." He sprinkled the salt across the floor along the closed door.

Knowing that the threat of evil promised to endure, Magdalene's nerves shattered. "But he'll open the door and walk these halls, breathe this air! No matter how clean the other rooms are, he'll continue to infect them!"

Claudio placed a hand over hers that held the crucifix. "I will come every week and do this to keep you and *Signora* Melling safe. Now, tell me where you have felt the manifestations of evil and I will concentrate on those areas."

"The parlor, dining room, kitchen, hallway, my bedroom, and Alexander's room." Images of her moments with Alexander and the times she was assaulted when alone continued to flash through her mind. "Eliza's room even had a chill air. And it tries to come for me when I'm in the bath!"

Silent sobs fueled by all the moments she'd been ruled by indiscretions shook her body as she followed Claudio through the dining room and parlor. When they started up the stairway, they were met with a continuous blast of icy air. Magdalene had to grip the banister to climb. Claudio increased the volume of his incantations and they were struck with renewed vigor at the top.

Claudio, not stopping his prayers, pulled Magdalene close and wrapped one end of the stole around her for protection. They turned right, and meticulously went from room to room, beginning with the men's bathroom and then Mr. Melling's bedroom. Its door hissed and crackled as much as his den's when struck with the blessed water. Claudio laid a trail of exorcised salt across that room as well. Mrs. Melling's doors did not offer rebuttal, but when they reached Alexander's, a screech echoed through the air Magdalene was sure would wake the household.

"It is empty?" Claudio asked.

Magdalene nodded.

"Let us go in."

The looming shapes of the covered furniture in the cavernous room were too much for Magdalene to face. She turned on the gaslights, the warm glow softening the odd angles of the covers. Claudio walked the room, sprinkling the salt in the corners and spreading the water, Magdalene watching as she clutched the cross with white knuckles.

While the deacon left a pinch of salt in the far corner, Magdalene was engulfed with the smell of brandy and sandalwood. The sensation of Alexander's caresses moved over her skin like raindrops on a summer afternoon. Familiar longings wormed through her veins, enticing her need to feel wanted. She dropped the crucifix to the carpeted floor and quietly closed the door. With a determined saunter, she crossed the room.

Upon turning around, Claudio doubled his efforts to keep praying despite Magdalene's persuasive efforts to distract him. When he started into *Ave Maria*, she dodged his path and shrunk to the far side of the bed. Upon his third recitation, she curled into herself beside the headboard and whimpered.

Claudio brandished the holy water at Magdalene. "Satan, be gone! You have no hold on this daughter of God. *Exorcizo te...*" he tumbled into Italian, offering more prayers as he slowly made his way to her—Saint Benedict's cross outstretched. Inches from touching the cross to her, he paused. "I do not wish to hurt you. Be not a vessel for demons, *signorina*," he whispered, pressing the crucifix to the top of her head.

Expecting searing pain in her shaken state, Magdalene only felt the weight of the leaden cross. She turned upward and kissed it.

"Forgive me, Claudio." She took his hand. "I weakened."

He pulled her up. "I feel it wearing me down as well, but take heart. We are almost done."

His words began anew as the two moved out of Alexander's bedroom. The small guest room was blessed without issue, but Claudio stopped at Magdalene's door. She reached ahead and opened it, motioning him inside.

He held her gaze a moment. "But you stay out here. We must not be unaccompanied in a room together, do you understand?"

Reluctant to be alone, she nodded.

He took the holy Bible from under his arm and passed it to her. Then he refilled the aspergillum with the water bottle he'd slipped into his pocket. Before entering the room, he crossed Magdalene and himself. She stood, rooted to the hall floor as the invisible tentacles of the demon grasped around her ankles, trying to make her move into the bedroom. She watched in agony as Claudio cleansed the space. When he sprinkled the bed with holy water, she felt the demon's hold dwindle. Appearing to be done, Claudio looked at Magdalene and then placed his trappings on the desk. She could tell something was different about him but it wasn't until an arm's length separated them that she noticed the devil's fire burning in his eyes.

"The room is purified from the evil that besieged you. Come with us now." He reached a cold hand across the threshold. "We can make it ours, Magdalene."

Her knees buckled. She grabbed the doorframe with one hand, the Bible tumbling to the floor. A card with an image of the Virgin Mary and a printed prayer fluttered out, landing on Claudio's shoe. He jumped back as though burned. Magdalene thrust her crucifix at him, catching him on the hand. He hunched over and screamed in pain.

Down the hall, a door opened.

"Magdalene, dear!" Mrs. Melling's arms were around her as she slid to the floor. "Did George—" Upon seeing the deacon withering in pain, she winced. "Claudio!"

Magdalene sobbed on Mrs. Melling's shoulder and Claudio heaved himself toward the desk, taking hold of his crucifix and aspergillum.

Mrs. Melling looked over the deacon's vestments and instruments as she pulled her robe closed. "An exorcism!"

"Please, I must finish what we started or it will all be in vain." Claudio stepped over the women in the doorway, continuing the Rites by sealing her doorway with salt. At Magdalene's bathroom there were scratching sounds, as though something tried to escape the deacon's path. He opened the door with his stole and disappeared within.

"Magdalene, what is going on here?" Mrs. Melling peeled her off her shoulder, holding her back so she could look her in the face. "Why did you not tell me our cottage needed purifying? Did you bring something with you?"

Magdalene wiped her cheeks with a sleeve and sucked in her breath to quiet the remainder of the sobs. "It was here all along. I've been besieged by demons since arriving, things I can feel but not see, in dreams, and at times through heinous temptations."

"Oh, my dear." Mrs. Melling petted her arm. "Are you safe now?"

"I hope to be, after Claudio is done."

The deacon came out of the bathroom, still praying and sprinkling. He paused by the stair door at the end of the hall, then turned and blessed the linen closet before reaching the attic door. A screech like a wildcat shattered the quiet and the knob rattled without being touched.

He turned to Mrs. Melling. "May I?"

"Dear Eliza… Yes, bless it all."

He hesitated.

Magdalene, recalling the words Alexander spoke in her dream about Claudio and Eliza, knew Claudio would have to face his own demons within the chamber. She fought the urge to go with him, for she knew she would be no help to him there. "Mrs. Melling, could you accompany him?"

"But you, dear girl—"

"I'll be fine." She reached across the floor to retrieve the card with the Virgin Mary and brought it and the Bible to her lap. She passed the crucifix to Mrs. Melling, and motioned to Claudio. "He needs someone."

As soon as Mrs. Melling entered the stairwell, a gust of wind ripped down the hall, slamming the door shut behind her. Magdalene felt sick at sending Mrs. Melling into danger—what she'd promised Alexander she wouldn't do—but knew she could never be in the attic alone with Claudio.

Twenty-Five

Though drained from her ceaseless prayers, Magdalene knew she was better off than Mrs. Melling and Claudio. Ten minutes later, they stumbled down the attic stairs still gripping the crosses, their countenances haggard.

Before any of them could speak, the kitchen stair doorway opened at the end of the hall. "Is everyth—" Rosemary took in the sight of Mrs. Melling in her night clothes, the deacon in ritualistic vestments, and Magdalene on the floor, eyes swollen from crying, and gasped. "Do y'all need help?"

"Yes." Mrs. Melling stiffened under the gaze. "We need a hot breakfast. It's been a taxing morning. Magdalene, Claudio, wait for me in the sitting room while I dress." With all the dignity one can possess in her house coat, Mrs. Melling disappeared past the door at the opposite end of the hall.

Offering no further explanation, Claudio helped Magdalene stand and the two retreated to Mrs. Melling's sitting room. Claudio took an armchair, rocking back and forth while unceasingly repeating *Ave Maria*.

After watching the color slowly return to his face, Magdalene had to know what had happened in Eliza's room. "Was it stronger than in the other rooms?"

Claudio stopped reciting, but continued rocking in his stationary seat. "Not any more than the others, but this room held certain memories that I had previously atoned for. They were brought to the forefront of my mind."

"I know that is where you and Eliza—"

"How do you know this, *signorina?*" His voice was strained.

"Alexander told me in the nightmare I keep having."

Claudio clutched the cross and shook the now empty aspergillum. "Then there is more than just the infestation. While the house is diabolically infested, the demons manage moments of oppression and possession. The devil knows how to fuel our weaknesses to turn us to sin. Your dream, revealing things you could not know, could be either."

Hearing more than she expected, Magdalene's heart sank. She didn't want to admit she had weaknesses that demons could exploit to make grievous sin appealing. It wasn't her attraction to Alexander. It had to be something deeper, but she wasn't ready to understand.

"Mrs. Melling still doesn't need to know all the details," Magdalene said. "She needn't know about Alexander's struggles or your relationship with Eliza—it would break her heart."

"Yes, but no lies. If she asks plainly, we shall not bear false witness."

Magdalene shuttered at the thought of being laid bare, but agreed.

Mrs. Melling emerged from her room in an off-white tea dress with three-quarter length puff sleeves.

"Oh!" Magdalene covered her mouth after the exclamation escaped.

"It is time to move out from the sadness." She took a deep breath. "I feel like a new person. It has been too long since I was prayed over. Do you think the evil spirits are what have troubled my sleep these past few months?"

Claudio went to Mrs. Melling. "It is possible, *signora*."

"Can I stop taking the medicine?"

"Wait, see how things settle. We were unable to properly bless a few of the rooms we have reason to believe are most affected."

Mrs. Melling's eyes narrowed. "I see. Well, when you come Wednesday, those spaces will be unoccupied. You have my permission to do the Rites but I do not wish to be present during them. Witnessing Eliza's space was more than enough for my heart."

"I'm sorry," Magdalene said. "I thought we could do it without you having to find out."

"Do not shy away from me. We are all stronger than we look, but what a way to spend Saint Patrick's Day!"

***

Mrs. Melling, Claudio, and Magdalene were finishing in the dining room when Mr. Melling yelped from the hallway and staggered in. The atmosphere in the room grew fusty. Still in yesterday's clothes, he looked like his night of binging wasn't worth the discomfort he currently experienced. He gazed at the people around the table with squinting eyes.

"Supper already?"

"No, brunch." Mrs. Melling's voice was clipped. "We are just finishing. You may help yourself. There are some leftover eggs and biscuits."

"Something feels odd in here." He moaned. "I need coffee."

"It is already by your seat." She stood and motioned to Claudio and Magdalene to do the same. "Rosemary will be in shortly to check on you."

In the hall, Magdalene pointed to the den. "Should we—"

"No." Mrs. Melling kept walking toward the parlor. "He shall be here all weekend so there is no use trying to clear the air."

Knowing that Mr. Melling and his spaces still harbored demons caused a quiver in Magdalene's middle.

"I must go now." The deacon's words further rattled Magdalene. "I will come Wednesday, but I hope to see you at Mass tomorrow."

Mrs. Melling embraced him. "Thank you for helping us, Claudio. Magdalene, stop by the carriage house and have the Campbells bring him to town."

Magdalene kept her pace unnaturally slow as the two collected Claudio's things from the hall table and exited the front door. With trepidation, they went around to the back porch to pack the items into his bag. Rosemary stood at the screen door watching them.

Magdalene managed a smile. "Mr. Melling's in the dining room now. He might need assistance."

Knowing she was sent away yet again, Rosemary frowned but set off.

"I wish you could have made a clean sweep of the place, but thank you for all you've done." Magdalene put an affectionate hand on his arm. "I wouldn't have survived much longer."

Claudio handed one of the crucifixes back to her. "Keep it until I return."

She shifted uncomfortably. "I'm scared of Mr. Melling. After supper yesterday, he said some things that lead me to believe he'll physically harm me."

"Before you rise and before you lie down to sleep, pray unto the Father for protection. Keep a prayer in your heart, in all you do." With the first three fingers of his right hand, he did the sign of the cross and muttered an Italian prayer over her. Then he kissed both cheeks and smiled. "God will watch over you, *signorina*."

The two ladies spent the rest of the morning in the sitting room, the door closed against unwanted intruders. Several times Magdalene heard Mr. Melling cry out in pain when he went in or out of a room and looked to the fast approaching one o'clock dinner hour with trepidation.

She need not have worried. Mr. Melling could barely eat and stayed no more than five minutes at the table before retreating to his room.

Mrs. Melling looked at Magdalene with a shrug. "Part of me feels sorry for him, the other wants him to suffer a little while longer." She crossed herself. "I shall have to confess for that."

Not wanting to be alone, Magdalene stretched out on the sofa in the sitting room while Mrs. Melling took a nap. It proved a blessed hour of sleep for herself, the best she'd received since arriving at Seacliff Cottage.

Supper was a quiet affair as well. Mr. Melling claimed stomach pains and stayed in his bedroom the remainder of the night. Magdalene completed her bath without disturbance and sleep arrived slow, but was restful when it came.

Magdalene awoke at half-past six, surprised to see that she'd slept the whole night with no nightmare or remembered dreams. She dressed in her blue Sunday finery and descended the stairs to the kitchen. Brewing both coffee and tea, she fingered the wooden bracelet hanging freely on her wrist. Now that Mrs. Melling was privy to the happenings, she no longer felt the need to hide it, though it sometimes caught inside her sleeve.

Mrs. Melling was the first one down, wearing a splendid gray dress suit trimmed with fur.

"Good morning. You look lovely today," Magdalene said.

"Thank you. Yes, it is a good day, at least for me. I stopped at George's room. I do not think he is going to make it to church. You can ride with me. The Methodist church is just a few blocks down the road from the Italian congregation so it is no trouble."

"I thought it might be best to go with you to show Claudio my thanks."

"Do not worry about that. He will understand you wanting to develop relations within your own sect. Why, I shall probably begin going to an English-speaking Mass soon myself. Alex was right last week when he said the Italian church was Eliza's place. We kept with it out of respect for her."

The two ladies took their tea at the corner table. Then they went on their separate stairs to finish getting ready.

In case she changed her mind, Magdalene brought the folded mantilla with her to the stable yard and found Douglas wiping down the seats of the Great Arrow. He was in the same outfit he'd worn when he first met Mrs. Melling, but this time his shirt sleeves were rolled up and he had a plaid cap that matched his vest.

"Morning, Miss Magdalene." He tipped his flat cap.

Magdalene tried to let the sensation his charm caused roll off her without flickering around her belly, but it didn't work. "Hello, Douglas. Do you get to bring us to church today?"

"Aye. It's appropriate that my first official driver duty is to take Mrs. Melling to the Lord's house, isn't it?"

"Yes." Magdalene, feeling shy because of the easy way he smiled at her, fingered the bracelet.

Mrs. Melling came around the house. "Mr. Melling is too poorly to make it today. Douglas, do you think Mr. Campbell would be willing to stay in the house and listen out for him while we are gone?"

"He was going to ride with me to show the way, but we were by the church when we brought the deacon back yesterday, so I think I could manage, if you help steer me straight."

"Of course. Bring him out and I shall instruct him on what to do."

Douglas came back from the little house with his uncle and a pair of goggles hanging from his neck. Mrs. Melling gave instructions for Mr. Campbell to help himself to anything in the kitchen and to check on Mr. Melling every fifteen minutes. Then the two ladies settled in the backseat of the automobile with a light lap blanket across them to protect their dresses from dust and set off with Douglas at the wheel.

When they grew closer to Daphne, Mrs. Melling gave directions to the Methodist church, with the understanding that Magdalene would walk to Church of the Assumption if she finished before they returned for her. When Douglas came around to help her out, she left the lace head covering folded on the seat.

"I figured you were a Catholic girl." He pointed to her bracelet.

"No, sorry. That was given to me by a friend as a talisman. Thank you, I'll see you soon."

The pastor stood in front of the whitewashed wood building to welcome those arriving. Magdalene met numerous friendly people and hearing the word of God preached in a familiar way was a balm to Magdalene's soul. Afterward, she accepted a ride up the road by a fisherman's family and climbed into the back of the wagon with the children. When they pulled up outside the Italian church, her eyes roamed to Douglas leaning against the automobile, arms folded across his plaid vest. He watched Magdalene stand in the rickety wagon and rushed over to help. His steady hands, as well as his leg bent into a step, were necessary for her to return to the ground.

She called her thanks to the family, looked at Douglas, and laughed. "It was much different climbing in than it was getting out. Maybe the companion of a fine lady shouldn't be seen pulling splinters from her dress."

"May I?"

She nodded and he walked around her to check for snags on her dress.

"You look as fine as you did when I left you."

She felt her face warm and looked at the dusty ground as she smiled.

"*Signorina!*" Claudio dashed across the churchyard like a school boy. He embraced her and kissed both cheeks. Taking her hands, he noticed the rosary on her wrist and brought it to his lips as well. "It is good to see it on another lovely young woman. May my sister rest in peace." He did the sign of the cross.

Over his shoulder, Magdalene noticed Douglas step back, frowning slightly.

"Does Mrs. Melling need assistance?" she asked.

"No, she is speaking with Father Angelo." Claudio turned slightly to include Douglas. "Thank you for getting my ladies to church today. I hope you enjoyed Mass."

"Aye, it reminded me of the time I attended a Latin Mass during Lent when I was a boy. You have a nice congregation here."

"Many thanks." Claudio smiled. "You are welcome anytime. As are you, *signorina*, though I am happy to see you found a chapel more to your own liking. Was it good?"

"Oh, yes. Everyone welcomed me and the sermon was just what I needed to hear."

"*Fantastico!*"

Mrs. Melling, accompanied by Father Angelo, approached the group.

"So you made it back," Mrs. Melling remarked. "I hope you had a favorable experience."

"Yes, thank you, Mrs. Melling. Good morning, Father Angelo."

"*Mia figlia.*" He took her hand and kissed it. "Daughter, I trust your soul is less troubled."

Magdalene, unsure how much the priest knew, smiled politely. "Yes, thank you, Father."

Upon arriving home, they found Mr. Campbell sitting vigil in the front hall. He'd brought in a chair from the kitchen so he could keep track of everything in the house.

He stood to give his report. "There was much moaning, restless slumber, and he drank coffee when awake."

"Thank you, Campbell. It was a relief to know you were here. And do not worry about Douglas. He did a wonderful job. Would you two care to take dinner with us?"

"No, thank you, ma'am. We better see to the horses and automobile."

"Would you two mind accompanying Magdalene to the shore when you are done? That is, if you did not already have plans."

"No, that sounds like a fine idea. Douglas hasn't had the chance to go down yet."

Magdalene beamed. "Thank you, I'd like that very much."

After a light dinner, Magdalene changed into an everyday shirtwaist and skirt. Expecting to go wading again, she left off her hosiery and loosely tied her boots over bare feet. She double checked with Mrs. Melling, who stayed in her sitting room with the door open to listen out for Mr. Melling across the hall.

"Just be back by five, dear. Have fun."

Magdalene skipped across the yard to the gate. Douglas led Janus into the stable but called out that he'd be back in a moment.

The harsh words Mr. Melling spoke Friday night slipped into her mind, causing her to stay in the side yard rather than join Douglas in the stable.

Mr. Campbell exited the carriage house and approached Magdalene. "Seacliff Cottage feels different, Miss Magdalene. Well, except Mr. Melling's room. It's got bad spirits in there if I've ever felt one. Is that why he's poorly?"

Magdalene nodded. "The deacon blessed most of the house Saturday."

"Figured as much when we had to give him a ride home yesterday morning. Hopefully, you won't be further troubled. You looked a mite scared last week."

"Thank you for bringing me out this afternoon. The fresh air is most agreeable."

"These old bones don't trek down to the shore much, but it wouldn't be right to send you alone with Douglas. Not that I don't trust the lad, of course."

"Oh, I know, but thank you all the same. I need to be back by five. Do you have a timepiece?"

"Mine stopped working last month, but Douglas does."

He joined them, minus his driving cap and vest. "I do what now?"

"Have the time. We need to get her back to the house by five."

"Aye, it's no longer on display, but I'm keeping it with me." Douglas patted his pants pocket and then offered his arm to Magdalene, who willingly accepted it.

They took the lead, Magdalene pointing the way to the path, and Mr. Campbell followed behind them. The shimmering blue bay reflected the clear sky above. Mr. Campbell settled himself in the Adirondack chair by the cypress trees and the others paused long enough to remove their footwear. Douglas rolled his pants up to his knees and the two set a straight course for the shoreline. The tide was high but on its way out so it didn't take long to cross the sand. Magdalene tried not to giggle when he stumbled beside her but a few slipped out.

"Don't be too hard on a fellow." He pretended to tweak her nose.

"I was the same way last week and Mrs. Melling and Claudio laughed at me."

"He's a good friend of the family?"

"Very much. And he's been a great help to me. I already consider him my closest friend."

They paused, their feet sinking into the packed sand as the bay inched closer to their toes.

"I hope to become someone you can rely on as well." Douglas turned to gauge her reaction.

Smiling, she met his stare. "I'd like that, very much."

Then she lifted her skirt halfway to her knees and splashed into the water above her ankles. Douglas laughed and joined her. "This will be the place to come in the summer. Uncle Simon says the heat's enough to make him want to swim back to Scotland come August."

"Yes, it's miserable. The beach will be a blessed relief for me, too. There was a stream nearby where I grew up, but it was often fouled with livestock. I used to fill a pail at the pump and soak my feet in it each afternoon."

"On the porch, in a rocking chair?" he asked.

"Yes."

He chuckled. "I can see you doing just that, Maggie. May I call you Maggie?"

The way he said the name with his lilting accent weakened her knees. To battle the impending swoon, she kicked a spray of water at him. "Only if you can catch me!"

Twenty-Six

Weighted down by her skirt, Douglas overtook Magdalene before she could pass beyond the cypress trees. He reached for her arm and trailed his hand until it reached hers. She slowed, migrating to the packed sand so she could release her skirt.

Slightly breathless, they stood side by side, still holding hands.

"So Maggie it is." He released her hand, but held her gaze.

Overcome with the gentleness of his blue eyes, Magdalene started walking the way she'd previously ran.

"If you don't like it—"

"But I do." She glanced over her shoulder to see if Mr. Campbell watched, but they were far enough up the beach not to be seen around the trees. "You say it lovely, too. The Mellings just don't seem to be the type to like nicknames. I'm not sure how they'd take to it."

"I understand your concern, but I'm not speaking to them. The worst that could happen would be Mrs. Melling asks me not to call you Maggie, then I won't—at least while she's around." He arched an eyebrow mischievously. "But I don't think she'll mind. After all, your Italian friend has a pet name for you, it's only fair that I do as well."

Magdalene laughed. "So he does, though I've never thought of it that way."

"You shine when you're happy. I hope to make you smile every time we meet."

A pleasant hum vibrated in her chest that she wished to downplay. "Good luck to you. I can be most stubborn when I want to."

"All the worthwhile ladies are." He offered his arm. "Let's get back to where Uncle Simon can see us. I don't want to be accused of impropriety or place you in an uncomfortable situation."

Holding his arm as they walked back, Magdalene couldn't help but compare Douglas to the other men with whom she'd had relationships. The one whose arm she held at the moment was truly more a gentleman than many of the sides of Alexander she'd witnessed during her few days with him. Douglas seemed a polished version of William, with the bonus charm of his accent. If it wasn't for the fact that Mrs. Melling already wished them a couple, she'd have lost her heart for him. As fond as she'd become of the lady of the house, she wasn't ready to forgive her for thinking she'd been the only one making flirtatious advances with Alexander.

Magdalene and Douglas sat in the sand beside Mr. Campbell, Douglas leaning against a cypress and Magdalene propped up by her hands behind her, legs stretched in front. After an hour of idle chatter, Magdalene and Douglas waded in the water one more time. When the three of them made it back to the top of the red cliff, Douglas walked Magdalene to the gate.

He hooked his thumbs into his pockets. "Thank you for spending the afternoon with my uncle and me. I enjoyed my time with you."

"I had fun as well. See you tomorrow."

"Most assuredly."

When Magdalene entered the kitchen door, the aroma of tomato soup filled the air and Priscilla latched onto her legs. "You went to the beach without me!"

"Afraid so, little one. You weren't here when we left, otherwise you would have been invited."

"Truly?"

Magdalene laughed. "Yes, Priscilla, truly."

"Mama, we come early on Sundays!"

"Now, now." Rosemary waved a finger. "We've got our own things to do before we come over."

Priscilla stuck her lower lip out, her eyes clouded over with the threat of tears.

"We'll be going back during the week, too. Just you wait." Magdalene patted her on the head as she continued on through the room.

"Between you and the captain, there'll be no living with her," Rosemary remarked.

Magdalene washed and found Mrs. Melling in the sitting room.

"He still hasn't eaten anything. I have Rosemary preparing his favorite soup for supper, so hopefully that will entice him. Oh, Magdalene, did we do the right thing?"

Fearing that she would be accused of wrongdoing, Magdalene rushed to defend the actions she and Claudio took to protect the house and everyone within. "Yes, we had no other choice. If you could have felt—"

Mrs. Melling tapped the arm of her chair nervously. "I did. Those fits and the daily headaches, those must have been related because I have felt better this weekend than I have for months. I thought I wanted him to suffer, but now I am ready to forgive him and pray for his peace."

"That's very good of you." Thinking on the harsh words Mr. Melling had spoken to her, and all the anguish his follies heaped upon the rest of them, Magdalene wasn't ready for a change of heart. The sensation of the tentacles, the swirling passions and regrets—no! They were too fresh to forgive when she pondered upon all she'd been through. Not to mention Claudio, Eliza, and Alexander, though she was sure the siblings would have found trouble on their own.

"You may take your supper where you like, I am going to sit with George until I go to bed. Please inform Rosemary to send up the tray for two when it's ready."

"Yes, ma'am." Magdalene hurried past Eliza's portrait and Mr. Melling's door on her way to the back stairs. She let Rosemary know what the instructions were for the Mellings and asked if she could take supper with her family in the kitchen.

"Of course, there's a fourth chair ready for you whenever you want it."

***

Magdalene awoke in the predawn hour to her door rattling the bench. It sounded as though someone clawed at the wall. She retrieved Saint Benedict's crucifix from under her pillow and crept out of bed, muttering a prayer of protection. A few feet from the closed door, she strained her ears to understand what happened in the hallway.

She couldn't make out the noise, so she risked pressing an ear to the door and heard labored breathing and some sort of mumbling.

Fearing for Mrs. Melling's safety, she quietly lifted the bench and set it aside. With great caution, she turned the knob, keeping the crucifix outstretched in her other hand.

Mr. Melling in a quilted gray robe that caused him to look like something half dead leaned against the wall opposite her room. "You did this to me!"

Startled by the intensity of his anger, she jumped. He lunged at the doorway, but stopped short like he'd hit a glass wall. She raised the cross to his eye level so he could see she was protected.

"This is my house. I'm master here, you must stop this nonsense!"

"Evil is no longer welcome." She brandished the cross in the doorway.

His roaming eyes made her feel naked in her nightdress. "We were here well before you and staked our claim. This is our house, no matter what you talked the deacon into doing."

From down the hall, the echoing chimes of the parlor mantel clock rang up the stairs like a trumpeting call to the dawn as it struck six o'clock.

"Lydia comes," he whispered, a glint of malice in his eyes as he licked his lips. "I'll deal with you later."

Mr. Melling stalked away, staying as far from the blessed doors along the hall as he could in his weakened state. Magdalene replaced the bench. Pacing the room, she mulled over how she could help Lydia. She hurriedly put on her striped wash dress and opened her window, sitting by it while she brushed her hair, so she could watch for the maid's arrival.

Magdalene couldn't concentrate enough to successfully attempt the pompadour style, so she did a hasty single braid the length of her hair like she did every night. Not long after securing the end, she spotted Lydia in the lane.

She leaned out the window. "Lydia! Stop, Lydia! Don't go in!"

Lydia entered the side gate, her hair perfectly secured under the lace headpiece and her white apron crisp and straight over her black dress. "What's this?" She stopped under Magdalene's window.

"Don't come in yet," she called down. "Mr. Melling's been sick this weekend. It would be best if you waited until he left for the ferry before reporting for work. I'm sure the Campbells would be happy to allow you to sit in their house while you wait."

"Nonsense. I need to collect my pay and fix Mr. Melling's coffee."

"I know you were paid Friday, same as I. There's no reason for you to come in."

"If he's been poorly, he'll be more than eager for a cup of coffee."

"Lydia, don't come inside the house. It isn't safe!" Fearing she grew too loud, Magdalene leaned out the window further, and lowered her voice. "Please wait until he leaves. Go to Mr. Campbell and tell him I asked if you could wait there."

"So you think you can order me around now? Isn't that just like a lady's companion to take airs." Lydia shook her fist up at Magdalene. "You're jealous and uppity to boot! You can take your fake concern and use it to pad your corset. If you really cared, you'd come speak with me face to face. But I don't rank high enough for you to be bothered to walk down here and bring me to the carriage house yourself." Lydia threw back her shoulders and disappeared onto the back porch.

Magdalene brought the window down too hard, causing the glass panes to tremor. She groaned, sick for cowering when she should have protected the virtue of another woman. Magdalene started back to pacing, unsure if she should go downstairs and confront the evil or awaken Mrs. Melling and have her deal with it. Or the third option of hiding away in her safe haven. But there might be a fourth to choose from—fetching the Campbells and having them drag Lydia out of the house. But how many minutes had passed since Lydia entered? Was Mr. Melling waiting for her in the den or was he still upstairs?

Not being able to forgive herself if she stayed safely in her room, she grabbed the crucifix off the table and hurried down the stairs. The aroma of coffee filled the kitchen—the bowl with the freshly ground beans sat on the side board and an unheated kettle of water stood on the stove—but Lydia was nowhere to be seen.

Magdalene went through to the hallway. "Lydia?"

All the rooms were empty, except the possibility of the den, which she saved for last. As she stepped toward the closed door, a chill went up her spine. The sounds of a struggle came through the wood door.

"You stupid girl," Magdalene muttered. Then, confronting one of her worst nightmares, she knocked on the door with the cross because she didn't want to touch anything belonging to the unblessed space in the house.

"Leave us!" Mr. Melling bellowed.

Magdalene took a deep breath. "Not until I know Lydia is all right."

"You insufferable wench!" Lydia cried out. "Mind your own business!"

Magdalene reeled back as if struck by the words. Shivering, she felt the oppression of the evil seeping from the doorway toward her. She rushed into the kitchen and out the back door. Plopping on the gazebo swing, she leaned forward and tried to quiet her erratic breathing while holding the crucifix to her forehead.

"Maggie, is everything okay?"

Magdalene raised her head and turned toward Douglas at the fence. She wiped at a few stray tears that had escaped down her cheek and nodded.

"It doesn't look like it from here." He came through the gate, looking handsome as ever in brown pants and an ecru button-down shirt. Lifting his earthy tweed cap, he nodded toward the crucifix. "You keep a lot of Catholic relics around. Is that typical of Methodists in this country?"

Magdalene laughed-hiccupped and shook her head. "No, there's nothing typical around here."

Douglas kept to the outside of the gazebo, but looked straight at her troubled eyes and rubbed the stubble on his chin. "Is there anything I can do?"

"It's out of my control as well as yours." She flipped the crucifix around, looking at the medallion on the back as well as the depiction of the savior on the front. "Just pray. Pray for the well-being of everyone touched by this house. And if someone—whether myself or someone who says I sent them—ever comes to your door, give them shelter no matter the hour."

"Of course, Maggie." He reached an arm through the lattice and touched the back of her hand. "You can count on me."

Moved by his tenderness, Magdalene managed to thank him and sent him on his way before she broke into heaving sobs. But Douglas wasn't far enough away for her to disguise the agony. He hopped the picket fence and passed a white handkerchief through the lattice to her.

"Maggie, you must give me something to do."

She wiped her eyes and nose before looking up at him. "Make sure Mr. Melling is on the ferry when it pulls out of Montrose. And if for some reason he misses it, race north to catch it in Daphne. He must get to town today."

Douglas clenched his fists. "Has he—"

"No, he hasn't done anything to me, though I wouldn't put it past him. The trespass isn't mine to announce, but what shall we do if he doesn't leave?" Her fear was so prominent on her face she could see the matching concern on Douglas's countenance.

"I'll be sure I have him on the ferry, even if I have to place him there myself."

"Douglas!" Mr. Campbell called from inside the stable.

"Are you sure you're safe?" Douglas asked.

When she nodded, he took a step back.

"I'll look for you before I leave and as soon as I get back."

Twenty-Seven

Douglas wasn't gone for more than a minute
when pots clattered in the kitchen. Peering in the window, Magdalene
saw Lydia light the gas stove to boil water. She entered and shut the
screen behind her. The maid's hair was half down and her apron
wadded on the floor at her feet, but she hummed.

When Lydia turned around, her smile turned to a scowl.
"There's the thorn in my side, Miss Magdalene Jones of Seven Hills."

"Are you not hurt? Upset?" Confusion furrowed her brow.

"Upset at you! Who goes knocking on Mr. Melling's door at
six thirty in the morning, tell me that? Especially when you knew I
was in there. You're not the friend I thought you were."

"I'm not the friend? I was trying to protect your virtue!"

"Go on and wave your cross and shout, you hypocrite!
Because of you, my best apron got torn. I'll have to waste my
precious time mending it when I could be cleaning and get done
quicker." She lifted her chin, her long, straight nose high in the air.
"Now go fetch Ruth's sewing box for me. She keeps it next to her
chair in her sitting room."

"I'll go, only to help right the wrong you *think* I inflicted on
you, though it's a heinous thought." Magdalene tucked the crucifix
into her waistband. "But I suppose to one interrupted in sin,
everything seems bad."

Lydia stomped across the room and raised her hand to slap,
but Magdalene caught the maid by the wrist.

"Don't ever try that again," she said through gritted teeth.
Then she pushed Lydia's hand aside and climbed the back stairs.

In her anger, Magdalene didn't give thought to Mr. Melling,
but she stopped short by the top of the front stairs before reaching

his open bedroom door. Hoping he was in the bathroom, she rushed for the sitting room and locked the door behind her. Magdalene lifted the sewing basket off the floor and set it on the chair while she collected her thoughts. Part of her wanted to wait until she was sure Mr. Melling was gone, but the other part of her thought it best to get back to Lydia so she wouldn't be alone.

Bravely, she gripped the basket in one hand and opened the door with the other. After she'd closed the door and started toward the far side of the hall, a door opened behind her. Magdalene hoped it was Mrs. Melling—awakened by her comings and goings—but she quickened her step, just in case it wasn't.

"Stop, Miss Jones," Mr. Melling commanded.

She slowed, but didn't stop. "I'm in a hurry to get this to Lydia."

"You work for me, not her. You would do best to remember that when you begin to worry more over her situation than your own place in this household. Now come here, Miss Jones."

Before turning around, Magdalene slipped Saint Benedict's cross out of her waistband with her free hand and tried to hold it casually as she did the basket in the other. Mr. Melling, now dressed in a three-piece suit and polished black shoes, stood on the other side of the stair landing. She stopped just before the stairs, keeping more than six feet between them. He had returned to his full imposing self—not the moaning, ashen man of the weekend—and she was leery of his calculated moves.

"Whatever you did this weekend that set me ill, I trust you not to repeat it." He sauntered toward her, but stopped to look at his pocket watch, as if she were wasting his time. "I assume it has something to do with that cross you're carrying about today. It's really not an attractive look for a young woman."

Mr. Melling paused to allow Magdalene a chance to reply. When she held her gaze on the floor, he continued. "I cannot abide being ignored when speaking with someone. Look at me, Miss Jones, so I am sure you hear my words."

"Yes, sir." Not caring for his drooping mustache or his shrewd eyes, Magdalene stared at his left ear.

"It was unwise of Ruth to only give you two day's testing for your employment. If she had used better forethought, she should have asked for a two-week trial before deciding to keep you permanently. If that were the case, you'd be on the ferry this morning on my command. But seeing how she has taken a liking to you, and she was a dear nurse to me yesterday, I don't wish to upset her by taking you away."

"Thank you for considering her feelings." Magdalene wanted to add that she didn't think him capable, but she held her tongue, though the thought manifested itself on her face.

"You're a charlatan, Miss Jones. You kept your impertinence hidden during our interview." He stepped within arm's reach of her. "I sought a demure country girl, not a tenacious woman with eyes open to the ways of the world."

"I'm sorry to disappoint you."

"You're no disappointment."

Magdalene flinched as he raised his hand, but he merely fingered a tendril of hair that had come loose from her braid. She held her ground and chanced to look his in eyes—cold and hard like Alexander's when he only cared for himself.

"You're an upset to my plans, but I enjoy a good fight."

When he started to run the back of his hand down her cheek, she met him with a point of the crucifix against his vest. "Don't touch me. Ever."

He lowered his hand and smiled. "Yes, the perfect tussle to keep boredom away when I'm here." He moved to knock aside the cross, but recoiled when his bare hand touched it.

"What would your priest in Mobile think of you not being able to touch a sacred symbol? Does he know what you've been up to?" Magdalene asked with a sneer. "You're a pathetic excuse for an honorable man, Mr. Melling. Why don't you try confession sometime? I hear it works wonders."

She spun around to leave, but he caught her by the braid and pulled her back, wrapping an arm across her chest from behind, pinning her limbs to her sides in the process. Panicked, she dropped both the basket and the crucifix and tried to fight free. He wrapped the other arm around her shoulders at the base of her throat.

"Don't try to lecture me," he whispered in her ear. His hot breath on her neck caused fear to boil beneath her skin as he tightened his hold. "We're master here."

The chill wind blasted through the hall. Frozen with terror, Magdalene could do nothing more than try to breathe within the constricting grasp. The more she squirmed, the more arms it felt were holding her until it seemed like she was bound to the front of Mr. Melling with ropes. In her struggle, the rosary bracelet fell out of her cuff and dangled against the heel of her palm. He lumbered forward, pushing her along with him until she pressed against the door to Alexander's room.

"Alex is still too weak from his ordeal last year to best you, but I'm stronger." He dropped one arm to open the door and they stumbled into the bedroom. He kicked the door closed, leaving the room in darkness. His hold on Magdalene weakened and she fought to free her arm with the bracelet. He jerked her around to face him and shook her by the shoulders. "You did something to this room as well! What gives you the right to take control of my house?"

She still gasped for breath, but she managed to speak. "Good will triumph over evil."

With a growl, he shifted his hands off her shoulders, seeking to pull her toward him. Before her arms could be pinned, she took the tiny crucifix and drove the wooden symbol into the palm of his probing right hand.

Mr. Melling howled in pain and fell back against the wall. Using the light from under the door as a guide, Magdalene lunged for the exit. She rushed out of the room, nearly tripping on the sewing basket in the hall. All she could feel for a moment was relief that she hadn't been attracted to Mr. Melling—the evil hadn't been able to get within her.

Lydia came through the back stair door and stared at Magdalene in disbelief. "I heard a door slam. What did you do?"

Magdalene, still quaking and breathing heavily, clenched her fists. "It's what *he* tried to do. I merely defended myself."

Lydia rolled her eyes and pushed past her. "One doesn't simply go against Mr. Melling. Now—oh! What did she do to you?" She dropped to her knees inside Alexander's room to help her employer.

Just after the parlor clock struck seven there was a knock at the front door. Lydia fawned over Mr. Melling, so Magdalene picked up her crucifix and the basket and made her way downstairs on wobbly legs. Relief to see Douglas standing on the porch filled her chest.

"Thank you for coming. He's taken a turn for the worse, but should recover once he's out of the house." She pointed to the stairs. "He's just inside the room at the top. Lydia's with him."

Magdalene stayed downstairs. Listening from the hall, she heard Lydia question Douglas.

"I'm paid to get Mr. Melling to and from the ferry, as well as transport Mrs. Melling around as needed. I was told to be ready to bring him to the Montrose pier for the morning run, and that's what I'm going to do."

"Don't be a fool. He's in no shape to go to work today."

"Get me out of here!" Mr. Melling sounded strained, but forceful.

"Aye, sir, that's what I'm here for. Now, if you could just get out of the way, miss."

Magdalene ducked into the parlor as they descended the stairs. When she heard them at the front door, she crossed the room to peer out the window.

"You take care of him," Lydia fussed. "Oh, he hasn't even had his coffee."

Douglas had parked the automobile directly before the front gate. Mr. Melling's labored walk caused the driver to support him around the waist with his right arm. The man leaned into Douglas as he cradled his right hand against his chest, but with each step away from the house he straightened. By the time they reached the little gate, he stood on his own.

Lydia hurried over from the back door with a steaming cup. She smiled as she leaned against the shiny car while Mr. Melling drank his coffee. Douglas spoke, but Magdalene couldn't hear the words. Mr. Melling passed the cup to Lydia with the exchange of a few words, and then took her hand for a moment before climbing into the backseat. Lydia returned toward the back of the house with a smile.

Mr. Melling waved Douglas over and showed him something in his right hand. Douglas took off running in the direction of the stable. Magdalene, though curious to see what would happen, felt it her duty to get the sewing basket to Lydia like she'd promised.

"Here's the kit. I'd appreciate it if you could finish by nine so I can return it before Mrs. Melling is awake."

"You poor, simple girl." Lydia took the basket from Magdalene and picked her apron off the kitchen floor. She brought the things out the back door and sat in Mrs. Melling's rocking chair.

Torn between finding out what caused Lydia's excitement and not playing into her games, Magdalene hesitated. The remembrance of Mr. Melling's dirty hands touching her hair helped her choose fixing her hairstyle over giving insufferable Lydia attention. At her dressing table, she set down the cross, undid her braid, and brushed through her hair. This time she was successful in placing it up in the Gibson style pompadour.

Whether she wanted to deal with Lydia or not, she needed to watch for Douglas. He'd promised to check with her when he returned, to assure her of Mr. Melling's departure. As honorable as he was, Magdalene didn't think he would allow something simple like the impropriety of entering the house to stop him from keeping his word. Feeling more composed and ready to ignore any snide remarks, Magdalene went out to the gazebo with a cup of tea. Lydia, hunched over her apron, stitched the lace trim back onto the fabric.

"You could sit with me," Lydia called out to her. "Isn't my companionship more agreeable to none?"

That was questionable, but Magdalene saw no reason to prick at her. "I'm not sure. We've both said and done some cruel things this morning."

Lydia squared her shoulders. "I'm willing to forgive your silly remarks about sin and all that. You know nothing of love."

Magdalene took the rocker next to Lydia. "I was engaged four years back."

"Four years!" Lydia scoffed. "You're a real old maid now, Mags."

Bristling at the nickname, she took a breath and continued. "Mr. Melling isn't about love. He's all about control and power. How loving is it of him to break his marriage vows?"

"He says he respects Ruth too much to divorce her."

Magdalene couldn't stop the harsh laugh from escaping. "That's rich! Lydia, it's the complete opposite of respect. If he cared anything for her, he wouldn't be cheating. He's been with her a quarter of a century. What makes you think he'll be true to you when he can't value the mother of his children?"

Lydia stabbed her apron with the needle and worked a tiny stitch. Her mending consisted of a row of tiny Xs going along the lace trim. "Shows what you know. Their marriage was stagnant for years, but I have the passion now, not Ruth. He's mine!"

"If you think a man like him can belong to someone, then you're the naïve one. You're not the first conquest and you most surely won't be the last." Magdalene got out of the chair and paced.

"Don't be upset because he turned you down." Lydia glared at her.

Magdalene stopped, both fists at her side. "He did *what?*"

"When I found him on the floor in Alex's room, he told me what happened. He said you lured him there and then struck him with a hex when he wouldn't go along with your advances. That makes me wonder why you chose that room. Have you had your way with a man in there before?"

Fists still clenched, Magdalene's arms trembled with anger. Now it was she who wanted to slap—more like punch—the other woman. "You've insulted me one too many times. I've never heard anything so ridiculous in my life!"

Lydia tied off her stitch and broke the dainty thread with her fingers. "It all makes perfect sense to me now. All that blood in Alex's room the morning he left was—"

"No!" Magdalene shouted. "Don't even speak such lies! You have no idea what's happened within these walls. And if you do, it's only your small part of the evil that's infested this home. You're a piece of the blight here and should leave."

Lydia smiled. "I'll gladly leave and you'll be sorry when I do. You'll wish you never stuck your nose into my business. Just don't be jealous you didn't end up with one of the Melling men. You had your chance and lost."

"I wouldn't want one," she snapped back. "They're the most insufferable lot I've ever known!"

The sound of an engine coming up the lane rumbled through the cloudy morning. Magdalene's fists loosened when she saw Douglas alone in the automobile.

Lydia stood, shoved the sewing basket at her, and tied on her mended apron. "I see your type, Mags. You prefer the working boys who don't know how to shave properly. Be sure to keep the hay out of your hair. Ruth wouldn't like that." With the final cutting remarks, she let the screen door slam behind her.

Exhausted by the verbal battle, Magdalene forced herself to meet Douglas at the fence. She knew he would come to her, but she wanted their conversation to take place away from the house. She held the basket behind her with both hands and waited while he parked the automobile.

"If I hadn't seen it myself, I wouldn't believe it. I thought you were crazy when you said he'd be better when he was on his way, but I've never seen a man get his strength back that quickly. Is there anything you wish to tell me, Maggie?"

She looked up at him, curiosity in her brown eyes. "No…it's been a trying morning."

Douglas scratched at the stubble along his jaw. "There was something else miraculous besides Mr. Melling's returned strength.

He kept it hidden from the maid, but it seems he burned the palm of his hand. It was festered with blisters."

Magdalene's eyes widened, remembering his scream of pain when she touched the crucifix to him.

"I went to get a wet rag and he wrapped it around his hand to ease the pain. When we got to the top of the ferry landing, he unwrapped it and nothing was there."

"Nothing?" She put a hand on the fence and leaned forward, the sewing basket dangling by her side.

Douglas shook his head. "Aye, it was as if it never was, though I saw it plain as anything before."

"Is the demon really as powerful as that?" she asked under her breath.

"Is the what?"

"Nothing." Magdalene gripped the fence.

"He had a story about it." Douglas studied her face.

Afraid that Mr. Melling told the same thing to him as he did Lydia, her heart sank. She'd never be able to look him in the eyes again. "If it's the same thing he told Lydia, it's a heap of lies," she said defiantly.

"Give me some credit," he rolled his words. "I might be new here, but that doesn't mean I'll fall for anything. It would be impossible for someone wielding the cross of Saint Benedict to inflict black magic. Especially if the supposed curse happens to be the same size and shape of said person's rosary." Douglas reached his hand to hers on the fence. With a finger, he freed the bracelet from the cuff of her sleeve. The cross hung from her wrist and he gently touched it, an eyebrow arched in wonder. "Aye, just the size and shape of this. Now, is there something you wish to tell me, Maggie?"

Softened by the fact that he didn't believe Mr. Melling and he understood the signs of protection, she decided to confide in him—just enough for him to understand the breadth of the turmoil.

"Claudio gave me the crosses to help protect me against the demons in the house. Apparently, the evil spirits started causing trouble last year when Mr. Melling…first entertained sin. The demons spread their domain, affecting others in the house in different ways, but this past week seems to have been the culmination of the infestation. Claudio exorcised most of the house Saturday, but couldn't get into Mr. Melling's rooms while he was home. The blessings appeared to have aggravated the demon within Mr. Melling, and caused him to be extremely ill this weekend."

"What manner of evil have we found ourselves besieged with? Why did my uncle not warn me?"

"I don't think he knew of the extent of it. It's only within the house that the demons seem to take hold. Don't be angry with him for not knowing what wasn't revealed to him."

He patted her hand. "I know Uncle Simon to be an honorable man. But how did Mr. Melling get over his aversion to the blessed house?"

Magdalene felt her cheeks warm. "He kept in his own rooms this weekend, and then when Lydia arrived this morning, they…"

Douglas shook his head. "There's no need to go on. As you said earlier, it's not your trespass to speak. Mr. Melling did tell her he'd send for her before we left—however he means it, I don't know. But why did you have to defend yourself against him? That is, if it isn't too painful to discuss."

"I had to go to Mrs. Melling's sitting room upstairs to get the sewing basket for Lydia." She lifted the basket for good measure. "She ripped her apron while she…whatever it was that happened behind closed doors. Mrs. Melling can't stand her, so I volunteered to fetch the basket for her."

"And did Mrs. Melling hear anything this morning?"

"She's on medication to help her sleep and doesn't get up before nine, except on Sundays." Douglas nodded his understanding, so Magdalene continued. "I was coming out of her sitting room, the basket in one hand and Saint Benedict's cross in the other, when Mr. Melling came into the hall and bid me to stop. He accused me of meddling with the house and making him ill, which I suppose is true, but not for the reasons he proclaimed. I said some harsh words, as you can imagine—"

"Aye, I can." Douglas smiled despite the seriousness of the situation.

"When I turned to walk away, he grabbed my braid and pulled me to him, trapping my arms and nearly cutting off my breathing. I'm sorry to say I panicked and dropped the basket and the cross, so intent on getting out of his grip I couldn't think straight."

"It will be difficult not to give him my right hook when I collect him Friday."

Fearing Douglas would do something rash if she continued too long, she condensed the final actions. "While struggling to get free, the bracelet came out of my sleeve and I was able to touch his palm with it. He shouted and fell to the floor where you found him."

"I'm sorry you had to go through something so frightening." He placed his hand on the fence post adjacent to hers. "Call for me if you ever need help. I'll sleep with my window open, no matter the weather."

Magdalene looked at the ground, pretending to study the green sprouts of daylilies that were coming up along the fence while she tried to tame the emotions threatening to bubble over. "Thank you. That means a lot, though I hope I never have to take you up on it."

Twenty-Eight

Magdalene spent the remainder of the day keeping both herself and Mrs. Melling out of Lydia's way. The maid hummed and danced as she worked, which caused more alarm than her being grouchy. Over lunch, Mrs. Melling remarked that the house didn't feel as settled as it had over the weekend, but Magdalene reminded her that the deacon would be there in two days to complete what he'd started.

After supper, Mr. Campbell came to the front door to ask after the women but declined an invitation inside. That night, Magdalene experienced the nightmare with Alexander again, and over their morning tea on Tuesday, Magdalene voiced her concerns.

"I don't think we should have anyone over until Claudio completes the Rites tomorrow."

"The public spaces are fine and I have practically invited the Campbells for dessert today."

Fear of taking advances with Douglas—or him turning into a carnal demon—drove Magdalene to stop the social call another way. After the midday meal, she stole away and found Douglas cleaning the stalls in the stable.

She wasted no time as she picked a path through the hay. "I have a favor to ask you."

With a smile, Douglas rested an arm around the end of the pitchfork handle and his other hand straightened his leather suspenders. "Anything, Maggie. How may I be of service?"

"Don't come to call at the house tonight. Keep you and your uncle away, please." Embarrassed by the pleading tone that leaked into her voice, she looked down.

He raised his hand to reach out to her, but upon seeing it streaked with dust, he lowered it. "Is there new trouble?"

"No, the same, but I don't want anyone over until Claudio comes tomorrow. I wouldn't want something to…happen to someone. I don't think it's right to unnecessarily expose people to the evil."

"We were over last Thursday without trouble, but I understand your need to try to control the situation by limiting guests."

"Oh, I knew you would!" Magdalene gushed. "Mrs. Melling thought I was being silly."

"Uncle Simon won't like it, but maybe we can happen by at tea time, if you take it on the back porch."

"That would be perfect. Thank you, Douglas."

At half-past two, Magdalene swung in the gazebo with Priscilla and Mrs. Melling read in her rocking chair on the other side of the porch. The Campbell men came in the back gate, scrubbed clean from their morning chores, and Mrs. Melling welcomed them to share the afternoon tea. When the refreshments were brought out, Mrs. Melling called Priscilla over to eat at the table next to her, thereby freeing the other half of the swing for Douglas. He brought Magdalene her tea and a plate of food and they settled into a conversation about horse tack while Mr. Campbell and Mrs. Melling discussed going into town for a shopping trip. The pleasant afternoon led to a quiet evening.

On Wednesday, the curtains in Magdalene's room billowed softly in the cool morning breeze. At tea the day before, Douglas suggested leaving her window open in case she needed to scream for help—he'd be more likely to hear her that way. She sprang out of bed without praying and opened the drapes to look across the yard at the carriage house. In the back of the supply wagon parked by the stable, Douglas slept in a bedroll. Magdalene gazed at his form innocently at first, but then the nagging desires crept in.

Call to him, and he will come to you.

"I will not call him to danger," she replied in a firm whisper.

She turned away from the window and witnessed a creeping mist seep into the room from under the hall door. It slithered across the parquet floor. Magdalene looked to the bed, where Saint Benedict's cross was tucked under her pillow, and to the vanity, where the rosary bracelet lay in plain sight. Between her and both locations the expanding mist rose like bay waters blocking all chance of redemption. It lapped against her bare ankles and teased the hem of her nightgown.

An appendage of the ethereal mist coiled around her legs and made its way to her chest, constricting so she did not have enough lung capacity to cry for help. She should have called for relief when she had the chance, but her obstinate need to play the martyr ensnared her once again.

"Maggie!" Douglas's voice called from outside the window. "Maggie, are you all right?"

With the diabolic hold on her body, Magdalene could neither move nor reply. But she did not want to surrender her will—especially with Douglas nearby. In an attempt to fortify her mind and soul against possession, she visualized the chapel she'd attended since birth in Seven Hills with its white washed pine walls, oak pews, and the pulpit her father had helped build when the new preacher came three years ago. It was the church she was supposed to be married in, but that wavering thought wasn't what she needed at that moment.

The door to her room burst open, momentarily scattering the vapors. Seeing her held hostage in the swirling haze, Douglas sprang into action, trudging barefoot through the thickening mist. "I'm coming, Maggie!"

All thoughts of the one-room chapel in Seven Hills faded and were replaced with the figure before her. The buttons on his shirt were undone two-thirds of the way, exposing a smattering of russet curls across his broad chest. His brown leather suspenders hung from his waistband, his khaki work pants riding low on his hips because of it. Magdalene squeezed her eyes shut, a moan escaping her parted lips.

"Don't give in, Maggie! Look! Look at me! I'm almost there!" His desperate voice as he fought his way through moved her to give him hope, though it could become his undoing.

She looked and was met with Douglas's bright eyes less than four feet away. She tried to speak, to warn him not to touch her, but rather to get one of the talismans from elsewhere in the room. The demon's hold on her still too strong to talk, she managed to shake her head.

Douglas stopped. "Can you move or speak?"

She shook her head with more effort.

"Do you have protection?"

Again, she struggled to shake her head.

As if he felt more exasperation than fear, he threw his arms into the air. "In the name of the Father, and the Son, and the Holy Spirit, the devil shall be banished from this room!"

The mist dispersed. Upon losing the support of the unseen arms, Magdalene fell to her hands and knees.

Douglas helped her up. "Are you all right?"

"Yes," she rasped. "How did you do that?"

"Do you not read the Bible? All followers of Christ have the power to cast out devils. Surely you've done so in some way in your time here."

"Well, yes, but you commanded with such competence and flourish!"

"Aye, it's all in the wrist." He held up an arm and gave a waving motion with a flick.

Overcome with relief and joy—for neither she nor Douglas turned into molesting fiends—Magdalene collapsed against his shoulder with unabashed laughter.

"There's that smile I promised each time we meet. Now where's your rosary?"

Still trying to collect herself, Magdalene pointed to the dressing table. He walked her over and placed the talisman on her. Catching sight of her reflection, Magdalene gasped and stepped away. She'd lost count of how many men had seen her in her nightgown since living in Seacliff Cottage—more than she ever planned in her lifetime, that was for sure.

"I take it you're ready to get dressed." Douglas, gallant enough to look away now that she was self-conscious, stepped toward the door. "I'll wait for you on the back porch."

***

Lydia had not arrived when the Wattses pulled in at nine. By then, Douglas worked in the stable with his uncle and Magdalene sat in the kitchen, Saint Benedict's cross on the lap of her black skirt. Not feeling talkative, she retreated to the sitting room before the Watts family entered the house.

Half an hour later, Rosemary came with the morning tray. Seeing the closed bedroom door, she looked to Magdalene and whispered, "Lydia ain't here. No matter what, she's always been here by nine. Should I tell Mrs. Melling or will you?"

"Let's wait until dinner before we say anything," Magdalene said. "She might not have been able to find a ride or there could be word by then."

At noon, Mrs. Melling remarked on the quietness of the house when Rosemary brought in a platter of cornbread.

"Miss Lydia hasn't shown today," she replied.

"I cannot say I am disappointed, but I will have to have a word with her Friday."

After lunch, Mrs. Melling gave Leroy the task of tidying up the parlor and sent Magdalene out to remind Douglas that he needed to collect the deacon.

She found Douglas under the hood of the Great Arrow, tinkering with some of the gears.

"Everything in good shape?" she asked.

"As good or better than anything else on the road." He wiped his hands on a cloth hanging from his waistband.

Magdalene thought back to the way he looked when he rushed into her bedroom and blushed. "Mrs. Melling wanted me to remind you about bringing Claudio in from Daphne and to check for mail at the post office in Montrose. It's a block east of Main, on Adams Street."

"Uncle Simon pointed it out to me." He pulled his watch out of his pants pocket since he wasn't wearing his vest. "I'll be there, still plenty of time. Now tell me why there's sadness to your eyes today. Still upset over me being in your chamber this morning?"

Magdalene's face heated further, but she gave him a bashful smile. "It's not that, though I can't thank you enough for helping me. Lydia still hasn't shown. I remember you said something about Mr. Melling wanting her when he left Monday."

"Aye, he took her hand and said he'd send for her, though I didn't understand it at the time. Do you think he's called her to Mobile?"

Part of her felt relief at the thought—the less sinful activity in the house the better—but the other half felt pain for Mrs. Melling. "I wouldn't put it past him. He was filled with vile intentions that morning, but bless Mrs. Melling's heart if he has."

They stood in silence a few moments before Magdalene spoke.

"Tell Claudio what happened this morning, as well as on Monday, so he knows the guards he placed are wearing thin. I might not get a chance to inform him privately."

Douglas assured her that he would.

Promptly at two, a knock sounded on the front door. Leroy saw Claudio and Douglas into the parlor and Mrs. Melling asked him to have Rosemary ready the tea after she greeted the deacon. Claudio took Mr. Melling's fireside seat, placing his bag by the chair.

Mrs. Melling turned her attention to the chauffeur. "What is the news, Douglas?"

"Mail, for both you and Maggie."

Her hand went to her heart. "Maggie? Oh, how charming! Our dear hearts must have precious names."

Magdalene wished she could disappear into the velvet of the settee for surely she was as red as it. Douglas looked slightly embarrassed himself as he delivered the envelopes to Mrs. Melling.

"Stay for tea, Douglas. Take a seat with Magdalene for now."

Magdalene glanced at the envelope, expecting it to be from Aunt Agnes, but it was on stationary from the Point Clear Hotel and postmarked Fairhope. Her stomach dropped to her toes.

Mrs. Melling had already glanced at her own mail and set them on the side table. "Nothing from Alex. All these can wait, but what do you have, Magdalene?"

"I'm not sure. It's from this side of the bay."

"Go on and open it, we shall not be offended if you ignore us while you read."

With foreboding, she slid her finger under the envelope flap and removed the folded paper.

> *Mags,*
>
> *Remember how I always told you I would move up in life? Today is the day. I received a telegram from George inviting me to the main house on Government Street. I'm sure you'll remember that's where he originally wanted me to work, but considering the situation of my extended family here, I thought it best to stay close.*
>
> *I fear this will be my final invitation, so I must take it. Be happy for me, even if you think me wretched, for I will get what I deserve soon enough. Be a dear and inform Ruth that I'll see her at the end of summer when she returns home, that is if George still wants her when he'll have me every day.*
>
> *Sincerely,*
> *Lydia*

When the words sank in, she wished she'd stopped reading while she still had the chance.

"Maggie?" Douglas gently laid a hand on her shoulder.

"It's as we feared." She dropped the letter, covered her face with her hands, and cried.

"Claudio, get that letter." Mrs. Melling held out her hands to receive it. "I need to know what has pained our Magdalene."

"No, Mrs. Melling." Douglas handed the letter to Claudio. "Let the deacon read it and break the news to you."

She folded her hands in her lap and tilted her chin up defiantly. "Next, I suppose I shall be taking orders from the cook."

Claudio set to smooth Mrs. Melling's pride. "Some days, *signora*, it is wise to take advice from those we often counsel ourselves."

Douglas kept a comforting hand on Magdalene's shoulder and passed a fresh handkerchief to her as her sobbing slowed.

"*Padre Santissimo!*" Claudio crossed himself and muttered a few more lines in his native tongue. All eyes were on him as he folded the letter. "May I speak freely, *signora?*"

"Of course, dear Claudio. I trust you with my deepest heartaches." She glanced at the others sitting on the settee. "And since everyone else seems to be privy to the letter's content, I see no reason to send them out."

"I should like to take this to Father Angelo to get his opinion on the matter, but I think it would be wise to send this, along with a letter of explanation of the happenings within this house, to the priest at your congregation in Mobile." Claudio leaned across the space between the wingback chairs and took Mrs. Mellings hands into his own. "Your husband's sins are most grievous and can no longer be ignored."

Mrs. Melling pulled one of her hands free and clutched it to her chest. "What has he done?"

"He has sent for Lydia to come to your home in Mobile. With the words she used in this letter, there can be no denying the true purpose of her relocation, with or without the disguise of being a maid."

"I will be shamed, never step foot in the city again!" Mrs. Melling dabbed her eyes with a handkerchief. "I knew something changed last summer, but I did not think he would ever be so bold as to regularly consort with a servant no matter how good her coffee is."

At the mention of coffee, Douglas looked to Magdalene with a raised eyebrow.

"I suppose he will no longer come to us on the weekends, but it is just as well. There is nothing I could say to him." Mrs. Melling touched her forehead. "I feel a sick headache coming. Magdalene, could you help me to bed?"

"Yes, of course." She crossed the room, tucking Douglas's handkerchief into her pocket as she went.

"I have permission to walk the full house, do I not, *signora*?" Claudio asked.

"Yes, I shall not shut myself in. Do what you must. And please send the Wattses out on an errand after I am in bed, Magdalene."

"What shall I say to them?" she asked as they slowly climbed the stairs.

"Tell them I am in the mood for something exotic. Something fresh and sweet, but not too rich. That should keep them busy."

Magdalene removed Mrs. Melling's shoes so she would not have to lean over, and helped her settle on top her bedspread, covering her with a blanket she kept folded at the foot of her bed. She did her best not to look at the crucifix with the skull and the postmortem photograph of Eliza on the side table, but she shuddered when it happened.

She left both the bedroom and sitting room doors ajar. After pausing to hang an item on her bedroom doorknob, she hurried toward the back stairs. Rosemary wasn't keen to hear Mrs. Melling's request.

"Shall I leave Leroy here?" She untied her apron and called out the back door for Priscilla, who played in the side yard.

"No, we'll be fine."

"In the house unchaperoned with two men while Mrs. Melling is in bed?" A hand went to her hip.

"Mr. Campbell is just outside and Douglas won't be in here much longer." Magdalene smiled reassuringly. "Besides, Claudio is practically a priest. Nothing could happen."

Twenty-Nine

Claudio and Douglas stood before the fireplace, deep in conversation. A thorn of jealousy pricked at Magdalene's heart to see the two being social, as if there wouldn't be room for her in either of their lives if they befriended each other.

One of them must choose you. One must have you.

"Mrs. Melling is resting and Rosemary is gathering her family, but let's wait five minutes to be sure they're gone." Magdalene made a production of dropping onto the settee, both arms outstretched on either side of her along the back of the seat. She kicked a foot out and crossed her legs at the knee. Both the men turned and looked at her. "After all, we don't want to be chanting and sprinkling water all over the place with the Watts family looking on like we're some sort of sideshow." She laughed bawdily.

"Did you happen to nip a drink while you were gone?" Douglas cautiously approached her.

Magdalene laughed again and patted the spot next to her. "Not at all, but there's plenty in the corner if you wish to pour something for us."

He looked back at Claudio as if for unspoken advice. The deacon shook his head and set his bag in the wingback chair.

But Magdalene wasn't going to let the deacon control what they did. She jumped out of her seat, took Douglas by the hand, and pulled him down with her so they landed on the dainty sofa in a tangled fashion. Douglas managed to straighten himself, leaning away from her pressing body that hugged his left arm as she sat curled against him.

"Tell me, *signorina*," Claudio spoke as he sorted through his black bag, "what was different this morning?"

"My window was open so I rushed out of bed without praying, hoping I'd see a glimpse of this man." She squeezed Douglas's arm as though he were her special catch. "He was out there like a knight guarding his princess in the castle."

The hint of a smile tugged at the corner of Douglas's mouth. Seeing her chance, she rested her head on his shoulder and looked across the room at Claudio as if to dare him to try separating them.

"*Signorina*, did I not instruct you to pray fervently, morning and night, as well as keep a prayer in your heart all day?" He stepped toward the settee with Saint Benedict's cross in one hand and the aspergillum in the other.

Magdalene ran a hand across Douglas's chest, letting it rest on his opposite shoulder as she nuzzled into him. "He's going to hurt us," she whispered pleadingly into his ear. "Please don't let him hurt us."

"There's no need for all that, Claudio." Douglas waved him away. "She's just feeling vulnerable after all that's happened. Give her a minute."

"I do not believe that, and you are a fool if you do." Claudio looked at the two cuddled together and fingered the crucifix in his hand. "Check her wrist for the rosary. If it is missing, you will know she is not herself."

Magdalene released Douglas, falling back against the curved side of the settee. With her body draped before him, she placed one hand on the lap of her black skirt and the other across her chest. When Douglas reached for her, Claudio held the cross before him.

"Stop. I will check her."

Douglas retreated to the opposite corner of the settee. Outside, a wagon rattled down the lane. Knowing they were now alone, Claudio hastened his movements, depositing his things on the nearby side table.

Pretending the deacon wasn't there, Magdalene looked directly at Douglas. "It's two against one. We don't have to let him boss us around just because he brought a bag of trinkets. We have the upper hand because we know where the other girl hid her book of sketches."

Claudio took Magdalene's hand from her lap and felt around the cuff of her white shirt for the bracelet. "You know where Eliza hid her sketchbook?"

"For one so gifted in recording all the details, she's not very imaginative in hiding private things."

"Where is it?" Claudio gripped Magdalene's hand. "Please, *signorina*, tell me so I can find it before her mother does."

"It's higher than the tallest tide. Always close, always dry." Magdalene giggled and rubbed her legs against Douglas. "Now, why do you want a book full of pictures from the moments you've atoned for, preacher boy?"

Letting her arm fall, Claudio grabbed the other and found nothing there either.

"See, Douglas?" He stepped back. "I told you this is not Magdalene. She has abandoned the holy symbol. At the moment, she is nothing more than an instrument of the devil."

Magdalene stood and circled Claudio with the fluidity of a tigress. "You look pleased to announce that, but you don't want anyone else to have me because you can't." Then she bent over Douglas, one hand resting on the back of the settee, the other tracing his jawline. "Do you want to suppress your life as he has, or do you want to feel passion burn like the flame of life that it is?"

"I'm ready for the fire," Douglas replied, taking her face in his hands and drawing her closer. Their lips met, and a second later, Magdalene dropped onto his lap as her hands immediately explored the buttons down the front of his shirt.

Having been hypnotized by her pacing, Claudio watched in astonishment as the seduction occurred before him before springing to action. "*Ave Maria!*"

Douglas stared at Magdalene as if he didn't know where she'd come from, but he made no effort to remove her from his lap. She, on the other hand, sucked in her breath through clenched teeth. Seeing his opportunity, Claudio grabbed Magdalene around the middle and pulled her toward the hall. She kicked and hissed. The deacon struggled for the front door, praying over her as they went.

"Don't let him take us away from you!" she called from the hallway.

Hearing her cry out and still being dazed, Douglas ran for the damsel in distress. He pulled Claudio to a stop by the sleeve of his cassock and punched him in the face. His bloody nose was immediate, most of it gushing onto Magdalene's white shirt. Momentarily ceasing his prayers, but not loosening his hold on Magdalene, Claudio spit out the blood that had poured into his mouth and faced Douglas. He lifted one hand to him and performed the sign of the cross while he recited in Latin.

"Dear God, what have I done?" Douglas's eyes were horror-filled as he beheld the bleeding deacon holding Magdalene.

"Open the door!" Claudio once again had both hands around Magdalene as she struggled to get free.

"No! Douglas, no! Our place is here with you." Magdalene squirmed within the deacon's grasp. When her eyes beheld the shocked looked on Douglas's face, she turned her efforts to the one who held her. "You think you've won, but I'm stronger than a weak stable boy."

"Do you not remember the humble babe born within a stable? He is on my side."

"Do *you* not remember Eliza? Her will was stronger than yours." Claudio's arms loosened. She smirked and moved in for the final stab. She stopped struggling and held her ground a moment. As his grip further slackened, she drove against him and licked his cheek, taking in some of the blood in the process. "You taste like fear."

Douglas yanked the front door open and helped Claudio throw her onto the porch. She curled into herself on the floor boards, laughter slowly dying into moans. Still dripping blood, Claudio retrieved a handkerchief from his pocket and held it to his nose.

"Can you fetch me the crucifix and the aspergillum, please?" he spoke around the cloth.

"Did I see her..." Douglas looked down at Magdalene's withering, blood splattered form with disgust.

"Yes, but this is not Magdalene—this is a demon using her body. Fortunately, she will not remember any of what happened and we do not need to remind her."

"But I remember. I had her in my arms and we—"

"You were only oppressed. You temporarily gave in to your temptations. She, on the other hand, is possessed and has no control over her faculties. Please get the items for me, quickly. It will be easier to exorcise her while the demon is weak."

When Douglas rushed inside, Claudio knelt next to Magdalene, a hand on her shoulder to keep her down. "Why did you do and say that to me?"

Magdalene leered at him. "It's what Eliza told you your first time together, when you were shivering in—"

"*Silenzio!*" Claudio pulled his personal rosary out from his cassock and pressed it to her forehead. He prayed over her, holding her down while she writhed and groaned. When Douglas brought the requested items as well as the deacon's bag, he helped restrain Magdalene while Claudio draped the purple stole over her.

Mr. Campbell came from the back yard. "What in the name—"

His nephew held up a hand to silence him, and he came up quietly. He leaned his old bones against one of the white columns and watched the scene before him. With the aspergillum and Saint Benedict's cross in hand, Claudio completed the ritual for exorcising the demon with no more struggles from Magdalene, then he did it three more times, to be sure.

After his final pronunciation, she raised her head from the floor, looked the deacon in the eye, and whispered, "Thank you."

Then she fainted, Claudio catching her by the shoulders to lower her gently back down.

*   *   *

The deacon sat back on his haunches and wiped his brow with the sleeve of his cassock. "A false sense of security is the ultimate enemy."

"What do we do with her?" Douglas looked upon Magdalene as though she was less than human.

"She's been through the ringer, ain't she?" Mr. Campbell remarked. "It looks like you boys still have your work to do. If you get her into the carriage house, I'll watch over her."

Claudio went to stand, and his legs gave out from under him. He grasped the doorframe to keep himself upright.

"You rest a minute. I'll get some tea on, and then Douglas can bring her over."

"I want to bless your house before bringing her, for her protection as well as your own."

"Give me—and yourself—five minutes and then come for a quick spot of tea and the blessing. When you get back, Douglas can bring Miss Magdalene. That way, there will always be someone here." Mr. Campbell went into the house and came back with a kitchen chair for Claudio and a decorative pillow from the parlor that he slid under Magdalene's head.

With his uncle gone, Douglas questioned Claudio. "She'll remember nothing?"

"Nothing from the time she came back from bringing *signora* to rest."

He leaned against the column, picking his fingernails nervously. "So are we to carry on like nothing happened with her, even though she and I kissed like drunken sweethearts and she tasted your blood?"

Claudio rested his elbows on his knees and held his head in his hands. "It wasn't her. She's innocent in all this."

"But you said yourself she should have prayed this morning. She circled you like she wanted to eat you alive and enchanted me. Does that mean I'm attracted to demons?"

"No, *amico*. It means you are human because you find a pleasant woman attractive." He gestured to Magdalene reclined on the porch with both hands. "Look at her! Even exhausted and covered in blood, she is beautiful. I nearly fell under her spell twice in the last week. I assume it is rare for us both to agree on the attractiveness of a woman with us coming from opposite ends of Europe as we do."

Douglas looked down at her and then away, not wishing his feelings to overwhelm him. "So she's a temptress?"

"No, no, she does not attempt the evil actions alone. The devil within this house is manipulating her weakness—whatever it is—to beguile us. Though the first time it happened, it was just her, pure and simple, on the beach. I am human, as are you. But we must put aside the natural man and be strong. *Signorina*, Maggie, as you call her, has defended herself against much more than we will ever know in her days here. She is strong, but not perfect. You tell me you've not taken a bite without blessing your food or gone to bed without kneeling before the Lord and I will allow you to harbor resentment toward our *signorina*." Claudio stood to leave.

"I'm trying to place the blame elsewhere and it isn't working. Thank you for setting me straight." Douglas put out a hand, and Claudio shook it.

Then Claudio placed a hand on his shoulder, pausing on his way. "Remember, she spoke truthfully when she answered my questions. She rushed out of bed to look for you. Hold to that."

"I'm trying to forget the feel of her kisses. I want to erase them from memory, though they're the best I've ever had." Douglas kicked at a leaf on the porch. "I suppose that's not the best topic to discuss with a man of the cloth."

"As one training for the priesthood, no. But as a friend, it is fine. Pray and cleanse yourself. I will need your help when Magdalene is safely with your uncle."

Thirty

Magdalene awoke cradled in Douglas's arms. He walked toward the backyard and over his shoulder she could see Claudio staring after them from the porch.

"Stop, please. What's going on?" And then, seeing the drying, brownish blood stains on her shirt, she screamed. "Claudio!"

As the deacon ran to them, she asked to be put down and Douglas obliged. Her legs were weak so she held his arm to steady herself. With her other hand, she felt her face for injury.

Seeing the dried blood on Claudio's face, her heart quickened. "What happened?"

"The demon possessed you, but just briefly. You are now yourself." To help her believe, Claudio did the sign of the cross and placed Saint Benedict's crucifix in her hand. "All is well, no?"

"No! Did I attack you? Why is there blood on us? Why is Douglas carrying me away?"

"He is taking you to stay with Mr. Campbell while we exorcise the house completely." Claudio spoke extra slow, as if he hoped to keep her calm through his voice. "*Signora* Melling is resting inside, but she gave us permission to do so. Do you remember the letter you received?"

She thought back and then leaned into Douglas as her knees once again gave out. "Lydia. The letter was too much for Mrs. Melling."

"You accompanied her upstairs and returned not yourself," Claudio said.

Thinking of what Alexander had done while under diabolic influence, she immediately reddened and hung her head. "I must have been an animal. You never said I didn't hurt you."

"No, *signorina*, you didn't strike me. That was Douglas, trying to defend you."

She looked to Douglas, whose arm she still held. "Were you touched by evil, too?"

"Not completely." He patted her arm and tried to smile.

"But enough to battle Claudio. Tell me everything so I can apologize."

Douglas opened his mouth to speak, but Claudio spoke quicker and placed a hand on each of their shoulders. "Be assured you are not accountable for what you said or did. There is no need for remorse. Nothing you did physically harmed anyone. Now, Mr. Campbell has tea awaiting you. Sit and rest with him while Douglas and I sort out this house." He kissed her on both cheeks and sent them away.

As they exited the gate, Douglas looked down at her hand resting on his forearm. "We don't mean to shuffle you off, but we want to get as much done as possible before Leroy and Rosemary return. We don't want to look like a sideshow to them."

"What an odd thing to say. I must have made a spectacle of myself. I hope you'll forgive me."

A look of relief passed over his face. "As Claudio said, there's nothing to forgive." He paused on the front stoop of the carriage house, his eyes softening as they looked upon her. "Ask my uncle for one of my shirts so you can soak this one. I'll see you soon, Maggie. Don't lose heart."

Mr. Campbell met them at the door and helped Magdalene over the threshold. The main room held a kitchen, dining, and living area all in one, with a door open to a modest bedroom off in the back left corner and a closed door in the other corner, beyond the ladder to a partially enclosed loft. The furnishings were simple but clean. He showed Magdalene her place at the small dining table and promptly brought the kettle over.

"Please, if I may. Douglas said I could borrow a shirt so we could clean mine."

"Of course, and you'll want to wash up as well." He walked her to the door in the right corner.

She closed herself in the small washroom and spent the first minute staring at her reflection in the weathered mirror hanging over the sink. Shame once against crept over her as she thought of the night Alexander had clawed himself in an effort to free the demon. But with the evil he'd given in to—all the pursuing of her and attempted murder—he had still remembered what he'd done. Why did she not remember what happened? It had to be awful for Claudio to want to protect her from the truth.

When she removed her blouse, she checked her body for wounds but found nothing. She washed her face and hands, and then she reached for what she recognized as Douglas's Sunday shirt from one of the hooks on the wall. He had worn it when they went to the shore and it still smelled slightly of the beach—the bay, car polish, and Douglas. She slid her arms in and buttoned it over her chemise, recalling how startled she'd been to wake up in his arms. If it wasn't for not knowing how she'd come to be there, she would have enjoyed the moment. For now, she relished in his scent and the scandalous sensation of being in his clothes.

She kept silent as she took her tea and biscuit while Mr. Campbell started rinsing her shirt. He didn't question her when he joined her at the table. They both sat staring out the window at Seacliff Cottage. After finishing, Magdalene looked across the table at the weathered man and asked what she desperately wanted to know.

"Did you see what happened? What did I do that caused me to be cast out?"

"Dear girl, you weren't cast out. You're here because they wish to protect you." He rubbed his forehead as though pained. "I heard shouting and came around the house. The blood was already spilled. The deacon had you on the porch with the purple stole on you. He knelt beside you with his holy water and the cross, speaking who knows what in that language of his. Douglas held your legs still as needed. They treated you with compassion, if that's what you're fretting over."

"Oh, not that. I trust Claudio with my life. It's just…never mind. Do you think we can sit outside?"

Mr. Campbell let her have the lone rocking chair on his small porch and brought one of the straight back chairs they'd used at the table for himself, setting it in front of the screened door. Magdalene dispersed her anxiety by rocking and rubbing her hands over the hard-to-see blood spots on her black skirt. She knew enough about Claudio to know he would not give in to her demanding to be told what transpired during her possession. If she was to learn anything, it would have to be through Douglas.

***

An hour later, Claudio and Douglas exited the kitchen door at Seacliff Cottage. The deacon wore the white surplice and purple stole over his cassock and clutched something to his chest. He slumped into one of the rockers, hung his head, and wept. Not fearing repercussions, Magdalene ran for him.

When she got to the porch, Douglas held out a hand to stop her from going to Claudio. He touched the sleeve of his shirt she wore and looked at her as if she was completely new to him. Then he took a firm hold on her elbow and brought her back to the carriage house.

"Uncle Simon, I need you to take the carriage to Claudio's church and bring Father Angelo here. Tell him it's an emergency. I'm sure Mrs. Melling would insist upon it. In fact, let me go check on her. She might want to ride."

"But what happened?" Magdalene's voice was panicked. "What's wrong with Claudio?"

"These things are taxing on the soul." Douglas rushed back to the house, leaving Magdalene to stand on the porch while Mr. Campbell readied the horses.

After shaking off the initial pain from being cast aside, Magdalene walked back to the fenced yard. She settled on the swing across the porch from Claudio, though she wanted to throw her arms around his shoulders and cry with him.

"No, Douglas," Mrs. Melling's voice came through the screen door. "You must drive the automobile. It is faster." She came out of the door, tying a sun hat on her head with a mint green scarf.

"But who will stay and—"

"Your uncle is more than capable of watching the house and keeping an eye on them." Mrs. Melling stopped by Claudio and laid a hand on his shoulder. "Hang in there, my dear boy. Help is on the way."

Douglas glanced at Magdalene and tried to muster a smile, but it looked pained. As soon as Magdalene offered a nod of acknowledgement, he rushed ahead to hold the gate for Mrs. Melling.

When Douglas drove away with Mrs. Melling, Mr. Campbell set to work putting the carriage horses back in the stable. Claudio raised his head, not bothering to wipe away the tears that streaked his olive skin. Slowly, he unfolded his arms, revealing a red leather book he'd clutched to his chest.

Magdalene gasped, causing Claudio to look at her for the first time.

"Are you well now?" he asked.

"I'm much better off than you." She approached him slowly, to allow him time to tell her to leave him alone if he did not wish for her company. "Is that Eliza's sketchbook?"

He fingered the worn cover and nodded.

Magdalene sat in the rocking chair beside him. "How did you find it?"

He locked gazes with her, his brown eyes nearly drowning in sorrow. "You told me where to find it."

"But I've never seen it before."

"The demon told me through a riddle while it possessed you. I did not understand the clues, about being above the highest tide. I thought it might have been on the cliffs. Douglas figured it out while we were blessing the house." He looked around. "Where is he?"

"Gone with Mrs. Melling to collect Father Angelo. He figured it was time for reinforcements."

"Oh, *é la cosa migliore*. It is for the best. I am on the ledge between doing more harm instead of being helpful." He dropped the book on his lap.

"Where was it?"

"On top of the tank of the toilet in your bathroom. That is why you were plagued so in that room. This book is filled with sin." He held it to his chest once again.

"And Mrs. Melling had her heart set on finding it."

"She must never see it!" He jumped out of the chair, a wild look in his eye. "We must burn the book before they return."

"The kitchen stove?" Magdalene went for the door.

"No! No, *signorina*, neither of us must step foot into the house. No one except Father Angelo will be safe until we are all blessed and the cleansing completed."

"But the Wattses are due back anytime."

Claudio took her arm and started across the yard. "We will watch for them, but this must be destroyed." He marched them out of the gate and into the Campbells' little house. "You stay by the window."

He stoked the fire within the stove through the oven door, and then opened one of the lids.

"Don't try to burn the cover. The leather will stink up the house and take much too long to destroy," Magdalene warned from her spot by the table.

One by one, he ripped page after page of sketches, crumpling and dropping them through the hole in the cook top. Mr. Campbell looked in at the door, but went back to the stable to give them their space. Claudio muttered to himself in Italian but every once in a while, Magdalene caught words she understood such as *Eliza* and *amore*. Then he sobbed and surely must have been blind to what he did because of the tears. Each time he brought paper toward the opening, his stole came closer to falling in as well.

Magdalene led him to a chair. "Let me finish for you, Claudio."

"No, I must be the one!" His knuckles were white around the book.

"It's not safe for you by the fire. You sit there and pull the pages for me if you must. Remember, the burden is no longer yours alone. You've given it to the Lord."

He remained silent but opened the book and tore the next page. Magdalene held her breath as she watched a detailed sketch of a bare-chested Claudio reclining in a pile of pillows in the attic bedroom be wadded into a ball. So perfect it was, she could see the exotic colors of the fabrics though black ink was the only embellishment. He handed it to her and it pained her to burn something created with such care, but she dropped it into the stove, feeling the rush of heat the new fuel created.

Consumed with Eliza's talents, Magdalene wanted to keep one of the pictures to study the technique so she could improve her own. It would be easy for her to walk to the stove and hide the picture rather than drop it into the fire. When taking the crumbled page, she looked at the next one displayed, so she could judge which would be the best one to take. She knew better than to nick one of the more intimate portraits—and there were many of those. It needed to be one she wouldn't be embarrassed to be found with, in case she wasn't as sneaky as she thought.

Then she saw a self-portrait with more clarity than a Da Vinci. A charcoal sketch of Eliza nestled against Claudio's neck, their bare shoulders melting into the edges of the page. Claudio's eyes were closed, his lashes an elegant fringe along his closed lids. Eliza's three-quarter profile had no distortion—common in less-skilled artists like herself. Her eyes were half closed, a dreamy smile of contentment on her full lips.

Magdalene raced the current page to the stove and hurried back to snatch the picture from Claudio before he could completely wrinkle it. She smoothed it against her skirt as she walked to the stove. Looking over her shoulder to check that he wasn't watching, she slipped it behind a collection of cans on the shelf above the stove.

"We're almost done," she reassured Claudio.

"I cannot continue." He shoved the book at her, and buried his head in his arms on the table.

Pleased with the opportunity, Magdalene took the book to the stove and flipped through the remaining dozen sketches.

While she was engaged to William, she'd taken an overnight trip to the city with Aunt Agnes to shop for her trousseau. They had stopped at the university to visit one of Aunt Agnes's cousins, and Magdalene managed to steal away to the art section of the library. Looking through books of the Renaissance masters, she saw many nudes, but to her distress the final page of Eliza's book was a full-length drawing of Claudio. She hastily ripped the page and shoved it into the stove, burning her thumb on the edge of the hole in the process.

She rinsed the burn in the sink and checked her soaking shirt. The sounds of an automobile coming up the lane rumbled through the open windows.

"Claudio, they're back. Let me finish with the stove and then we'll go meet them."

She pulled the rest of the drawings out of the book and scanned them, settling on one that featured the attic with just a glimpse of the sleeping form of the deacon on the bed in the corner. Magdalene added it to the other behind the cans on the shelf. She tore at the end pages adhered to the leather cover to loosen them and crumpled the remaining pages, dropping them into the fire. She opened the door on the front of the stove to peer in, making sure all the pages were sufficiently burned, before closing the lid.

She haphazardly tossed the leather cover into the loft, figuring Douglas would help her dispose of it. Then her attentions were once again on the deacon.

"Come, Claudio." She helped him stand and linked her arm through his, trying not to visualize what each curve of his muscles looked like under his cassock. "Let's meet Father Angelo."

Thirty-One

When Magdalene and Claudio reached the gate, Father Angelo, Mrs. Melling, Mr. Campbell, and Douglas had convened on the back porch.

"There you are, my dear Claudio." Mrs. Melling shepherded him into her arms. "Douglas told Father Angelo all that you were able to accomplish before weakening, so he is going to complete the Rite and bless the house. It's about time, too. The Mellings had this cottage since after the Civil War, and while we have done remodeling, a spiritual sprucing is just what it needs."

Magdalene, annoyed with the frivolous way Mrs. Melling tossed about the serious troubles, stalked to the gazebo and threw herself into the swing. She ignored her chattering, and sighed in relief when the priest quieted Mrs. Melling so he could pray over Claudio.

When done, he said something to Claudio in their native tongue and then he turned his wizened face to Mrs. Melling. "I have not had the opportunity to see your home. Could you please come with me to make sure I do not overlook any of the rooms?"

"Of course, Father. Oh, Douglas, be a good fellow and put the box on the table in the kitchen. If you could check for anything that needs to be placed in the icebox, that would be wonderful."

Douglas took the box he held inside, his uncle continuing to hold the door for him after Mrs. Melling and Father Angelo entered the house.

"I'll be heading back to the horses now, but holler if you need something."

"Thank you, Mr. Campbell," Magdalene said.

Douglas emerged from the kitchen, first looking at Claudio in the rocking chair and then down the way at Magdalene in the gazebo.

He turned back to Claudio and the deacon stood. Douglas picked up the rocker, following him down the porch. He set the rocking chair across from the swing.

"You take your pick," Douglas told Claudio.

He chose to keep to the rocker, so Douglas sat beside Magdalene with a timid smile.

Magdalene did her best to sit upright, though she felt odd casually sitting on a swing with the man she liked with all the turmoil of the afternoon. "Don't tell me Mrs. Melling made you stop and go shopping while you were in town."

"No, we passed Leroy and Rosemary on their way back not long after we pulled onto the main road. Mrs. Melling had them turn the things over to us and gave them the rest of the day off so they wouldn't be put in harm's way."

"*Buonissimo.*"

"That was thoughtful of her," Magdalene said. "I'm impressed, though it probably has more to do with protecting her family's sensitive information than the welfare of their souls."

"Bitterness is not good for you, *signorina.* It pinches your face."

"As opposed to my shirt," Douglas chimed in, "which looks great on you."

The flippant nature of Douglas's remark made her furrow her brow, at which Claudio pointed to her. "There! The pinching continues."

Magdalene's stern face dissolved into laughter, as light as the spring breeze that passed through the lattice. It felt good, but then she remembered being upset about Mrs. Melling's nonchalant attitude and she returned to being serious. "There will be a day for joy, but it's not today."

"The devil wants us to be miserable, Magdalene. Do not give in to those feelings. We need to find joy as often as we can, especially during the dark days. Do not feel guilty for smiling." Claudio held her gaze and forced himself into a grin.

"Do you feel better now?" she asked.

"I do." He leaned back in the chair, pushing into a rocking motion with his worn black boots. "Did you finish burning the pages?"

"Of course." She felt a rush of guilt over the pages she'd tucked away.

"I am sorry you had to see them, *signorina*. I did not know Eliza was so thorough with her sketches, she did them so quickly and often when I was asleep." Claudio stammered. "It brought back my shame all over again."

Douglas reddened, helping Magdalene understand that her shame over lying was taken for embarrassment due to the intimate subject of the sketches.

"They were beautiful, though." Both men looked at her, Claudio with surprise and Douglas with mortification. "Her technique. She was very talented for someone so young. Much finer than anything her mother has shown me of her work."

"And what do you know of art?" Douglas challenged.

"I sketch myself and know how difficult it is. A few years back, I went into Mobile with relatives and stopped by the college. I snuck away from my aunt and spent an hour in the library looking through books with the likes of Da Vinci and Raphael. Believe me when I tell you her work is just as good. She understood how to capture the human form at all angles, which is no easy task."

"It is her subject matter that needed improving," Claudio said in a fit of self-depravation.

"I'm not so sure," Magdalene teased. "From what I saw, you could have modeled for some of those Roman statues."

"Of all the vulgar things for a lady to say—and to a deacon!" Douglas stomped down the porch.

"Come now," Claudio called. "She was only mocking, like I did to her about looking pinched and you did about her wearing your shirt."

Douglas, on the far side of the kitchen door, mumbled something.

"What's that? Come back so we can hear you, *amico*. Your Maggie and I tease each other. That is our way. If she does not behave herself, I shall begin calling her *posseduta*. Now, what was it that you said?"

Douglas, the stubble on his face looking red in the sinking light of the sun, came hesitantly back to the gazebo space. "I said I wasn't joking when I said Maggie looked good in my shirt. I can't help it if I enjoy the sight of the first woman to wear my clothes."

"I did not know you were a *romantico, amico*."

But Magdalene had guessed as much. Embarrassment for being too brazen with her jokes made her wish she could take them back as to not offend Douglas. "I'm sorry for crossing the line with my banter. I can be most outlandish and stubborn at times. I suppose that's why my aunt wanted nothing to do with me."

"Her loss, our gain, as they say. Do you not agree?" Claudio looked to Douglas.

"Aye, my experience in America would be much different if you were not here. To think I'd have to judge all young women by the likes of Lydia and her coffee. What was that all about?"

Magdalene shook her head slowly and smiled. "Still not the right time."

"Do I want to know what it is you speak of?" Claudio asked.

"No," Douglas and Magdalene both said at the same time. All three of them laughed.

"See, now we are good. With this summer ahead of us, we will need all the ties of friendship we can hold. Now, as I was inquiring earlier, *signorina*, where is the rest of the book?"

"The rest?" Her heart pounded in her chest. "The pages were all burned."

"No...*libro da copertina*." He made his hands into the front and back of a book, opening and closing them. "The outsides."

"The cover?" Douglas asked.

"*Sí*, the book cover. You told me not to burn it because of the smell."

Relief flooded her gut. "Of course! I tossed it into the loft. I thought that was Douglas's room and he would help us dispose of it." She touched his hand, resting on the swing between them. "Is that all right?"

She could tell he was still upset over her teasing Claudio because only one side of his mouth curled into a smile. "Aye, I'll take care of it."

"Then I can survive for another day." Claudio leaned back and closed his eyes.

Douglas and Magdalene sat in an awkward silence, not wanting to disturb the weary deacon. For the most part, Magdalene kept her eyes averted from Douglas, but every minute she chanced a look. Typically, he would look away, as if he'd been caught staring, a strange mix of amusement and annoyance in his eyes.

The fifth time it happened, he held her gaze and opened his mouth to speak, but then Mrs. Melling came to the kitchen door.

"Claudio, Father Angelo needs the incense. We're ready for the final stage and he's invited everyone to walk through and pray with him." Mrs. Melling came on the porch and watched as the group sitting amiably in the gazebo stood. She was all smiles until noticing Magdalene for the first time. "What are you wearing, Magdalene? And in front of Father Angelo. Go and change at once!"

"I can't." Magdalene shifted her arms uncomfortably. "There was an accident with my shirt and I don't want to go into the house until it is purified. You all go, I'll wait outside with a prayer in my heart."

Mrs. Melling stepped closer to study the shirt. She looked at Magdalene and then to Douglas, and back to the shirt. A smile struck her face the moment she understood. "Well, it is a bit forward for a woman, but it does not look bad on you. Maybe if it was tucked in…yes, that would improve things."

"No, go on without me, please." She waved Claudio and Douglas forward. "I'll be fine."

She waited a few minutes after they were all inside before rushing across the yard. Mr. Campbell worked in the stable and she easily retrieved the pictures from the shelf over the stove. Laying them on the table, she smoothed them more and then folded them neatly into quarters before tucking them into the waist of her skirt. Then thinking they might be noticed through the odd fit of Douglas's shirt, she went into the bathroom and tucked them into her stockings.

Deciding she needed an excuse to be in the house, she rinsed and wrung out her shirt, happy to see the stains were gone. Feeling bold, she climbed the ladder to the loft with her shirt to hang it to dry where Douglas would have to look upon it. She needed to get him to talk about what happened and she felt keeping her possession fresh in his mind would work the best.

The red leather cover from Eliza's sketchbook lay open on the floor near the foot post of the brass bedframe. She placed it gently on the made bed, running her hand along the sky blue coverlet. After looking around the sparsely furnished loft—bed, highboy dresser, and a straight backed cane chair—she felt the proper place to dry her shirt would be the tall headboard of the bed. She stretched the sleeves across the top bar and the front of it hung without touching his pillow. As she had wrung it properly, it did not drip, so she felt no guilt in hanging it in so personal a space.

Magdalene returned to the porch swing with minutes to spare before the group returned.

"Are you positive you cannot stay?" Mrs. Melling asked the priest as they exited the house.

"We must return to the church, but thank you for the offer. I will see to sending Bishop Allen an account of the troubles facing your family so he can see to things on the other side of the bay."

"I am much obliged, though I wish there was no need for it."

Claudio stopped at the table to pack his bag and Douglas continued to the yard to ready the automobile. He lifted a hand in greeting as he passed Magdalene and she smiled in return.

"Come, *mia figlia*." Father Angelo motioned to Magdalene. She joined the group near the door. "I must bless you once again. You will indulge an old man his peculiarities, no?"

"Of course, Father." She had no trouble being open with Claudio's spiritual leader, though his face seemed harsh and judgmental.

From a small bottle he placed a drop of holy oil on his finger and made a cross on her forehead and then the full sign of the cross while he prayed in Latin. Afterward, he embraced her like a child and whispered, "Do not let secrets darken your spirit. Confession is good for the soul."

The texture of the pages hiding under her skirt irritated her leg but she smiled and nodded her agreement.

In the twilight, Douglas drove away with Claudio and Father Angelo in the back of the Great Arrow. Mr. Campbell could be seen through his opened window preparing supper for him and Douglas. Magdalene, with a sigh, turned to Mrs. Melling.

"It's been a day, Magdalene. I'm ready for it to be over." She held out her arm, and tucked Magdalene against her side. "Rosemary purchased an odd selection of treats this afternoon in an attempt to appease me. I think we should indulge ourselves with them for supper. If you can prepare tea, I'll see to the food."

"Sounds like a wonderful plan."

Walking through the back door, Magdalene immediately felt a chill, but only skin deep. She shivered and looked to Mrs. Melling. "It feels so cold and empty."

"Empty because the evil spirits are gone. Cold because the ovens are not in use and none of the fireplaces have been lit this afternoon. See to the tea and I'll set the table. And please be sure to change your shirt before you come to supper."

Magdalene set the kettle on the gas stove and then ran up the back stairs to her room. She closed the curtains and tucked Eliza's sketches into her own sketch book before changing into a ruffled pigeon front blouse and a fresh navy skirt. Even though Mrs. Melling didn't notice the blood stains on the black one, she knew they were there. Her hair was a fright, but her time ran low. She pulled it out of its pompadour—already half out on its own—and quickly brushed through it. On her way back to the kitchen, she braided her hair, finishing it in front of the stove.

Minutes later, she carried a tray with the china teapot and two cups and saucers through the swinging door of the dining room. The ladies enjoyed strawberry short cake and blueberry scones with their tea under the light of the gas chandelier.

Magdalene gathered the dishes, feeling the damp chill more. "The air has the hint of a spring shower."

"Go see if Douglas would light the fireplaces for us, but just the bedrooms. I don't think I'll be sitting up tonight, though I feel better than ever. Bring the rest of the cake to the Campbells, but save the scones for our breakfast."

Magdalene readied a plate for the men and hurried across the yard. Douglas answered her knock at the door, looking surprised.

"Thought you were finished with me for the day, didn't you?" She beamed at him.

He slipped out and stood uncomfortably close to her on the little stoop. "Aye, especially after your display of laundry on my headboard."

"When you say it like that..." she stammered. "I didn't mean anything by the location, I just wanted it out of your uncle's way and spread out properly."

"Mm-hmmm." Douglas scratched his chin as if he were bored and refused to make eye contact.

"I'm here on an errand from Mrs. Melling. She'd like you and your uncle to have the rest of the strawberry shortcake that Rosemary bought at the bakery today and would appreciate it if you'd be willing to light two of the fireplaces. That's something Mr. Watts usually does for us in the afternoons."

With a resolute expression, he nodded and took the cake. "Thank you. I'd be happy to help."

He brought the cake in to his uncle—who Magdalene heard give a whoop of joy—and came back a minute later with her damp shirt. He looked like he wanted to throw it at her, but he handed it to her respectfully. A few sprinkles fell from the dark sky as they headed across the yard, but Magdalene kept her pace and Douglas stayed by her side.

"I must have behaved horribly for you to be so put off by me." She kept her voice low on purpose, but a pleading tone slipped in without her bidding. She stopped just shy of the back porch, to the left of the muted rectangle of light coming through the screen door.

"Not completely." Douglas started to reach for her arm, but pulled back at the last second. "Claudio said it's better if you don't know."

"Easy for him to say! He's never had chunks of time missing from his life." She stomped across the porch, but paused to hold the door for Douglas so it wouldn't snap at him as she had.

"I know you must be frustrated. I was when he'd told me I'd been oppressed, though sometimes I wish I didn't remember."

"I was simply horrid, I must have been!" Tears threatened to overspill her eyes. She placed her shirt on the back of one of the chairs and then gripped the wood.

This time, Douglas followed through with reaching out to her. He cradled her elbow with one hand. "It's not just your actions that have me distraught. I walloped a man of God in the face and—"

"Here I am thinking it's all about me, while you're wrestling with guilt, too." Realization struck her that he was about to tell her something else when she'd cut him short. "I'm too selfish."

"It's that stubborn streak you've warned me about, but I didn't mention it for pity, only to explain that my moods aren't all directed at you." Douglas smiled and gently squeezed her elbow. "Forgive me."

"Of course, that is if you can excuse my behavior—"

"Magdalene?" Mrs. Melling's voice rang through the house. "Is that you?"

As much as she hated to, she turned away from Douglas and pushed through the hall door. "Yes, I just got here with Douglas," she called out.

He rested his hand on the small of her back for a moment, causing Magdalene's body to react with racing chills—the good kind.

"I'm in the parlor," she called.

The room at night, without the cheerfulness of a fire in the hearth, was somber even with the gaslight sconces at intervals around the walls. Mrs. Melling looked out of place sitting in Alexander's preferred spot beside the decanters, a new bottle of wine next to it and the table stocked with clean glasses.

"I thought it proper to offer a drink after a day like today, as a toast. Should we get Campbell, too?"

"That won't be necessary, Mrs. Melling. He's more than pleased with the cake, thank you. I'd be happy to toast with you ladies, as a representative of the staff."

"Hush with the formalities," Mrs. Melling gushed. "What will you have?"

"Whatever you ladies take is fine with me."

"Magdalene?"

"I've no fondness for brandy"—Mrs. Melling laughed at that—"or any other hard drinks." Magdalene's cheeks went pink, knowing that Mrs. Melling found humor in her slighted reference to her son.

Mrs. Melling raised her glass and the others followed her lead. "To a clean house and new beginnings."

"Here, here!" Douglas raised his glass higher.

"Yes." Magdalene, not knowing the socially acceptable protocol, as that was her first toast, kept her voice soft. She waited until the others drank, all standing in the corner in a triangle of connection, before sipping.

"Magdalene, from what I have seen, is a slow drinker," Mrs. Melling remarked to Douglas. "I am going to take mine upstairs while I ready for bed. Have Magdalene show you up when she is finished."

And with that, Magdalene and Douglas were left unchaperoned with a bottle of wine in a dimly lit parlor, as if the lady of the house was happy to invite mischief back into it. Douglas motioned to the small settee against the back wall. Magdalene nodded, and sat down. He picked up the bottle and offered to refill her glass.

"No, thank you. I'm not used to drinking, that's why I'm slow."

He poured his glass to the top and recorked the bottle. "Just don't tell my uncle," he said as he sat on her right.

Who needed evil spirits to tempt when the memories of past indiscretions swirled in one's head? She drank more from her glass, and to keep from thinking of her time with Alexander, brought the conversation back to the day's events.

"From driving out demons to toasting with the lady of the house. It's all in a day's work."

"Aye, America is a fine country. Never a dull moment." Douglas gave her an easy smile. "Good and bad, highs and lows."

"What were the best and worst parts?" she asked.

"In hindsight, I think they were the same. Though in the moment, I would have chosen the worst differently."

She turned toward him, propping her right arm on the back of the settee. "Intriguing, but I'm guessing you won't tell me more."

He downed the rest of his wine, placed his glass on the table. "I can't."

"But how can the best and worst have been while I was possessed? It makes no sense to me."

"I hardly understand it myself. It was like a dream turned nightmare for a while."

That Magdalene understood all too well, and she tried for more. "My nightmare is not knowing what I did that turned my friends against me."

"We were never against you, Maggie." He took her hand and held it between them. "Well, I was briefly, after seeing you…but Claudio explained that it wasn't *you*."

She gripped his hand in panic. "My God, what did I do?"

"It was when he dragged you outside, after I'd hit him… He'll be mad at me for telling."

"He doesn't have to know." Her words were rushed, her mouth dry. She took another sip while waiting for Douglas to decide if he was going to speak or not.

"You'll never tire of seeking the truth. It was easy for Claudio to say not to tell you when he doesn't see you every day."

Magdalene laughed. "Am I that persistent?"

"There's my smile." He studied her face for a moment. "But yes, you're relentless."

Whether it was the look in his eyes or that she expected to be shocked by what Douglas told her, she realized he still held her hand. While she decided between leaving it and pulling away, he started running his thumb along the inside of her wrist, melting her heart further, though it only made it lurch back when he spoke.

"You—your body—struggled against Claudio's efforts. Then you stopped, and as he relaxed his hold, you turned to him, licked his bloodied face, and told him, 'You taste like fear.'"

She recalled Alexander's dominant position over her when he'd ripped her gown, licked her, and said those vile words. And then the malicious smirk on his pale face…

Douglas caught her glass before it dropped. He placed the wineglass by his own and wrapped his arms around her shaking form.

"Claudio was right. I shouldn't have told you. I'm sure you didn't really taste much blood."

"The demons are cruel!" she cried out. "It's not so much the act, though it's reprehensible, it's the words that go with them."

Douglas paused. "Claudio didn't seem shaken by what you did until you spoke those words."

A dry sob turned hiccup escaped Magdalene. "Then she used those words on him. Or rather, the demon did."

"You mean Eliza?" he asked.

"Yes, and now I'm just as tainted as the Mellings."

"How did you come to have those words spoken to you? Is that something Mr. Melling—"

Magdalene shook off his comforting arms and stood. "We mustn't keep Mrs. Melling waiting. She'll be too pleased with herself if we're down here any longer."

She stepped to the side table and drank the rest of her wine before turning to the hall. When Douglas exited with her, she paused to shut the lights off. Halfway up the stairs, she ran back down to lock the front door. Seeing Douglas waiting above made it easy for her to imagine he waited to accompany her for the night. She successfully brushed aside the impure thought until she returned to his side and he placed his arm around her protectively.

"Now you're withholding information from me," he said. "It's my turn to be persistent."

Magdalene smiled. "If it's a battle of stubbornness, I think I'll win."

Thirty-Two

It seemed nothing more than Mrs. Melling's scheme to keep Magdalene and Douglas together for her to have to accompany him to the fireplaces upstairs. For all his assisting Claudio that day, he knew his way around the rooms as well as anyone. They passed through the chilly sitting room and Magdalene knocked upon the bedroom door.

"Come in." Mrs. Melling sat in bed, her blankets pulled up to the chest of her modest nightgown. Her face was nearly as pink as the walls as she looked at both their faces for clues.

Douglas went right to work with laying the wood from the brass holder beside the fireplace into the hearth.

Magdalene stayed near Mrs. Melling. "I locked the front door before we came up and turned the lights off in the parlor. I'll do the same in the kitchen when Douglas is done, but is there anything else I should do?"

"No, Magdalene. You've been most helpful. So have you, Douglas."

Once the fire burned well, he replaced the screen and said his farewell to the lady of the house. At Mrs. Melling's request, Magdalene closed both her bedroom door and the sitting room door on their way out.

In the hall, they both paused in front of Eliza's portrait. "I expected her to be the root of the evil," Magdalene said. "If she were alive, I'd owe her an apology."

"She does have an air of mischievousness. Combined with her sultry eyes, I'd say she was a recipe for disaster. Poor Claudio."

Magdalene sighed. "After seeing some of those drawings, I'd like to think that if she'd lived, they would have run away together."

Douglas looked at her. "And just how much of them did you see?"

"Glimpses of the last half—when I had to help burn them after he grew too distraught. How much did you see?" She challenged.

"I found it while he recited the ritual and flipped through it, not realizing what it was. I don't understand how someone committing such a grievous sin would wish to record the moments. There's too much opportunity for it to fall into the wrong hands. And the fresh pain it caused Claudio was terrible. I was afraid it weakened him beyond repair, but he seemed in better spirits when he left."

"I'm worried as well. I hope Father Angelo keeps a close watch on him for melancholy." Magdalene turned away from the painting and resumed walking to her room. The desire to run her hand along the rich, glossy woodwork struck her, followed by fear that she shouldn't have drank the rest of the wine.

In her room, she turned the gaslights on and paced while Douglas set the wood in the hearth.

"It's time to tell me the meaning behind those words," he said to her over his shoulder.

She walked the room twice more, wrestling between trusting Douglas with the truth and saving her reputation. Then she decided the events today already tarnished his vision of her being the perfect woman. Magdalene dropped to her knees beside him and stared at the young flames.

"It was right here." A single tear rolled down her cheek. "Alexander licked my cheek and told me the same thing before he tried to take me."

"Oh, Maggie." An arm went around her and with his thumb he wiped the tear drop that hung on her chin. "Your days here have not been kind to you, yet you survive. That shows your strength and fortitude."

"But I've been a wretch, too. My thoughts and actions have been swayed from time to time, as you witnessed today. But I pray I didn't make a complete mockery of myself."

"No, Maggie. You were merely flirting. I was the one who acted out of turn."

"You?" A tender vulnerability in his blue eyes, a slight frown on his lips made her heart feel like it was between an anvil and a hammer, white hot from the flame and taking a beating.

"And that was after Claudio warned me you weren't yourself. You spoke of allowing the flame of passion to burn within and all my yearnings for you since the first time I saw you took over." Tentatively, he touched her cheek with two fingertips. "I took your face in my hands and kissed you. Deeply."

Magdalene tilted her head toward Douglas's fingers. He cupped her cheek in response. "And then?"

"Then you dropped into my arms and we continued until Claudio started in with *Ave Maria*. That made me pause and it drove you a little crazy. That's when he started pulling you toward the door. You called to me about not letting him separate us and I clobbered him before I realized what I was doing. It wasn't all you."

"Sounds like I did plenty of beguiling." She hung her head.

"No, it wasn't you, Maggie."

"But it was my body, even without my soul in control. My lips, yet I have no memory of what you enjoyed." Magdalene shifted to face him, losing his arm around her in the process, and raised a hand to her own face. Then she reached from her mouth to his and ran her fingers along his jaw. "Did it roughen my skin?"

Douglas's mouth twisted into a smile. "You had no complaints."

"Will you give me a memory now?" She tilted her head and softly brought her hand from his unshaven chin to his shoulder.

"Maggie," his voice was breathless and he pressed his forehead to hers, "not today but soon, I hope."

Douglas hurried out of the bedroom and made it halfway down the back stairs before she caught him, taking his left hand. He turned, looking up at her in the flickering gaslight within the narrow space. "You put up a great argument, but I've given in too many times today for me to live with myself if I move forward with another."

Magdalene descended the last step separating them, their bodies meeting in a surge of heat. Douglas put a hand on the single rail and the other wrapped around her waist. Her body had memories and expectations of their own. She instinctively wrapped her arms around his shoulders and kissed the spot where his ear met his jaw. He nestled into her neck.

"Maggie, we shouldn't," he murmured. "You need time to heal and I'd feel like I took advantage of you."

She clung to Douglas, her mind racing between his logic, the drive to please him, and her body's immediate needs. The situation was like those with Alexander, but this time the choice was up to her to heed his warnings and sound judgment or play into her primal yearnings. Being encircled in his arms, the rhythm of his heart beating against her body, and his mouth provocatively near her neck pushed her to choose immediate gratification.

Her hands traced down his strong shoulders and arms and then ran up his chest, causing him to straighten. They held each other's gaze for several seconds before Magdalene leaned in to claim her kiss.

"Douglas?" Mr. Campbell's voice rang out from the kitchen.

"Lord bless him." Douglas exhaled and looked up at her. "My uncle just saved us both."

Their arms unraveled from each other and they straightened their clothes before going down the remainder of the stairs and through the swinging door.

"Sorry for the delay, Uncle. Their fires were completely out and both Mrs. Melling and Magdalene were eager to chat about the day."

With a hollow feeling in her heart, Magdalene gave her thanks, returned Douglas's shirt, and said goodbye. She locked the back door, retrieved her own shirtwaist from the chair, and retreated to her room. The fire burned bright and pleasant, reminding her of Douglas's warm body.

***

Magdalene didn't wake up until after eight in the morning. Though her thoughts had been filled with Douglas the night before—delaying her ability to fall asleep—once sleep had come to her, she found it deep and complete. She pulled the curtains open with high hopes for the day. Though the sky blanketed in gray wasn't cheerful, she had no fears of having gone too far with Douglas when she pursued the kiss. She'd decided she was grateful for Mr. Campbell's interruption, even after a few hours of annoyance.

The yard was empty, but a buffing rag had been left on the hood of the automobile. That meant Douglas wasn't far away. Magdalene hurriedly dressed, stuffed the rest of her laundry—including several of Douglas's handkerchiefs—into the linen collection sack and sprung into the kitchen with a light heart.

"Y'all have about driven me mad," Rosemary said, turning from the sink where she readied a bucket of hot, soapy water.

"Sending me out on a goose chase for sweets and then turning me around before I can bring them back."

"Sorry, Rosemary." Magdalene set the kettle on for tea. "It's not all my doing, though they were delicious. Mrs. Melling would like the rest of the scones sent up with the tea."

"Things sure have changed since you got here." She gathered rags from a cabinet and hoisted the bucket out of the sink. "I had the inkling we should come early today, and I'm glad I listened to it. Blood stains in the front hall, of all places!"

Magdalene sucked in her breath. "Yes, I'd forgotten about that. It was too late in the day for it to be seen when I next passed through there."

Rosemary paused by the hall door. "Do I want to know how it came to be there or should I just ask if it's anywhere else?"

Magdalene, smiling in relief, shook her head. "It shouldn't be anywhere else, unless some dripped on the front porch. It was Claudio. He had a bloody nose."

"First Alexander, now the deacon!"

Magdalene shrugged. "Spring fever, I suppose."

She followed Rosemary into the hall. Leroy had the front door propped open, studying the oriental runner and the woodwork in the natural light. Rosemary passed him the bucket and rags.

"She says it was the deacon this time." Her voice full of skepticism.

"It was!" Magdalene cried out.

"I believe the lady." Leroy winked at her. "The house seems clear and happy today, despite the stains."

"That would be the work of Claudio and Father Angelo. They blessed the house." Magdalene smiled at Leroy and then his wife before ducking into the parlor to retrieve the wine glasses, but they'd already been removed.

Rosemary, watching from the hall, shook her head. "Already done, child. That and the dining room. Y'all make it difficult to miss half a day of work when I have to work double the next time."

Rosemary kept a close eye on Magdalene, so she dared not take her tea on the porch or walk to the stables that morning. She followed the cook up the back stairs with Mrs. Melling's breakfast at nine thirty. Rosemary piddled around the sitting room until the lady of the house emerged in a stunning ecru tea dress.

"I am afraid there is a dirty glass in my bedroom this morning, Rosemary."

"Not the worst thing I've seen today, ma'am." She hurried into the bedroom to make the bed.

"She really is the best worker," Mrs. Melling told Magdalene, loud enough to be overheard. "The few times she complains, she does it with humor."

"Saying things in a way to be remembered is the only way to set things right. No one remembers the grumbling, just the fun," Rosemary called out.

"We did have a most frightful day." Mrs. Melling sipped her tea. "The best is being free of Lydia, even if it creates a hole in the staff. Rosemary, do you think we need a new girl three days a week or do you think we could get by with someone twice a week with the men gone?"

Rosemary, done with tidying the bedroom and bath, paused to think it over. "A good worker should be able to keep the house with two, with the option to bring her in more days if needed. Do you have someone in mind, ma'am?"

"No, but are any of the ladies at Little Bethel Baptist in need of a job?"

"A sweet lady named Zora Baker just moved in with her married sister after their mother died over in Africatown. She's a fine girl, nineteen, and looks to have found a beau already, so she'll be settling down soon."

Magdalene frowned behind her cup, unsure if the remark was meant to sting her or refer to Lydia. Possibly both. But did she really care what the cook thought of her? Yes, especially since Rosemary had been nothing but kind to her the past two weeks. She chanced a look at the cook, and she winked at Magdalene. Satisfied no harm was meant, she settled back in the armchair and enjoyed the day.

While Mrs. Melling took a nap after the midafternoon tea, Magdalene finally had the opportunity to go outside. She headed straight for the stables, but other than the sounds of the horses nickering, they were silent. The carriage house's door was open, so she walked toward it. A few feet from the house, Douglas slipped through the screen, carefully shutting it behind and holding a finger to his lips. He gave her a half smile and led her down the lane, toward the front of the main cottage.

"What's wrong?" she asked as they came to a stop near the front yard gate.

"Uncle Simon's resting. His joints are burning with aches. He says he gets it from time to time, especially when it's damp. That drizzling weather last night stirred up his pain."

"And he got out in the night air because I'd kept you longer with talking and…" She hung her head.

"It's not your fault, Maggie." He put a hand on her arm. "I was just as happy to linger."

Magdalene looked up at him through her lashes. "Even in the stairwell?"

"Aye, especially then." He dropped his hand and motioned for them to keep walking.

"I've managed to amass quite a collection of your handkerchiefs these past few days. I sent them all out with my laundry, but I'll be returning them once I get them back."

Side by side, they strolled in a big loop in the red dirt lane. He looked at her with a smile. "Keep one, if you'd like."

Magdalene smiled with relief. "I was up half the night worrying you were angry."

"Frustrated at first because I didn't want to take advantage of you, but you managed to persuade me." He fingered her hand as if he wanted to hold it. They both turned their heads toward the other. "Uncle Simon was a Godsend. If he hadn't come, I think we'd be the ones hurting today."

"Is it wrong of me to want a kiss that I can remember? You have such strong feelings about what you experienced I think it's fair that I have the chance to know what your lips feel like." She knew she blushed at her words, but she wanted to be truthful with Douglas.

"Sweet Maggie." He took her hand and squeezed. "I brought you out here to walk so we could speak freely, but still be in the open. This way no one in the house can imply anything negative about our time together. I respect you and want to keep you safe. We don't want to be sneaking around for stolen moments, but I promise you, if by chance we're given a private minute or two, you'll have your kiss. Of that you can be sure."

Thirty-Three

On Friday afternoon, uneasiness disturbed the household. No word had come from Mobile, and both Magdalene and Mrs. Melling were praying over Mr. Melling. The former's supplications were that he would stay in the city with his sinful ways, the latter that he'd confessed his sins and found favor in the sight of the Lord once again.

The ladies, as well as the Campbells and Wattses, took their tea together and were on the back porch at three o'clock when Captain Walker came up the shore path. He wore a leather messenger style bag across his shoulder and a set look to his mouth that made one think he wasn't happy.

"Captain Walker!" Priscilla squealed, and ran to meet him at the gate.

He removed his hat and bowed to her with a quick, easy smile that erased any tension he previously held. Then Priscilla had him by the arm and nearly shook it off with her eagerness.

"You leave him be, Prissy!" Rosemary called. "Ain't no way to treat a guest."

She dropped her grip, tucking her hands patiently behind her back while the captain removed a peppermint stick from his pocket.

"Thank you, Captain Walker." Priscilla ran her candy to the gazebo swing and jumped next to Magdalene, who laughed at her exuberance. The little girl looked at Douglas, who leaned against the lattice across from the swing. "Told ya he'd bring one to me if I was a good girl."

Hat in hand, the captain approached the porch, waiting to be welcomed by Mrs. Melling.

"Good afternoon, Captain Walker. We're just finishing our tea, but there is plenty if you'd like to join us."

He inclined his head and stepped onto the porch. "Thank you, Mrs. Melling. A bit of tea sounds just the thing."

"I don't know if there's any tea for those who spoil children," Rosemary teased.

"Even ones who personally went to the farmer's market in Mobile to find the best sugar snap peas for you?" His crooked smile negated a few years of aging that he'd taken on from more than a decade of working on the water.

"You know how to sweet talk your way out of anything, don't ya, Captain Walker?" Rosemary said before going into the house, her husband following.

The captain, still smiling, turned to the lady of the house. "That comes from months of trying to win over my girl. While others were battling Spain, I fought for her heart."

Mrs. Melling, her hands clasped in her lap, nodded. "I remember the stories of your wife before you were married. Quite the fuss in the paper about her liaisons in the Tampa colored camps."

His smile faltered somewhat. "You can't believe everything you read in the papers, but Claire sure had it rough that year. She didn't let others stop her from doing what her heart felt was right. She helps the island midwife these days and is as big-hearted and headstrong as ever. Motherhood hasn't changed her any more than fatherhood has been able to make a gentleman out of me."

"You do your best and are quite respectable in any case. You will have to bring your family sometime, Captain Walker. I would like to meet Claire and the little ones. I am sure Priscilla would enjoy playmates for an afternoon as well."

"Thank you, Mrs. Melling. I'll see what can be done."

Mr. Campbell excused himself, waving Douglas along with him. Before they left, the captain asked after the automobile, opening a discussion on the glories of the car from both Mrs. Melling and Douglas. When Rosemary brought out a fresh cup of tea, the others dispersed and Magdalene joined Captain Walker and Mrs. Melling at the rocking chairs.

The captain, after taking a sip of tea, turned serious. "I'm afraid I'm the bearer of bad news today." He opened his satchel and pulled out a thin envelope and a bank pouch. "I'm not sure what all is in here, I just know that Mr. Melling remarked he wouldn't be coming home today."

Magdalene's sigh of relief was eclipsed by Mrs. Melling gasp.

"I feared as much, but it still smarts." Mrs. Melling looked to Magdalene. "I think I would rather read this inside. Come with me."

Magdalene helped her stand, then took the items from the captain. "Thank you."

Realizing her rudeness, Mrs. Melling turned back to Captain Walker. "I did not mean to spurn you, Captain. Was there anything more?"

"Just the groceries and goods from the city, as Rosemary sent the order last Friday. I'll send the men up with it."

"Yes, and then please join us in the parlor." Mrs. Melling nodded to Magdalene and they went through the kitchen door that the captain held open for them.

Mrs. Melling settled into her chair by the unlit fireplace. When Magdalene tried to hand her the items, she waved her off. "You open the letter and read it to me."

Magdalene, sitting opposite, opened the envelope with trembling hands. She pulled out the folded stationary and stared at Mr. Melling's looping handwriting, bold and proud like his personality.

> *Dearest Ruth,*
>
> *It has come to my attention that you took it upon yourself—or perhaps you were urged by a certain companion— to involve the church in our private affairs. I will not tolerate you interfering with where I decide to place our employees. Lydia is needed at our home in Mobile. You may have forgotten, but this is where you are supposed to live. I have had to take over the running of this house as you have been overwrought with mourning and hiding at our summer cottage. If you had been here to see that the house was kept properly, I would not have seen fit to bring over our excellent maid. As you've left me no choice, I have put my trust in Lydia's capable hands.*

Magdalene, red with anger for his unjust accusations on Mrs. Melling's behalf, paused to look at the lady.

"Please, continue, Magdalene." She brought a lace-trimmed handkerchief to her cheek, reminding Magdalene of Douglas's plain hankies she had tucked in her own pocket, which brought her an ounce of comfort.

She cleared her throat and continued.

I do not know when I will wish to visit, but each Friday I will send through Captain Walker money enough to pay the salaries of those working at the cottage, including enough for a replacement maid if one is needed. I personally think your headstrong companion could use hard labor—but I leave that to your discretion now that you know all the trouble she has caused you. Besides the salaries, I will enclose an ample sum to keep you content with whatever frivolities you wish to indulge in, as well as an automobile allowance for Douglas so you need not use your funds on those expenses.

If you ever want more than is provided, be sure to send word. I will continue to pay the grocery and goods bill that Captain Walker brings over, according to his list from Rosemary, as well as his transportation fee. Be sure to tell Mr. Watts to inform the mercantile in Daphne to bill me at the office, as I will not be in monthly to settle the tab. It will make me feel better to know that you aren't using your money on necessities and I will be able to keep the books, as always.

Now, dear Ruth, think about the situation you've placed yourself in. If all goes well, I will see you at the close of summer for Alexander's wedding, if not before. We shall see how it all works out in the meantime.

Sincerely,

George

Magdalene wanted to ball the letter and throw it into the fireplace like Claudio had done with the sketches, but she simply folded it and stuffed it back into the envelope with an exasperated sigh. Mrs. Melling looked broken beyond anything she'd witnessed, hunched over in her chair, wet handkerchief in hand.

"This is not your fault," she told her. "Blame me for his leaving if you want, but do not blame yourself for any of it."

"It is my fault, hiding myself away here."

"But it isn't! He started on this path last year—you told me so yourself. Blaming your rightful grief for his own abhorrent actions is just proof of his vileness."

Leroy saw Captain Walker into the parlor. He looked at Mrs. Melling, crying in her chair, and Magdalene with her fists clenched.

"I'm sorry to see that my suspicions were correct. Please don't hate the messenger."

Mrs. Melling made no effort to move so Magdalene took the lead. "We don't blame you in the least, Captain. But if I may ask, did you see Mr. Melling this week?"

"Briefly this morning, before he went into a meeting. I check in at his office for any additional orders, but I rarely see him. The day with the automobile was an exception, of course."

"And how did he seem?" Magdalene asked.

"He was all smiles, but his eyes weren't joyful, if that makes sense."

"Completely. One cannot experience joy while living beneath the shadow of sin." Magdalene, fed up with sitting idly in her anger, walked the length of the room.

"You know I cannot abide pacing, Magdalene. Go"—she waved her hand without looking at her—"take yourself outside until you calm down. Captain Walker will sit with me."

Magdalene stopped by the captain to get his opinion on the matter since he wasn't asked if he could stay long. He gave her his boyish grin and held up both hands to signal ten minutes.

"Thank you," she whispered.

Magdalene exited the front door because she knew the kitchen would be busy with unpacking the grocery order. The deckhands from Captain Walker's steamship were drinking lemonade on the back porch. She heard one whistle at her as she passed the fence, but she didn't turn to acknowledge the attention. In her minutes of freedom, she wanted to find Douglas. She went inside the stable and stood on the far side of the stool where he oiled a saddle so she wouldn't cast a shadow on his work.

"Which one of those shipmates whistled at you like you're a school girl?" he questioned without looking up from his work.

"The cute one I winked at."

Douglas jerked up, but upon seeing the smirk on her face, he broke into laugh. "You got me, Maggie."

When the rush from teasing and seeing the handsome smile that made her feel like a coal burned through her settled, the joy left her eyes.

He started back on the circular motion with the oiled rag, but asked, "What is it?"

"The letter from Mr. Melling." She said his name as if it were venomous. "He basically blamed me and Mrs. Melling for everything and said he probably wouldn't see her until the end of summer, when they expect Alexander to return with a fiancée. He's going to send food and money like we're exiled in a faraway tower."

"I thought you'd be happy he isn't coming. I've been trying to remain calm so I won't—"

"Do what you did to Claudio?"

"Aye." He rubbed the oil extra hard in one spot.

"I would be happy if he didn't lay so much blame on his wife in the process. She's been sobbing ever since I read the letter to her. Not to mention he's abandoning her for another woman—at least temporarily. It's awful for Mrs. Melling, no matter my personal feelings."

"I'm sorry for the pain it's causing you, but I'm glad he's not coming." Douglas stepped back to look at the saddle.

"You did a great job. I used to clean and oil saddles while my father shoed the horses to make a little spending money. It's a lovely piece. Feminine." Magdalene analyzed the fine cut and scrolling pattern that had been burned into the leather around the edges of the saddle. A hand went to her mouth. "Oh, it's Eliza's, isn't it?"

Douglas wiped his hands on a dry rag and nodded. "I found it up in the hay loft gathering dust. Uncle Simon said Mr. Melling told him to dispose of all of her tack when Flora was put down, but he couldn't throw away the good equipment. He hid it where the family never goes. It'll rot away if someone doesn't keep it up. That accident was really hard on Uncle Simon. His letters after it were nothing but sadness and complaining of poor health. That's why I decided to come."

"I'm glad you did." She swayed back and forth slightly, not sure if she should step toward him or keep the few feet between them. "I only have a few minutes, the captain is sitting with Mrs. Melling but he has to leave soon."

"Aye, let's get the wharf rats out of here. I don't like the way they look at you."

"They were perfectly respectable when I rode over with them when I arrived."

"But that was with the captain watching over them. I'll see you to the front gate."

He offered his arm to her. No whistles sounded, but Magdalene felt the eyes of all four men on her as Douglas brought her to the front of the house. Stopping at the white picket fence, he held the gate open for her, and then pulled it closed when she passed through.

She turned to him, a silly grin on her face. "Thank you for escorting me back. Now I feel like a school girl being walked home for the first time."

"I've escorted you several times now."

"But not with an audience of jealous deckhands."

He threw his head back and laughed.

"I almost forgot why I went looking for you." Magdalene pulled his handkerchiefs from her pocket and passed them over the gate.

Douglas flipped through them and looked at her with a raised brow. "I told you to keep one, don't you want to?"

"Yes, but these were all laundered and your smell has gone from them." She felt her face grow warm. "I thought you could keep one with you for a while, and return it to me later."

He brushed the tip of her nose with his finger. "Aye, just like a school girl."

"But you'll humor me, being the romantic that you are." As confident as she was in his mutual admiration, she phrased it as a statement rather than a question.

In response, he kissed the top hanky and put it into the chest pocket of his shirt. "This one's for you, the one by my heart."

Thirty-Four

On Sunday afternoon, when the Wattses came
to prepare supper, they brought along Zora so Mrs. Melling could
meet her. Magdalene and Mrs. Melling were in the wingback chairs
beside the young fire. Zora Baker sat on the settee, Mrs. Melling
inquiring after her experience and skill levels with everything from
ironing to scrubbing to meal preparation while Magdalene stroked
the handkerchief Douglas had slipped to her when he helped her out
of the automobile at the Methodist church that morning. She didn't
hear much of the sermon because she was too busy holding the
handkerchief to her nose, not caring if her pew mates thought her
plagued by sickness.

After Mrs. Melling sent Zora to help Rosemary in the
kitchen, she turned to Magdalene. "I think she'll do well, don't you?"

"Yes. She has a lovely smile," Magdalene said, for the young
woman's pleasant, round face was all she could recall from the
meeting.

"Did you hear a word she said or were you too busy mooning
over Douglas's handkerchief?"

Magdalene stuffed it up her left sleeve, beyond Claudio's
rosary, and stared at Mrs. Melling like she had a serpent wrapped
around her.

"It is his, is it not?"

Magdalene nodded, causing Mrs. Melling to laugh—
something she hadn't done for days. "I told you that the two of you
would be a fine match."

"It's still much too early for any of that talk." Magdalene
stood.

"Oh, go." Mrs. Melling waved her away. "I know that pacing look when I see it. Be back in time to wash for supper."

Magdalene ran up the front stairs to her room. She stopped by her dressing table, pulled out her up-do, brushed through her hair, braided it, and then adjusted the ties on her Sunday dress. Satisfied with her reflection, she clipped her mother's chatelaine scissors to her waistband, and then skipped down the front stairs and out the door to avoid the hubbub of supper preparations in the kitchen.

The first of the wisteria was beginning to bloom, so she settled herself sideways on the gazebo swing, stretching her legs the length of it. She admired the pale lavender cones of the wisteria blossoms and their heavenly scent. With the vine sprouting for the season, the lattice wall behind the swing was curtained from the yard. She hoped Douglas would be able to spot her through the blockade.

Magdalene was about to give up hope when he came down the lane from the direction of the carriage house, whistling a jaunty folk tune. Douglas paused at the fence halfway to the gate and looked at the house as if he wished she'd come out. She shifted forward on the swing and waved. Hopping over the fence, he ran across the lawn with a huge grin on his face.

In the gazebo, he straightened his tartan vest. His face was Sunday smooth from his morning's shave, but Magdalene decided then she preferred the rugged stubble he collected during the week best.

"I almost didn't see you in here." He motioned to the vines along the back wall. "It's a most convenient privacy screen. May I?"

Magdalene nodded and then held her breath as he sat next to her—leaving mere inches between them. "I was hoping you'd be out," she said. "I have until supper. What about you?"

The hand on his lap shifted to the narrow space on the swing between them. "My uncle's already in bed. He takes his Sabbath rest seriously these days."

"Mm, that's good." Magdalene leaned a fraction of an inch toward Douglas, and looked down at his hand beside hers. He wiggled his fingers, causing her to giggle. When he made no effort to take her hand, she took his instead. "You might have all evening, but I don't."

"You always surprise me, Maggie." They swung, holding hands, in silence for a few minutes. "You can put your head on my shoulder, if you'd like."

Magdalene wanted more than that, but she accepted his offer. "I'm happy to say I've neither soaked your handkerchief with tears nor had to wipe my nose with it." His shoulders shook as he laughed, causing her to lift her head. She took the change in position to turn toward him. "I wanted to give you something in return and finally decided on what it will be."

Douglas looked about, as if seeking an audience. When he saw no one, he turned his attention back to Magdalene. She had her folding scissors unhooked from her waistband and passed them to him. Then she pulled her long braid over her shoulder, and held out the tip of it.

His face shone pure tenderness. "A lock of Maggie's hair. Aye, you know me well. And I like your hair best that way, though I expect I'd enjoy it even better all the way down."

Rather than fall into fantasy with visions of her hair being undone by Alexander's experienced hands, Magdalene tried to focus her attention on the present, but the appetite had slipped in. She no longer craved Alexander, but the desire for impassioned touch coursed through her body. Douglas curled the lock of hair he'd snipped and tucked it lovingly into the back locket of his watch.

Near breathless with longing, Magdalene leaned closer, placing a hand boldly on his knee. "You carry a piece of me. Now it's time to make memories."

"Maggie..." As he bent his head toward hers, the hand she'd rested on his leg moved to his neck, caressing around his collar. When their lips met, Magdalene responded by shifting her body closer. Douglas pulled away after a few seconds and studied her. Her breath heaved and her lips parted with expectation for more.

"I see that look in your eyes," he said, "but I think we should go back to holding hands."

"It's not fair." She turned so her back was against the swing. Douglas did the same and their shoulders touched as he took her hand.

"If you think it unjust, you need to decide what's more important to you. Instant gratification or respectable courtship to nurture true love. One road is easy and short, the other challenging and long, but worth the journey from what I understand."

Magdalene laid her head on his shoulder and sighed. "I want both. Is that too much to ask?"

"You know the answer to that, Maggie." His thumb caressed her wrist. "Don't make it more difficult than it needs to be, you'll only hurt yourself."

***

Three weeks passed. Much to Magdalene's disappointment, she and Douglas averaged only a kiss a week and brief moments of holding hands. Mr. Melling had still not returned, but he kept his word to the finances being taken care of, so no one wanted for anything monetarily, though Mrs. Melling was forlorn most of the time. Zora fell into the pattern of life at Seacliff Cottage, arriving with the Watts family on Tuesdays and Fridays.

Claudio came each Wednesday afternoon, performing a simple blessing over the house, as well as both Mrs. Melling and Magdalene. On those afternoons, after the spiritual needs were seen to, the household—Wattses and Campbells included—convened with Claudio at the shore. Douglas and Claudio often kicked around a football he'd brought from Scotland. Those hours on the bay were when Mrs. Melling seemed the happiest. Whether it was the blessing, the fresh air, or both, Magdalene did not know. The deacon did not visit every weekend, as the threat of Mr. Melling wasn't there at present, but he sent a letter those Saturdays he did not come. Mrs. Melling most often received a letter from Alexander on Fridays, who was then in New York, so plenty of Saturday afternoons were spent in the sitting room replying to correspondence.

After her first month at Seacliff Cottage, Magdalene received only one letter from Aunt Agnes. Barely a page long, it was filled with much ridicule over her selfish action in taking the job across the bay, along with warnings to stay morally clean. Only the final line gave her what she sought—information on her father. He could sit up in bed now, but was still unable to feed himself.

On April fifteenth, Easter Sunday, after having attended a sunrise service, the household napped after their typical noon Sunday dinner. At three o'clock, Mrs. Melling knocked on Magdalene's door and urged her to hurry along.

Magdalene, wearing a new rose-colored tea gown with more lace and ruffles than she was accustomed to, pinned on the white hat with a cluster of pink flowers above the wide brim Mrs. Melling had purchased for her to go with the new dress. She felt silly in it until she looked in the mirror and realized she was a respectable woman, not a spurned country girl. When her white silk gloves were in place there was nowhere in the world she could not conquer—as long as no one peered under her ruffled hem and saw her boots were losing their shine.

She met with Mrs. Melling in the parlor. Her gown was robin's egg blue and her bonnet black. The two ladies went out the front door and around the back of the house to the forest trail. They walked silently toward the mausoleum site, where they had journeyed each day for the past week and a half. The supplies and building crew had arrived on time and the ground had been graded and the eighteen-inch foundation set—a glaring white scar in the otherwise serene clearing. That past Friday saw the addition of two marble steps leading to where the door would be.

"Go on to the cliffs if you wish, Magdalene. I'll be fine." Mrs. Melling settled herself on her bench.

Magdalene continued on to the edge of Ecor Rouge. She did not think it wise to sit on the boulder in her delicate dress, so she paced the ledge. Gazing at Mobile Bay, her head full of visions of Douglas because the bay reflecting a mostly sunny sky reminded her of his magnificent eyes. Magdalene turned at the sound of someone approaching from the southern trail. Her chest swelled at seeing Douglas in his crisp white shirt and new gold vest, the same color as his watch chain.

"Is this all right?" He looked around. "I saw you and Mrs. Melling go by the house and figured she'd be going to the site."

Magdalene nodded and slipped his hanky into her sleeve. "She's there now, but released me while she ponders. We're alone at last."

They each stepped forward and Douglas took her gloved hands in his and swung them back and forth a few times. Magdalene closed the last step between them and tilted her head to him with a curving smile of welcome on her lips. He tasted of fresh bread and she freed her hands to place her arms around his shoulders as their kiss continued.

Douglas's hands went to her waist, but moved hastily to her arms so he could pull her away from him. "No need to rush, Maggie. I'm not going anywhere."

"I've been waiting days for this. Just once more?"

Her pouting lips and sad eyes seemed to summon his base desires. His arms encircled her and pulled her to him with a force that reminded her of Alexander. She shuddered there in the sun and ran a finger across his lips to be sure it was really him and not a specter of the other man before she accepted his mouth to hers. A minute later, she realized her hands had mussed his hair and were now running the length of his vest and across his broad shoulders as their kiss turned deeper.

Magdalene pulled away.

"Oh, Maggie…" He licked the taste of her off his lips and closed his eyes. "You're all I want in this life, but we must be careful."

"That makes a good memory to hold to. Are we about even now?"

He laughed and squeezed her hand. "More than even, because this time it was fully you and fully me. You can stop chasing your demonic actions. It's time to focus on us and the future, not the past. Agreed?"

She nodded and turned to look across the quiet bay.

Douglas drew a protective arm around her and she leaned against his side. "And this spot is an improvement over the dreary parlor. I'll remember it always."

Thirty-Five

The end of April signaled driving lessons for
Magdalene. The rest of the week stayed the same, but on the days
Zora came to clean, Mrs. Melling settled herself in the back of the
Great Arrow and watched over Magdalene and Douglas in the front
seat. On Tuesdays and Fridays, they took their noon meal at
restaurants in Daphne, Fairhope, Loxley, or whatever town on the
Eastern Shore their drive took them for the day. Tuesdays they
stayed out as late as supper time, but on Fridays they returned by two
o'clock so they wouldn't miss Captain Walker's delivery.

May eighteenth, a mild day with springtime temperatures
holding in the upper seventies, found the trio still out at half-past
one. Mrs. Melling, Magdalene, and Douglas finished their boiled
peanuts and sodas from Zundel's Store south of the Point Clear
Hotel, and returned to the automobile. The two ladies buttoned their
dusters to protect their dresses and Douglas fastened his beige
driving jacket to keep his shirt and vest clean. Magdalene climbed
behind the wheel. Her sun hat was tied on with a gauzy blue scarf
and she wore her own pair of goggles, much to the shock of Mrs.
Melling. The goggles were a gift from Claudio and Douglas the week
before in celebration of her passing the driving test Douglas prepared
for her after a month behind the wheel.

"We need to hurry back, but not too quickly, Magdalene,"
Mrs. Melling said as Douglas helped her into the backseat. She settled
in next to a huge potted palm she'd picked up for the parlor at a farm
in Silverhill. "And please don't tell Rosemary what we ate for dinner."

Magdalene laughed, imagining what Rosemary would say
about the lady of the house dining on peanuts and fizzy drinks, then
waited with one hand on the seat and the other on the wheel. As

soon as Douglas slid onto the leather bench next to her, he ran his hand over hers, interlocking their fingers in a brief, squeezing hold that was over much too soon. But Magdalene never put on her gloves or started the automobile until she'd felt Douglas's comforting hand in hers, reassurance that whatever happened, he was beside her.

The air off the dirt roads swirled behind them as Magdalene pushed the automobile to twenty miles per hour on the straightaways, slowing for turns and oncoming traffic—usually horse driven wagons—like Douglas had taught her to do. Those moments with the hum of the motor and the wind rushing by, her beau beside her, and endless possibilities ahead were the highlight of her week. She would almost give up trying to sneak kisses from Douglas if she could drive every day.

When Magdalene parked the automobile in front of the barn, Douglas hopped out to assist Mrs. Melling to the gate.

"I'm going to freshen up before the captain gets here," she called to Magdalene. "I suggest you do the same. Don't be long."

Magdalene took that as permission to stay with Douglas a few minutes. She stood and removed her gloves, hat, and goggles.

"My lovely raccoon," Douglas teased as he removed his own goggles and displayed the similar clean eyes and face browned with dust.

"It's most handsome, on you, though." Magdalene felt the grit of the road in her smile lines.

He stopped in the stable for clean cloths, filled a bucket at the pump to wash the Great Arrow, and cleaned his face at the spout. He rinsed one of the cloths and brought it along with the others to the car.

Magdalene, still standing by the driver's door, looked at him curiously when he came toward her with the wet rag. "I'm going to wipe your face. Mrs. Melling said you needed to freshen up."

Magdalene laughed and took his free hand in hers. "I don't think she meant with a cleaning rag, but go ahead."

He stood close, head bent in concentration. He swiped across the middle of her forehead first and then made little circles around the sides.

"Are you polishing me?" Magdalene giggled, the rough cloth tickling her skin.

"Hold still, Maggie." He folded the rag to a clean side and went for her nose. When she flinched under the touch, Douglas placed his other hand on her waist, reaching around to the small of her back and nudging her closer to hold her motionless. He washed around her nose and then her right cheek. "There's my girl."

His possessive touch and tender words stirred Magdalene's insides. He leaned in to kiss her clean cheek but she turned at the last moment so he made contact with her lips. Startled, he pulled back and looked around the yard for prying eyes. Seeing no one, he kissed her on the mouth with purpose.

"I think you missed a spot," Magdalene said. He came at her, eyes shut, but she playfully shoved him away. "No! My face, you goose! You only got one cheek and missed my chin completely."

He laughed and tugged on her braid, which had fallen over her shoulder. "Can't blame me for trying."

Douglas wiped at the other spots on her face and then helped her out of the duster. When he folded it over her arm, his touch lingered on the sleeve of her white blouse. "You did great today, Maggie. I hope to see you later, but if not, please stay away from the wharf rats."

She smiled suggestively and wiggled her shoulders. "I can't stop them from looking."

His sturdy hands rested on her hips for a moment and he kissed the top of her head. "They can look and be jealous all they want, so long as they don't call out to you like those fishermen on Zundel's Wharf today."

"After that scolding Mrs. Melling gave them, I doubt they'll do that again."

Douglas smiled at the memory. "The lady looks out for you as much as I do. I suppose I have to share you with her while you're working, but I'm glad you're mine."

"I best get inside now." Magdalene stepped away.

"Wait." Douglas took her hat and driving accessories from the seat. He passed them to her before she dashed across the yard.

As much as Magdalene enjoyed Douglas's attention when he washed her face, she had to properly clean herself in the bathroom. She descended the front stairs the same time Leroy answered the door. The butler stepped aside to let the captain in, and Magdalene met him at the bottom of the stairs.

"Welcome, Captain Walker."

The captain offered his arm. "Shall we go together?"

Magdalene accepted his chivalry and they entered the parlor arm-in-arm.

"I was worried you would not be presentable in time, Magdalene." Mrs. Melling looked her over. "But I wish you had taken more care with your hair. Even in that ghastly braid you insist on putting it in, it still gathers dust in the driver's seat. You should go out to the back porch and brush it so it does not dirty your room."

"Right now?" she asked.

"No, in a minute. Captain Walker has already seen your scraggly appearance, so there is no rush."

Captain Walker delivered the money pouch and an envelope to Mrs. Melling from his satchel before sitting in the chair across from her. She tucked the small bag between herself and the arm of the chair before opening the letter.

Rosemary served tea to the captain first, then Magdalene because Mrs. Melling was studying the letter. From the looks of it, she read it no less than three times before looking up. She set the paper in her lap and motioned Rosemary over for her cup.

After the cook left, she declared the news. "George will be here next weekend to oversee Eliza's homecoming. Is it not wonderful?"

Magdalene's stomach rose to her throat. She could think of plenty of words to describe the situation other than "wonderful." She made no remark, so the captain filled the void.

"That will be good for you, Mrs. Melling. He must plan on coming on the ferry because he made no mention of it to me."

"The mausoleum will be completed by the middle of next week. They're setting the roof as we speak. Would you care to see it?" Mrs. Melling asked.

"It would be a privilege, thank you."

"Magdalene, you may take my things to my sitting room and then see to your hair."

Magdalene tromped up the stairs. She read the spiteful letter and laid it and the pouch in Mrs. Melling's armchair before collecting the brush from her bedroom. Blinded by the dread Mr. Melling's impending visit created, she rushed down the back stairs and into the kitchen full of deckhands with boxes of groceries and household supplies.

Leroy and Zora were unpacking things at the table and Rosemary looked up from the list she was checking things off from. "You go on through, sugar. Ain't no time to talk."

A deckhand held the screen open for Magdalene and she stepped onto the porch with a sigh, only to be met by two more eager faces.

"Come to sit a spell with us?" One raised a cap from his head and leered at her, setting her nervous stomach to churning.

Though Mrs. Melling had told her to use the back porch, she was sure the lady didn't think through the afternoon's visitors and Magdalene wasn't in the state of mind to play coy with flirting men. "No, just passing through, thank you."

She rushed across the lawn before either man could think to open the gate for her, and flew to Douglas, buffing the automobile. His vest was removed and shirt untucked.

"You look a mite green, Maggie. What's wrong?" His Scottish brogue was thick, showing his concern. He dropped his cloth and reached to her.

She thrust her brush at him and then doubled over the bucket of dirty water, vomiting. With her stomach empty, she sat back in the dirt and sobbed into her hands. Douglas rushed for a cup and a fresh cloth, which he filled and dampened at the pump. Kneeling beside her, he delicately lifted her chin and wiped her face for the second time that afternoon.

"Here, catch your breath and then take a sip to rinse your mouth." He held the small tin cup before her with one hand and gently rubbed her back with the other. "Don't worry about talking until your head's set to rights."

Tears fell for a minute more, in which time Douglas momentarily set aside the cup in favor of retrieving a handkerchief from his pocket to pass to her. "Here's another for your collection."

Magdalene's mouth turned up at the corner and she was able to calm her breathing as she dried her face. After rinsing her mouth three times, Douglas helped her to the stable and pulled the saddle stool to the shady space just beyond the doorway—far enough in that someone would have to look closely to see, but in plain sight to avoid being accused of hiding. She sat side-saddle on the curved stool and he kissed her forehead.

"Now, tell me what's wrong."

"Where's my brush?" A panicked look crossed over her face. "Mrs. Melling sent me here to shake out my hair from the day's drive. Please, my brush!"

Douglas retrieved it from the Great Arrow's running board and brought it directly to Magdalene. She calmed some, and turned the wood handle over in her hands while she thought.

"Was it one of Mrs. Melling's letters that upset you?" Douglas tried to get to the root of the trouble. "I saw her head for the tomb with Captain Walker."

"Yes." Magdalene gave a trembling sigh. "She wrote last week to inform Mr. Melling the mausoleum would be complete before the end of the month and she was unsure how to proceed with the logistics of having Eliza's coffin moved. She told me after she'd sent the letter. If she'd told me before, I would have set Claudio or the captain or Leroy up with the task. As it stands, his condescending letter informed her she was to remember how weak and stupid she is and that she needs a man like him to keep her and take care of everything."

"Surely it couldn't have said all that."

"His words are so biting, it might as well have." With the brush in her lap, she pulled her braid to the front and untied the sky blue ribbon from the bottom. She stuffed it into her pocket, and then undid the braid, one strand at a time.

Her hands visibly quaked and Douglas took them into his own. "What else is it?" Inches from her face, his blue gaze searched her brown eyes for clues. She clenched his hands so tightly the pain registered on his countenance.

"We've all been happy but she had to ruin everything. He's coming next Friday!" Magdalene fell against his chest and sobbed.

Douglas wrapped his arms around her, hugging her close. "'Tis his house. We can't keep him out, but we'll do all that we can to fortify it against him."

Thirty-Six

Next Friday afternoon, an uncomfortable silence fell over the parlor. Mrs. Melling, adorned in a lacy green tea gown, smiled in her fireside chair, but Claudio and Magdalene both wore frowns on the settee. All week, Magdalene had pleaded to Mrs. Melling to stop her husband from coming, but her begging fell on deaf ears. The lady of the house was convinced only her husband could handle such a pressing matter. She did consent to allow Claudio to stay the weekend, though the deacon himself proved harder to persuade. Looking at him seated stiffly beside her, she felt sorry she had placed him in the situation, especially when Leroy brought him to the small guest room adjacent to Magdalene's chamber earlier.

"This is not proper!" he had exclaimed.

When he brought his concerns to Mrs. Melling, she dismissed his claims as unreasonable because she trusted both him and Magdalene and there was no alternative because Alexander's room was shut for the season and she would not place him in the attic room with the bohemian display unsuitable for a man of the cloth.

Captain Walker had come and gone with his weekly delivery. The fact that there wasn't a money pouch proved the nightmare was real. A short note instructing Douglas to pick up Mr. Melling from the Montrose dock was all the captain brought to Mrs. Melling.

Magdalene prayed for Douglas's safety and level-headedness from the moment he drove away. When the sounds of the automobile came up the lane, she ran to the window to check. Mr. Melling drove, Douglas at his side with goggles atop his plaid flat cap. It was difficult to read the chauffeur's face from the distance since he hadn't had his weekly shave in five days, but his arms were crossed and he wasn't smiling.

Magdalene returned to the settee, fingering the cream ruffles on the skirt of her new tea gown.

"Is Douglas all right?" Claudio whispered.

"He didn't look too happy about giving up the wheel."

"That will be the least of our troubles, *signorina*." The deacon's voice was grim.

Moments later, the front door swung open. A sharp intake of breath in the front hall signaled Mr. Melling stepping into the house.

"Ruth, dear, I'm home," he said, not sounding as chipper as he could have.

Leroy went by with his luggage as Mr. Melling entered the parlor. His eyes swept the room but settled on his wife by the fire.

"Ruth!" He crossed the room, took her hands in his, and kissed her cheek. "You're looking splendid. Your health must be much improved. I'm happy to see you're being well taken care of in my absence."

He turned, stared at the two on the settee, and grunted slightly as he sat in his chair. "Miss Jones, you look well. And it's nice to have Claudio over for supper."

"Claudio is staying the weekend," Mrs. Melling informed her husband. "It has been so long since we have had a proper guest, we thought it would be nice to have more time to visit this weekend, especially if we are able to bring Eliza home within the next two days."

"Oh, I'm sure." Mr. Melling's icy glare turned Magdalene cold all over.

In the hour before supper, Mr. Melling was introduced to Zora, whom he didn't seem to have an opinion on, and then excused himself to see to the salaries in his den. Minutes later, he called for Zora, and then Leroy. When he called Magdalene's name, Claudio went in her stead.

The conversations over supper were mostly the husband and wife, speaking across the others from the head and foot of the table. Often, Mrs. Melling would draw Claudio into a discussion, but Magdalene was ignored. After supper, the four gathered in the parlor. Without asking for their preference, Mr. Melling poured wine for everyone, which seemed to please Mrs. Melling. After half an hour of watching Mrs. Melling fawn over her husband, Magdalene asked to be excused for the night.

"Of course," Mrs. Melling said. "We'll have a full day tomorrow, I'm sure."

Magdalene opened the window as soon as she got to her room.

Douglas sat in the rocking chair on the front stoop of the carriage house, but he ran to her, standing under the window. "Is everything okay in there?"

"Miserable, but nothing's happened so far."

"Leave the window open, like we discussed. You know where I'll be."

Magdalene wished he could be in the house with her—sitting guard outside her door. Instead, he'd be sleeping in the wagon like he did that night nearly two months before. "It means more than anything to know you're there." She blew a kiss to him and smiled as he tried to catch it before it fell.

She lowered the window halfway and pulled the sheer curtains together, leaving the heavy drapes open. After completing her ablutions in the locked bathroom, she returned to her room in a new nightgown and robe ensemble. Not wanting to go to bed, she sat at her desk and retrieved the now familiar drawings she'd saved from Eliza's sketchbook. She wasn't fool enough to tote them around in her own book. She left them in her desk, under her stationery set, and pulled them out to study before trying to use the techniques in her own sketches. She had copied the sketch of the attic room—minus Claudio—several times in her own book with increased skill, but the proper contours of the faces in the one of Claudio and Eliza still eluded her. Most of her attempts landed in her own fireplace. Tonight, she didn't draw, only stared at the curves of the handsome face, the fringe of lashes on his resting eyes.

A knock at the door roused her. She tucked the picture under her sketchbook and crossed the room as she tightened the sash on her robe.

"Who is it?" she called.

"It is I, *signorina.*"

Having just studied his face, Magdalene felt eager to see the real person and hastily opened the door.

"You do not look yourself. Are you well?"

She stared at his mouth, the way his lips followed the set line of his jaw when he was concerned. "Yes, quite well."

"They have all gone to their rooms. I will bless your door and put exorcized oil on the knob to deter its use from outside sources."

He paused, staring at Magdalene in return. "Do I have food within my teeth, *signorina*? Wine on my chin?"

She laughed. "No, Claudio, you are unblemished. It's just…" She moved quickly to avoid a reprimand and ran her hand along his jaw. "You have such exquisite lines."

He snatched her wrist and stared at her, a blaze of resentment in his eyes. "What manner of mischief do you play at?"

"Nothing, Claudio." Her whisper held more than a little fear.

"Lies!" He backed her into the room and shut the door behind them. "I demand you tell me at once."

Magdalene retreated toward her desk. "I mean no harm, Claudio. Don't be angry with me."

"There is foul play, whether you mean it or not. Those are the words Eliza would tell me as she made her pictures. 'Your lines are exquisite, *amore mio*. They beg to be drawn.'" He stood before Magdalene and fingered the collar of her robe. "Do you wish to draw me, *signorina*?"

"Yes," she whispered. "I want to try to capture how Eliza managed the proper shading to get the contours perfect. I've been studying—"

"How can you study what no longer exists?"

The panic manifested as wide eyes and a frown, allowing him to read the answers.

"What did you keep? Where is it?" The anxiety spewed from his mouth and grasped for the truth.

She backed to her desk, trying to get out of his way. He looked past her, saw the book on her desk, and grabbed it. Only after he had her sketchbook in his hand did he see what it had covered. Dropping the book, he pushed Magdalene aside and slumped into the desk chair, staring at Eliza's drawing.

Hurried steps thundered up the back stairs and then the bedroom door flew open. The anger in Douglas's eyes cooled slightly when he saw Claudio at the desk. "I heard voices and saw two silhouettes against the window. I feared Mr. Melling had come." He quietly shut the door and looked between the two, settling on Claudio. "But by what means are you in her room with her dressed for bed?"

Claudio stood with the picture. "I came to set protections about her door before retiring. She came to the door in her nightclothes with longing in her eyes for my 'exquisite lines.'"

"But it's not like that!" Magdalene looked to Douglas, fear in her eyes. "He makes it sound wrong when I merely—"

"You have been harboring this picture, but *I* make it sound wrong? You have betrayed me most severely, Magdalene. You know I never wanted to stay the night in this house, yet you pushed and pushed for me to do so, pleading with *signora* to entreat me to stay until I felt to decline would be most grievous to her. It has all been part of a trap for me."

"No!" As soon as she said the word, doubt crept into her mind. Did she fully understand what danger she placed Claudio in when she begged for him to stay the weekend? Did she do it on purpose, in an attempt to pain him or to trap him unto herself?

"Maybe I was selfish to ask you to come, and for that I'm sorry. My fear of Mr. Melling surpassed my judgment."

"But why do you have a picture from the sketchbook?" Douglas stood before her, a pained expression on his face. "You told us you destroyed the rest of the drawings the afternoon we found it."

"I did!" Hysteria edged into her voice. "I burned them all!"

Claudio gave a bitter laugh. "Even I without mastery of the English language know that is a lie."

Magdalene turned to Claudio. "I burned them all, except the two I kept."

He shook her by the shoulders. "Two! Are you mad? These works possess the sin they were wrought in. Where is the other?"

"Come, Claudio." Douglas came up between the two and put a hand on his arm. "Give her space. She's scared."

"You should be scared! You have invited evil into this house after we worked so hard to cleanse it. Blood was spilled to protect you from the same fate as Eliza, yet you mock our efforts by your dishonest actions." The deacon released her shoulders with a shove, but Douglas steadied her.

"I'm sorry, Claudio. I couldn't make myself destroy all of the art before I had a chance to learn from her masterpieces. I didn't think it wrong."

Claudio wrinkled the drawing in his fist. "Did you walk out with them proudly in your hand or did you slink out with them hidden?"

Both of them stared at her, a mixture of disappointment, anger, and betrayal burned among the three. It felt like one against the world at that moment, but Magdalene had to see the picture she'd poured over once more. She leapt for Claudio's hand, tearing the picture from him, and spun toward the alcove with her treasure. Huddled in the corner beside the bed, she fingered the dark lines of the sketch and muttered praise for its gorgeous lines and provocative forms.

"All my things are still in my room," Claudio told Douglas. "I stopped by to let her know what I was going to do. I dare not leave either of us alone with her to collect my supplies, nor do I wish to leave her alone until both the pictures are disposed of. How do you wish to proceed?"

"I'm right here and don't enjoy being discussed as a naughty child that needs a talking to." Magdalene stood, straightening her robe with one hand, the other clutching the drawing. She stepped past the bed to the center of the room, displaying the rosary bracelet on her wrist. "I am myself, flaws and all. You both speak of protecting me, but do you give thought to the situation you've put me in? If Mr. or Mrs. Melling were to find out I had not one, but *two* men in my bedroom this evening, I would be cast out from my employment into a state of retched homelessness."

"You have placed yourself in this position, *signorina*. Do not blame us."

"But you"—she poked Claudio in the chest—"came to my door and found fault with the way I looked at you."

She turned to Douglas. "And you burst in like a madman."

"Aye, out of concern. Under no other circumstance would I enter unannounced or uninvited." He kept his voice low, soothing, and he gently touched her cheek. "All you need to do is throw the drawings into the fire. Then we'll leave."

"Anything to buy my peace and keep my job." She marched past them and stopped before the low burning fire. She looked from the sketch to Claudio and sighed. "You were her muse and she reached her artistic pinnacle. Do you realize what you had together?"

Claudio crossed the space and raised his hand to slap Magdalene, but Douglas grabbed his arm midair. They scuffled a moment, until the deacon regained some composure and stepped back.

Douglas came to Magdalene's side. "Don't you see, Maggie? To Claudio it's not art, but a painful reminder of his sins. He sees you stabbing him with it like a huge thorn. It's not right to torment him. Let it go."

With tears in her eyes, she wadded the paper and tossed it to the center of the logs. The fire blazed red and yellow and swallowed the paper in a curling, shrinking mass. She turned to Claudio. "You should have run away with her. You had perfection and—"

"I killed her!" Claudio collapsed on the floor, his black cassock fanned around him. "We had planned to run away that night. I had the train tickets in my pocket but the Lord would rather take her home than send her into a life of shame with a failed priest. I am certain it was punishment."

"Our God is one of mercy, not punishment." Magdalene kneeled beside him. "Just as surely as I know you can forgive me, God forgives you."

"But why else should her horse rear so wildly that an experienced rider like herself could not control her? And why would it happen close enough for me to witness but do nothing to stop it?" His eyes showcased the anguish in his soul.

Magdalene wrapped her arms around him, leaning her head against his shoulder. "I don't know and the answers may long be hidden."

Douglas, looking down at the two, shifted his feet as if he were uncomfortable with the scene of his beloved in her night clothes comforting another man. He cleared his throat but they made no effort to move.

"Flora was a sturdy, gentle horse and trusted Eliza, even during night rides." Claudio went on. "We met there often and there was no reason for that night to be different other than we were going to leave."

Magdalene rubbed the deacon's shoulder. "Where did you meet?"

"Jackson's Oak. I was waiting in the surrounding tree line when she rode in. Before I could emerge, Flora reared up and threw her. Eliza's head hit one of the roots. I heard it from where I stood. I heard it for weeks afterward every time I lay down to sleep. I hear it now."

Magdalene, overcome with the desire to comfort all his capacities, touched his face and then ran her fingers through his short hair. "What can I do to quiet the sound?" Her voice was breathy and her lips parted into a seductive smile.

"Maggie!" Douglas yanked her from the deacon's side and held her at arm's length. "Come to your senses! It doesn't matter that you wear the cross, you're swayed."

Seeing the concern on his face, Magdalene's own countenance softened, causing Douglas to relax his hold on her. The passion at odds within her took the opportunity to fling herself into his arms, her hands roaming up to his face, where she guided her lips to meet his. Douglas resisted at first, then she felt his body relax as he returned her affection.

"*Amico! Signorina!*" Claudio took them each by an arm. "We must destroy the second picture!"

They ignored him until they needed to take a breath. Douglas looked at him first. "Sorry, Claudio. Now I understand why you didn't want to leave either of us alone with her."

Magdalene shrugged her shoulder with a lissome movement that slipped the collar of her robe loose. Claudio, back to his full faculties, brought his own rosary forth and touched it to her forehead before she could react. "*Ave Maria, piena di grazia…*"

Her eyes went wide before she grew weak. Douglas caught her as she fainted.

***

Magdalene awoke with a jerk, her arms reaching out from under the blankets into the dim room. The fire crackled within the hearth, but the gaslights were off. Remembering the passionate kiss she shared with Douglas before Claudio broke them apart, she sat upright. The blanket fell away from her, revealing her nightgown. Her robe was on the dressing table stool, and in front of the fireplace Claudio dozed in the armchair and Douglas sat leaning forward on her desk chair, seemingly lost in thought.

"Douglas," she whispered.

Magdalene held her hands out to him and he gathered them in his own, kissing her cheek.

"What time is it?" she asked, keeping her voice as low as possible.

"Just after one. Claudio fell asleep last hour. Don't worry, all's been quiet in the house. The Mellings don't know we're here."

"But why are you?"

"Claudio wouldn't leave until we destroyed the other picture, which we found in the bottom of your desk. And then he didn't want to leave until he spoke with you after you fainted. He wants to judge your spirit, I'm sure." He sat on the edge of her bed, eyes wandering as he leaned closer to whisper. "You look fine. Clear eyes, and everything."

"Clear eyes?" She raised an eyebrow like he often did. "Is that the best you can say to a woman when you've put her to bed?"

"I really don't know." She loved the way he stammered and blushed. "As Claudio is my witness, we were respectful. I've never been in this situation before. I wish you'd stop fainting on us. What would you have me say?"

"Try me." She reached for his face—her favorite look and feel with his five-going-on-six-days' worth of maturing beard, and ran her hand down his neck.

"Maggie, you're even more glorious by firelight." He kissed her gently on the lips. "Never in my dreams did I ever think I'd see you to bed—to be here with you—before we made any vows. I'm not sure I can control myself." His next kiss urged her to reciprocate.

There is no want, only need.

Magdalene coaxed his hands around her body as she caressed his shoulders and back. Then she lay down on her pillows, bringing him with her. Their necking led to craving for more.

"My Maggie…" Douglas shifted so he could tug the blanket down, but Claudio pulled him off the bed and cuffed him in the face.

"Do not turn this into a den of sin!" Claudio pushed Douglas toward the opposite side of the room before turning to Magdalene, his crucifix in hand. "And you, *signorina*. Tell me, are you alone?"

"No, my handsome deacon." She sat up, her head cocked to the side. "I'm kept company by two men, at least one of whom tried to ravish me."

"Maggie, it wasn't like that," Douglas protested from his spot before the fire, a hand covering one eye.

"The *posseduta* jests, *amico*. And now you need not feel guilty for the bloody nose you gave me last time. Your eye will be as black as my hair by midday." Claudio inspected her wrists. "Where is the rosary I gave you?"

"It was gone when I woke. You're the ones who disrobed me, what all did you take from me?"

"*Dio ci aiuti!*" Claudio raised his hands in defeat. "It is bad enough normally, but God help us when her humor is perverted by the devil."

"Do you think it humorous to defile an unconscious woman?"

"No, *signorina*, and that is precisely my point. You are the one joking about it, not us."

"You're no fun tonight, Deacon."

"Because I am in no mood for this." He turned to Douglas, still nursing his eye in the armchair. "I think it best I bless her, hope she passes back out, and then seal the door with the Rites until sunrise. Then in the morning we can take her outside and pray for her deliverance."

Douglas agreed, so Claudio pressed his rosary to her and prayed over her in Italian until she fell back on her pillows, dazed. Then he climbed upon the bed to retrieve the crucifix from the wall above her headboard. He nestled it into her arms and covered her gently with the bedspread as her eyelids fluttered closed.

Thirty-Seven

Magdalene, Claudio, and Douglas

gathered at the table on the back porch. They had completed the prayers and blessings before half-past eight and were enjoying tea and coffee, grateful that Magdalene only suffered from oppression rather than a full possession. When Mr. Melling stepped outside, the three quieted.

Only Claudio was polite enough to greet him. "Good morning, *Signor* Melling."

He leered at all of them, his eyes lingering on Magdalene. "Yes, so it is. Miss Jones, fix me a cup of coffee and bring it to me in my den. And I mean for her to do it," he added, gazing upon the deacon. Then he turned to Douglas, sitting across the picnic table from Magdalene, his eye swollen and purple. "I don't approve of my driver looking like he participates in pub brawls, or taking breaks with *my* house girl."

Douglas stood. "Yes, sir."

Mr. Melling watched while Douglas went across the yard, glancing at Magdalene from time to time in an apparent attempt at reading her feelings for the man. But the three friends had already decided not to let Mr. Melling know of their deep ties of friendship— or in the case of Magdalene and Douglas, their developing romance. Magdalene stayed stoic, never once mooning after Douglas's retreating form nor reminiscing of their encounter in the early morning hour. Without comment, she gathered both hers and Douglas's dishes. Claudio took his and held the door open for her and then Mr. Melling. When he had disappeared into his den, Magdalene sighed.

"Monday can't come soon enough." As she placed a clean saucer and cup onto the silver tray, a shiver ran down her spine. "Remember that teacup that flew across the room at Alexander?"

Claudio looked up from rinsing dishes at the sink. "Of course."

"I thought it was Eliza, trying to tell him she loved you. But if everything that happens around here is related to demons, does that make Eliza one?"

"That would be blasphemy. Demons never had a body, that's why they seek to control ours. They know our thoughts, fears, and weaknesses and play upon them to trick us. That's all it was, a diabolic trick to make us think she was haunting us." He wiped his hands and came to Magdalene, blessing her with the sign of the cross. "Do not be afraid of what you cannot see, for there are angels standing with us, more than the devils that stand against us."

"So angels will attend while I serve Mr. Melling his coffee?" Magdalene poured the steaming liquid into the cup.

"Of course, and the procession shall be led by me."

He walked ahead of her, crossed the hall, and knocked on the door for her.

"Come in!" Mr. Melling boomed.

Claudio opened the door and waved Magdalene in. Mr. Melling sat on his sofa, facing the hideous display case of birds before the closed window, his back to the door.

"Shut the door, and bring me my coffee."

Claudio nodded to her, closed the door, and stood against the wall between it and the desk.

Magdalene hesitated, scared to get any closer to Mr. Melling though Claudio stood as protector. Realizing Mr. Melling might turn around if she took too long, she hurried forward, nearly tripping on the edge of the oriental runner.

"Careful, girl. You might have the lines of a woman with grace, but your actions speak otherwise. Lydia, on the other hand, is all grace with the lines of a country girl. But it works for her. I'd like to see if what you have is equally effective."

Not wanting to accidentally touch him, Magdalene held the tray out for him to take his own cup. "Well, I haven't broken any dishes or stubbed any toes since I've been here, so that must count for something."

"Sarcasm in a woman is not attractive."

Magdalene wondered how he tolerated Lydia, but figured the maid probably played the meek damsel in his presence. "I'll save you the discomfort and be on my way."

"No need to shy away from me." He replaced his cup on the tray she still held before him. "You and I seem to have a misunderstanding. Sit with me and let's see if we can come to better terms."

"I'm sorry, sir, but I don't think it's proper for us to be in here together. Besides, it's almost time for me to see to your wife."

"I have the feeling Ruth will be sleeping a bit longer than usual today. She might have a headache, too. Have the powder at the ready." He smirked, the droopy corners of his mustache partially obscuring his smile. "Sit with me a minute, Miss Jones."

"I respectfully decline, Mr. Melling." She placed his cup and saucer on the side table and stepped away, clutching the tray to her chest like a shield.

"You don't understand. There is no choice, only commands that you must obey in my house."

"I'll follow nothing contrary to what is right." She turned to go. Out of her peripheral vision, she saw him reach for her backside. Swinging the tray as a weapon, she brought it toward him to strike, but he dropped his hand at the last second to avoid being struck.

Claudio and Magdalene retreated through the door without a backward glance from him, but they knew his anger was kindled.

Magdalene waited in the sitting room until after ten for Mrs. Melling to stir. When Magdalene entered the bedroom, she was surprised to see a smile on the lady's face because she looked like she didn't feel right and she still lay in bed. An empty wine bottle and two glasses stood before Eliza's final photograph on the side table. Magdalene's stomach churned.

"Bring my tea and headache powder. I want to take my tea before I rise today."

"Of course." She fetched the tray from the sitting room and powder from the medicine cabinet.

"He came to me last night, Magdalene," she said. "Like young lovers, he brought me wine and romance. It felt like I was twenty again, but now I feel even older than forty-five. It was worth it, though. I feel as though he is coming around."

Sickened, Magdalene couldn't pretend happiness for Mrs. Melling's sake, nor could she lie and say her congratulations. She decided to remain mute and hope the lady of the house wouldn't pay enough attention to detect her distaste.

***

Not long after Mrs. Melling, Claudio, and Magdalene came to the parlor, Mr. Melling was off in the automobile to see to the mausoleum business in Montrose. The lady of the house sent Claudio and Magdalene to the site, to make sure the men who did the final touches cleaned the area properly.

The walls of the sepulcher were luminescent in the dappled light of the late spring day. The four gables of the roof towered over them, meeting in the center of the building to support an even taller dome, the cross on top above all save the trees. The arches and columned details made it look more cathedral than Seacliff Cottage itself, save the massive, scrolling M over the door.

Claudio opened the sepulcher door and stepped into the marble crypt, motioning to Magdalene. "Come, see how much cooler it is inside."

She shook her head and stepped back.

"It is not yet a consecrated place, *signorina*. Now is the only time you will have to experience it without disturbing someone's resting place." He reached out a hand to help her up the stairs.

She stepped inside the narrow corridor, appreciating the stained glass window depicting a dove in flight across from her. Then her eyes roamed to the walls that were lined with stone. One slab rested upon a black cloth on the marble floor. Where the stone would go was a gaping shelf nearly the length of the wall, just tall and deep enough for a coffin to be slid into place.

Magdalene shivered in the biting air. "That's enough for me." She jumped off the top step and waited for Claudio as he picked up a few stray pieces of lumber that were in the clearing.

Mr. Campbell, struggling with rheumatism, was smoking his pipe in the rocking chair on his stoop when they returned. He asked that the wood Claudio found be placed beside the stable and welcomed them to stop in to see Douglas.

Douglas had a bucket beside him and a scrubbing brush to wash the walls of Janus's stall. He stopped his work and joined the others in the central part of the stable.

"Your eye looks worse than it did this morning." Magdalene tenderly touched his cheek below the affected area.

"It's the sweat that keeps dripping into it as I work. It stings like the dickens." He moved to put an arm around her, but she shied away from his shirt, wet with the toil of honest labor.

Magdalene placed one steadying hand on his damp chest and carefully kissed him so as to not sully her ruffled shirtwaist. She removed his handkerchief from her pocket, mopped his brow, and placed it in his hand. "Try wearing a cotton cap or bandana to absorb the sweat. I request a fresh one sometime soon."

Douglas smiled but then winced from the strain it placed on his swollen eye. "It'll have to wait until I'm cleaned up. Claudio," he said as he turned to the deacon, "how would you feel about taking Janus for a ride? I don't feel safe taking him when I've only got one good eye."

"*Sí, amico,*" Claudio said.

"I'd love to do that sometime." Magdalene took Douglas's hand. "But not while Mr. Melling is here, of course."

"Alexander's tack wouldn't be right for you."

"What about Eliza's? You said it's all in the loft and I know you've been keeping the leather oiled. May I go look at it all?"

Douglas nodded.

"She had specially made riding clothes with split skirts to allow her to ride as a man." Claudio looked to Magdalene. "Do you only ride sidesaddle?"

Magdalene blushed. "No, I belted on and rolled up the cuffs of my father's trousers to ride."

Douglas pecked her on the cheek with a playful kiss. "I'd like to see that."

"I'm sure you would." She turned to the ladder and climbed the rungs to the loft.

She found the saddle hanging on the wall on left side of the stable, above where the riding horses had their stalls, though Janus was the only one left on that side of the barn. On the floor under the saddle she found a crate draped with an old saddle pad. Magdalene settled herself on the floor next to it and removed the dusty cover.

Below her, Douglas readied Janus for Claudio to ride. She paused after removing the bridle to listen to snatches of conversation from the men, grateful to have both of them in her life. The bits and brushes from the crate were all in good condition but Magdalene wasn't sure if they would survive the summer humidity without proper storage and care.

"Behave yourself, *amico*," Claudio said to Douglas, "or I will punch you in the other eye when I get back."

"I'll hit him myself!" Magdalene called out.

"And wound me with your sarcasm, too." Douglas's strong laugh soared to the loft.

Magdalene giggled to herself as she pulled the final item from the crate, a handsome green and brown saddle pad. She shook it a few times and laid it on her lap to refold it. When she took the farthest corner in her hand and brought it toward her, something snagged on her skirt. Reaching around the other side, she pricked her finger. She stuck her index finger in her mouth to ease the pain and turned the pad around.

On first inspection, she saw nothing. Then, leaning closer, she saw a few tiny spines of a burr poking through one of the quilted squares, four spots down and three squares in from the corner. Running her finger along the stitches marking that patch of the pad, she felt little bumps where usually flat lines would be. She tested the other seams and found them smooth. Magdalene brought the pad to the nearest loft window, open to allow a cross breeze to pass through the stable. In the direct sunlight, she could easily see that the stitches marking the area where the burrs stuck through was sewn with intricate little Xs instead of the standard straight marks of a machine or traditional sewer.

"Where have I seen…" she muttered. Then she gasped. "Douglas!"

She rushed for the ladder. "Douglas!" she shouted again as she slung the saddle pad over her shoulder and stumbled down the ladder so fast he had to catch her five rungs from the bottom because she lost her grip.

"What is it, Maggie?"

She didn't mind the dampness of his shirt as she clung to him, his arms around her. "I know who killed Eliza!"

"What?"

Magdalene freed herself and ran for the door. "I must show this to your uncle!"

Mr. Campbell wasn't on the porch.

"Wait, let me check on him first." Douglas entered the little house and Magdalene watched through the screen door as he placed a loving hand on his uncle's shoulder.

Douglas waved her in, and motioned for her to sit across from his uncle at the table. The last time she'd sat there was with

Claudio when they were burning the sketchbook. Now that the days were warmer, no fire burned in the stove when food or drink wasn't being prepared.

"Mr. Campbell, I've been sorting through Eliza's tack and I made a discovery that could explain why her horse threw her." Magdalene ran her fingers along the edge of the pad.

"I saw nothing wrong with the saddle pad when we got Flora home." He rubbed his hands, massaging the gnarled joints on his fingers.

She turned it quilted side up on the table between them. "I didn't see it at first, but something snagged my skirt and then I pricked my finger on it. See?" She pointed to the offending square. "There are a few burrs sticking out."

Mr. Campbell and Douglas leaned in, Douglas ventured to touch it, then pushed around the stitching, which caused more spines to poke through the brown fabric.

"Well, I'll be." Mr. Campbell whistled. He held the pad up to gauge where it would rest on the horse. "It would have given Flora a prick with each movement on Eliza's part because it's near where her left knee would be. By the time she made it to Jackson's Oak in Daphne, Flora would have had enough with the pain and reared to adjust her rider."

"But who would do such a thing?" Douglas asked.

"See the stitches done up with Xs? I've seen someone sew like that in my time here." Both Douglas and Mr. Campbell looked to her expectantly. "I watched Lydia with my own eyes mend her torn apron like that."

"But why would she?" Douglas asked.

"I'm a fool!" Mr. Campbell cried out. "Flora had scratches on her side. I knew she'd run through the woods, so I thought the wound happened then. I should have inspected her tack properly."

"Don't blame yourself, Uncle Simon. One doesn't expect foul play when it comes to accidents."

"But the maid was hanging around the stables the week of New Year. I remember her remarking how she thought it odd Eliza was staying over here with all the balls and carnival events to see to in the city that time of year. I should have known something was off because the girl had said next to nothing to me in the months since her hire."

"It's not your fault, Uncle." Douglas's hands were on his shoulders again. He looked to Magdalene. "Now that we know, who should we tell?"

"I'm of no use now that they have an automobile. I'll confront Mr. Melling. If he gets upset and fires me, there's little for me to lose."

"But, Uncle Simon—"

"Now, see here, boy. Would you rather your Maggie be placed under his wrath or yourself be dismissed? I'm the logical choice. It's the final act I can do to save the memory of the fine horse he had slaughtered, not to mention young Eliza's life."

With resolute nods, Magdalene and Douglas agreed. They left the saddle pad on the table and stood to return to work. Hand-in-hand, they crossed to the stable, a heavy silence between them. Being distraught when she clamored down from the loft, she didn't notice Claudio's cassock hanging from a peg on the wall until then. She pointed to it.

"He took it off to ride." Douglas went back to collect the wash bucket from beside the stall. "He should be back soon."

"We need to report to Mrs. Melling about the mausoleum site, but he needs to know about the burrs. And Mrs. Melling, too. When shall we—"

Douglas, hands full, stopped before her and kissed her lips. "You should wait until Mr. Melling is told before telling his wife. Claudio, on the other hand, needs to know as soon as possible so he doesn't find out another way."

She walked with him out of the stable the same time Claudio emerged from the path to the beach and Mr. Melling drove up the lane. Claudio rode Janus into the stable, avoiding the speeding car, and dismounted inside. Douglas dumped the dirty water from his bucket in the bushes and hung the pail from a fence post before going in the stable to see to the horse.

Magdalene waited outside the stable door for Claudio, not making eye contact with Mr. Melling. He exited the automobile with a huff and made straight for her.

"Did I not inform you during your first days here that you were not to enter the stable?"

"Blame me, *Signor* Melling." Claudio stepped out, still buttoning his cassock. "I asked her to accompany me while I saw to a quick ride. Now that it is done, I see that it was most selfish to leave her idle while I trotted about on Alex's fine horse."

"And what of my wife? Did you leave her alone to go gallivanting around with Deacon De Fiore?"

"No, sir. She sent us to check the mausoleum site, which we saw to first. Claudio's ride took a scarce ten minutes and we're headed back now." Magdalene took the arm Claudio offered and stepped away from Mr. Melling.

Mr. Melling put a finger to Claudio's shoulder to stop him. "You left my girl out here unchaperoned for ten minutes? While I'm not too keen on her tramping about with you, the company of a deacon is better than none when it comes to young ladies. Ten minutes is more than enough time for mischief when stable boys are concerned." He glared at Douglas, who paused in the doorway, saddle in hand. "Just how did you come by that shiner?"

He shrugged. "I tried my luck with a pretty girl and lost the battle against her chaperone."

Magdalene fought the urge to smile so she wouldn't give anything away. Claudio stayed silent beside her.

"You aren't using my automobile to hit the town at night, are you?"

"No, sir. I have my limits, however humble my position in this life."

Mr. Melling harrumphed. "See that my car shines before I take it out again after dinner. I still have work to attend to."

Thirty-Eight

Midday dinner consisted of Mrs. Melling prattling about Eliza's homecoming while her husband looked like he'd rather be anywhere but there. When the meal concluded, Mrs. Melling excused herself for an afternoon nap so she would be fresh for the later events. Claudio and Magdalene retreated to the shade of the gazebo where she endeavored to tell him of her findings in the stable.

"But why would the maid want to harm her? Did she know we were to leave that night? I know she was not a confidante of Eliza's for she hated Lydia more than her mother does."

"Maybe the hatred was mutual, but whatever the reasoning, it was by her hand that Eliza was thrown from Flora. It's not your fault any more than it was Eliza's. No matter your mistakes, someone had evil intentions."

"Thank you, *signorina*." He took her closest hand and held it as they swung. "But what shall we do for justice? Leave it for God?"

"That depends on Mr. Melling. Mr. Campbell is going to bring it to his attention. Perhaps he will involve the law when he sees the evidence."

"We can only pray."

Magdalene yawned, put her head on Claudio's shoulder, and closed her eyes. Minutes later, Claudio squeezed her hand. Magdalene turned to him.

"*Signor* Melling is in the yard and it sounds like Campbell is talking with him," he whispered.

Unseen through the leafy green of the wisteria vine, Magdalene strained her ears to understand the voices in the stable yard. Just as she was about to speak, Mr. Melling's voice boomed out.

"You were to destroy all that cursed horse's tack! What gives you the right to harbor information?"

His response was too low to hear.

"Too much time has passed and nothing could be proven! Why do you wish to cast suspicion on the maid after all these months?"

Magdalene held her breath though she couldn't hear Mr. Campbell's reply.

"You can't even follow directions, Campbell! You're worthless to me now!"

The car door slammed and the Great Arrow's engine roared to life. Mr. Melling sped down the lane, a cloud of dust swirling in his wake.

***

Magdalene and Claudio were in the parlor, hands linked in prayer, when Mrs. Melling joined them at three o'clock.

After Claudio's "Amen," they raised their heads.

"It is good to see you both attending to your spiritual needs." Mrs. Melling took her seat by the unlit hearth.

"We're trying to protect ourselves." Magdalene shifted on the settee. "The atmosphere is changing for the worse within the house."

"Nonsense, I have felt splendid since George returned."

"You had one of your headaches this morning," Magdalene reminded her.

"That, dear girl, was from drinking too much wine last night. Do not look for trouble where there is none."

Magdalene wanted to explain about the saddle pad, but knew she must allow time for Mr. Melling to tell her first. It wasn't her place to spread information of such disturbing nature when the man of the house hadn't had the opportunity to do so first. Knowing better than to argue with her over her husband's evil ways, Magdalene looked to Claudio to carry the conversation.

As he and Mrs. Melling were discussing the glories of candlelight Mass, Mr. Melling drove up the lane. Magdalene shivered when he entered the room.

"The hearse will be here between four and four thirty," he announced. "I want everyone who lives or works on this property to be in attendance. I'll inform Watts to tell the others."

Claudio looked to Mrs. Melling. "I shall begin my prayers, if that is all right."

Mrs. Melling dismissed him and then went to Magdalene. "Fetch the dress you wore when we dedicated the mausoleum site from the attic."

"But, Mrs. Melling, isn't that displaying too much skin before supper?"

"My dear, the sleeves are elbow length and the neckline only displays the base of the throat. Just wait until you have a proper evening gown, Magdalene. Your life will change in an instant."

She saw Mrs. Melling to her sitting room, and then continued down the hall, her heart growing heavier with each step as she passed the portrait of Eliza, then beyond Alexander's closed room to the door leading to the attic.

The stairwell was hot and stuffy, and more so in the top floor of the house. Magdalene left the doors ajar and entered the room that had been one of her artistic obsessions the past two months. Claudio may have destroyed the original, but she had several copies of it she'd drawn with her own hand.

Shaking the image from her mind, she quickly crossed to the wardrobe, willing herself not to stop and stare at the entrancing room. With the cream and black gown in hand, she retreated to the stairs, shutting the attic door behind her. The open door at the foot of the stairs summoned her to freedom. She rushed down the steps and straight into Mr. Melling.

Gripping her upper arm, he pushed her back into the stairwell, closed the door behind them, and turned off the gaslights. "Now it's time to have that little chat, Miss Jones."

Magdalene felt his hot breath on her cheek, spreading a rash on her skin with his vile intentions. Grateful the borrowed dress pressed between them added an extra layer of protection from his repulsive body, she shrunk further behind it. "On your orders, I'm to be in my finery and ready within the hour. There isn't time."

He ran a finger across her lips. "I can help you out of your dress."

She tried to squirm away, but the heel of her boot struck the bottom step and she fell back onto the stairs, Eliza's dress on top of her.

"Yes, sit back and relax." His felt his way up the gown. She winced with each touch though it was just a slight impression through the coverings.

"No!" She kicked, striking his shin, and thrashed her arms, which struck him haphazardly on the face.

"Curse you, wench!" He used his hands to defend his face from her flailing arms but he fell upon her in a most distressing way.

"Get off me!" she shouted before he clamped a hand over her mouth and thrust his knee into her thigh to stop her from kicking. Her body quaked in panic.

"Accept that I've won you." His voice blended into that of Alexander's the night he towered over Magdalene on her bed. The only relief she felt was that she could not see the cold eyes of Mr. Melling in the darkness. He tore Eliza's gown from her lap and his hands groped up her legs.

The stairwell door pulled open with a burst of fresh air and light.

"Have you no shame, *signor*, that you must accost young women in the dark?" Claudio, commanding a strong spiritual presence with his white surplice over his cassock, pulled Mr. Melling by the collar like he was vermin in need of tossing out. "You are the most abhorrent man I have ever had the misfortune to know! You learn that your mistress played a role in murdering your daughter, yet you spend your free minutes trying to defile one of the only virtuous people remaining in this house."

Mr. Melling broke his fall against the far wall. He immediately turned on Claudio, arms raised to strike. The deacon faced him as he pulled the aspergillum from his pocket and flicked holy water at Mr. Melling's face. He went down to his knees, screaming in agony and covering his eyes.

Claudio helped Magdalene off the stairs and shook out her borrowed dress. He escorted her around the heaping form of Mr. Melling to the bathroom and told her to lock herself in.

Magdalene undressed and washed, hoping to remove the feeling of Mr. Melling's unwanted advances. A knock came at the door, causing her to jump and clutch her towel.

"*Signorina*, he has withdrawn to his room. I will stay here until you are ready." The deacon's languid voice eased her fears that crept around the edges of her stomach.

She placed her hand on the closed door and leaned her forehead against it. "Thank you, Claudio."

Dressing now with purpose, she tightened her corset and pulled the gown over her head. The taffeta and silk were smooth against her skin and the ruffles brought more volume to her bosom.

She'd forgotten how she enjoyed the gown the few hours she'd last worn it. Smiling to herself in the full-length mirror, she adjusted her puffed sleeves and then pulled apart her messed pompadour hair. Having no brush in the bathroom, she raked her fingers through the main snarls and cascaded her hair around her shoulders before opening the door.

Claudio leaned against the opposite wall, head bowed and his hands clasped around a Saint Benedict's crucifix in prayer. She tiptoed to him and kissed his cheek. Immediately, his eyes blinked and his mouth opened with a look of astonishment.

Magdalene battled the urge to fall upon his lips. Knowing she was tainted from her encounter with Mr. Melling, she did not wish to bring harm to her friend, though blithe enough to want to enjoy the moment. She fingered her way across his chest and bit her lip provocatively.

"Lust not after her beauty in thine heart; neither let her take thee…" His words from the Psalms trailed off as she collapsed against him in weakness. He walked her toward her bedroom.

She squirmed with discomfort as he nudged her through the blessed doorway, one hand clinging to his vestment. "Don't leave me."

Claudio stroked her loose hair and then did the sign of the cross over her. "I shall be right here waiting for you. Finish readying yourself. Douglas has never seen you dressed so fine, be sure your hair and countenance match the ensemble."

The door clicked shut, but she hardly noticed. She stood, transfixed at the name Claudio had uttered—Douglas. All passions churned within her and a breeze rustled her flowing dress. Remembering the way she'd lured him to her bed during the night while Claudio dozed by the fire stirred her emotions to one thing— she must have Douglas.

Thirty-Nine

Mrs. Melling stood on the porch,

watching for the hearse carrying Eliza's remains to arrive. Magdalene and Claudio, together on the settee, ignored the red eyes and blistered lids of Mr. Melling across from them. He'd informed his wife he'd gotten shaving cream in his eyes, but the two friends knew better. Claudio fingered the cross hanging over his surplice and Magdalene repeatedly smoothed her skirt over her lap.

"It's coming!" Mrs. Melling called through the open front door. They joined her on the porch. "Claudio, you take the lead. Show the driver where he can bring the carriage to the beginning of the path."

The hearse, a shiny black carriage with two men on the driver's bench, halted in front of the house until the deacon passed. Then it crept behind him to the end of the lane. Mr. Melling offered his arm to his wife and they started for the back gate.

Magdalene followed the couple, anxious to see Douglas's reaction to her rich gown and fanciful hair. If she could have gotten away with it, she would have braided it into a wreath circling her head, but she knew Mrs. Melling would not have stood for such countrified ways on her special day. After a few attempts, Magdalene managed the softest pouf of fashionable Gibson Girl hair she'd ever made. The loose wave framed her face magnificently with the knotted bun pinned up in the back. The whole style reminded her of the reoccurring dream with Alexander in the attic room that she had months back. Her stomach lurched with the thought of being one step closer to seeing it fulfilled.

Around the back of the house, all three members of the Watts family joined the procession. Douglas, freshly shaved and wearing his tartan vest, came up behind them with his uncle on his arm. Magdalene made no effort to make contact, keeping her gaze on the opening doors at the back of the hearse that revealed the white box inside. The driver and his assistant stood on either side of the coffin and pulled it to the edge of the carriage.

The Wattses came to a stop beside her. "Thank the Lord they transferred her to a new coffin," Rosemary said, squeezing Priscilla's hand. "I was afraid they'd bring her in the one from the cemetery with dirt still clinging to it."

Imagining those who had to transfer the five-month-old remains from one coffin to another, Magdalene shuddered and took a step back.

Mr. Melling turned to those assembled. "Deacon De Fiore will lead the procession to the sepulcher. Watts and Douglas, you will need to assist in the transportation. Come now."

Douglas came up behind Magdalene and touched her exposed forearm—sending tingles racing up her skin. "My uncle will escort you." And then, in a whispered breath, "You're flawless."

She couldn't hide the smile that broke across her face like the morning sun after a stormy night, though her heart sank at seeing the rise of new colors around his blackened eye. With Mr. Campbell securely on her arm, she focused on the happenings before her. Leroy in a gray Sunday suit and Douglas in his plaid vest were an odd pair on either side of the rear of the coffin behind the matching black suits of the professionals.

Pausing before the marble tomb, Claudio blessed the space in his native tongue. She could hear the catch in his voice as he neared the end, and her heart ached to comfort him. The hearse men took either end of the coffin and carried it inside, Douglas and Leroy stepping to the opposite side of the doorway from the Mellings.

When all was said and done, the two strangers returned to their hearse and the Watts family hurried ahead to finish the final supper preparations. Claudio, giving Mr. Melling several harsh stares, hovered beside Mrs. Melling as she wiped her eyes by the mausoleum's steps.

Douglas came to Magdalene and his uncle, several paces away from the others. "Thank you," he said to her as he took his uncle's arm from hers, his fingers once again causing electricity to course through her body.

"I hope to see you later," she whispered.

***

After supper, Mr. and Mrs. Melling retired upstairs, he because of the discomfort of his eyes and she with the excuse to nurse her husband. Claudio and Magdalene were given leave to sit in the parlor with the fire, one of the last of the season.

After the Watts family left for their own home, Claudio removed his cassock and sat by the hearth in Mrs. Melling's chair. Magdalene rested on the settee and studied his form. She itched to attempt drawing him but knew better than to do it, for the pain it would cause him would be difficult to forgive—especially after her previous trespasses. So she set her mind on Douglas, her yearning for him swelling as a wind whispered through the room.

Claudio turned to her with a sharp movement. "Did you feel something?"

"No. You look nervous tonight."

"I am worried about what *Signor* Melling might try. If he is willing to accost you in the middle of the afternoon, I fear what he is capable of in the dark of night."

"Sit with me, then." She switched the cross of her legs. "Protect me from the evil."

Claudio jumped out of his seat as though he would run to her, but set to pacing the room instead. "We should not be alone, *signorina*, but I am concerned that bringing Douglas back a second night would be risking too much in the possibility of him getting caught."

"It sounded like Mrs. Melling was going to wrap her husband's eyes. I doubt he'll be roaming around anytime soon."

He stopped before her. "Later is when I fear his mischief, but it's the now I fear our own."

She stood, placing a hand on the shoulder of his white shirt. "Then bring me Douglas. You can claim him as your guest if they find us all in here. Surely entertaining in the parlor is more appropriate than the two of you in my bedroom." She ran her hand down his arm, causing him to quake.

"I should not have removed my vestments. I am too exposed and weak in this state." His eyes searched first her face, then down the length of her body. His laugh was hollow. "Yes, I will get Douglas. We can beat each other senseless to protect you if needed."

With Claudio gone, Magdalene removed her boots, tucking them at the bottom of the stairs. Then she poured herself a dash of

---

brandy, filling the room with the woodsy aroma and stirring her passions with memories of Alexander's hands caressing her. She missed the feelings the touches created—knowing she was needed and adored. Her whole being wanted that now, but with Douglas. She twirled around the room in her stockinged feet when Claudio and Douglas let themselves in the front door.

"There is no music in this house," Magdalene said as she passed them. "Father used to play his fiddle after supper, but here there is nothing. Claudio, do you think we could talk Mrs. Melling into getting a gramophone?"

"We could try. I know they have one at their home in the city." Claudio took his previous seat by the low burning fire and rubbed his temples.

Douglas, handsome in his vest, stepped into her path. "May I have this dance?"

She curtsied, her eyes beguiling him. "Only if it's a ballad and you hold me close."

Douglas kissed her hand and she placed the other on his shoulder. He placed his right hand snug at her waist. They box-stepped around the parlor, carefully avoiding the furniture. After they did several passes, Magdalene pulled him down with her onto the little settee on the far wall.

"Would you like a drink?" she asked.

"I won't turn one down after today. Might take the lingering sting from my eye."

Magdalene kissed his brow before turning to Claudio. "And what of you? You appear to have a headache."

"Yes, some wine might do, thank you, *signorina*." The deacon placed a hand over his closed eyes.

Taking advantage of the privacy, Magdalene shifted toward Douglas and kissed his cheek below his swollen eye. "Was it worth it?"

He took her nearest hand and ran his fingers from her palm to her elbow and back. "Aye, though you teased me terribly after. I'd never hurt you, Maggie."

"I know." She leaned into him for a full kiss that lingered.

He wrapped his arms around her and pulled her until she was nearly in his lap.

"But sometimes," she said between kisses, "I think I'll end up hurting you."

"Then I'd welcome the pain." He trailed kisses around her neck.

A moan escaped Magdalene as he nestled into her, his lips making their way back to her face without the friction of a beard, though she would have enjoyed the extra sensation. *This is true love— the give and take of pleasure.* She convinced herself that it all led up to this moment of lust and she wasn't going to let anything stop her.

"*Signorina*, my wine, please," Claudio, his eyes still closed, called from across the room.

Magdalene, flushed with the heat of the moment, shimmied free from Douglas's arms. He joined her and poured the wine which she brought to the deacon.

"Thank you." Claudio briefly opened his eyes to accept the glass. "You look hot, *signorina*. Keep away from the fire."

"Yes, of course." She slowly made her way across the room, watching for his eyes to close again. Then she dimmed the gaslights. If he asked about them, she'd say it was for his headache.

In the corner by the decanter set, Douglas had her glass at the ready. She downed the red wine in three gulps, not wanting to waste her time drinking when she could be kissing him. But the drink in his tumbler was different, and he was in no hurry to finish it.

"Can you believe they have a twenty-year-old bottle of Scotch whisky from my hometown? I found it in the bottom cabinet, barely touched. I only took a smidgen."

Magdalene sniffed the pale amber drink. "Mm, smells like vanilla."

He took a sip and swished it around his mouth before swallowing. "There's nothing like it," he said.

"Let me taste." Rather than go for his glass, she went for his mouth. With a sigh of contentment, she spoke one word, the hunger dripping from her lips. "More."

He downed the rest of the Scotch and set the tumbler on the side table with a *clink*. His hands were around her, caressing her back through the smooth fabric of her gown. Her ruffled front flattened between them as she returned his embrace threefold, savoring the taste of his mouth, hands grasping at his clothes.

"Maggie, I love you." He kissed below her left ear, causing her to quiver with ecstasy.

Douglas followed her lead as she went toward the upholstered armchair in the dark corner. There wasn't a wall light there and the potted palm from their trip last week hid the chair from the doorway. Magdalene glanced across the room at Claudio. He still gripped his forehead.

Her eyes returned to Douglas and she ran her hands across his vest, pushing him until the back of his legs bumped the chair. "Have a seat."

He sat without question and she curled into his lap, resting her head on his shoulder. She stayed like that, breathing in his scent and relishing his gentle strokes up and down her arm. Then the creeping wind of iniquity returned, rustling the palm fronds and stirring unsatisfied desires.

There came a moan from across the room. "*Dio aiutami. Dio aiutami,*" Claudio murmured. Magdalene, thinking the deacon dreamed, ignored his pleadings.

But Douglas looked concerned, trying to see his friend around Magdalene. To refocus his attention to where it belonged, she trailed kisses from his smooth cheek down to his neck, where she opened the top two buttons on his best shirt. Feeling the rush of his full attention, a groan of pleasure escaped her as his hands trailed over her silky dress from her hips to her knees.

"You torture me, Maggie." He buried his head on her ruffled bosom, her heart pounding under the layers. "Put me out of my misery and marry me that I might take you as I yearn to."

"*Dio aiutami!*" This time the pleading could not be ignored.

"Claudio!" Magdalene took his hand, surprised by the chill on his skin when he sat so near the fire. "Wake up, I think you're dreaming."

"If only it were a dream." He shifted his head back and forth, but did not open his eyes.

"What is it, then? Why are you so cold?" she asked.

"It has me." He clung to her arm and his grip crept up to her shoulders. "And it wants to have you."

Claudio had her inches from his face when Douglas pulled her from his grasp. "Go!" he told her. "Go to the porch!" Then he put both arms under Claudio's armpits and pulled him to his feet, half-walking, half-dragging him to the door as he recited a Hail Mary.

"Thank you, *amico.* I was foolish to tempt the demon by removing my holy garments. If these headaches are what besiege Mrs. Melling, I have more sympathy for her." He leaned against the nearest column. "We should not have brought you in, I should have sealed Magdalene in her room even though it was early. I am sorry I failed you both."

"But you didn't." Douglas encircled Magdalene and pulled her to his chest. "You gave us more time together, and that's everything."

"But I felt the yearnings in the air. I heard the sounds of pleasure though I could not see. Truly, I placed you both in moral danger."

Scared of sharing how far her cravings were willing her to go, Magdalene allowed Douglas to answer. First, he hugged her closer, resting his chin upon her head for a moment, his heart beating beneath her cheek from her nestled position of safety.

"Only if you hadn't called out when you did. Your voice pulled us to safety as well." He loosened his embrace so he could look at Magdalene's face. "While I meant what I said, the passion could be our undoing. I don't want to ever hurt you, Maggie, and I know that you're in danger of losing that which is most precious every moment we spend alone. I think we need to stay apart so we can be together properly in the future."

"No! That would hurt me even more. Our moments together are what bring joy to my days." Her hands snaked into his opened collar and pulled him to her mouth.

Claudio, as if knowing this was his friends' final display of craving, faced the front yard, his rosary in hand. Seeing the deacon turn away, Magdalene released her inhibitions in an attempt to show Douglas how she felt. He indulged her a minute, giving in to the pleasure of the other's touch. In her fervor, she lost all modesty. Her hands worked their way under his shirt, skimming the patch of hair below his navel. He pulled away with a sharp intake of breath.

"We needn't cross a line we can't turn back from."

With a sob in her throat, Magdalene ran into the house before the tears could fall.

Forty

Sunday morning dawned brightly through the open window. Stretching, Magdalene shifted on top of her bedspread. Her face was crusty from tears and the gown rumpled. She moved slowly across the room to the window. Douglas slept in the back of the wagon. Though still upset over him turning her away, she smiled to herself. Magdalene realized she hadn't barred her door with the vanity bench and had to admit her impassioned state was reckless to her well-being. After gathering fresh clothing, she went for the bathroom, tripping over something in her doorway.

She caught herself before falling into the hall and looked down. "Claudio!"

He rubbed his eyes and sat up. "I am sorry, *signorina*. Are you all right?"

"Yes, I just wasn't expecting someone to be on the floor. What are you doing here?"

"After Douglas left, I brought your boots up. I could hear you crying so I did not wish to disturb you. I sat and waited should you need help during the night."

"You mean in case I decided to throw myself at someone again?"

Claudio stood. "No, *posseduta*, I knew you had your fill for the night. Your soul was spent, ripped in two between your longings and your internal compass." He cradled her chin in his palm. "Douglas is honorable—stronger than I ever will be in the matters of denying the natural man. He told me he asked you to marry him."

Magdalene turned her face away from the deacon's touch. "It was in a moment of passion, I won't hold him to it. He must despise me and my wickedness."

"He does not. He told me it is the desire of his heart to grow old with you and asked for my help in clearing the way, both spiritually and by smoothing things with the Mellings if needed." He put his hands on her shoulders. "I vowed my service to the both of you. I mean to see you through to your wedding, to help you both stay unblemished before the Lord."

"You're going to sleep at my door every night? Follow us on our driving lessons?" her voice rose with annoyance.

"Not every night, and not every lesson, but I will be watching for my dearest friends."

"Claudio, the pestering angel."

He shrugged, laughing. "Is there a more noble profession?"

"I can think of plenty."

Magdalene continued to the bathroom to dress. She missed washing her hair the previous night, but didn't have the time for it that morning. Dressed in her blue Sunday ensemble with braided hair, she descended the back stairs half an hour later. In the stable yard, Douglas wiped down the automobile. As she waited for her water to boil, she watched him out the window, enjoying the way he moved, strong and determined. She smiled to herself upon remembering how it felt to be in those arms, feeling the steady beat of his heart and soft lips.

The kettle whistled, causing her to jump. When she turned toward the stove, she walked right into Mr. Melling.

"Enjoying the scenery?" His eyes were healed enough to glower at her.

"It's a beautiful Sabbath morning." Magdalene stepped around him and turned off the stove, praying Claudio would come down. She felt Mr. Melling deliberately moving behind her, closing in on her with each step, so she retrieved the kettle with a hot pad. "May I fix you some coffee?"

"Yes, Miss Jones." He ran a hand down her braid that reached her waist, his hand lingering by the blue ribbon at the end of it. "It's good to see you remember how to be polite."

"I was raised to be polite, but if you don't remove your hand, I'll be forced to empty the contents of this kettle over your head."

His laugh was full of scorn but he stepped to the side, straightening his suit. "It's obvious your time here has only strengthened your stubbornness. I almost wish to stay on so I might tame you."

"And what of your mistress? What would Lydia do without you?" Magdalene knew mentioning her was a mistake the second the words were in the air, but she gathered the cups and continued her work.

"Give me more credit than that, Miss Jones. I'd never have a maid as a mistress." He pulled one of the chairs out from the table and sat, legs sprawled most distressingly. "A maid to help me settle in after a long day, yes. A maid to see me off at the beginning of each work week, yes. A maid to keep things in working order, oh, yes." He made a lewd gesture with his hands and smirked as she turned away. "A maid is a gentleman's prerogative. A mistress denotes mystery, power, and sophistication. I'd never be fool enough to bring my mistress into my home. She is for travel, wowing important guests, and escaping the mundane."

"You, sir, are no gentleman. I've met farmhands more respectable than you." She practically threw his coffee cup onto the table and backed away from him before his lecherous hands could stop her.

He stood, using his height to its best advantage. "Adding a lady's companion would be just what I need to fill my time. Then I would be satisfied wherever I go without wearying poor, old Ruth."

Claudio burst through the swinging door from the hall and came straight for Mr. Melling's throat. "I have heard enough from you!" He pushed the man, larger than him by at least thirty pounds, to the far wall, trapping his neck beneath his forearm. "You are an adulterer and harboring a murderess!"

As Claudio shoved all his weight against him, he used both hands to relieve the pressure from the deacon's arm. Unable to fight back, Mr. Melling's face turned red.

"No wonder your own daughter loathed you. She could not wait to get out from under your wicked thumb and confided in me her plans to run away. She did not want your twisted authority or your money! Eliza was willing to run away with nothing just to escape you!"

"You...lie!" Mr. Melling managed to sputter.

Claudio's eyes were wild with rage. "No, you are the one who deals in lies, not me!"

Scared, lest another murder happen within the family, Magdalene flung open the back door. "Douglas!" She screamed so loud she grew dizzy with the effort.

She gripped the doorframe as he hurdled over the fence and dashed to the backdoor. He took her by both arms. "What is it?"

"Claudio…" She pointed to him and the mulberry-colored Mr. Melling.

He crossed the tile floor and wrapped the deacon in a bear hug. "Claudio, think of your vows. Do not throw away all you've labored for to get back at one with bloody hands. You would lose your life if you take his."

Claudio pressed harder against Mr. Melling, causing him to sputter and gasp.

"Maggie and I won't make it without you. You must offer protection for us, not retaliation for Eliza."

Claudio dropped his arm and stepped back, Douglas moving with him.

Mr. Melling slumped to the floor, gasping for breath and brushing tears from his eyes. "You've sealed you fate. Father Angelo will never ordain you to the priesthood when he hears of this."

"Do you forget that it was Father Angelo who sent word to Father Quinn about your sinful state of affairs in March? Do you really think your words hold more weight than mine with this holy man?" Mr. Melling's purple face paled. "You are to leave on the afternoon ferry back to Mobile and not return until the end of the season. Do you understand?"

Mr. Melling nodded.

"Then collect your coffee and go crawl into your hole. You are not welcome here." Claudio turned his back to him and looked to Magdalene standing by the counter. "Is there any tea for me? I need some chamomile to calm my nerves."

***

Mrs. Melling sent Claudio and Magdalene to Daphne for church by way of the carriage because, for reasons unknown to her, her husband wouldn't allow them to take the automobile, with or without a chauffeur. As Mr. Campbell's hands were too pained to hold the reins, Douglas was their coachman, much to the chagrin of Mr. Melling.

The ride was leisurely compared to the automobile Magdalene was now used to. She passed the time by asking Claudio questions, some silly, some serious.

"Do you really think Douglas and I are good for each other?"

"You are a striking pair." He smiled at her from his seat on the opposite bench.

"Making a handsome couple is one thing, but having a lasting relationship is different."

"You are equals—matched in spiritual gifts, wit, and upbringing."

"But he's Catholic and I'm Methodist. How could that ever work out? Who would ever agree to marry us?"

"When I receive my *sacri ordines*—my holy orders—I shall do it myself."

"But won't you be moved after your training here is finished?"

"Yes, I could be transferred to another parish, but do I not merit you planning your wedding around?"

Magdalene felt her laughter in her belly.

Douglas rapped the roof. "Everything okay in there?" he shouted.

Claudio moved to the edge of his seat and cracked the door open. "All is well, *amico*," he called. "I am merely planning your wedding."

Douglas gave a *whoop* of joy before Claudio closed the door. Magdalene looked at his familiar lines and wanted to run a finger over his smiling lips.

"I could kiss you right now." She leaned forward. "But I'll be good. It's easy to control myself when I'm not in Seacliff."

"I will collect what else I need to cleanse the house after Mass." He switched seats to be next to her and leaned his head on her shoulder. "We were happy these past weeks. *Signora*, you, me, Douglas, Mr. Campbell, and the Watts family. We have led a joyous life since *Signor* Melling left with Lydia. I am sorry he came back, more sorry than for what I did to him this morning. Father Angelo will hear of it from my own mouth. He did not need to threaten to expose me."

"We're coming into town. I don't think resting on my shoulder would be good for your prospects of a getting that holy order."

"I shall miss the comfort of a woman's touch. Here, for that kiss you threatened me with earlier…" He kissed both her cheeks. "Since we have been together all weekend, I have missed greeting you so."

She blushed. "If it weren't for the fact that Father Angelo does the same thing, I'd have to tell Douglas on you."

He moved back to his own bench, his smile fading into a frown. "It is good to be out of the air of Seacliff Cottage. I have not been myself this weekend. I will seek blessings for both of us from Father Angelo before we return."

Leaning across the space between them, she took his hand in hers. "Claudio, if Douglas had not come when he did, would you have killed Mr. Melling?"

His intense brown eyes held her gaze. "*Sí*, I was prepared to."

Forty-One

Claudio blessed everyone and exorcized the home Sunday evening, and again on Monday morning before he left. When he came to visit Wednesday afternoon, the Rite was completed before everyone walked to the beach for a picnic tea. Then once more, on his Saturday visit, after which he collapsed on the swing and refused to be social, much to Magdalene's disappointment.

Since the previous weekend, Douglas refused to sit or walk with Magdalene unless another adult was with them. She begged that he would allow visits when she played in the yard with Priscilla, but he stood firm in his decision. Magdalene relied heavily on the twice-weekly visits from Claudio for her time with her friend as well as her beau. The only added bonus time was Friday afternoons, when Captain Walker brought the weekly delivery. Douglas was sure to be seen about with Magdalene, often walking between her and the deck hands, who took their time with their lemonade in the ever growing heat of the summer afternoons.

Those few pleasures, as well as the outings in the automobile with Mrs. Melling on Tuesdays and Fridays, were what kept Magdalene from being too rash with what she thought she needed. Though she received no more than the firm hand squeeze before starting the engine each time behind the wheel, she sat beside Douglas for hours as well as took dinner with him and Mrs. Melling each of those days. Mrs. Melling was quite amicable about the growing relationship between Magdalene and Douglas. Though she didn't push for a union like she did at first, she watched over them from the backseat like a mother hen and smiled knowingly at their shared glances during meals. Once they returned from their drives, she hurried inside as soon as Douglas helped her out and called over her shoulder for Magdalene to take her time.

Each time in June when Magdalene hovered over Douglas's shoulder as he checked the fluid levels and wiped off any accumulated grime or mud from the vehicle, he gave her clipped responses to her attempted provocations. She usually stomped into the house after being brushed off for a quarter of an hour. Then she'd listen to Mrs. Melling ramble about the latest letter from her cousin, Edith Warrington, about all the fine ladies Alexander had danced with at some fancy party or another in Newport, which got her feeling worse because those ladies at the party had the touch of their dancing partner—even if they were condescending men who would look upon a blacksmith's daughter only if they were possessed.

After their Friday drive on July thirteenth, a sudden thunderstorm rolling in from the gulf caught Magdalene and Douglas unaware. He took her by the hand and dashed into the stable. They were both drenched and chilled from the sudden change in temperature from sultry to cool. Staring at one another, they were unsure what to do with their newfound privacy.

Her hand still in his, Douglas reached his other to wipe the rain from her face. His affectionate touch awoke her displaced passion. Magdalene's free hand went to his chest and she knew from the racing of his heart that he felt it too. Like the swell of electricity accompanying a lightning strike, they both needed to tend their stored appetites.

"Maggie." He breathed her name before covering her lips with his.

Magdalene's hands were all over his wet shirt, feeling each muscle she'd watched him use as he cared for the automobile and horses but was forbidden to touch. She kissed his salty neck. "You still want me?"

His hands went to her hips and he walked her backward until she was pressed between him and the ladder. "That was never the question, and you know it."

She fumbled with the buttons on his shirt. "But I want to hear you say it."

He gripped the ladder behind her and kissed her softly. "Upstairs. I'll show you how much I love you."

Her eyes momentarily widened with the enormity of the moment. Maybe Mr. Melling was right to be concerned—she would be tarnished in the stable, but at that moment she didn't care. After a nibbling kiss, she turned and hurried up the ladder. At the top, she looked around the loft, lit in the storm darkened air by occasional flashes of lightning. Eliza's things were still in the corner, haunting the space with the reminder of her untimely death.

Douglas came up behind her and wrapped his arms around her waist, swaying slightly to a song only he heard. "Wait here," he whispered.

Rummaging through supplies behind her, he came back with a horse blanket that had been folded away for the season. He shook it open, spread it on the slope of a hay pile and took Magdalene's hand. She lay back with a sigh and he dropped to his knees beside her. Douglas's fingertips traced the curve of her cheek, settling on her lips, where she kissed them. Her free hand went into his half-opened shirt and reached around his back to pull him closer. Magdalene could see the battle between his desire to revere her and feed his physical cravings displayed on his countenance.

"I'm yours, Douglas." Her brown eyes shone in a flash from the storm.

He collapsed beside her and pulled her to face him as he caressed from her shoulder all the way to her hand that rested on her hip. He didn't remove his gaze from her eyes. "I want you every day, Maggie."

They indulged in several more kisses—Magdalene's aching to be loved further incited with each touch. She undid another button on his wet shirt. "We might not get another moment like this."

"All for the better." He encircled her waist and kissed her eyelids. "I don't trust myself."

"I trust you, and you said you'd never hurt me." She ran her hand over his short beard and gave him an alluring smile.

Douglas's hands went up her back until he gripped her shoulders from behind and drove their bodies together. Magdalene caught her breath as he rolled so she was on top. She quickly adjusted her skirt and legs so she straddled him, secure in the fact that she would not remove herself until they were closer than they had ever been. Then she felt something hard against her thigh and gasped.

Understanding her fear, he smiled. "Do you still trust me?"

She nodded, biting her lower lip.

He found the edge of her skirt and reached underneath, feeling his way to her left knee. Her face and neck flushed as his hand skimmed between her upper leg and his hip. As if sensing the fear mingled with excitement coursing through her, Douglas sat up enough to kiss her, his hand still in the forbidden zone—where it seemed to Magdalene all of the blood within her body flowed. Light-headed, she stared into his soft, blue eyes.

"I'm nearly there," he assured her.

For the first time with Douglas, shame crept into Magdalene's emotions. Then the memory of Alexander pressing on though she begged him to stop rushed through her mind like wildfire, spreading distrust and fear. The whinny of a horse below startled her more. She scrambled off him and sat trembling on the end of the blanket. Douglas, hand in his pocket, removed a tiny box which he set aside to pull her back to him. She curled in his lap, much like the May night of Eliza's homecoming, when they cuddled behind the palm tree in the parlor. He smoothed the loose hairs that had curled in the rain around her forehead.

"I'm sorry I frightened you. I knew I needed to get the box out of my pocket when I saw that you'd felt it."

"I thought…" She turned away, her face heated.

"Maggie, it is a means to it, but not today." He kissed her cheek and ran his hand over her braid.

She turned halfway back, still not ready to look him in the eye after her foolishness. "What is it?"

"Your birthday present. I don't want to wait until Monday to give it to you because we'll never have the private time on the trip to Pensacola. It needs to be official, even if there's no write-up about our engagement in the social pages." He opened the little wood box like a clam shell and slipped the gold ring with a tiny speck of sparkle in a pronged setting onto her left ring finger. "Magdalene Renee Jones, will you be my wife?"

"Yes." She kissed him. "Yes." They kissed again. "Yes!"

They did not come up for air until the sun peeked through the western window.

Douglas kissed her on the forehead and buttoned his shirt. "The storm's passed. I need to get you back to the house before I lose my job."

"Do you think, since we're engaged now, you can loosen our restrictions a little?" She stood before him and ran her hands over his shoulders. "Let me kiss you from time to time, so when we have a brief window of privacy like we just did, we aren't starved for each other's touch."

"It might be safer that way." His lips lingered on hers. "I'm determined to bring you to our wedding bed undefiled, though it seems futile at times, such is your power over me."

He handed her the ring box as a keepsake and folded the blanket away before they climbed down the ladder. On the main floor of the stable, she paused to share another moment before they journeyed out, relishing his tender touch on her cheek.

They passed the automobile, hand in hand. "I'll have to mop it out soon," he said, referencing the rainwater in the windowless car. "Next time, I'll be sure to put the tarp over it before pulling you into the barn."

"Maybe just spend more time being aware of the weather instead of ignoring me."

"Maggie, I hear and see everything you do when you're out here with me. I feel your breath on my neck when I check the oil. I see the curve of your chest when you lean over the door while I'm wiping the dust off the seats. You bring havoc upon my concentration."

She squeezed his hand. "You never said anything so I figured you weren't interested."

Douglas laughed. "I didn't say or do anything because I didn't trust myself to speak without revealing my heart's secrets or touch you without giving way to the desires that run rampant through me when you're nearby."

"It's good to know I don't have to try so much. Next time, I'll just blink."

Smiling, Magdalene and Douglas went in the front door and walked into the parlor still holding hands.

"There is news, I hope, because I had wonderful news in my letter from Cousin Edith." Mrs. Melling waved the letter they'd collected at the Montrose Post Office on their way home.

"Yes, Mrs. Melling. You'll be pleased to know that Douglas and I are engaged."

Mrs. Melling clapped her hands. "Oh, I knew it the moment I first saw you two together in this very room! Many congratulations. We shall share a bottle of champagne tonight after supper. You and your uncle will come at seven."

"Thank you." Douglas stepped toward the door. "I need to finish my work now. I'll see you both later."

"Go on, Magdalene." Mrs. Melling waved at her. "See him to the door."

When Magdalene returned to the parlor, Mrs. Melling was all smiles. "We shall begin shopping for your trousseau next week. I bet we could find at least one thing in Pensacola." She waved her letter. "And there looks to be something else we will need to shop for."

"What's that?" Magdalene feigned excitement.

"Alexander has taken an interest in Miss Beatrice Kirkpatrick. Edith says he danced exclusively with her at the last ball and he hinted at taking her to a concert the next week."

"How nice for him." Magdalene shifted in the wingback chair.

"And Edith informed me the Kirkpatrick family is often written about in the New York papers. Remind me to ask Captain Walker to bring us some next week. She is supposed to be quite lovely, as is her mother, who has royal relations by marriage of a cousin to an English duke." Mrs. Melling sighed. "It is too early in the season for engagements—oh, not for the likes of you, dear, but in society—so I do not expect news in that regard for another month. But I will keep an eye out for the perfect dress or pattern suitable for a mother of the groom. You shall need something yourself, and you must not buy a thing without me there, Magdalene. Promise me."

"Really, Mrs. Melling, there's no need to fret over my clothes."

"I insist. God took from me my opportunity to be the mother of a bride, but through you, I have a second chance." Tears glistened in the corners of her eyes.

"Of course." Magdalene smiled, a bit of sadness creeping in at the mention of Eliza's passing—her murder that Mrs. Melling, if she knew about, refused to speak of.

"And your twenty-third birthday Monday will be extra glorious, though I wonder about the respectability of taking an engaged couple on an overnight trip."

"Nothing will happen, you can be sure."

"That may be, but people would talk and I cannot abide slanderous gossip. Though gossip about becoming related to a duke through marriage is fine."

"Can you not request his room as far away as possible at the hotel?" Magdalene asked.

"That, my dear, would draw even more attention to the situation and guarantee discussion. Perhaps we should go it alone…"

"I've not yet mastered the art of changing a flat tire, nor do I know how to fix any of the mechanical issues that might go wrong."

Ignoring Mrs. Melling's laughing expression, Magdalene continued. "What if Mr. Campbell came along, then Douglas would have a chaperone as well?"

"We shall figure something out. But you look like you were caught in a storm, and that is no way to greet the captain. And you might as well dress in something presentable for supper and the post-supper toast. Seven o'clock will be here before we know it."

Forty-Two

The birthday trip to Pensacola began with Mrs. Melling buying Magdalene a bathing suit, which she put to use that Monday afternoon. The mohair, two-piece navy sailor set trimmed in white with knitted tights and lace on slippers turned Magdalene into a water sprite. The laughing gulls and excited conversations of the other vacationers were drowned in the noise of the breaking waves where she played. Worried for her safety, Mrs. Melling sent Douglas to the shop to rent a suit so he could watch over her.

When he waded out in his navy suit, Magdalene blushed to see his bare legs well above his knees. They were just as toned as his arms, which were bare beyond his shoulders, the perfect cut to accentuate his physical appeal—the white star on the suit's chest further drawing attention to his broad strength. Her own arms were exposed up to the capped sleeves of the sailor dress, and her skirt cut above her knees, though her legs were covered with dark tights.

"I'm supposed to protect you from the powers of the gulf," Douglas announced when he reached her side. "But who is to protect me from the allure of Maggie?"

"If you so much as touch my arm when I am not in need, Mrs. Melling will have you in a crab boil." Magdalene lay back, floating on the surface while the waves were quiet.

He smiled down at her laid out before him. "But what she can't see won't upset her."

He belly flopped over the next wave, motioning Magdalene another six feet out so they were beyond the breakers in shoulder-deep water. He reached his hand underwater and took hers, fingering her ring, before letting go.

"I'm yours, Maggie, no matter what, but it's good to know you have shapely knees."

Her laughter carried over the water and rolled to shore. "And you, Douglas Campbell, are much to be admired in that suit. I think you left a trail of swooning women on your way to me."

She balanced on one foot, bobbing when the next wave elevated the water. In the calm, she extended her left leg until her slippered foot poked him in the stomach. He seized her ankle and ran his hand up her stocking until he reached her knee. With the next swell of the water, the current pulled them closer. Douglas dropped her leg and returned to holding her hand.

"I noticed several chapels on the way here," he said. "I'm sure we could find a priest or pastor in one who would join us."

Magdalene splashed out of reach. "I've promised Claudio we'd wait for him to have his holy orders, you know that." They drifted further out, causing them to tread water.

"All I know is that it's getting more difficult to stay my desires. Claudio of all people would understand. He's happy for us, no matter what."

"Maybe, but do you really think Mrs. Melling would allow it? It's probably too close to an elopement for her gossip-worried brain."

"There's one way to find out." His arms flowed back and forth in a sweeping motion as he stayed afloat.

Magdalene smiled, considering the possibility of swimming into those fluid arms. "We'll ask, but first, how long can you hold your breath?"

"I've never much paid attention."

"Try it." Magdalene ducked under and kicked away from him. When she surfaced, he was still submerged. He came up seconds later in the same area he went under. She licked the gulf water from her lips, remembering the taste of Douglas's neck—the summer tang of hard work—when he'd proposed Friday afternoon.

Douglas, understanding what she wanted to do, shook his head. "It's too dangerous. We could surface before realizing it. Let me go speak to Mrs. Melling instead."

Magdalene dove under and headed straight for Douglas, but she passed him—brushing his knees with her hand in the process— and rising a couple feet beyond him.

"You torture me, Maggie."

"We'll try it once, where the waves break. That should push us under for a few moments. Watch me."

She swam toward the shore, stopping where the swells crested in chest deep water. When the wave approached, she dove under. The force of the water rushing to the shore pushed her down and then tossed her back for the next wave to do the same. She struggled to stand and looked back at Douglas, her chest heaving for breath.

"It doesn't look safe." He came closer.

"One try, please. Dive for me and I'll dive for you. After contact, we can push each other away so we don't surface too close together."

Douglas raised an eyebrow, which cause Magdalene's heart to drop to her stomach in a delicious swirl of emotion.

"You have a devious mind," he said.

"Only when it comes to you."

They waited a few minutes until a larger wave rolled in. With a nod, they dove under. Their bodies tumbled together under the current. Magdalene grasped for his arm but wasn't quick enough to get a hold. Douglas hooked his arm under hers, but was unable to lean in for the kiss she wanted. They both came up closer than planned and sputtering for air.

Magdalene turned to him, longing in her eyes as the sensations from the salt water on her lips and the water lapping her bare arms made her yearn all the more for his touch. The memory of his body passing hers underneath the wave brought exhilaration to her already quickening pulse.

"I know that look, Maggie. If we were in Seacliff Cottage, there'd be no stopping you."

She threw back her head and laughed as the pelicans swooped toward the gulf. "You know me too well, faults and all."

He let Magdalene lead the way to the shoreline. Once in knee-deep water, she looked over her shoulder at him as he approached. The wet suit clung to his body, further defining everything she wanted to explore. He returned the appreciative glance, and when he was alongside her, he whispered. "Aye, *very* shapely legs, Maggie."

She kicked up a giant splash like she did the first time they went to the bay together and he had asked if he could call her Maggie, and then took off running. Afraid if she stopped she'd fling herself into his arms, she ran to the edge of the hotel property before turning back. Douglas with Mrs. Melling on his arm and a robe around his swimsuit, headed toward her.

"Really, Magdalene! It is one thing to frolic like that on the bay when it is just us, but to make a spectacle at the resort is quite unladylike." Mrs. Melling handed her a hotel robe. "What will the talk be in the dining room tonight?"

Magdalene tied the robe on over her suit. "I'm sorry. I must have swallowed too much salt water."

"The fact is, Mrs. Melling, Magdalene and I are both giddy with our coming nuptial." Douglas looked at the lady as they headed for the sun deck. "We were wondering if we could see about being married by one of the local ministers tomorrow."

"Out of the question!" Mrs. Melling snapped. "We must have time to prepare a proper trousseau."

"But I don't need the finery that someone like you is accustomed to. I have a hope chest at home that can be sent for, and you've already been so generous with purchasing new clothing for me—"

"And I will continue to do so, Magdalene. The fact of the matter is Douglas's letter to your father went out in today's post, and I will not allow you to be married until we have word back from your family. It would not be proper."

"Thank you for safeguarding her reputation, Mrs. Melling. I'm glad you care for Maggie so much."

"You are quite welcome. Now leave it to me. I shall have the best plans for your special day when the time comes. As for today, let us focus on your birthday." She patted Magdalene's arm.

They met Mr. Campbell on the sun deck. He took his free time there because the salt air brought relief to his rheumatism and color to his ashy complexion.

"You go to the room and shower, Magdalene. I believe we will have time to shop before our supper reservation. I shall be up as soon as I see that Douglas's suit is changed from a rental to a purchase. Your matching suits are too quaint to pass up. Consider it part of an early wedding gift. And remember, gentlemen, you might not see us until checkout time tomorrow. I hope you enjoy your evening as much as we will enjoy ours."

Resentment toward Mrs. Melling snaked its way into Magdalene's thoughts. The easy way her employer dismissed hers and Douglas's wedding ideas, the slight of not taking supper with the

Campbells, and the condescending tone in which she'd spoken to Magdalene all constricted around her mind.

Showering did little to help because Mrs. Melling had laid out clothes for her while she was in the bathroom. The pink and white promenade dress with white leather boots that buttoned up the side with a special button hook was much too fussy for her taste. She felt like a doll in Mrs. Melling's care when the lady insisted on lacing her corset for her and was none too gentle about it. Magdalene felt new sympathy for Eliza as Mrs. Melling helped pull the dress on because Magdalene could not bend enough to adjust it properly over her undergarments. Nor could she button her own shoes.

"Next time," Mrs. Melling said, "be sure to put the boots on before the corset."

"Yes, ma'am." But Magdalene didn't want there to be a next time.

"You'll be sure to turn lots of heads, if only we can do something with your hair."

Knowing it to be better to play along, Magdalene spoke up. "I read an article in last month's *McCall's Magazine* about heightening a pompadour."

Mrs. Melling clapped her hands. "Perfect! I do not want to see a braid in your hair unless you are in the water or behind the wheel—and only then because you insist on it."

"Douglas likes the braid."

"And a braid is fine around the house, as well as to play and sleep in, but when you are out around town with me, I need you to look like a proper lady, not a country housewife, even if that is the station you covet. I know being out in society is new for you, but part of being a lady's companion is having a radiant disposition to turn the heads of people my way. Women my age no longer merit attention but we still want all eyes upon us when we enter the room. We rely on younger relations or the fresh face of our companions to draw the crowd to us. That, my dear, is you when we are outside of Seacliff Cottage. Do you understand?"

"Yes, ma'am," she said through gritted teeth.

"Did you ever play princess when you were little?"

Magdalene nodded, not trusting herself to speak.

"Consider this an extension of that. Hold your head high and do not forget the weight the Melling family holds along the Gulf Coast."

Magdalene wanted to let Mrs. Melling know exactly what she thought of her precious family, but held her tongue. She needed to keep the job until she was married and she did not wish to jeopardize either Douglas's or his uncle's employment.

"Yes, ma'am." She turned to the dressing table and set to work on making her hair presentable according to Mrs. Melling's standards.

"And tuck that ring into a drawer for safe keeping. I would not want something to happen to it while we are about town." Mrs. Melling smoothed Magdalene's dress. "Life is going to be quite different from now on as we await news of Alexander's engagement."

THE END

BONUS

"The Portrait of Eliza Melling"
The Possession Chronicles #4.1

Sean Spunner paused before a gilt mirror in the ornate entry of the rebuilt Battle House Hotel. He adjusted the seam of his old skeleton costume over his left shoulder. Repurposed from the 1904 masquerade, it was Sean's fourth occasion wearing the skin-tight suit. The last time had been over five years previous when he helped kidnap Alexander Melling for a bachelor party. Pleased his regular hours at the gym kept him physically fit at the age of thirty, he gave himself a half-smile as he pulled a black mask over his eyes.

The elaborate ballroom was decked out as a haunted forest for the 1910 Halloween Flirts ball. The familiar feel of the creepy surroundings pricked at his memory. The forest, half composed of canvases depicting pine trees, were painted by his love for the 1905 ball when she crafted all the scenes for the graveyard theme.

Eliza.

Eliza Rose Melling.

The woman of his dreams.

Sean's fiancée, taken from the world five winters ago, was the reason he came to this dance every year since he escorted her. Staring at the towering pines expertly detailed with craggy bark and shimmering needles, he couldn't help but finger one of the canvases that Eliza had touched. *Created!* A bolt of energy flowed up his arm. It reminded him of the excitement he felt whenever he was in her presence. The pleasure they shared with each contact. Eliza had been his match in every way.

Seeking to quiet the ghost in his mind, he looked about the room for a familiar face. The crowd looked younger than ever—mostly those in their teens during their first year out in society. Spotting one of the gym regulars, Sean made his way to Chuck Brady dressed as a jester.

"Brady!" Sean's hand slapped the young man's colorful silk-clad back.

"Spunner." He passed him a flask. "Nice skeleton suit."

Sean took a swig and grinned. None of the people in attendance would know the significance of the Mystics of Dardenne skeleton suit—worn to their masquerade the year they were raided and many of their guests were hauled to the police station for immoral behavior.

"The room is full of fresh faces tonight." Chuck lifted his pointed hat, exposing his wavy black hair to two young ladies passing beside them. The girls—one gypsy and one fairy—leaned together and giggled before continuing on. "Take one of those first-timers out on the dancefloor, Spunner."

Sean laughed and passed the drink back to Chuck. "I know those two from the cathedral and I can honestly say I'm twice their age."

"Don't exaggerate."

"I'm the father's lawyer of that gypsy and remember him talking at the Aethelwulf Club last fall that he was debuting his daughter at fifteen to get her to stop complaining about not being able to attend balls. And the one with her is the little sister of my best friend's wife. I know for a fact she hasn't graduated as I've dined with her at supper parties."

"Then why are you here, old man?" Chuck took a shot from his flask.

"Memories, I suppose." Sean plucked a leaf off a potted ficus and rubbed it between his fingers before going for the refreshment table. He gathered a sampling of shrimp before taking a seat against the wall in defeat.

I shouldn't have come.

He closed his eyes and focused on the music. The string quartet made him envision gliding around a similar dancefloor with Eliza—hands roaming her curves.

I should have stayed home rather than resurrect these memories.

But Sean knew if he was at home, he'd be staring at her painting. It had been almost five years and he still ached for her.

He thought he'd dreamt the tap on his shoulder, but it happened again. "Mr. Spunner? Wake up, please. I'd like a dance with you. It's ladies choice."

"I wasn't asleep." He looked on Sadie Marley with a slight touch of nausea when he opened his eyes.

She giggled and stepped back, her fairy costume shimmery in the dim light. "You were daydreaming at least. Come on."

Sean looked at her outstretched hand and did his best to let her down softly. "Miss Marley, I really wasn't planning on dancing tonight."

"Then why did you come, Sean Spunner?" *The question of the night.* "We've had supper at John's house enough times to be on a first name basis. I'm Sadie, in case you forgot."

"I remember, Sadie. And thank you for the invitation." With a slight smile, he accepted her hand—the gentlemanly thing to do. He never felt like such a fool as he did following the lead of the sixteen-year-old to the dancefloor and was glad none of his old friends were there to witness how far he'd fallen.

When he took her in his arms to waltz, it was as awkward as it was half a lifetime ago when he had to practice dancing with his cousin before her first cotillion. Sean breathed a sigh of relief when the score was over.

"I look forward to telling John that I rescued the oldest man in attendance from being a wallflower. I 'll see you at the next supper party." Sadie giggled before walking away.

He inwardly groaned and headed for the punch bowl. The liquid was blessedly spiked with a liberal amount of whiskey. Sean stood at the table and refilled his glass twice before claiming a chair on the edge of the dancefloor.

The quartet switched out with a ragtime band. Half the young crowd left the space as the others immediately started to cakewalk. Those that watched from the sidelines took interest in one couple in the middle of the floor. People began to crane their necks and lean in to get a better look. Curiosity got the better of him. Sean joined the ring of spectators closing in on the dancers. The guy was a fair-headed chap in a Union Army costume but the young lady, garbed in a simple black witch's dress, captivated him. It was probably the combination of her dark braids and womanly curves, but Sean could only see Eliza. She would have kicked up her heels and shimmied like a woman set loose as well.

He made his way to the edge of the crowd when everyone clapped and stared as the couple passed. A fleeting glance from the young woman showcased her piercing blue eyes. They didn't have the violet tint like Eliza's, but it was enough. He knew if he didn't leave, he'd make a fool of himself before long.

He stumbled out of the Battle House and collapsed in his automobile until he caught his breath. Firing the engine, Sean willed his hands to quit shaking as he removed his mask. John Woodslow, his best friend, had a fine house a few blocks west so he headed there. Shadowed figures were silhouetted against the parlor drapes as the doctor and his wife hosted a Halloween party, which Sean respectfully declined an invitation to. Looking back, he realized he should have accepted. He knew John's wife—ever the thoughtful hostess—would have paired him with a lovely young woman that was probably a better match than her little sister of any of the other girls at the masquerade.

But then Sean would have missed seeing Eliza's trees—and her double in the form of the dancer. Truth be told, Eliza was a double herself. He'd only loved two girls in his lifetime and both were taken from him in most horrific ways. His first love, thirteen years previous, was another dark-haired beauty with blue eyes and womanly curves on her still budding frame. Yellow fever took the first, a horse riding accident the second. Dare he chance a third attempt?

He thought he wanted to.

John might complain about his wife, but Sean knew his friend was happy. He worked long hours at the hospital and enjoyed relaxing at home, whether with his family or hosting friends. The doctor still came to the men's club a few times a month, but he didn't stay too late and never divulged any indiscretions.

John's well-settled in life and love and it's high time I was too!

Sean drove down Government Street and stopped in the middle of the road before the Mellings' mansion. All was quiet, the widows closed—no lights or laughter. Not that there was ever much joy within those walls save for the impish fun of Eliza and her brother, Alexander. Now it was a gilded prison for widowed Ruth Melling, just as Sean's house was to him. And he wanted out.

He doubled back several blocks and parked in the drive of his towering Federal style home he'd purchased to impress the Mellings. Its flat, imposing brick façade did little to welcome him when he returned, but he couldn't give up the place he shared the ultimate closeness with Eliza for the first—and later the last—time.

Sean grabbed a bottle of brandy from the credenza in the parlor and stalked up the stairs to the master suite.

"What good is a master suite when one lives alone?" he asked aloud as he plopped into the armchair beside the fireplace.

He drank straight from the bottle and stared up at the self-portrait Eliza painted for his Christmas gift in '05. Tendrils of her nearly black hair skimmed her ivory back, bared to the viewer as she clutched a purple silk sheet to her glorious chest. Bright eyes and playful smile taunted him over her shoulder from the frame above the mantel.

"I promised I'd never forget you when we were parted." He took another drink. "I've kept my end of the bargain nearly five years. Is it enough?"

Eliza shook her head, causing her hair to ripple across her flawless back. "Never, Sean Spunner. You're my greatest passion and I must remain yours."

Sean's heart lurched as her figure stood, turned toward him fully and stepped out of the painting. With a fluid grace, she floated to the floor like a falling magnolia petal. She kept hold of the sheet, but like her form, it was barely there—a hint of purple clasped to her generous breasts. Her blue-violet eyes were misty with intrigue.

Standing before him, she smiled triumphantly. "You look like Alexander in your bone suit, drinking brandy and lamenting his lost lover."

He pressed against the back of the chair to get as far away from her as possible. "You're not here."

"I am, my darling." She lowered the sheet and cold air tickled his face as she leaned closer. "And in my natural glory."

Sean licked his lips and pointed to the painting, trying to ignore the ethereal form he could see the mantel through. Hiding his fear, he lashed out in anger. "Go back! I can't speak to you and you most certainly should not be speaking to me."

"My likeness is still there." Eliza motioned to the framed painting. "I stand before you in my current form. Am I as beautiful as you remember?"

Goose flesh pricked his arms beneath the costume. He wanted nothing more than to touch her—to feel her giving flesh beneath his palms—but the terror of what he might *not* feel overcame his impulse to caress.

"You're everything I remember, Kitten."

When she moved to climb into his lap, Sean jumped to his feet. He skirted around—through—the phantom and shivered as he glanced back from the door. The apparition drew closer.

"Stop!" His knuckles strained around the bottle.

Miraculously, Eliza obeyed, though she always preferred to give orders rather than take them.

"If you insist on haunting me, please get some clothes on. It's cruel for you to flaunt what I can no longer have."

Eliza laughed and shimmied in a provocative sway. That dangerous smile—the one his Mystics of Dardenne brothers all warned him about—flashed across her pretty face as she tugged the purple sheet around her. "Have you had anyone since me, Sean?"

He took a swig from the bottle and stalked to the hallway.

"Have you?"

He turned. The opaque figure now wore the royal blue Regency gown Eliza dazzled in at the Halloween Flirts ball they attended together. Her hand trailed her décolletage as she eyed his tight suit with an appreciative leer.

"You haven't!" She shrieked with cruel laughter.

Sean hurled the brandy bottle and it smashed on the wall behind her.

"I loved you with my whole heart, Eliza Rose Melling. Our six months together was the best in my life. Please don't spoil those memories by your actions tonight."

Sean stopped at the credenza downstairs and poured himself a glass of Irish whiskey, hoping it would somehow negate the anxiety over his dead fiancée following him around his house.

"That's what you need," Eliza said with a soft voice. "Go back to your roots rather than my brother's antics."

He took a shot and readied another. "I'm beginning to think Alex had the right idea all along."

"Staying drunk to numb the pain?"

He spoke forcibly around his trepidation. "Trying to replace the loss with other intimacies."

"You wouldn't dare, Sean Spunner! You loved me too much." Eliza's eyes were wide with fright, kissable lips downturned, and body—though not solid—held stiff with indignation. "It took you over seven years to open your heart after your first love died. I demand that long, at the very least."

"What I felt for that girl—"

"Winifred." Eliza sneered. "I know all about her now. There are some benefits in death. We had a nice heart-to-heart about you. Well, after she nearly clawed my eyes out for what I—never mind. She was a little hellion, I bet."

"She was a young woman grieving her family when I knew her."

Eliza's hand shifted over her bosom once more. "I bet you were more than ready to hold her close in her despair. And it appears your preferred type was patterned after dear little Winnie. For fifteen, she sure had some big ones. Not to mention her sky blue eyes and dark hair. I feel positively used after meeting her. I'm not one to settle for being a stand-in."

Sean set his glass on the table and choked on bitterness. "You pretentious Melling! But for all your bluster, you're jealous of a girl who's been dead more than twice as long as yourself."

Not knowing how else to get away from her, Sean went for the stairs.

Right on his heels like a January wind, she followed. "But you were so sweet with her. She told me you kissed her on the lips on her deathbed. Kissing a girl with yellow fever is mighty heroic, Romeo. Weren't you afraid to die?"

Gripping the banister, he turned and unleashed his fury. "I was ready to die after watching the life leave her beautiful face! Weeks before she grew ill, I knew I was going to wait for her and told her cousin as much. Winnie was the sweetest, bravest girl I've ever met. Wild, yes, but that made her all the more wonderful. She'd climb a tree on a whim without thinking twice, hanging upside-down though her knickers and ripped stockings were showing and her aunt would holler at her for it."

Eliza *tsked* and twirled a lock of hair around a finger. "Must you always fall for the naughty ones?"

Sean's knuckles went white around the handrail. For a moment, Eliza flickered solid and he almost sprung at her—to slap or kiss, he didn't know which.

"You were the naughtiest, Eliza."

"I should hope so." She gifted the notorious Melling smile of venom and charm before flying past him into the master suite.

"Get out of my room!"

Still grinning, she pointed to her painting. "Obviously you want me in here."

He slammed the door and knelt at the hearth in hopes a fire would chase the chill—and the ghost—from his bed chamber.

Eliza drifted about his room as he stoked the flames. "If you have a chill, you know I can warm you."

"You can do nothing for me in your current state."

"Oh, I bet I could." She perched on the side of his bed and motioned to the sketches she'd given him during their courtship— framed in a neat grouping at eye-level on the side wall. "How often do you sit here to look upon me while you work yourself into a frenzy to find release?"

Ignoring her, Sean locked himself in the bathroom and started a shower. He lathered and scrubbed in an attempt to wash the thoughts away and bring a bit of sobriety to his night. If he'd drunk too much, perhaps Eliza would leave as his mind cleared.

He opened the shower curtain and grabbed for a towel.

"You're still a fine specimen, Sean Spunner, though I thought it was a cold shower you're supposed to take to cool impulses." Her voice came through the steam trapped in the space.

Tucking the towel about his middle, Sean glared into the fog until he caught the outline of Eliza—now draped in a white nightgown. "Have you no shame?"

"None." She smiled and maneuvered closer. "But don't ask questions you know the answers to."

He shook the water from his brown hair and went for the door. Eliza raised both hands in front of Sean's chest. Trailing her hands over his abdomen, she followed each muscle. His bones ached and his teeth chattered.

"I'd draw you if I could, Sean." She looked ready to devour him. "I might have to settle on tracing every line on your body with my tongue."

"You'd kill me." He shoved through the mist. After a vigorous rub down with the towel, he pulled on his robe and stepped into his slippers.

"You've trembled before me and said those words before, but it was no hardship as I recall. You wanted me to put you out of your misery. Don't you remember the night you brought me here after the Halloween dance?"

"Every day, and that's my problem." He dropped into the armchair and tossed another log into the fire.

"We warmed each other well." She sighed as though lost in memory. "These pictures are quite a scandalous collection. No wonder you haven't taken another lover. You couldn't bring a woman here with my nude sketches on display, not to mention the painting."

Sean stalked across the room, pulled the largest drawing from the wall, and returned to the fireplace. Pausing a moment to look upon the framed image—presented when he stayed overnight at Seacliff Cottage the first time—he remembered opening the envelope that held the sketch of his fantasy woman. He had even shown it to Deacon De Fiore who was a regular guest of the Mellings when they were across the bay. Now his dream girl was a nightmare he needed to exorcise.

With deliberate swiftness, he raised the frame and smashed it upon the mantel's edge.

"Sean!" Eliza screeched.

He tore the paper from the broken glass and threw it into the fire.

"You can't destroy me!"

"I've carried your memory long enough, Eliza Rose."

"No!" Her nearness sent ice down his neck. "You still need me."

"You're attitude tonight is making it easier to leave you behind."

"You used to love my sharp tongue. Besides, what will the maid say about this mess?"

"My housekeeper has complained about these for years. I'm sure she'll be more than happy to clean the glass off the floor to be rid of the 'unholy pictures'." He turned back to the corner to retrieve another one.

"Are you trying out for sainthood?" She kept her voice firm, but she winced when he broke the frame.

"I'm no saint, Eliza, but I do try to behave these days."

She laughed. "Once a Dardenne, always a Dardenne, as the guys used to say."

He shook his head as he watched the corners of the paper curl and burn until the image of Eliza's bare chest was no more. "That's true for some, but not all. I've matured since you last saw me. I no longer seek flings."

"Because once you have a Melling, you can never go back."

"You're as arrogant as your parents." He fed another sketch into the fire.

"Father approved of you. He wanted me to have a love-blinded dupe for a husband so you wouldn't inflict me with whorehouse diseases. But I think if he saw how you've behaved all these years, he'd lose what respect he had for you in standing up to Mother like you always did in my behalf." She looked at his gaping robe and smiled. "You're as handsome and fit as ever, but much too soft for George Melling to respect."

"I was never soft for you, Eliza."

She laughed and danced around him. "I had you just where I wanted, but you didn't have quite enough backbone to go completely against my parents."

"Because I didn't want to elope to the Smoky Mountains?" He tossed the last sketch into the flames.

"And don't forget refusing to join Melling and Associates because you didn't want my father's wrath upon your uncle's firm."

"We got through all that and enjoyed the holidays and New Year's Eve. We were going to spend a long weekend at Seacliff Cottage before—"

"That weekend at Seacliff was never on my schedule. I had my alternative plan set in motion."

Hairs rising on his arms, Sean stared at the devil masquerading as his lost love. "Another—what do you mean?"

Eliza shrugged. "You wouldn't get me away from my parents so I found someone who jumped at the chance."

Feeling his heart about to break as it had when he heard the news of her accident, Sean gripped the bedpost. "Who?"

"He loved me, you know. How could he not with my play of seduction and all the time we spent together across the bay." Her poisonous smile was back. "Mother adored him, much more than you. I bet she would have eventually accepted us, though with you she would have always kept a wall up because you crossed her one too many times. After my accident, she refused to hear your name spoke in her presence—did you know?"

Staring at her deadly eyes, he made no sound.

"You might have watched your first love die, but my lover watched me fall and carried my broken body home."

"Damn you to Hell, Eliza Rose! I was true to you even before we courted, but you … you were just what the guys said you were! You had me fooled but God saved me—and the deacon—when he took you from this life."

He found not an ounce of beauty when he looked upon her features. As though she felt the shift in him, Eliza switched clothing from the nightgown back into the Regency apparel. Sean shook his head and went for the mantel.

Eliza screamed.

He reached for the painting. "Will it destroy you if it burns?"

"No, but you'll regret it in the morning." Her voice was soft, coaxing. "You burned the sketches. Wait until you wake and decide if you can do without the painting as well."

Sean grunted, not wanting to agree that he already felt the loss of his collection.

Her arms wrapped about his waist but her coldness didn't penetrate the robe. "I did love you, Sean. Part of me still does."

"You were all I wanted," he whispered.

"We had fun together, but I had to get away from my parents. Blame my hatred for them rather than any lack of feeling for you."

Sean shook his head and stepped away. "You ended up just like your father—using people to your benefit without thought of how they're left when you walk away."

Eliza laughed—bold and loud—and glowed a rosy pink on her see-through cheeks. "I suppose I did. The Melling taint. I put poor Alex to shame, don't I? He never could measure up to Father's standards. I'm glad he finally put Father in his proper place, even if I wasn't there to witness it."

"He was a great friend."

"Was?"

"He ... when your father ... the fire at Seacliff after the hurricane."

"Alexander Randolph Melling!" she shouted with glee. "You did what I couldn't do—you escaped our hell with your life!"

"He's not—"

"My brother never crossed over."

"But he was said to have perished in the fire."

"He's another manipulative Melling, my darling. Don't underestimate us." She did a kissing motion at Sean's face and motioned over the mantel. "Will you keep me around another night? It is Halloween, after all. Five years ago was exquisite."

Sean bit back a chuckle. "Will you go and never return?"

She nodded.

"Promise me. And turnabout so I can make sure you aren't crossing your fingers."

"You know all my games now, Sean. I promise not to haunt you." Eliza slowly turned, her splendid gown fading to nothing so

---

she was left naked when she faced him once more. She winked. "But you still haunt my memories, Sean Spunner. You were the best—every time. Think of me—for another year or two at least. I couldn't stand to be second fiddle to a fifteen-year-old the rest of your life."

"I won't be in a rush to replace you—of that you may be sure."

Eliza rose off the floor. "And dear little Winifred. Whoever you find needs to be better than both of us together. You deserve an exceptional woman."

"Go, Eliza."

"And don't overlook her naughty side. You must have a touch of the debauched to satisfy your inner Mystics of Dardenne." She blew a kiss. "I love you, Sean. Remember me on your lonely nights."

He looked his fill at the heavenly figure before she stepped back into the painting. "And I love you, Kitten."

Fingering the canvas at the lowest glossy curl on her back, he smiled. "You were a minx to the end, but that was one of the reasons I loved you."

Sean stumbled to bed, dropping his robe and slippers on the floor before passing out. He stirred to life shortly after eight in the morning. His gaze immediately fell on the blank space on the wall by the bed.

Eliza—gone.

He sat up and looked to the hearth. Eliza's painting hung slightly crooked and a scattering of broken glass and frames were all over the floor.

But she was here.

Robe and slippers tugged into place, Sean crossed to the scene of destruction.

"It's a new day, Eliza Rose Melling," he said to her cheeky likeness before lifting the frame off the wall. "And a new season for me. Our time was wonderful, but I must say goodbye."

He opened his closet and shoved the portrait into the farthest corner.

"Rest in peace, wherever you reside."

THE END

Author's Note

My continued love and appreciation to my family for tolerating my possession by these characters while writing and editing this saga. This book—and the whole Possession Chronicles series—wouldn't be here without Sean Connell urging me to try writing horror. I can't thank you enough for the push to write outside my perceived comfort zone.

Thanks, as always, to my scattered critique group. MeLeesa Swann, Candice Marley Conner, Joyce Scarbrough, Lee Ann Ward, and Stephanie Thompson, you all are the greatest.

Special thanks to Heidi Hughes for answering my horse-related questions and the members of POSSESSED: Timeless Gothic Reads group on Facebook for creating a network to share Gothic literature, no matter the sub-genre.

And a special shout out goes to Michael Sachs for feeding my need for art and museums when I'm in his part of the world, because inspiration happens everywhere.

And to the membership of Mobile Writers Guild, Mobile Public Library workers, Angela Trigg at The Haunted Book Shop, the folks at Serpents of Bienville, and every other fabulous group/place where I find inspiration and support—thank yo

About the Author

While experiencing the typical adventures of growing up, Carrie Dalby called several places in California home, but she's lived on the Alabama Gulf Coast since 1996. Serving two terms as president of Mobile Writers' Guild and five years as the Mobile area Local Liaison for the Society of Children's Book Writers and Illustrators are two of the writing-related volunteer positions she's held. When Carrie isn't reading, writing, browsing bookstores/libraries, or homeschooling her children, she can often be found knitting or attending concerts.

Carrie writes for both teens and adults. *Fortitude* is listed as a Best History Book for Kids by Grateful American Foundation. She has also published *Corroded*, a contemporary teen novel about friendship and autism, several short stories that can be found in different anthologies, as well as a multitude of Southern Gothic novels for adults.

For more information, visit Carrie Dalby's website:

carriedalby.com

Ingram Content Group UK Ltd.
Milton Keynes UK
UKHW010921100423
419916UK00004B/203